THE CIGAR SEED

Paul Chiswick

THE CIGAR SEED

ISBN-13: 978-1499274929
ISBN-10: 1499274920

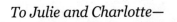

To Julie and Charlotte—

Hibiscus flowers are cups of fire,
(Love me, my lover, life will not stay)
The bright poinsettia shakes in the wind,
A scarlet leaf is blowing away.
A lizard lifts his head and listens—
Kiss me before the noon goes by,
Here in the shade of the ceiba hide me
From the great black vulture circling the
sky.

Sara Teasdale (1884-1933) – in a Cuban garden

About the Author

Paul Chiswick resides with his wife in a North Warwickshire village. He lived and worked in the Far East as a Civil Engineer before undertaking a second successful sales career in the IT industry. He now divides his time between writing, helping unpublished authors get into print and promote themselves, and producing living memories from static images.

The Cigar Seed is his second novel. His first, *Through Glass Eyes*, is available on Amazon. He has also written a book of short stories, *Shorts for Christmas*.

More about Paul and his writing can be found on his website www.paulchiswick.com

Bayonne, early June 2006

Terese Rodriguez walks briskly along the quiet Bayonne street, squeezes the balled tissue in her fist and curses, wishing she had never mentioned the last diary of Ernesto 'Che' Guevara. If only she had kept her mouth shut nobody would be any the wiser.

Now it is too late. Once the idea sparked in Peru's mind, he won't let it go until it becomes reality.

She shivers as she recalls his words. *That's it! We'll use the virus at the airport . . . They'll be on their knees after that. All we have to do is get it out of Cuba.* She laughed, said he must be joking, but he simply glared at her, jaw tight, his look telling her he could not be more serious.

Never in her wildest dreams could she have come up with such a plan.

Nightmarish. Impossible. Suicidal.

Brilliant.

She pauses outside the smoked glass door of a converted Colombage house sited close to the River Nive's east bank. To the left of the door a rectangular stainless steel plaque inscribed **El Correo** indicates this is the local office of the Basque Country's most popular newspaper. Beneath it there is a grey intercom, a single white button set in its centre.

Jabbing the button once, she says, 'Terese'.

An automatic lock disengages with a sharp clunk. Pushing open the door, she enters a small, cream-coloured reception area, walls bare except for two pin boards crowded with newspaper cuttings. A bespectacled, middle-aged woman, who would not look out of place in a library, peers up at her from behind a counter layered with open newspapers.

'Good morning, Terese. Are you OK? You look a little off-colour.'

She dabs her nose with the tissue. 'I think I'm starting with flu, Frantziska.'

'Poor girl. Perhaps you should take the day off. I'll ask Frederic if he'll cover for you.'

'No, don't bother, I'll be fine.' She tilts her chin at the papers. 'Anything of interest in the nationals?'

The receptionist sifts through the papers, plucks out a copy of *El Mundo* and passes it to her. 'This might raise a few eyebrows.'

Splashed across the front page is the headline:

ETA NO LONGER A THREAT
DAYS OF TERROR ARE OVER SAYS SENIOR POLICE OFFICER

She sucks in her breath. Peru will raise hell when he reads that.

'I'm going out for a couple of hours. If anyone calls, take a message and say I'll get back to them.'

'Will do.'

He has blood on his hands, but that doesn't trouble his conscience one iota, metaphorically speaking. He takes care not to be in the vicinity when the bombs go off or the victims of the assassinations have their brains splattered in a red mist. He is completely unaffected by the devastating results of his organisation's actions and will do whatever needs to be done, without a second thought.

His principles tell him theirs is a just cause, one worth dying for if necessary and one for which the indiscriminate doling out of injury and death is unavoidable if they are to achieve their ultimate goal.

Many do not agree with him, but then, they do not walk in his shoes.

He hides his emotions, plans his moves like a chess grandmaster. Following a strict regime, he keeps his body taut, lean as a skinless chicken breast. Outwardly, he appears mild-mannered, someone to whom temper is alien, but he delights to deceive. A narrow scar marks his forehead from left eyebrow to hairline, made by the tip of a switchblade as it narrowly missed his eyeball: a marginal error that cost his assailant his life when he retaliated, drawing on years of training received at the hands of some of the world's deadliest exponents of unarmed combat.

That incident changed his views on life and death.

They call him 'Le Fanatic' behind his back. That makes him swell with pride. When in his company, they call him by the name the priest gave him twenty-eight summers before.

Peru.

As the sun hangs motionless in an azure sky, he sprawls lazily on the grass under the dappled shade of a twisted oak tree, sucking in deep drafts of Lucky Strike. This is his favourite spot in the whole of the city; a place where his thoughts are set on edge by the harsh mewing of gulls overhead then smoothed by the comforting sound of the lazy Adour carrying its heavy waters to the Bay of Biscay. He puffs curling smoke rings into the luxuriant foliage above, his thoughts turn once again to the outlandish plan he has conceived. It is daring, devastating, and possible. ETA has attempted nothing as ambitious since the bungled assassination of King Juan

Carlos in '95. A successful outcome will see the glorious name of Peru Echeverria, liberator of the Basque people, written into the history books.

However, before he can reveal his plan to the commando, he will have to deal with Salbatore and that is not going to be easy. No one has yet dared openly to challenge the leader. Peru has been waiting for the right moment. For the past month he has secretly canvassed the support of the others, support they gave willingly.

By midnight, Salbatore Vasco's reign will be over.

He stubs the cigarette out on the sole of his shoe, studies the woman as she approaches, her steps hurried. His eyes scan the far distance to make sure she is following the prescribed procedure. She is. Fifty metres behind her stands another, much shorter figure, sporting a red and white soccer shirt.

Terese kneels on the grass beside him, brings her face close to his, lips puckered.

He holds up his hand, palm outwards. 'Not here. You never know who's watching.'

The kiss dies. 'Did you see the headline in *El Mundo* this morning?' she says.

'How could I fucking miss it?'

'It's a pretty convincing argument. The guy's been accurate with his facts. He—'

'Look, if they think we're out for the count because we've been quiet since that hotel fiasco, they've another think coming. I told Vasco it was a stupid idea, but would he listen to me? Like fuck he would.'

Every time he thinks back on it a thousand needles pierce his skin. They attempted to blow up a hotel in Villajoyosa, but a stupid idiot of a lifeguard moved the sports bag containing the bomb from the hotel reception to the pool's storage locker when he was unable to find its owner. The explosion failed to damage anything

4

except a small house close by the hotel's pool. Admittedly, Vasco couldn't have foreseen that, but why were they blowing up a hotel in the first place? That gaffe had the governments of both France and Spain laughing at them and the mocking press coverage of their incompetence and ineffectiveness went on and on, concluding ETA was unequivocally a spent force, a shadow of its former self. The commando's embarrassment was almost insufferable. After that, they swore never to allow such a mistake to happen again.

Vasco's latest folly involves a nightclub. A nightclub! Clearly, his once well-oiled brain is seized beyond repair.

He grips her forearm, locks eyes. 'Are you prepared for tonight?'

He feels her tremble. Uncertainty? Excitement? Fear?

'Peru, do you think it's such a good idea? I mean if the others change their—'

'Are you stupid? Of course it is. You saw how they reacted after Villajoyosa, after all the shit thrown at us. Do you think I'm about to tell them I've changed my mind and we'll simply carry on with Vasco leading us God knows where? How do you suppose they'll take that news, eh?'

'Well, I don't think—'

'No, you don't think, Terese . . . that's your problem. If you did, you wouldn't doubt what I'm doing, would you?'

'OK, OK. But are you sure they'll support you? All of them?'

He takes his hand off her arm and places it on her shoulder. 'I can guarantee it. Once tonight is over and done with I will tell them of my plan for the airport.'

'Do you really think it will work?'

'There are a few minor difficulties to overcome, but I don't see why it shouldn't.'

'But Cuba—'

'Is just another country. OK, I admit it won't be a walk in the park. The place doesn't conform to any rules we understand. In a place like that, anything can happen. All we've got to go on is the internet, your research and what Martina's father has discovered.'

Five men and two women huddle in a candlelit corner of the Chat Noir Cafe, a dingy restaurant overlooking the oily waters of the Nive. Nothing distinguishes them from any other group of ordinary young people enjoying a balmy summer evening. Outside the night is inky black, washing out the moon and stars. The air smells damp, earthy, its heaviness deadening the sounds from across the river. Coal-grilled meats and fish, sheep's milk cheeses, wine, and cider lay on the heavy, stained-oak table around which they sit. Usually, they would be laughing and joking until the serious talk begins, sloughing their way through the dishes spread before them without a care in the world. Not this evening: the food is barely touched and the carafes of wine are emptying fast.

As Salbatore Vasco runs through his plans for the Santesteban nightclub there is much nervous shifting on seats, silence cloaking the group.

When he finishes, he leans towards Peru. 'Well, what do you think?'

Peru drains his glass, places it on the table, leans back in his chair and crosses his arms over his chest. 'It's pathetic and you know it.'

Everyone freezes. This is it. This is what Peru told them to expect.

Salbatore clicks his tongue, shakes his head.

6

Peru knows exactly what the leader is thinking. This isn't the first time they have locked horns. They almost came to blows over the plans for the debâcle at Villajoyosa when Peru argued the futility of the exercise. That time it was behind closed doors and Salbatore got his way.

This time, it's out in the open.

'Peru, you're beginning to get on my nerves. Why is it you dismiss every idea I've come up with recently? If you think you can do better, let's hear it, eh?'

Five pairs of eyes lock on Peru. Now it is time for him to strike, but he will have to tread very carefully. Salbatore won't simply roll over and forsake the position to which he believes he is entitled by right, and he has talents they will continue to depend upon. No one comes anywhere close to his knowledge of and skill with explosives and many of their operations demand explosives, carefully placed and timed.

He rests his elbows on the table, clutches his left fist in his right hand.

'OK, Salbatore, let's try to be reasonable. Let's examine what this operation . . . proposed operation . . . is and what it will achieve.'

Raising his right hand, he extends the index finger. 'One, the target: the Casa Magico nightclub. We've never done nightclubs before and never carried out an operation in such a godforsaken place as Santesteban.'

Salbatore's face is impassive.

Peru's middle finger joins the index finger. 'Two, the intention is to cram a van to the brim with Semtex and blow the building? Do I have that right?'

'Precisely.'

'Without warning?'

Salbatore rolls his eyes. 'Don't be stupid, the intention isn't to kill anyone. We'll give the authorities

7

plenty of notice. They won't anticipate that, it's not the way we usually operate.'

'Then we blow the building?' Peru spreads his arms, palms skywards, and shrugs.

'Got it in one.' says Salbatore, winking.

'I don't see the point.'

'It worked at the football stadium, didn't it? Look at the embarrassment it caused the authorities. This time—'

'The football stadium got us a headline, that's all. I—'

'Look, we've tried violence and it doesn't work. Somehow, we have to gain the support of the entire population, not simply those who agree with what we're trying to achieve. Ghandi got it right in India. I'm even going to call this new approach the Ghandi Way.'

He grins, as if he's revealing the secrets of the cosmos to a bunch of Neanderthals.

Philippe, the youngest in the commando, raises his hand. 'Excuse me, Salbatore. Why the Casa Magico?'

Salbatore lets out a long, exasperated sigh. 'Listen up everyone, this is really important, so I'll go through it one more time. Yes, the town is a backwater, but it's not the town that matters, it's the nightclub, which just happens to be located there. For those of you who follow football, it won't come as a surprise why I've chosen the place. For those of you who don't, I'll explain. One of the world's greatest strikers is the Brazilian genius Horatio, who now plays for Real. He loves nightclubs but he detests publicity and is constantly on the lookout for places where he and his friends can enjoy a good night out without being hassled by the paparazzi. If they do discover where he hangs out, he simply goes elsewhere. Right now, he's enjoying a brief spell of obscurity at the Casa Magico. It won't last and soon he'll move on again. His inner circle is mostly wasters from rich French and Spanish families and they all want to bask in Horatio's limelight. As long as he's there, they'll be there. It's these people we're going to scare shitless.' He pauses while his words sink in. 'But if we blow them up we would lose all credibility with those influential families. There you have it, QED.'

Philippe frowns, scratches his head. 'So why do we need to be credible with the families?'

'We need to be credible so we can use the Ghandi Way on other occasions in the future, that's why.'

'Salbatore,' says Peru, 'I'm really trying not to be difficult, but ETA isn't meant to be a joke. We've been hauled over the coals once before and it wasn't a particularly pleasant experience, was it? We're fighting . . . at all costs so the oath demands . . . to free our people from imperialist rule. Surely, if we adopt this Ghandi Way, or whatever you call it, the world would never take us seriously again. ETA would become a complete laughing stock. I don't—'

He jumps as Salbatore smashes his fist down on the table. 'Look, it's a great idea and that's all there is to it. Trust me. Let's just get on with the job, eh? Now, can we continue?'

It is a serious miscalculation of the group's mood.

On cue, Martina, a stocky redhead, raises her hand. 'Look, this is a democratic group and I'm sorry, but I don't agree with you, Salbatore. As Peru says, we're committed to free ourselves of the oppressive powers that subjugate us. If it takes violence to achieve that aim, then so be it. I'm not about to go soft on that.'

A murmur of agreement rolls round the table.

'My father died for this cause,' adds Jorge, Martina's cousin. 'He would have done anything to see Basque liberation. You know that's what it's going to take, Salbatore. Anything. Frightening a bunch of rich kids wouldn't have been what he had in mind. If he were here now he would demand we do whatever . . . and he would mean whatever . . . is necessary.'

Peru inhales deeply. Now is the time to make the move he has rehearsed many times in his mind.

'Do you honour the oath, Salbatore?'

There can be only one possible response.

'What? Of course I do. What a pointless question.'

'To the letter and spirit: in thought and in action?'

'Don't be stupid man, you know I do.'

'Then I have a plan that will glorify us all.'

Salbatore smirks, leans back in his chair. 'You? A plan? Hah! When did you ever have a plan?'

Peru looks at the others in turn. Their eyes are afire, awaiting the coup de grâce.

'Who wants to hear it?' he says.

Without hesitation, five hands shoot skywards. Salbatore's face darkens and his mouth stretches to a pencil-thin line.

Peru clears his throat. 'Some time ago, I met with Martina's father. He told me of a startling discovery. Through his contacts he learned of the existence of a secret laboratory close to Guantanamo in Cuba. For many years, this laboratory has been experimenting with the deadly Ebola virus. Recently, it made a startling breakthrough. The head scientist, a dissident Russian, has discovered a way of transmitting this virus in the air. Previously, the only known way it could spread was through physical contact. That's startling in itself, but then he received further information. Leaked intelligence from a very senior Cuban official claims this scientist has succeeded in developing a strain several times more virulent than the naturally occurring one.'

'Mother of God!' says Philippe, crossing himself.

'I got to thinking if we could get hold of the virus, we could do some real damage.'

A snort issues from Salbatore's nose. 'If you think my ideas are crazy then I don't know what yours are. How do you propose we obtain this virus? Catch the next plane to Cuba and ask politely if they'll give it to us? You want to lead this commando? You're fucking mad.'

'Ah, that's where you're wrong, Salbatore. If you let me finish, I'll explain.'

'Go on, I'm all ears.'

'As you know, Terese is a great fan of Che Guevara and— hold it. Terese, why don't you tell us what you found out?'

All eyes switch to Terese, normally the least vocal of the group.

'At school I was friendly with a girl whose father was professor at the Sorbonne. We shared an unusual interest, the history of revolutionary movements. One day, when we were in the main library, we accidentally stumbled across the diaries of Che Guevara, which we found fascinating. The excitement of it still makes me tingle. We devoured them, reading them from cover to cover. We took the sentences apart, spent hours analysing their meanings. We ate, drank, and lived his adventures with him. He was under our skins. His beliefs became our beliefs, his struggles our struggles. Then we made a discovery that changed our lives. A discovery so amazing we would never forget it.'

She looks at Peru. He nods.

'The most surprising thing we discovered was that Guevara is a bastardisation of Gebara, a name from the province of Alava. It transpired Guevara's great-great-grandfather was a Basque. We couldn't believe it—our hero a son of the Basque Country!'

There is a collective intake of breath.

'Go on,' says Peru.

'In the last of his diaries I came across a passage that caught my eye. Guevara wrote of a child of his who was born whilst he was in Mexico. This child—'

'Hilda,' cuts in Martina. 'I remember she was the daughter of Che and Hilda Gadea, his first wife.'

Terese shakes her head. 'It wasn't Hilda, Martina. That's why this particular passage struck me.'

'Was it Aleida?'

'No, Aleida was born much later after he divorced Hilda and left Mexico. This child was a boy. You won't have heard of the mother, as she isn't mentioned in any of his other diaries. She was a married woman called Carmen Fortunato, wife of an old comrade of Castro.'

'Wait a minute,' says Martina. 'Are you saying he had an affair with a married woman?'

'It wasn't an affair. He describes it as a moment of drunken passion.'

Salbatore coughs, drums his fingers on the table. 'Look, this is all very interesting, but what has it to do with the virus?'

'I'm coming to that. The Fortunatos and Guevara agreed to send the child to live with a distant relative. Right here in this city.'

Gasps explode around the table.

'I still don't follow,' says Salbatore. 'Again, I ask, what has this got to do with the virus?'

'After the revolution, Carmen Fortunato and her husband raised three boys. The father never told them about their half-brother. You can see how shameful such a revelation would be in their society. We also know the husband was connected with the virus at several points in his past.'

'Ah, now I get it. You think blackmailing this man would be the way to get the virus?'

'Well. Peru thinks—'

'It has a good chance of succeeding,' says Peru, finishing the sentence for her.

Salbatore puffs out his chest. 'Well, Mister-Have-I-Got-A–Plan, I can see a problem straight away. No doubt others will have read the diaries and know of this affair. If so, it'll be common knowledge. That's hardly a good basis for blackmail, eh?'

Peru's eyes narrow. 'Nobody will have read the diary.'

'How can you be so sure?'

'Because it was never published.'

'Never published?'

'That's right. Never published. So no one knows of this child except Carmen Fortunato and her husband. And that's where my plan comes in.' He reaches under the table, pulls out a knapsack and places it on top. Undoing the straps, he flips it open and takes out a rolled up sheaf of paper. 'Now, who's in favour of hearing it?'

All except Salbatore raise a hand. One by one, he attempts to stare the others down, but they meet his eyes without blinking.

'It's sheer bloody madness, Echeverria. You'll get us all killed.'

Peru leans forward, points his finger at Salbatore. 'The oath says whatever the cost, Salbatore, whatever the cost. Now, are you with us, or not?'

Beads of sweat bubble on Salbatore's forehead and dark circles dampen the underarms of his shirt.

'Well? Are you or aren't you?'

Salbatore nods once, his face dark as thunder.

'Good. Then I'll explain it. Oh, and I suggest we abandon the nightclub idea. Hands up those who agree.'

For the second time that evening five hands shoot up. Salbatore slowly raises his hand as if it is pushing against the weight of the universe.

Sleep slips away from Terese. She curls into herself and tries to shut out the world, but the world won't play ball. Sliding out of bed, she slips on her nightdress and pads down the stairs into her kitchen. The house is silent except for the refrigerator's low hum.

She is still numb with shock.

Each member of the commando has particular skills, palatable and unpalatable. Peru and Salbatore are experts in unarmed combat and survival. Martina is the communications geek. Jorge is almost as knowledgeable as Salbatore about explosives; a reliable deputy in times of need. Philippe is the mechanic, a tinkering genius. Miguel knows the city like the back of his hand. Terese has a sharp nose, an ability to sniff out information, a skill she hones in her calling as a journalist. When Salbatore wanted to know where Horatio's latest playground is, she arranged to meet a junior groundsman at the Estadio San Mames. Tempted by a decent meal with a pretty woman, the young man passed on gossip from the dressing room.

Apparently, millionaire footballers have tongues as loose as their limbs.

She had almost fainted when Peru thrust her into the limelight during the meeting. That certainly hadn't been expected. Backstage is where she belongs, where she wants to belong. Never in her worst nightmare would she have expected what was to follow after the others departed.

Peru asked her to remain. She supposed he wanted to thank her for her support and then spend a few passionate moments together. Once he began to put his plan into operation he would be that focused they would have little opportunity to spend time together.

'It went just as you said it would,' she said, looping her arm around his.

'Yes, though I'm not sure Salbatore can be trusted.'

'I'm sure he'll be OK when he comes to realise how brilliant your plan is.'

'I hope so.'

She squeezed his arm. 'I'll miss you when you're in Cuba.'

He smiled, pointed to his chest. 'Me? I won't be the one going to Cuba. It will have to be a woman.'

It felt as if she had stuck her fingers in an electrical socket. A woman! That meant it had to be either her or Martina.

'I don't understand, Peru. Why does it have to be a woman?'

'Think about it. This man . . . this Major General Fortunato . . . he's supposed to be ruthless, right?'

'Yes, but—'

'So can you imagine how he would react if confronted by a man?'

'Well, I—'

'Christ, Terese! He would kill him!'

'But why would he be different with a woman?'

'I don't suppose he would, but it might just make a difference. Anyway, a woman would have a certain advantage. You know . . . '

He didn't have to finish the sentence. She took his meaning. 'Surely you wouldn't expect—'

'Do I have to spell it out? We did promise to do anything—*anything*—for the cause.' He leaned closer and smiled. 'Who knows best the story of the bastard child?'

'I-I guess I do.'

'And Martina is known to the authorities, isn't she? Thanks to your father, you're the last person they would suspect of having a connection to ETA.'

'I don't like the direction this conversation is taking, Peru.'

'Listen, Terese. You know the story like the back of your hand. You'll be able to figure out how to put the squeeze on the old man.'

Her veins ran cold as his words sank in. 'Send Martina, please. She's a tough nut. It takes a lot to intimidate her. She would know how to handle the Major General.'

His eyebrows arched. 'Too risky, it would attract attention. Besides, Martina has a short fuse; she would get his back up in seconds. No, it needs somebody with, shall we say, a *gentler* disposition.'

She raised her hands, palms outwards as if warding off a blow. 'No way, Peru, no way. All I do is research.'

His hand gripped her wrist, tightened, the smile no longer on his face. 'I'm not asking you to go, Terese.'

'Thank God for that.'

'As your leader, I'm ordering you.'

Wednesday, 5th July, Havana

The Cuban security guard walks with a measured tread along the line of passengers waiting to have their passports and visas checked. He has a heavy beard, a peaked cap emblazoned with a single red star and a Kalashnikov slung over one meaty shoulder. His black eyes challenge each new arrival.

As he approaches, Terese feels the queue press against her. An excited chatter filled the Havana air as her fellow travellers scampered across Jose Marti Airport's scorched concrete apron. Now, they are silent as if an unseen hand has turned a collective volume control fully anticlockwise.

The guard stops next to her, almost touching. She smells sacking mingled with cordite.

Her heart stutters. Rivulets of sweat trickle down her ribcage.

She is already wound up as tight as a watch spring.

Taking a deep breath, she tenses, braces her legs. Then looks up and stares hard at the guard.

His eyes narrow as he raises the rifle . . .

The Air France flight from Paris touched down just as the shimmering Caribbean sun melted into the horizon. After a delayed takeoff, the plane landed fifty-eight minutes late. For the hundredth time she runs the calculation through her mind. She has twenty-one days to complete her unwanted mission: thirty thousand two hundred and forty minutes. On the face of it, it seems plenty of time, but this is a completely new experience and, given all the unknowns, the loss of fifty-eight of those minutes could make the difference between success and failure.

Time is not what worries her most. The callousness of Peru's plan fills her with doubt. When ETA recruited her she swore an unbreakable oath to liberate her people. She spoke with conviction, her commitment unquestionable. However, hers is the commitment of a theorist, not an executioner. Liberation warps into an altogether different dimension when she watches colour footage of innocent people rendered blind, bloody and limbless as a direct result of the organisation's handiwork. The prank at the football stadium was a rude awakening as to the utter havoc they could wreak if they put their minds to it. Minutes before the match kicked off in the Estadio San Mames, they phoned the police with the unwelcome news that ETA was about to explode two hundred kilograms of cloratite to shake the evening up a little. The fans certainly felt the adrenalin rush as the stadium loosened its bowels and emptied in record time.

That incident made very interesting headlines in both the French and Spanish national dailies the next day, the papers crucifying the hapless Spanish Minister of the Interior.

A bomb scare is intolerable, but a cancelled match? Unforgivable.

What they are about to do is far worse than the stadium. This time it will not be a hoax. This time it will be for real. This time Peru is in charge, determined to attain ETA's Holy Grail by infecting hundreds of people in Barajas Airport with the world's most destructive virus. A haemorrhagic fever will wrack their bodies for days until finally they die. There is no known cure. Their suffering will be painful beyond imagination.

She has it in her gift to alter the course of events and save those poor souls who will be in the wrong place at the wrong time. All she has to do is catch the next plane home and to hell with the consequences.

That is what she should do. Yet here she is, making it happen.

To her amazement, the others voted to go along with his plan. Her heart screams it is unforgivably wrong and, if she did believe in God, she would kneel down there and then, pray Peru will call it off. But she has no God and Peru has a point to prove.

She cannot believe he has sent her instead of Martina. His reasons are plausible, but transparent. For months, she had worried he might ask her to go to Cuba, but never really believed he would. With hindsight, it was clear as daylight that was always his intention. For reasons known only to him, he is testing her resolve, waiting to pounce the moment she shows the first sign of weakness.

It's on your head, she says to herself. *What's it to be? Innocent deaths or the cause that puts fire in your belly and the man you love? Your choice.*

Perhaps she should return empty-handed, make an excuse and ask for a second chance. Forget it. If she has learned one thing about Peru, it is that he abhors failure.

No, failure is not an option.

Perhaps fate will intervene. Chance can play the devil when it has a mind to. Even if she were successful in her mission circumstances might conspire to prevent the horror going ahead.

There is always hope.

But right now she has a job to do.

Only half a dozen men in Cuba are aware their country possesses the Ebola virus. One is Major General Eduardo Fortunato, now an old man, but no ordinary old man. Until his recent retirement, he was one of the most feared men in Cuba, wielding the power of life or death. If Peru's plan is to succeed, she must confront the Major General and convince him to do the impossible.

Give her the virus.

Shortly before eight o'clock in the evening her taxi deposits her in front of the Hotel Telegrafo in Central Havana, a short walk from the domed Capitolio Nacional, the building housing the island's Senate and House of Representatives. The hotel, one of the city's oldest, is not a random choice: it is the ideal location for what she must do the following morning.

She enters, takes in the high ceilings and supporting arches replete with modern furnishings giving it the feel of a modish art gallery; too garish for her tastes. The smell of stale cigar permeates the air; clearly, punitive non-smoking laws have yet to reach these shores. After registering, she takes the lift to her room on the second floor, declining the services of a grinning porter with the expectant eyes of a gundog. She drops her rucksack on the floor, crosses the room and peers out of the window. On the far side of an oil-smeared ribbon of road, she watches figures criss-crossing the shadows thrown by streetlights across a large rectangle of ground her guidebook identifies as the Parque Central. Illuminated by a lozenge of yellow light, thirty or so people crowd round an imposing statue of Jose Julian Marti Perez, national hero and a symbol of the Cuba's bid for independence from Spain in the nineteenth century. They sing and sway to the rhythm of a samba beat, music and laughter drifting in the air.

20

The restfulness is strangely at odds with her experience at the airport, where she clenched her fists in an effort to calm herself after the face-off. Why did the guard single her out? She is not some head-turning blonde with an hourglass figure and a sway like a drunk on rollerblades. Men find her attractive, but she does not consider herself beautiful, certainly not glamorous; not glamorous enough for a gun-toting gorilla to single her out. Maybe he had perverted sexual preferences, misled by her unwomanly close-cropped hair and combat trousers. Maybe he was short-sighted. Maybe he was simply a bully who got his kicks from tormenting new arrivals in his country. Whatever the reason, she resolved not to be intimidated. She stood her ground, determined not to flinch. For an agonising moment, she held his eyes, heart hammering against her ribs. Just as she was on the verge of buckling, his beard parted in a nicotine-stained grin. In tortured English, he welcomed her to Cuba. Then, as quickly as it arrived, the grin vanished and he resumed his slow, methodical pacing up and down, seeking out his next victim.

After the long flight and nervy encounter, she feels weightless. Her body begs for rest, but thoughts race around her head, careening around her lover, her fiancé and her interfering father.

Peru, a man she once worshipped, has changed. A cold, hard skin now blankets the passion that once burned between them. On the rare occasions they make love in one of the safe houses, he is remote, indifferent, his mind elsewhere. She sees him watch, without a trace of emotion, images of carnage flash one after another on the news programmes. She thought his obsession with removing Salbatore was the cause of his indifference. Now that Salbatore has reluctantly passed the baton, she realises the root of his ambition reaches much deeper.

With the old Peru, she knew exactly what to expect. Of late, he is like a man who has grown a dual personality. One, she thinks she loves: the other, she is not sure she wants to understand.

Fabien is her fiancé, a kind, generous and sensitive man who loves her unconditionally and isn't afraid to show it. Brand Manager at Oromundo, one of her father's smaller companies, he is bright, attentive, and courteous; a son of one of the city's oldest and most respected families. The Mendiolas are highly regarded, reputed to be asset rich, but suspected cash poor. Unlike many of the landed gentry, he has chosen to work for a living rather than laze about a stately pile all day, bemoaning his lot. Her relationship with him was Peru's idea and, as always, she went along with it.

She thinks back to when he first suggested it, late one evening after a meeting in the Chat Noir.

'Terese, I'm worried your old man's getting too close for comfort. Martina has noticed his thugs keeping their eyes on you a lot recently. Sooner or later they're bound to connect you to ETA and if they do . . . well, I don't have to tell you what that would mean. I think we need to find you a boyfriend. A decoy if you like. Someone your father won't try to frighten off. Someone he's comfortable with.'

Her mouth twisted into a smirk. 'That narrows the field considerably.'

'Yeah, well, I've been thinking. He'll have to have a high profile, ideally a good social standing.' He stroked his goatee. 'You know, I think Fabien Mendiola would fit the bill perfectly.'

Her jaw dropped. 'Fabien Mendiola? You must be joking! They say he's as shallow as a toddler's paddling pool! If you think I'm cuddling up with *him*, then you have another think coming. I wouldn't—'

'Come on, Terese. It's only for a short while. Think about it. One, Mendiola is from one of the oldest aristocratic families in town; your old man would approve. Two, he's clean living, above scandal and therefore none of your newspaper colleagues would have the slightest interest in him. Three, he's weak, and you'll have no difficulty controlling him. Four—'

She held up her hand. 'Don't tell me, let me guess. He's employed by Groupe Rodriguez so my father already knows everything there is to know about him.'

'Got it in one.'

It seemed a good idea at the time, although she was not convinced. Then the 'short' while grew into three months, then six: six months during which she has deceived Fabien. He represents everything Peru detests; inherited privilege, breeding and wealth. Of course, the rumours proved to be true. Fabien confided in her that his family are strapped for cash, but too proud to divest themselves of family heirlooms, relying instead on the continuing tolerance of a bank that is fast becoming impatient with its highborn clients. Recently and completely unexpectedly, he cranked their relationship up a gear and suggested they get engaged. She reluctantly agreed, fearing a refusal might anger Peru; but there was a proviso—she made Fabien promise to keep their engagement a secret. That left him sad and disappointed. Nevertheless, he accepted it was her wish and said he would never pressure her. She would know when the time was right to announce it to the world.

He really is a very, very decent man and, in her life, decent men are thinner on the ground than a summer snowfall.

Her conscience needles her constantly, reminding her she is using the poor man solely as a means to a dishonourable end. From time to time, she thinks about expressing her uncertainty to Peru, but she never does, courage always failing her. At some point soon, he will order her to discard Fabien like a worn out pair of shoes when he has served his purpose. Disconcertingly, she feels needed when in Fabien's company, as if she's at the centre of his universe. With Peru, she will always be on the periphery, a handmaiden to his ego and ambition.

Viktor, her father, openly refuses to keep his nose out of her life. Most times, she doesn't give it a second thought, but on the flight from Paris an article in the airline magazine covering Bayonne's annual Aste Nagusia festival caught her attention, reminding her of the way he treats her; controlling, cajoling, and bullying as far back as she can recall.

It began when she was just seven years old. It was her second Aste Nagusia. Her mother, Marie-Louise, glowed with expectant pride at once again seeing her daughter parade with all the children from Les Beaux Arbres primary school. Terese herself had been bursting with anticipation for weeks, talking excitedly with her friends about the route of the parade, the gifts they would receive from friends and onlookers as they walked, and the various foods they would eat afterwards.

Then her father intervened. Six days before the parade, he joined Marie-Louise and her in the drawing room of their palatial house as they flicked through photographs of the previous year's festival. He was carrying three boxes that he laid on the table in front of them.

'This year, Terese, I want you to look really special,' he told her, looking down from his great height. 'This year, you will shine like the brightest star in the heavens. You are a Rodriguez, and people in this city look up to us.'

'But Papa,' she protested, 'I don't want to look special. I want to look the same as my friends.'

He brushed off her protest, opened the contents of each box in turn and laid them on the table. They contained a beautifully styled cream dress, a pair of cream ankle socks and the shiniest of red patent pumps. She can visualise the look of horror on her mother's face even now. It was traditional for the girls to wear white dresses, white ankle socks with a lace frill around the top and black leather pumps. Dressed in that way, they would all look identical. That was the intention and the custom, but it was not good enough for her father.

'There,' he declared a look of pride on his face. 'Aren't they beautiful? I had them made in Paris, especially for you.'

Tears welled up in her eyes. 'I'm not wearing those, Papa. I don't like them.'

'Of course you do. They're much better than what the others will be wearing. Now try them on so I can see what they look like.'

'I don't want to—'

He brought his face to within inches of hers. His breath was heavy with the smell of cognac, his eyes burning with anger. 'I'm not asking you, Terese. Put. Them. On.'

'No, I won't, I won't.'

'I won't tell you again.'

She resorted to screaming and tantrums. He boiled over, and lashed her across the back of her legs with the open palm of his hand leaving a bright red weal. It was the first time he had hit her. Her mother tried to make him see reason, but in vain. Marie-Louise knew better than to argue with a man who provided her with a lifestyle to which only film stars could aspire. Terese's teachers also petitioned him to change his mind, but they didn't try too hard. Monsieur Rodriguez was a patron of the school and, frankly, they depended on his financial support.

On the day of the parade all eyes were on her, the little girl who looked different to the rest. The effect was not the one her father had anticipated. The boys laughed at her and the girls tittered behind their hands. The women lining the route of the parade shook their heads and those who clucked to their friends were told to 'shut up' by their men folk. The men watched dutifully, mouths clamped tight, as many of them were in the employ of Monsieur Rodriguez. She was utterly miserable and everyone noticed it.

That attitude brought her two more lashings across the legs later the same evening.

That Aste Nagusia episode marked a turning point in their relationship. From that day onwards, she regarded her father with suspicion and fear. Gradually, she felt herself change from a bright, bouncy little girl into a wary, cautious individual who found it hard to trust him. She resisted every effort of her domineering father to control her. Viktor, a man without an ounce of empathy in his body, treated the situation as he would his business dealings—in the only way he knew how—by piling on more pressure hoping she would eventually crack. She did not. Terese had mined a seam of her father in her. She turned stubborn and resourceful. As she grew, the arguments and ensuing smacks became more frequent, but still she would not break. Her mother pleaded with him to desist, but he did not know how to give up; not until her mother was rushed into hospital with a perforated ulcer. That really shook him as his first wife had died nineteen years before from a debilitating illness.

She became the scapegoat for her mother's illness. Two weeks after the hospital admitted Marie-Louise,

26

Terese's cases were packed. Viktor put her on the train to Bordeaux en route to the Lycee Prive Largente, her new boarding school. The worm of hate began to wriggle its way deeper into her soul. Her father had taken away her friends, the mother she loved dearly, and the countryside she knew so well.

She breathes deeply, realising how much these three men have woven themselves in the fabric of her life. One wants her for her genes, one wants her for his own ends and one simply wants her.

Walking barefoot across the darkly-stained floorboards into the small bathroom, she pauses before the white enamel washbasin and looks at herself in the mirror. At first, she finds it hard to imagine the face staring back at her with the unfamiliar hairstyle is hers. All her life she has worn her hair long; loose or clipped in a ponytail. Peru complained bitterly after she cut it, saying it makes her look like a man. Fabien's reaction was very different. He complimented her on how much it suits her.

She doesn't give a damn what her father thinks.

Her eyes feel as dry as the Kalahari. She really needs to get some sleep and if her mind won't let her then sleeping pills will. Searching in her toilet bag, she takes out a bottle and tips one out. Returning to the bedroom, she opens the door of the mini bar and removes a small bottle of still water, unscrews the top, pops the sleeping pill in her mouth and gulps down a mouthful.

Lying on the bed, she sneaks one more look at the photocopied photograph given to her by Martina. The man in it wears a military uniform, his hair close-cropped. Taken some time ago, she wonders how much he has changed and if she will be able to recognise him. However, recognise him she must. If she doesn't find

Angelo Fortunato her mission will become a whole lot more complicated.

Peru finds the date on the calendar pinned to the back of the kitchen door, scores it with a red cross. His mouth stretches to a slit. Did he make the right decision in choosing Terese? The incident in the southern Philippines planted a seed of doubt in his mind. Terese and he passed four weeks with the Abu Sayyaf Group, a cause that sympathises with their own, has similar objectives and uses similar methods. He noticed the way she gagged as they watched films showing ways to silently stalk and slit the throat of an enemy and recordings of bombs exploding amidst civilian crowds, with the resulting bloody and fear-stricken aftermath. Then, one rain-soaked evening at the end of another muscle-straining day crawling through sodden undergrowth and wading in muddy ditches in the lashing rain of a torrential tropical thunderstorm, she expressed her misgivings as they huddled together in the narrow confines of their two-man tent. Anger shot through him as he grabbed her roughly, holding her arms in a vice-like grip.

'This isn't some kind of game like your old man plays,' he said. 'This is war and in war, if people don't kill, they get killed. If you can't handle that then it may be for the best if you get out now.'

She assured him instantly she could, but her eyes would not hold his.

Now he is mindful to watch her as the commando goes about its work. On the face of it, she appears to have made up for her lack of conviction. Nevertheless, he is cautious. People have let him down before and he isn't about to let it happen again.

He wanted to send Martina, of course he did. She is much better suited to the task than Terese. Martina has proven herself repeatedly, but there was a problem. Her father, in spite of the fact that he is a patriot to his core, would never forgive Peru if his only daughter was lost to him, and Peru depends on the man's contacts. Terese has yet to show she is worthy. He killed two birds with one stone by saying Martina's quick temper renders her unsuitable and Terese is the only available alternative.

Staring at the calendar, he wonders again if he has made the right decision. So much is at stake.

Perhaps I shouldn't have ignored my gut feeling. Perhaps I should have sent Martina after all.

6th July

The sleeping pill does the trick, coaxing Terese into the welcome blackness of sleep. Shortly before eight-thirty, she wakes, rises, showers, dresses and then leaves her room to take a light breakfast in the Telegrafo's capacious café. As she sips her glass of orange juice, sitting amid lozenges of sunlight filtering through windows set high in the structure's tall, brick arches, she dwells on the task before her. Today, she has to find Angelo. There is no guarantee she will stumble across him in this part of Havana, but it is as good a place as any to start her search. The Old City and its surroundings are a magnet for tourists and if tourists are there then so too is the money, and her research tells her Angelo likes money.

She finishes the juice, signs for breakfast then makes her way to the hotel lobby. Taking the photocopy out of her pocket, she approaches a smiling young man on duty at the porter's desk. A silver name badge, pinned to his lapel, announces to the world that his name is Carlos.

'Excuse me. I wonder if you could help me, please.'

'Certainly, senorita. What can I do for you?'

'I'm looking for this man. Do you know him?' She hands him the photocopy, expecting him to shake his head: after all, it is a long shot and she is prepared to make many such enquiries before somebody recognises Angelo's face.

His answer surprises her. 'Yes, I know him. He takes tourists around the city.'

'I don't suppose you know where I can find him?'

He grins, shows a set of straight white teeth. 'I know exactly where you'll find him. He'll be looking for business near the Hotel Parque Central.'

'Is that far?'

He laughs. 'Not far. Come, I'll show you.'

At the door, he points at a large building constructed in the Spanish colonial style directly opposite the Telegrafo. 'There, that's the Hotel Parque Central. The entrance is at the far end of the street. Most of the pony men gather there. Plenty of business, you see.'

'Pony men?'

'The pony men take tourists around Havana in their traps.' He jabs a finger at the photocopy. 'This man is one of them.'

'Ah, I see.'

Thanking him, she steps into the long shadow thrown by the imposing, pillared bulk of the hotel. The heat strikes her face like a hot towel and seeps into the underside of her feet through the thin soles of her sandals. Beads of sweat leach out of her upper lip and along her hairline. Cautiously threading her way through a dodgem string of bright yellow, one-eyed coco taxis, she crosses to the other side of the street and halts briefly at the edge of the park. She scans the photocopy quickly to refresh the image in her mind. Returning it to her pocket, she spots the entrance to the Parque Central Hotel, opposite which there is row of ponies and traps, waiting patiently beneath the protruding fingers of a clump of elephant-trunked palm trees. Groups of tourists in ones and twos slink past them, as if they wish for nothing more than to blend inconspicuously with their surroundings, invisible to the pleas of the welcoming, vibrant people who attempt amicably to relieve them of just a little of their cash.

As she begins to walk towards the ponies in the direction of the Old City, the smell of dung mixed with petrol fumes catches her nose. Sunlight filters through the trees' silvery foliage, spattering mottled patterns on the walkways. In the park, the sound of a spirited salsa drifts from a group around which a crowd has gathered.

A small knot of men sit huddled on the pavement, passing a can of Coke from one to another. None of them looks like the man she seeks. Perhaps Angelo has found a willing tourist and is already trotting along the streets.

Or maybe he isn't working today.

She glances at her watch. 10:07.

She scrutinizes the faces again. He definitely isn't there. Should she risk asking them if they know where he is? She dismisses the thought immediately; it might arouse suspicion. Her guidebook notes that people in this country are cautious about answering questions from strangers, knowing their answers may be misunderstood or misconstrued. If approached by a foreigner waving a photocopy it could set alarm bells ringing, something she wants to avoid at all costs.

Considering her options, she decides to wait in the lobby of the Parque Central Hotel and finds a seat where she has a clear view of the pony men's comings and goings. As she reaches the hotel's entrance, the uniformed attendant bows and holds open the glass door for her. Inside, people are busy checking out, their luggage piled high on the porters' trolleys. A dozen or so circular wooden tables are spaced around the marble-floored lobby and she finds one unoccupied, facing the entrance. Through the doors, she can see the pony men as they stroll up and down, their arms making imploring gestures as they try to attract customers.

She will wait here and hope to spot Angelo. If he does not appear in the next hour and a half, she will show her photocopy to the receptionist and enquire where she might find him.

'I bring you drink, senorita?' The high-pitched voice makes her jump. She looks to her side where a white-haired man leans towards her, skin the colour of coffee grounds and dressed in the hotel's livery, his mouth stretched wide in a toothless grin.

'A cup of coffee would be good, thank you.'

'Espresso?'

'Please.'

'Very well. Juan will bring one for you in no time at all.'

Five minutes later, he returns, places a cafetière and a white china cup and saucer on her table. 'Enjoy your day, senorita,' he says, before moving on to an elderly couple sitting three tables away.

Depressing the cafetiere's metal plunger, she fills the cup. Raising it to her lips, she peers over the rim, her attention caught by the neighbouring table occupied by two men. The figure of one overflows his chair, his corpulent body squeezed into an expensively cut, dark brown suit. His hands, resting on the table in front of him, sparkle with overstated gold rings; at least six or seven. Her first thought is he must be important to be so comfortable with such an ostentatious and rare display of wealth. He isn't a tourist; too relaxed, too self-assured: possibly a politician or dignitary. His companion, a beanpole with jet-black slicked-back hair, could easily be a down-and-out, his greasy suit is that crumpled. An angry, acne-riddled face, one eye that must be glass as it remains straight ahead no matter in which direction the other is looking, doesn't suggest Brad Pitt should worry any time soon.

An odd couple, she thinks.

She resumes her surveillance of the pony men, but, involuntarily, her ears tune in to the conversation taking place between her neighbours.

'What do you want me to do, Senor Suarez?' asks the beanpole.

'I think a little . . . persuasion . . . is called for, Adelmo.' The fat man drums his fingers rapidly on the tabletop.

The beanpole cracks his knuckles. 'As in—'

'Exactly. The contract signing is on the thirty-first of the month and there must be no last minute changes of heart. If Gomez puts any doubt in the others' minds there will be some serious consequences, some very serious consequences. The Frenchman is a very powerful man, a man it would not be wise to disappoint. Do you follow me?'

'I do, senor, but if he won't agree? Then should I—'

'Shush!' The fat man lowers his voice so she can hardly hear. 'Then you should shoot him, but be damned sure to make it look like an accident. Now, I must go, I have people to see. Meet me outside the tobacco factory at seven. And Adelmo . . . '

'Senor?'

'Do not fail.'

Rising from their seats, they shake hands and walk out of the entrance, the fat man beckoning to the door attendant, the beanpole heading in the direction of the Old City.

Terese weighs their words in the light of what she is in Cuba to do, and her stomach tightens.

11:25.

Waiting is playing havoc with her nerves. She gulps down a third cup of coffee, pays the bill. She slides back the chair, walks past the front desk and out of the hotel, having convinced herself that approaching the receptionist might not be her best course of action after all.

I'll walk round the park. By the time I've done that, he may have returned.

Crossing back to the park, she heads off along the road delineating the fringes of the Old City. As the tempo of her feet increases, she senses a presence next to her, matching her stride for stride. She puts it out of her mind, intent on avoiding the pavement's broken surface and water-filled potholes.

'Miss, do you want to take a pony ride round the Old City?' The male voice is soft, sibilant.

She resists the urge to respond. Her guidebook is clear. Havana's hustlers expect a refusal of their first offer. When that happens, they will then repeat it with a price incentive thrown in for good measure. Take him up on his first offer and she will only disappoint him.

She quickens her pace without turning her head.

'It's a great way to see everything and I only charge ten pesos.'

Out of the corner of her eye she glimpses the man and her heart skips a beat. There is a likeness to the photocopy, but she cannot be sure. It may be him, but the large sunglasses and dappled shadow thrown by a straw fedora conceal his features. She decides it is too much of a coincidence and waves him away.

'No, thank you. I prefer to walk.'

Her guidebook is clear on this also. Pestering her could land him in trouble. The authorities take a dim view of tourist harassment, especially women tourists.

'OK, but you don't know what you're missing. Angelo Fortunato is the best you'll find. Ask anyone.' He peels off in the direction of the Paseo de Marti.

She cannot believe her luck. Here he is, Angelo Fortunato, the son of a cragged revolutionary who marched and fought with Castro and Cienfuegos and became a legend in his own time. The Major General she must face. She wavers, turns and looks at his departing back as he ambles away.

'Excuse me, do you tour Downtown Havana?' she calls after his retreating figure.

He stops dead, silent for a moment. It is as if her question lingers, unheard, before sliding down the convolutions of his ear. He swivels on his heels to face her.

'Sure, I can take you to see Revolution Square, Jose Marti Memorial, Ministry of the Interior, the works. There are plenty of interesting places I can tell you about.'

'How much would it cost?'

He hesitates then holds five fingers in the air. 'Five dollars for three hours. That's fantastic value.'

'Make it three and you have a deal.'

He throws his arms aloft. 'But I could not cover my costs for three!'

Her heart is in her mouth.

Don't lose him now.

'Four. Take it or leave it.'

He tuts, runs his hand over his forehead. 'OK, OK. Four.'

'I want to go at two o'clock.'

'No problem. What's your name and nationality?'

She bites on the words before they come out. The fewer people who know her name, the better. 'Why do you need to know?'

He shrugs his shoulders. 'The government says I must submit these details to keep my licence. That's the way it is.'

Again, she wavers, uncertain. Then she makes her decision.

'Terese Rodriguez. I'm . . . I'm French.'

Five minutes past three and the air is blisteringly hot. Still, lifeless. The sun has sucked the greenness out of the grass, leaving behind a palette of burnt umber and russet. Occasionally, a snapping of tinder-dry leaves punctures the silence. The cracked, rock-hard earth cries out for the soothing relief of rain. Though it is almost the midpoint of the rainy season, the year is exceptionally dry. A smell of chicken roasting wafts from houses in the near distance.

By the side of the road, under the shade of an unruly sprawl of Royal Palms, Angelo's pony and trap stand motionless. After half an hour on the road, pausing only to buy a pineapple from a street hawker, they are taking a break, stretching their legs in Revolution Square. Fifty metres from where the pony rests they peer up at the monolithic, seven-storey-tall Ministry of Interior offices. A skeletal, metal sculpture of Che Guevara adorns the front of the cell-like building, its passionate intensity fuelling the inspiration for the iconic image that decorates everything from cups to T-shirts around the world. Coal-black, steel words—'Hasta la victoire siempre'—spill from its mouth and hang in suspended animation above the main door. A huge red, blue and white flag cascades from the top to the bottom of the unremarkable structure.

'Do you know he wasn't even Cuban?' Angelo says, pointing at the face and taking a swig of water from a half-full plastic bottle.

'No,' she lies, shaking her head. 'I always assumed he was.'

'So do most people. He was actually born in Argentina and studied medicine at the University of Buenos Aires, intending to become a doctor. Then, before he graduated, he took a year off from his studies. Alberto Granado, a close friend, and Guevara travelled on their motorcycles to the San Pablo leper colony in Peru to do some volunteer work. Guevara kept an account of the journey, which he later published as *The Motorcycle Diaries*. By the time he reached Peru he thought of South America as a single country. Shocked by the poverty, he declared that 'monopoly capitalism, neo-colonialism, and imperialism' caused the region's economic inequalities. Guevara spoke such big words! He graduated after returning to Argentina, but what he saw on his journey deeply affected him. He gave up medicine, threw himself into armed struggle. World revolution was his solution. After a short stay in Guatemala, he teamed up with Castro in Mexico and everybody knows what happened after that.'

'Fascinating.' Shielding her eyes against the glare of the burning sun, she squints up at the vast countenance of Guevara.

'Fascinating, yes, but his relentless pursuit of social justice got him killed in the end.'

I know what got him killed, my friend. I know everything about Ernesto 'Che' Guevara. I know where he was born, how he met Castro, when he became involved with the M-26-7. I know he oversaw the revolutionary tribunals and executions of suspected war criminals from the reign of the tyrant president, Fulgencio Batista. I know all this because since I was fifteen I've read every one of his diaries over and over and over again. I've hung on to every word, every meaning, every nuance. I know these things because I made it my business to know. I made it my business when I discovered that the man had Basque blood running in his veins and that he has an interesting connection to your father. That's why I'm here.

'"Always until victory",' Angelo translates, pointing at each of the words in turn. 'I'll say one thing for the guy; he had plenty of guts and he didn't know when to give up. Do you want me to photograph you with him in the background?'

She considers his suggestion. It will be interesting to see the effect the photograph has when she returns home. There will be plenty of teasing from her colleagues at *El Correo*. Peru will say she looks a true comrade, ready to die for the cause. As for Fabien, he is bound to comment on how beautiful she looks, beautiful and natural. Flattery is second nature to him and, although she does not care to admit it to herself, she is getting to like it.

'Sure. Do you know how to use this?' She hands him the compact, black camera.

He weighs it in his hands. 'Wow, a Nikon D70S. This is a nice piece of kit. Only tourists can afford these.'

As he admires the Nikon, she strikes a pose she thinks will impress Peru and please Fabien. Tall and slim, dressed in khaki shorts and mushroom-coloured T-shirt, she holds her back ramrod-straight, left arm by her side, right arm folded into a salute.

'You look as if you're on a parade ground,' says Angelo. 'Smile.'

An hour and twenty-five minutes later, an atmosphere thick with distillate-laden fumes spewing out from vehicles built during a less environmentally aware era envelops the pony and trap. There are hordes of people on the streets now, going about their daily business.

'Where in France do you live, Terese?' Angelo jerks the pony's reins, stirring it into a trot as he threads the animal through the chaotic late afternoon traffic on Avenida de Los Presidentes.

'Bayonne. Have you heard of it?'

'Bayonne? I don't think I have. Where in France is it?'

She studies the profile of the face half-turned towards her. A sickle-shaped scar stands out on his sunburned cheek and she can see a diminished image of herself reflected in the lens of his thin-framed, cheap sunglasses. Beads of sweat bubble on the dark stubble covering his upper lip and tiny rivulets chase the contours of his jaw. At his temple, beneath the battered fedora, there is evidence of the first signs of grey.

'It's in the south-west. Close to the Spanish border. Have you heard of Biarritz?'

He nods, slowly. 'Ah, I know of Biarritz. Many people from that place come to Havana. What do you do in Bayonne?'

'You're very inquisitive.'

'All Cubans are inquisitive, it's in our nature. I'm interested to know how people live in other countries. If you think I'm inquisitive you should meet my uncle.'

She already knows about the uncle. Felipe Caraballo is a bit player with but one important task to fulfil.

They reach the jumbled confluence of traffic at the junction of Avenida de Los Presidentes and Malecon. As they turn onto Malecon she finds herself surprised and shocked in equal measure. There is clear evidence of Soviet handiwork in the stark and characterless blocks of new social housing strewn out along the waterfront. Interspersed among them, in stark contrast, are many partially demolished houses waiting patiently for the promise of overdue regeneration to materialise. A substantial number of them bear scars from the hurricanes that bedevil Cuba. Only the previous year, Hurricane Wilma ripped up Malecon and its neighbouring streets. Unbelievably, people still live in these tired and worn-out shells, many clad in rusty scaffolding around which strangling creepers and dust-covered weeds claim a permanent presence.

It is plain to see the Russians skipped the country in a hurry before the job was anywhere near completed.

Anger wells up inside her. In the days when he valued her opinion, Peru and she passed many hours discussing the exploited people of Cuba. A plaything of powerful nations—first Spain, then the United States and finally the Soviet Union—invaders had plundered and pillaged the resource-rich country for centuries. When in '59 the M-26-7 finally threw off the yoke of Batista's corrupt regime, the people hoped that a new era of prosperity and equality would dawn. Not a chance. Old habits die hard, and the US wouldn't stop picking at the scab that was Cuba, fearing its communist leanings. Castro's unique hotchpotch of the political ideals of Marx, Engels and Lenin sustained the people only until '61 when he spat in the face of the Americans and welcomed the Russians warmly. Predictably, the Americans reacted by blockading Cuba and just as predictably the Russians countered by running the blockade. They bought the bulk of the island's sugar harvest and Soviet ships crammed into Havana harbour, bringing in desperately needed goods. Then the '80s era of Mikhail Gorbachev proved catastrophic for Castro, with Moscow pulling the plug on the Cuban economy by refusing to take its sugar. Still under the American blockade, and with its Soviet lifeline cut off, chronic shortages and empty shelves were inevitable. Tempers grew shorter as food queues grew longer. By the mid

'90s, many Cubans had suffered enough, thousands taking to the sea in a waterborne exodus to Florida in which many drowned. Luckless in its game of snakes-and-ladders, Cuba slid back to square one. Six years into the new millennium, the country is only just beginning to climb the rungs again, thanks to the renaissance of the tourist trade.

Angelo's voice cuts into her thoughts. 'From here, you can see my apartment in Casablanca. Look over there—the shining white building.'

Her eyes follow the line of his outstretched arm to a lump of bland ash-coloured concrete on the far side of the deep blue waters of Havana harbour. Indistinguishable from the ones they pass; one more testimony to Cuba's Soviet-trained architects.

'It looks very . . . attractive. You must have great views.'

'Terese, it's a pile of shit and my apartment looks out onto a deserted building plot. In another twenty years' time, it will be one more slum, only a high-rise one. What's your house like?'

It is inevitable he would ask this question at some point, leading to other, more probing ones. After all, he is only human and an impecunious human at that. A bony finger of guilt twists itself into her gut. No matter how much she tries to ignore it, that finger always digs deep and reminds her of a fact she would rather forget: she is the daughter of an extremely rich man, like it or lump it. Viktor Rodriguez always buys the most expensive and the best of everything, the prerogative of a billionaire several times over. That includes a rambling mansion in the most exclusive part of Bayonne.

'Oh, it's quite a large house in its own grounds.' Her answer is a half-truth. She now lives in a pint-sized house with a pocket-handkerchief-sized garden. Although at one time she *did* live in a huge house until she escaped her meddling father.

'How big is it? How many square metres? How many rooms?' He sounds like a small child begging for ice cream.

'Hmm, let me see. I guess about three thousand.'

His voice leaps an octave. 'Three thousand metres? Shit! That's twenty times the size of my apartment!'

She knows the questions will flow after that.

'What car do you drive?'

'A Porsche.'

Another lie.

'Which model?'

'911.'

'What colour?'

'Black.'

'Wow. How much do you make?'

'Make?'

'Earn. In your business.'

'That's personal.'

His sweat-varnished head is now swinging from side to side like a metronome. For the next five minutes, no words pass between them, the stillness broken only by the regular clip-clopping of the pony's hooves and the chug-chugging of cars streaming past them as they progress along the seafront.

'This place is just as I imagined it would be,' she says. 'Full of nostalgia.'

He nods. 'I hear that from many tourists. But you wouldn't think it if you had to live here.'

She is tempted to ask why not, but resists.

'You know, I have a friend called Rafael,' he says. 'People used to call us Los Gemelos—The Twins.'

'Why did they do that?'

43

'It goes back to when I was a small boy in primary school. I was my school soccer team's goalkeeper. During one match with a rival team, their centre forward kept backing into me whenever they took a corner. I finally grew impatient with his tricks and grabbed his shirt. He elbowed me on the nose, breaking it in two places.' He points at his nose, indicating where the breaks occurred. 'The centre forward was Rafael. But I got my own back.'

'What did you do?'

'Six months later there was a return match. As he tried to slip a low ball past me, I jumped with both feet on to his ankle, making sure it looked like a genuine challenge. There was a big *crack!* as my feet made contact.'

Terese winces. She hates the sound of breaking bones. The training films are full of them—fingers snapping, shins crunching, kneecaps . . .

'But I felt terrible for what I had done. I visited him twice a week for the next two months until his ankle mended. I found out we had a lot in common and shared a love of baseball as well as football. After that, we became the best of friends and went everywhere together. That's why people called us The Twins, we were that close.' He shows her his thumb and forefinger, almost touching. 'Now he's rich and I'm doing this.'

Her mind flashes back to the fat man with fingers full of gold rings. 'I'm sorry, I don't understand. I thought the regime here discourages people from becoming rich. So how come your friend is?'

A dark shadow passes across his face. For a moment, he appears lost in his own thoughts. 'Rafael no longer lives in Cuba.'

'Where is he?'

'He went to join his brother in Florida, thirteen years ago. Carlos was among the first to leave. All he took with

44

him was a bag full of clothes and a few personal belongings.'

She has read how the Cuban government reached an agreement with the Americans allowing twenty thousand of its citizens to emigrate every year.

'It must have been hard for Carlos, leaving his family behind for a strange country,' she says.

'Carlos is a survivor, a tough kid from a tough street. In Florida, he found a job crewing for a Chinese guy in the Keys. For three years he worked all hours, saved hard, kept his nose clean and eyes open. After that, he had enough money to buy a small tackle shop. That made him more money than he could have imagined. He also found himself a beautiful wife, the daughter of another émigré Cuban named Luiz. Four years later, he heard of a small Ford dealership for sale in Palmetto Bay. He got finance at the local Wells Fargo, spoke to the owner and went into the auto business. Rafael had recently demobbed and was worried about life in Cuba as a civilian. When Carlos asked him to come over, he couldn't leave fast enough. He applied for his papers and then boarded a ship bound for Florida as soon as he could. Now he owns an eight-bedroom villa on the outskirts of Kissimmee and a convertible Ferrari. Look.'

Reaching into his back pocket, he produces a crumpled photograph and hands it to her. On it, a short, swarthy man lounges against a shiny red sports car, his arm wrapped proprietarily around a much taller, raven-haired woman, who proudly rests her hands on a swollen midriff.

'Is that his wife?'

'Yes, Betty-Jo. They've been married three years. Their first child is due in October. I dream of a life like his.'

'Why don't you join him?'

'I can't.'

'Why not?'

'That's personal. You ask a lot of questions.'

'Must be my nature.'

He laughs. 'Perhaps we'll make you an honorary Cuban.'

Although no wedding ring decorates his finger, her intuition tells her he is married. 'Is it because of your wife? Won't she go with you?'

He shifts uncomfortably in his seat. 'No she won't, but that's only part of the problem.'

Her journalistic nose twitches. Talking to Angelo is diverting, and she desperately needs something to take her mind off the days to come. 'Do you want to talk about it?'

This time, he shows no reluctance. 'I have the dubious pleasure of being the son of a famous son of our country. Have you heard of Eduardo Fortunato?'

'I'm sorry, I haven't.'

One more lie, Terese. How easily they slip off your tongue.

'My father was a close friend of the Presidente until he retired. Back in the early fifties, Castro recruited him when Batista was in power. Unfortunately, like many of the people still in power, my father's loyalties and beliefs have failed to move on. He has a deep-rooted hatred of America and all things American. He considers anything remotely connected to that country, such as personal ambition and the pursuit of wealth, to be beneath his contempt. If I left Cuba for Florida he would treat it as an act of desertion and wipe his hands of me.'

'How does your mother feel about it?'

'Oh, she's not as dogmatic as my father. I think deep down she's accepted things here must change. They say you have only to visit Varadero to see proof of that. Of course, she would never let her feelings show. You see, she too was a revolutionary. No, my mother takes issue with me on a different matter entirely.'

'Which is?'

'She doesn't believe in divorce.'

'You're thinking of divorcing your wife?'

'I can't deny the thought has crossed my mind on more than one occasion. It would be difficult enough if only my mother frowned on divorce, but my religion does, too. I'm a Santerian and marriage is . . . well, it's sacred.'

'And divorce is always harder on children.'

Although in my case I would have welcomed it like a long-lost friend.

He harrumphs. 'Kids? We don't have any. That's another problem.'

'Oh, I'm sorry. I really didn't mean to be personal.'

'That's OK. My wife desperately wants children. It's me who doesn't.'

'You don't?'

He tilts his chin in the direction of the human river flowing along the street. 'They all look so content, don't they?'

'Who?'

'My fellow countrymen, smiles on their faces as they sell cigars and trinkets to the visiting masses. You would be surprised what misery a smile can hide. Take the Old City. The government spends much money on it to give the impression it's romantic, mysterious: all Hemingway and American gangsters. That's how tourists want to find Havana and that's the memory they'll take with them when they return home. But they don't see children playing in broken streets that haven't been maintained for the past thirty years and homes that are crumbling around them.'

'Like on Malecon?'

'Malecon? Ha! They were the good ones. If you were to see where my brother lives, you would be horrified.'

'But your apartment isn't like that, is it? It's new and I would imagine everything to be in good working order.'

'As I told you, it might be new but it was built to a tight budget. Besides, how do you think kids from the slums treat children from places like mine when they mix? It's a social disaster waiting to happen.'

'And that's why you don't want children?'

'I didn't say I don't *want* children. I can't bear the thought of bringing them up in this country as it is today. That's one reason why I want to go to Florida. Everybody knows it's a great place for kids with Mickey Mouse and Disney.'

She stops herself from contradicting him. America is one place she has no ambition to visit. Florida, she hears, is not a place for the Land of the Free's children. It's a place of escape for the nation's adults, and far from free.

'It sounds like you're caught in a cleft stick.'

He taps the side of his head. 'In here, a man can have his dreams.'

'Of course he can. Without dreams life is nothing. Tell me about your wife.'

'Her name is Maria. When I first met her, I thought she was the most wonderful thing that ever happened to me. We met at Rafael's birthday party. The second she walked through the door, I noticed her; legs that went on forever and hair the colour of roasted coffee beans. She was a work colleague of Rafael's elder sister, Lucia. I was a little drunk at the time and that helped me build up the courage to ask her to dance. We hit it off and started dating. At the time, I was in the army. Twelve months later, they sent me to Angola to fight. We thought we might never see each other again, so we married. It was a mistake.'

'I'm sure things will work out.' She passes the photo back to him.

'Wow, a mansion *and* a Porsche. I guess you must have plenty of money?' He slips the photo in his pocket.

'I guess so.'

A trio of girls sitting on the sea wall, hands covering their giggling, waves at them. Angelo waves back.

'What's it like to be rich, Terese?'

'Oh, I don't know, I don't think about it much. I suppose if you like to travel as I do, then it means you can go anywhere you wish.'

'The only place I want to go is America.'

'Then perhaps you should pursue your dream, regardless of the consequences.'

They lapse into silence again as he edges the pony gingerly into El Prado, the final stretch before returning to the Parque Central. There seems no concept of traffic control on this busy thoroughfare with suicidal pedestrians darting out across the road and engaging in a dance of death with the chaotic traffic. Few road users signal their intentions; not surprising, as many of the ancient cars lack indicators and most drivers seem reluctant to reveal what their next manoeuvre might be.

The Bayonne police would be writing tickets like demons possessed if people there behaved like this, she thinks.

She scrutinizes the man she hopes will lead her to his father. Dressed from head to toe in white; T-shirt, slacks, socks and sneakers—she already knows he is a devoted follower of Santeria, unlike the rest of his Catholic family and his bitingly sceptical father who abandoned religious beliefs as soon as he contracted the fever of revolution.

I know you're a man of principle. I know you're desperate to have the good things in life. I know you're very different to your father and brothers. We have a detailed dossier on your family, Angelo Fortunato. Martina and her father had to pull plenty of strings to get it. Anyway, enough polite conversation; it's time to reel you in.

'Angelo, have you ever been to Santiago?'

'Santiago? I was born there and my parents live in the city. Why do you ask?'

'I've decided that's the next place I want to see after Havana. Do you know of anyone who would drive me down there? It's a long way from Havana, but I don't want to fly and miss the sights.'

Ok, let's see if the fish bites.

Gently tugging on the pony's reins, he pulls into the side of the road and brings the trap to a standstill. Taking off his hat, he wipes his perspiring brow with the back of his hand and turns to face her. 'I think you'll have difficulty finding a taxi. At this time of year, the drivers can make a mountain of money ferrying tourists around the city. Very few would want to make the journey. You may strike lucky, but I think you'll have to catch a plane.'

Damn, damn, damn. Now, how am I going to get to meet your father?

He jumps out of the trap, holds out his hand and helps her step down. She hands over three dollars, adds another as a tip, thanks him and turns toward the Parque Central.

As she walks away, he calls her back, hands held up as if in apology. 'Please forgive me, I almost forgot. My Uncle Felipe drives a taxi for a living, so I could ask him if he would consider taking you to Santiago. I may even come with you. I'm long overdue a visit to my folks.'

She lets out a long sigh.

The fish is hooked.

Groupe Rodriguez Tower is blight on the landscape to most residents of Bayonne. A black-tinted glass cube, it is in stark contrast to the rustic beauty of its neighbours. Ten storeys high, it dominates the skyline.

People question how the company managed to secure planning permission for such a structure not in keeping with any of the city's other commercial buildings. They would not have to look far for an answer. Viktor Rodriguez knows exactly how to go about getting his own way in Bayonne. Stretching back many years, he has greased the right palms and built up a stock of favours, calling them in whenever he deems it necessary: favours in return for donations to local political campaigns, disbursements to schools and hospitals and contributions to charities. His generosity is legendary. However, such generosity comes with strings attached and he yanked several of those strings when he laid the plans for Groupe Rodriguez Tower on the table before the City Fathers. He grins when he thinks of the astonished looks on their complacent faces when Frederic Le Mesurier, the talented French architect to whom he entrusted the commission, first unveiled his sketches and preliminary plans for the preposterous building. As anticipated, their first reaction was to dismiss his application, but he accounted for them all, every single one beholden to him for some act of generosity. They knew it, and he knew they knew it. He stared them out, tight-lipped. They swallowed their objections, kept their opinions to themselves, and unanimously passed the application. It simply was not worth their while to fuss over a lump of glass and steel and risk the city's richest man withholding his support for their many public causes and, more importantly, personal needs.

Bayonne eats well, but it eats out of the palm of his hand.

Looking down from his office window, his vulpine eyes search the waterfront streets, tracking west to east along Avenue de l'Adour and down through the Allées Marine as far as the confluence of the Nive and Adour rivers. There is little activity today beneath a grey and threatening sky, the city lying indolent and passive. On the far side of the Adour is the Quai de Lesseps, the main railway line and the old, quadrangular Citadelle, nowadays a military installation. Beyond them, a degree or two to the west, his gaze settles on the area around Boucau. He picks up a pair of powerful Kahles binoculars lying on a small table adjacent to the tower's curtain walling, and scans the commune for Terese's small house. Once his gaze alights on it, he adjusts the focus until the details become clear. He never ceases to be amazed at what the binoculars are capable of revealing, even at such a great distance.

He wonders if she suspects him of watching her from his lofty perch. Of late, the upstairs curtains at the front of her house have been drawn, as if shielding a secret within. Then he recalls where she is and concludes it is probably nothing more than a need to prevent bedclothes discolouring in the bleaching rays of the sun whilst she is absent.

He carefully replaces the binoculars on the table, rubs his eyes and temple.

His hope for the future is out of sight and it is driving him crazy.

Skeletal hands clasped behind his back, his mind drifts to his wartime days. Working, living and fighting with the brave souls of the Free French created a rock solid foundation for his later business dealings. Know everything about everybody. Know your friends, but don't trust them. If you don't know who your friends are you'd better find out pretty damned quick is his mantra. People survive that way in this world. He learned that in '42 whilst fighting the Bosch. A Vichy sympathiser he fought alongside without knowing the man's true leanings infiltrated his group. He discovered the treachery one night when they illuminated a field with their torches to mark out the landing strip for the pilot of an RAF Lysander. The Germans were lying in wait. He was the only one to survive the subsequent massacre, left for dead, concealed beneath the bloody and broken bodies of two of his fallen comrades. The Germans captured the pilot and the British agent travelling with him.

He is always very careful whom he befriends.

Watching, questioning, and manipulating are an intrinsic part of his character. He built his extensive business empire with these tools, employing them still to keep it firmly within his iron grip. He should have retired long ago, but the business is his life, his whole being. Corporate smart-arses are *not* going to snatch it from under his nose and break it up in order to turn a quick profit.

Mostly, life has been good to him, but he feels a deep regret that neither of his wives provided him with what he wishes for above all else—a son and heir. His two wives (his first wife, Michelle, died in agony from cancer, slowly eating its way through her perfect body) both failed to produce a boy to continue the Rodriguez line. He dotes on his three daughters and lavishes as much money on them as any father could. However, when Michelle's daughters, Kalara and Lorea, reached the age when he thought they might be the future for his business, neither showed any aptitude whatsoever. That did not come as a surprise, as they are cast in the same mould as their mother as far as intellectual agility is concerned. Michelle, a second rate actress, attracted him by her legs not by her brains. She was the perfect accompaniment to a young, self-made man desperate to show his working-class parents and a stuffy, cocksure establishment just how smart he was.

Kalara is so lacking in ability she would have been a liability in the business, so he set her up in her own beauty salon. It confounds him as to why she married a lazy bastard called Julen Lizardi. All the man does is sponge off her. A good-for-nothing, a stranger to the word 'work' who sneaks off at every opportunity to be with some tart named Garrovillo. He makes a mental note to end that little liaison. A few well-chosen words from Oreaga will do the trick.

Lorea showed a little more promise. He arranged for her to join the business as a trainee accountant, hoping she would take an interest in the oil that lubricates the wheels of his empire. She did take an interest, but not in finance. Her interest focused on one Arnaud Foruria, her head of department. She became so fixated on the man, who happened to be happily married, that her increasingly flirtatious behaviour caused embarrassment to all. Either she or Arnaud had to go. Not a fair contest, as Arnaud's experience contributes a great deal to the coffers of Groupe Rodriguez's business. Viktor called in one more favour and Lorea found herself an assistant manager in one of the city's upmarket florists.

Terese is his only daughter by Marie-Louise, the woman with whom he fell deeply in love after the death of Michelle. Plain and unassuming, but with a huge heart and infectious personality, Marie-Louise could not be more different from his first wife. She brings out feelings in him that Michelle never did and gave him the one daughter with more than fresh air between her ears. Terese possesses the brain, the personality and the potential to one day hold the reins of power in Groupe Rodriguez if she chooses to. The problem is, she doesn't choose to. Five years ago, she opted to pursue a career in journalism, the one profession for which he has an intense loathing.

Time is running out for him. His mind is as quick as ever, but his body cannot keep up with it. From the very first day when Groupe Rodriguez Tower opened its doors, he spurned the use of the building's lift and insisted on taking the stairs to ascend the ten floors from the ground to his office. That ceased seven months ago when he found himself pausing halfway up, hands resting on knees, struggling for breath. Stubborn as a mule, he persisted, but it reached the stage where he had to stop on every level to suck in sufficient oxygen for the next floor. Finally admitting defeat, he condescended to using the lift.

The way news travels in Bayonne, if that leaks out the thing he most dreads will happen: the corporate vultures will begin to circle.

He is determined to make Terese succeed him in the business, come hell or high water, whether she wants to or not. He justifies his interfering on the grounds it is his paternal duty to keep a close eye on her and ensure nobody takes advantage until she comes to her senses and assumes her rightful place in his business.

Sooner rather than later.

The intercom on his desk buzzes. He takes a few short strides and presses the communication button.

'Yes, Argine?'

'Jacques Oreaga is here, Monsieur Rodriguez. He wishes to see you.'

'Send him in.'

His door opens and a man, stooping slightly, strides in. Oreaga is taller even than Viktor, shading two metres. Sallow-skinned, with a permanent five-o'clock shadow and mouth a stranger to smiling, he is Viktor's Head of Security and a longstanding friend: one of the best operatives when in the employ of the Directorate-General for External Security.

'Good morning, Monsieur Rodriguez.'

'Jacques. What can I do for you?'

'I have news of Mademoiselle Terese. It concerns Fabien Mendiola.' Oreaga places a photograph on his desk. In it, Terese and Fabien sit at a restaurant table, relaxing. Oreaga taps a finger on the image of Terese. 'I thought you might like to see this, monsieur. It was taken at Le Vin à Deux. Look at her hand on the table.'

Viktor screws his eyes up, studies the image closely and notices a thin, silver ring on the third finger of her left hand, barely discernible in the photo. 'Is that what I think it is, Jacques?'

'I think so, monsieur.'

'When did the engagement take place?'

'We have no way of telling without bugging one or other of them. To do that would be very difficult and not something I would advise. Bugging her house is one thing, bugging her person is quite another.'

'I agree, but there may be another way.'

It won't be necessary to plant a listening device on his daughter or on Fabien Mendiola. He has a less risky and far more productive plan.

Now it is time to put it into action.

Fabien Mendiola cannot fathom why he is being summoned to the top floor of Groupe Rodriguez Tower, but he knows better than to refuse a request from Viktor Rodriguez, chairman of his company and father of his future wife, although the man does not suspect that yet as Terese has demanded they keep their engagement a secret.

At six o'clock that morning, the phone woke him with its persistent ringing. Dragging himself out of bed and putting the phone to his ear, the gravelly voice of the top man rattled down the line and galvanised him into life from the pre-work stupor that is the customary start to his day.

There was no mistaking the directness. 'Is that Fabien Mendiola?'

'Yes, is this—'

'It's Monsieur Rodriguez here. Meet me in my office this morning, nine o'clock sharp. Don't be late.'

Click.

This is the way his Chairman treats people. Short, sharp and straight to the point without preamble or pleasantries. Rodriguez has a reputation for not respecting social etiquette in any shape. As a self-made billionaire, Fabien supposes the old man feels no need. Thankfully, at some point, he will retire and then he will be out of everyone's hair. What will happen then is a recurring topic of conversations whispered in quiet corners of the empire. His retirement might be a mixed blessing. One tyrant might be exchanged for many, masquerading as benefactors.

If he and Terese do marry, Rodriguez is a cross he will have to learn to bear. That is the one rogue speck of dust in the clean room: the flaw in an otherwise perfect diamond.

At nine o'clock precisely, Argine ushers him into the palatial office. Rodriguez commands him to sit in a large, leather chair facing his desk, welcoming him like a long lost son and, unusual for that time of the morning, inviting him to participate in a small cognac. Then, to his great surprise, Rodriguez announces he is to receive a promotion to the position of Marketing Director of Oromundo, along with a twenty percent increase in salary.

'I've been looking through your reviews, Fabien. They praise you very highly, very highly indeed. Your next career move has been on my mind for some time, but you know how it is . . . things get in the way. Now it's time for me to make amends. This promotion is long overdue. You deserve it.'

His mind goes into freefall, the helping hand up the corporate ladder taking him completely by surprise. He was not aware his blip even appeared on the chairman's radar. Lifting the glass to his lips, he sips the golden fluid, eyes never leaving Rodriguez.

'Thank you, monsieur, I'm most grateful.'

Then, without warning, Rodriguez changes the subject. 'I hear you're engaged to my daughter, young man.'

For a moment, his voice refuses to operate. Has Terese told her father, after she said neither of them was to tell anyone?

'Where did you hear that, monsieur?'

'Oh, I know everything that goes on in this city, Fabien. Nothing, and I mean *nothing* escapes my attention. I'm delighted she spends her time in the company of such a well-bred individual, but an engagement . . . well, that's another thing altogether, isn't it? Don't you think it would have been appropriate to ask me for my permission? What kind of man is it who doesn't do that?'

His stomach tightens. 'She told me not to ask you, monsieur. She said I didn't need your permission.'

'Is that right? What did you say?'

'I said I thought it was disrespectful, monsieur, but Terese insisted.'

'Did she? Well, well. I'm disappointed you didn't consult me first, but I suppose you were only honouring my daughter's wishes. She can be a little perverse at times.'

Perverse is not how Fabien would describe her. Determined, certainly: strong-willed, perhaps: secretive, possibly.

'Is there anything else you should tell me?' says Rodriguez.

'I beg your pardon?'

'I'm asking you, is there anything else I should know?'

'Like what, monsieur?'

'Like why Terese is in Cuba, of all places.'

The thought flashes through Fabien's mind. *How did he find that out? She hadn't told him of her holiday.*

'She's gone there for a break she says is long overdue.'

'Why didn't she book through one of our companies?'

'I don't know.'

Rodriguez fixes him with an icy stare. 'She's unaccompanied. Why aren't you with her?'

'It's my busy time at work, monsieur. She thought it best if she went alone.'

Swamped with work or not, he would have taken time off if she had asked him. The invitation never came and he let it pass, assuming she needed time out from her hectic job to recharge her batteries.

'Did she leave any information with you, such as her itinerary?'

Her words come back to him. *Don't ask me where I'm going, Fabien, as I won't know from day to day. I'm chilling out, OK? The last thing I want is a schedule.*

'I'm afraid she didn't, monsieur. She said she would phone periodically so I would know where she was.'

'That seems like a very loose arrangement. Doesn't it worry you?'

'She's very independent—'

Rodriguez, in the blink of an eye, covers the six feet between them and holds his face inches away, the vein in his temple wriggling like a fat worm. 'Damn it, man. I know she's very independent, but she's alone in a strange country and anything could happen.'

Fabien steels himself. He is on the point of saying it is as much a responsibility of Rodriguez's as his, but thinks the better of it. 'It's Cuba, monsieur, not Guatemala. I don't think there will be any problems. She's not the kind who . . .' He stops himself mid-sentence.

Rodriguez raises his eyebrows. 'Not the kind who?'

'She's not the kind who takes well to prying.'

'Prying? If you marry her, Fabien, you'll have to buck your ideas up. I expect you to *demand* to know what she's doing.'

'Monsieur, it's a little premature to talk about marriage.'

'Is it? She's twenty-five and by now she should be married. I was married to my first wife well before I was her age. I would advise you to give some serious thought to the question of controlling your future wife Fabien, if you haven't done so already.'

He bites his tongue as Rodriguez turns his back to him and stares out of the curtain walling. The weather is improving. The sky's canvas has lost its greyness, repainted a cornflower blue.

'Do you know what else she does with her life outside work?'

'Monsieur, I don't see what business—'

As soon as the words are out of his mouth, he knows he has made a mistake.

Rodriguez wheels and slaps the palm of his hand down on the big oak desk. 'It's a simple enough question. Do you or don't you?'

'I don't, monsieur, no.'

'Well, Fabien, that's not good enough, not good enough by half. Is it?'

'No, monsieur.'

'You should to do something about it, shouldn't you?'

'If you say so, monsieur.'

'Oh, I do say so. I'll tell you what you're to do. You'll find out exactly where she goes and what she does. I don't care how you do it, I don't want to know. Then you and I will have another little talk.'

'Monsieur, I don't think—'

'Good day, Fabien. By the way, good luck in the new position. I'm sure you'll make a good job of it. And Fabien . . .'

'Monsieur?'

'Remember that whatever goes up can always come down.'

Across the river from Groupe Rodriguez Tower, two T-shirted figures puff their cigarettes on the Quai de Lesseps, away from the early morning shoppers gathering in the central area of the city. On this, the quieter side of the Adour, several anonymous artists have scrawled their support for the separatist movement in colourful graffiti.

Peru's chest swells with pride as he tilts his chin at the artwork. 'Look Miguel, see how the people are behind us.'

Then he points at a number of tall, timber-frame houses dotted around the city, woodwork painted in the Basque colours of green and red. 'Those people are not afraid to support us. They know we're doing the right thing, the just thing.'

'If only there were more who committed to the cause.'

'There will be if we succeed in our endeavours. And succeed we will.'

Miguel is the person he most trusts in the commando. It is not that he mistrusts the others, simply that when it came to enlisting support for the showdown with Salbatore, the others were reluctant before he convinced them. Miguel showed no hesitation. That endears him to Peru who regards loyalty almost as highly as personal ambition. Nevertheless, Peru is shrewd and very careful not to show any signs of favouritism in public.

It is a novel experience discussing details of the project in Terese's absence. At one time they were so close; two intense people from very different backgrounds, thrown together when studying at the Sorbonne. One who rejects privilege and one who seeks to wipe it out altogether, both with a cauldron of social injustice boiling up inside them.

How things have changed.

'Do you think she'll pull it off, Peru?'

'That's in Fate's hands. She's aware of the timescale and if she's on track she'll soon confront the Major General. However, these things may take longer than we expect. Cuba is an unknown quantity. So I've allowed some contingency in my planning.'

'I thought you would have. It's a pity she's so far away. It would have been easier to acquire the virus somewhere in Europe.'

'Maybe so, but I doubt we could ever have snatched it from under the noses of the Russians or the British.'

He stubs his cigarette out, takes another as Miguel holds out his packet. They begin to walk as they light their cigarettes, staring across the river at the incongruous, smoked-glass office block. Crowned with three-metre high blue letters **GROUPE RODRIGUEZ** it dominates the narrow grey stone buildings lining the far bank.

'Do you worry for her safety?' says Miguel.

Peru vents a stream of smoke and does not answer for several seconds. 'My heart tells me I should, Miguel, but my head tells it not to be so emotional. Like you, I'm just a foot soldier and we can't afford to put personal feelings above the greater good. Salbatore knows that, you know that, we all know that. I don't think about anything other than the glorious days that will follow after we succeed in breaking the imperialists' grip on our country.'

He drapes his arm around Miguel's shoulder. 'You know, I've come to terms with the fact that I may never see her again. I've heard it said that people can disappear without trace in Cuba if the authorities have a mind. If it happens to a tourist, they can always find a scapegoat to pin the crime on; some poor, ignorant deadbeat dragged off the streets and beaten until he confesses. They don't exactly have a great human rights record. Even the Pope had a go at Castro when he visited in '98.'

Miguel nods. 'Yes, I remember hearing that when I was at university. I bet the Bishop of Rome had some fun on that visit.'

'We have to believe luck is on her side. She is right at the start Miguel, just the beginning. There is a lot more for her to go through yet. She and I have talked about different scenarios. We've considered all the possibilities, but life doesn't run on rails. There are many places where she could stumble and then we'll be back to where we were. I'll regard it as a personal failure. No doubt Salbatore would insist I be ejected from the commando and I would be disgraced.'

Miguel's face tells him he is aware of the humiliation Peru would suffer at the hands of the old leader if he fails in his very first mission. Salbatore's pride has been dented and it is plain for all to see he still harbours a grudge.

'It must be a heavy burden to bear, Peru. I pray Madame Fortune will smile kindly on both of you.'

Peru expels a ringlet of smoke and crosses himself. 'Madame Fortune will, Miguel. She's on the side of the righteous.'

Miguel aims his cigarette at the tower. 'Does it ever worry you that she's that bastard's daughter?'

'She hates him as much as we do, so I don't think we need have any concern on that score. And in answer to your question, no, it doesn't bother me at all.'

But it does, and the more he thinks about it the more it worries him as the hours tick away.

Thirty minutes later, after he bids Miguel farewell, he spots the headlines of a passer-by's *El Mundo* as he strolls along the Avenue de l'Adour.

A SPENT FORCE
ETA NOW A TOOTHLESS DOG

The headline makes him curse. The newspaper is squeezing the most out of the interview with the police officer and now the bandwagon is rolling everyone is jumping on it. He smashes his fist into the palm of his hand, causing the passer-by to look up in alarm. Now the news has made him angry again, but that is nothing new. He has been angry as far back as he can remember.

When he was a small boy, all he wanted was to follow in his father and grandfather's footsteps as gamekeeper to the Comte. He loved the wide-open spaces of the estate and the animals roaming on it. His grandfather, a vague figure in his memory, was a gentle, quiet man. His father is different. Giles is like dry straw in a drought; it doesn't take much heat for it to burst into flames.

Tragedy befell the family when Giles' quick temper got the better of him. He crossed swords with the Comte's son when he discovered the lad garrotting a fox. That cost the boy an angry lecture on how to treat wild animals. Later that day, the brat returned with his mother in tow and the Comtesse gave his father a public dressing down in front of all the estate workers. Peru, a year younger than the Comte's son, watched his proud father's shoulders sag under the weight of the Comtesse's scathing words. That night he heard his mother weeping, after which a blazing row broke out. Its pitch grew louder and louder until finally there was an almighty *whack!* followed by a deathly silence. At breakfast the next morning, after his father had left to set the traps, he came down to find his mother nursing a bruised and swollen left eye. She remained silent all through the meal and hardly noticed as he mounted his cycle and pedalled off to school.

Even then, he was prone to jump to conclusions. In his childish train of logic, it wasn't too big a leap to deduce the damage to his mother's face had come about because of that little prick, the Comtesse's son.

He pledged to do something about it. A week later, he came across the spoiled brat mercilessly teasing one of the Comte's horses.

'What are you doing?' he said.

'What's it to you, Echeverria? It's none of your business. They're our horses, not yours. You can get lost, idiot.'

'Who are you calling idiot?'

'Look around, I don't see anyone else, do you?'

'That's just as well, because I'm going to teach you a lesson in manners.'

The next day the Comte's butler called in person. He told Giles that his family must pack their belongings immediately and leave the estate, without argument. The butler said there was no place on this estate for troublemakers.

'Troublemakers?' said Giles. 'I don't understand, Emile. What trouble are we supposed to have made?'

'I don't know and it's not my business to know. I'm merely the messenger.'

'But where will we go?'

'I'm sorry, Giles, that's all I've been told to say to you.'

'That's fine, my friend, I understand. It doesn't take Einstein to figure out what's going on here.'

'No, Giles, it doesn't. I'm sorry, but I have no influence in the matter, otherwise I would plead your case. You're a good man, as was your father before you. Good luck to you and your family.'

'Thank you, Emile, the same to you.'

Giles moved his family in with a second cousin who lived in a sea-washed house close to the mouth of the Adour. Never a man to rest on his laurels, he found work unloading and loading small cargo vessels on the Quai de la Douane. The job is dirty and repetitive, but Bayonne does not offer much in the way of manual work for a man of his age. He detests it and gradually it is corroding him. In the past year, the heavy manual labour has taken its toll and his body aches constantly. Sleep is the only relief from the niggling pains that chew away at his shoulders and knees. His is a long day at the quayside, rising at six-thirty, clocking on at seven and working through until six.

Nowadays, with Peru doing a night shift managing his company's workers on the rejuvenation of the port, the only time he happens to see his father is in the hallway of the little house, as one comes in the other goes out.

'Did you know the Comte's family came to this land from Angouleme, Peru?' his father used to say to him. 'Angouleme, I ask you! The man's French! *And* he still has a huge estate there. What the hell right does he have to kick us out of our home?'

As he grew, those words, mouthed repeatedly, fuelled Peru's bitterness. Every waking hour filled with thoughts of rebellion. ETA's activities would often grab the headlines: a bombing here, a kidnapping there, with the occasional assassination striking fear into the hearts of the ruling classes. He pictured himself a fearless ETA warrior, daring and courageous, serving the cause, prepared to lay down his life. There was only one problem and a massive one at that. How could he join ETA? It was not as if he could post an application letter or casually stroll along to the nearest recruitment office for an interview.

He had to wait until he was an undergraduate to receive his answer and take the first steps on his journey. Access to the Sorbonne's internet proved to be of some value, if limited. In the days before Wikipedia established itself and the web was only just on the verge of becoming mainstream, his surfing enabled him to piece together snippets of information about the organisation, although it was scant and totally uncorroborated. Coupled with newspaper cuttings from the university's archives, he formed an idea of the structure and operation of the organisation.

It was a lot of hard work for very little benefit.

In the end, he need not have bothered.

ETA came to him.

7th July

Terese stands by the window and looks out across the empty road fronting the hotel. Havana has yet to awake and few people are out on the streets. In the Parque Central the trees stand still as statues, framed against the backdrop of a leaden sky. The only sound she can hear is the crowing of a cockerel, clear as a bell, which amazes her. Where could anyone keep a chicken in the heart of the city?

Her head begins to throb, bedevilled by the same recurring question. Why isn't Martina here instead of her? Martina is the hard-nosed one, the one whose father is not afraid to air his views in public. She volunteered for the mission but Peru said, "No, Terese is the one to go. Best if you remain here. Confront the Major General and you'll only end up in the nearest graveyard."

Thanks, Peru, kind of you to show me such consideration.

Slipping out of her towelling robe, she begins to dress when the shrill ring of the room's phone makes her jump. Putting the robe back on, she walks quickly over to the bedside table and picks up the instrument.

'Hello?'

'Miss Rodriguez? This is hotel reception.'

'Yes?'

'A Senor Fortunato is here for you. He says can you meet him in the hotel cafè? He has news for you.'

'Thank you. Tell him I'll be down as soon as I'm dressed.'

When she enters the café, he is sitting alone at a table, dressed as the previous day, only this time the sunglasses are absent. He looks tired, slouched on his chair, his face wearing a vacant look. Doubt assails her; she cannot help but think he bears bad news.

He holds up a hand in greeting. 'Hi. Would you like a drink? Maybe you'd like to try a Mojito?'

'A Mojito? What's that?'

'You'll see. I'll order one for you.' He beckons to a youth loitering behind the bar. The boy sidles over, emits a cursory greeting. Angelo fires off a stream of words. The boy nods and disappears.

She pulls out a chair and sits down, noticing how nervous and agitated he is.

If it is bad news, better to get it out of the way. 'Did you meet your uncle?'

'Yes, I called round at his apartment yesterday evening after I put the pony away. I told him about you and that you wanted to travel to Santiago.'

'What did he say?'

Before Angelo can answer, the boy returns and hands him a can of Pepsi. Wiping the table, he places a tall glass in front of Terese. The drink is colourless, packed with ice and has what looks like a sprig of mint immersed in it.

Lifting the glass to her nose, she sniffs the concoction. 'What did you say this is?'

'We call it a Mojito. It's very popular with tourists.'

'What's in it? I can smell mint.'

'It's made of six ingredients: white rum, sugar, lime, soda water, ice, and mint. Created in Cuba. Try it.'

She takes a sip from the ice-cold glass. The drink is cool, refreshing. 'Hmm. That's really good.'

He rolls the Pepsi in his hands, clearly struggling with some inner conflict, something that is making him uncomfortable.

He doesn't want to tell me his uncle can't drive me to Santiago. I knew it.

'Angelo, is there a problem?'

'No, not really.'

'Look, if your uncle doesn't want to take me to Santiago that's fine. I'll fly if I have to.'

'No, no. My uncle says it's OK. It will give him a chance to see my mother without having to pay the gas.'

Relief washes over her. She should thank him, talk about the arrangements, stand up and take her leave. The look on his face prevents her.

'Then what is it?'

He stands the can on the table, leans back in his chair. 'It's my father. I'm always like this when I visit his house. You could say we don't see eye-to-eye. I tell him one day Cuba will change and we'll have the things other people outside this country have. He says I'm a traitor because I dream of being wealthy. It makes for some very interesting discussions. I don't visit my folks as much as I should because my father and I always end up arguing. '

'Ah.'

'And because my brother, Oswardo, will probably be there. We don't exactly hit it off, either.'

'You've a brother?'

'Two. Oswardo and Ramon. Oswardo is a captain in the air force. Ramon is a doctor.'

'Your father must be very proud.'

'Of my brothers, yes.'

He shrugs, picks up the can, and takes a deep draft. She tries to imagine what his father is like. Martina was unable to provide them with a photo of Eduardo and very little information exists about him. Cuba is good at keeping its secrets. They may laud Eduardo in his country, but to the outside world, he is a nonentity.

Angelo rises, pushes back his chair. 'Excuse me, I have to go. My uncle says he will collect you here the day after tomorrow. Around ten o'clock.'

The day after tomorrow? Another day wasted?

'OK, I'll be waiting. Thank you very much for asking him.'

He reaches out his hand and she grips it in hers. They shake.

'Bye, Terese.'

'Bye, Angelo.'

Things at home have deteriorated since Angelo last visited his mother and father. Constantly harangued by Maria, he has taken to regularly visiting Ramon in his younger brother's crumbling, second floor apartment, sometimes staying overnight after stabling the pony.

A cardiologist at the prestigious Havana Hospital, Ramon is gentle, considerate, and sympathetic with a good ear for listening; highly regarded by his patients, staff and superiors. He is the cleverest of them, the medical postgraduate with an incisive mind and marvellously dextrous fingers.

"He has Grandma Estelle's magic in his fingers," their mother proudly boasts. "She was a wonderful seamstress. The whole of Vedado marvelled at what those fingers could produce."

Last night, Maria waded into Angelo as soon as he arrived home from a tiring day plying his trade. Rather than provoke yet one more scene (their neighbours are beginning to complain vociferously) he threw the day's earnings at her, spun on his heels, slammed the flimsy apartment door behind him and walked the two kilometres to Ramon's apartment. Luckily, Ramon was off duty. Angelo stayed overnight, sharing a bottle of rum and complaining about his lot into the early hours. Ramon listened as he poured out his troubles and swigged his drink, nodding and occasionally shaking his head, commenting with a wipe of his brow how lucky he himself is not to have followed his brothers into marriage. Oswardo and his wife are apart and his elder brother doesn't give a damn. Angelo and Maria are together, and it is torturing him.

Yet his problems seem insignificant when compared to others. The neglected building Ramon lives in is falling apart around his ears. Months ago, the tired old lift finally expired and no way on earth is it ever going to be repaired, even if it were possible. Carmen Rosa, an ancient neighbour so stick-thin she would vanish if turned sideways, lives two floors above Ramon. She now finds it impossible to leave her apartment. When the lift died, Ramon found her squatting at the foot of the concrete steps, crying and wringing her hands. She managed, with much pained effort, to descend the steps on her way out to the streets and on her return attempted to climb the steps, something the poor woman has not done for years. She simply did not have the strength. Tired and frustrated, she collapsed on the first floor landing and that was where Ramon found her. With the help of two neighbours, he carried her up three more flights to her apartment. She has not reappeared since. Now trapped in her small space, she has only a view of the Straits of Florida for comfort. She is not alone in her suffering. Miguel Morales, the bent-double widower on the fifth floor, lives in an apartment with a sieve for a roof, suffers chronic arthritis and spondylosis of the spine. Ramon, a good neighbour, spends more and more of the little spare time he has comforting them by handing out assurances the lift will be replaced soon, knowing the chances of that are next to non-existent. There is talk of resettling the residents in his block, but that is all it is—talk. Nothing has progressed in years. Ramon knows Carmen and Miguel will be in their graves way before that happens. God rest them.

After a late breakfast, the brothers decide to relive some of their childhood days and go fishing off Malecon. The sea is calm, gently lapping against the protective wall as they choose their spot and settle down on a small outcrop below a group of teenagers listening to the crackling strains of Pacho Alonso on a beaten up portable radio.

'Have you contacted Oswardo recently?' asks Ramon, baiting the hooks of his paternoster.

'No. Not for quite some time, in fact. Could be a year. Maybe longer.' He spits in the sea. 'I couldn't care less, really. He does what he does and I do what I do.'

'What is it with you two? Anyone would think you were suitors in some love triangle! Ma must wonder what on earth she gave birth to.'

'We don't see eye to eye and never have. A long time before you came along we fought like cat and dog. With our words, that is. I wasn't stupid enough to take him on if he challenged me to a fistfight or to wrestle him. No way! Pa coached him almost as soon as he could walk and, as a kid, he was big for his age and incredibly strong. It probably accounts for his psychopathic tendencies.'

'Come on, he's not that bad. I get a phone call from him a couple of times a month. I guess he's feeling lonely since Carina left and took little Eduardo junior back to her family in Varadero, although he would never say it.'

Angelo studies his handsome brother. At twenty-seven, Ramon, with his intellect and good nature should

74

be in a happy and loving relationship. How strange. Oswardo needs his woman, but he will not admit it; Angelo does not want his but is stuck with her; and Ramon does not appear to have an interest at all.

All flawed in one way or another.

'Ramon, I'm thinking I should visit Santiago again. Why don't you come with me? It would be a surprise for Ma. There's a French woman who Uncle Felipe has agreed to drive there. If you come too, I'll have a good excuse for leaving Maria at home.'

'I don't know, Angelo, it's hard to get away now the hospital has opened its services to the paying world. We've a tremendous reputation you know, although it can feel a little like a production line at times.'

'Come on. The money they pay you, you can afford a few days off.'

'Money? You must be joking! None of my colleagues does this for the money; we could do better driving co-co taxis! Ask Uncle Felipe, he'll tell you just how little money professional people get paid in this country.'

'Have you ever thought of emigrating? I hear people with your skills could make a fortune overseas.'

'Like Rafael you mean? Look, Angelo, I love my work, I love Ma and Pa, I love you and I love this country. The last thing I would think of doing is leaving all that behind me. Hell, at times I even love Oswardo.'

They burst out laughing.

'Then little brother, if you love your family so much, you should come with me.'

'I'll see what I can do, but don't hold your breath.'

They sit motionless, listening to the lapping of the Havana harbour waters on the seaweed covered rocks and the putt-putting of mechanical dinosaurs above them, as Havana's families go about their business.

Angelo fractures the stillness. 'I'm worried about Pa, Ramon.'

'Pa? Why, is he ill?'

'Don't be crazy, he'll probably outlive us all.'

'What's bothering you, then?'

'I can't put my finger on it, but ever since he retired he's been . . . different.'

Ramon places a hand on his shoulder. 'I hear retirement can do that to you.'

'Ma says he does the same thing every day. Walks to Moncada, sits staring at the place, walks home again.'

'He's a soldier. Routine is what they do.'

'I guess so, but—'

'Look, you've other things than Pa to think about—like how Marie and you are going to get your marriage back on track. Now shut up and let's fish.'

'

10th July

Angelo introduces Terese to his wife, Maria, and uncle, Felipe, in the Telegrafo lobby. The two men fuss over her like a long-lost relative whilst Maria skulks in the background, hardly uttering a word.

At last, Terese thinks, *I'm on my way to Santiago de Cuba and a meeting with Major General Eduardo Fortunato.*

'Look at all those poor souls,' says Angelo as the taxi passes the Capitolo Nacional. 'They'll be queuing for hours in this heat. No wonder offices are half empty on a Monday morning in this city.'

She notices a smile crease Felipe's face at Angelo's words. He leans across the dust-covered dashboard, turns the air conditioning up a notch. It makes hardly any difference to the four occupants of the Nissan, its overworked compressor crying out for a long-overdue service. He apologises, explains he is fortunate to have a car and one more reliable than the antiquated American autos his resourceful fellow citizens manage to keep going, one way or another. He laughs when he says, 'If they're foolish enough to attempt the journey from Havana to Santiago many won't get beyond Ranchuelo before succumbing to mechanical expiration!'

Four days after arriving in Cuba, she is leaving behind the verdant outskirts of Havana, Felipe's taxi trundling along the Autopista Nacional, the road that cleaves the island in two lengthwise. The trip, almost 500 miles, will take close to two days. Before they reach Santiago they will have an overnight stop on the outskirts of Las Tunas. She hoped to leave yesterday as Angelo promised, but soon realised that, in Cuba, there can be far more than twenty-four hours in a day.

Back home, she could have left a voicemail or sent a text message to Angelo's mobile. In Cuba, it is not so easy: cell phones are an unaffordable rarity, another of his complaints. Unable to contact him, she passed the day waiting, nerves jangling, as time ticked by. At one point, she feared she must have slipped his mind and, much against her better judgment, left the hotel and wandered around the Parque Central trying without success to find him. Then, as the light began to fade, he turned up at the Telegrafo and apologised, saying his uncle was going to be delayed by some important business: if she wished to make other arrangements, he would not be offended. She hastened to assure him it was OK; she was in no hurry.

They pass long lines of people standing, leaning, or sitting motionless, waiting for any mode of transport to take them to work in the city. Such patience impresses her. In Bayonne they would riot for less.

From the back seat, Angelo's words break into her thoughts.

'Cuba needs to change fast. If it doesn't, there won't be any work to go to and we'll all be begging for a living.'

Felipe chuckles as he parps the car's horn and waves at the driver of a dilapidated brown Chevrolet Fleetline chugging past them in the opposite direction. 'Please excuse him for his views, Terese. He's practising for when he has some stimulating discussions with his father.'

Angelo gives a snort from the back seat.

Felipe takes a piece of gum out of his pocket, pops it into his mouth. 'I hear you're a journalist?'

'Yes, I am. I work for the local paper, *El Correo*.'

'Do you enjoy the work?'

It is a simple question, innocent enough, but she is wary of striking up a conversation with someone she has only just met. What she really craves is sleep, not the effort of making small talk. She tossed and turned all night, reluctant to swallow another sleeping pill lest she oversleep, worrying if Angelo's uncle might be delayed again or worse, cancel.

'Most of the time I do. Do you like yours?' The words are sharp, too hastily spoken. She hopes her brusqueness has not offended him. If it has, it fails to register on his face.

'Not always if I'm frank with you. However, we Cubans have to be careful what we voice in public. It isn't wise at times to speak our minds, it could be taken the wrong way. That goes against the grain, but what choice do we have? Sure, it's not as bad as it used to be now the Presidente is confined to his bed. Though that doesn't mean we can throw caution to the wind. If you've heard of the Committees for the Defence of the Revolution, you'll know what I mean.'

She stares into the distance and nods. Her wonderfully informative guidebook is very explicit on the subject of the committees. It states the CDR officials are duty bound to monitor the activities of persons in their respective housing blocks and keep an individual file on each resident. The power they exercise generates fear and mistrust and is open to abuse. Many an innocent person has been spirited away in the middle of the night after a damning report from a CDR official, never again to reappear.

They drive mile after mile along the arrow-straight road passing fields of pineapples and mangoes as far as the eye can see, Felipe recounting his life during the Soviet years, when he held down a position as a professor of Spanish at Havana University. His previous standing in the academic community afforded him the opportunity to attend many conferences in the region, a privilege reserved for the most senior educationalists, government officials and military personnel. It allowed him to debate his views openly with international colleagues who were fortunate not to live under the harshness of a regime like Cuba's, and over the years the opinions of others substantially softened his original hard-line stance. He stresses once again he is always careful not to let such moderate views slip out, as others might construe them as a criticism of the Communist Party of Cuba, the PCC. He does not share his revised views with his sister Carmen, Angelo's mother, in case she mentions them to her husband in an unguarded moment.

He goes on to tell her that after the Soviets pulled out circumstances changed dramatically. The market for sugar disappeared. Cuba imploded. The outlook seemed very bleak for his country and times became very difficult at the university. Attendances at international conferences ceased and salaries were frozen as the cost of living spiralled. Then, like seedlings sprouting from sun-scorched earth after the first rains, promising signs of rejuvenation appeared in the welcome guise of tourism. Perversely, economic recovery arrived with a bitter twist for him and his professional colleagues. Cubans having access to the newly legalized US dollar through contact with the lucrative tourist industry find themselves at a distinct financial advantage to professional, industrial and agricultural workers. Unbelievably, taxi drivers now earn more than highly trained lawyers and doctors. He shrugs, says giving up the academic life was a hard choice to make, but not too hard. Divorce from his wife focuses him on the future needs of his only daughter, Adriana. He suffers a loss of status and some sniping from old colleagues with supposedly 'purer' principles, but it gives him a chance to talk freely with tourists and, of course, he makes far more money than he would ever earn in a lecture theatre.

After two hours of Felipe's non-stop talking, Angelo suggests they pull in at a roadside halt, popular with tourists travelling along the spine road. Grateful to be free of Felipe's droning, Terese feigns an interest in the flora as the others disappear into a small, stuccoed café. Half an hour later they reappear, call her over, scramble into the car and set off again. A hint of rum hangs about Felipe's person. She hopes he has not taken it as a lubricant for his overworked vocal chords.

In the blink of an eye, he is in full flow. 'I'll tell you another story whilst we've so much time, Terese. You'll find it even more interesting than the last one.'

She groans inwardly.

Pushing his steel-rimmed glasses up the bridge of his nose, he sinks back into the driver's seat. She turns, looks at Angelo who is staring disinterestedly out of the window. Next to him, Maria's eyes are closed, her head lolling from side to side with the gentle swaying of the car.

'When I was a small boy growing up in El Cobre, a small town close to Santiago, my family was visited by a man named General Gustavo Oliva. I would be about eleven or twelve years old at the time. Batista had returned to power after a bloodless coup d'état, grabbing the reins of power once again. Worse still, the US recognised his government. That was carte blanche for him and his corrupt cronies to make more money from racketeering. There was unrest brewing in the country, so Bastista sent Oliva to warn my father not to lend his support. My father, already deeply appalled and shamed by the corruption in Havana and remembering the way the city had welcomed American gangsters with open arms in the late '40s, told the general in no uncertain terms where he should stick his threats. That was a terrible mistake. Oliva merely shrugged his broad shoulders, spat on my father's floor and turned on his heels. Fearing the worst for his family and certain that Oliva would return soon, my father sent my mother, my sister Carmen and me to a sugar plantation owned by a friend of a friend—Angel Castro y Argiz.'

Terese's curiosity piques as she catches the name. 'Castro? No relation to—'

'I'll come to that. This brave man sheltered us for over a year, with my father paying occasional visits to see us. They would huddle together in conversation, my father doing most of the talking and the senor gravely nodding his head. Then one day, news came that there had been an attack on the Moncada army barracks in Santiago. It had failed and more than sixty were dead. Those who had survived fled into the Sierra Maestra. Senor Castro y Argiz took my mother to one side and whispered something in her ear. On hearing his words she let out an ear-piercing scream . . . I can still hear it all these years later . . . and immediately fainted. The next day, when she had recovered from the shock, she told us that our father had been killed in an accident. Those were her precise words, "in an accident". We suspected for years that he had been involved in the Moncada episode, but it wasn't so. Oliva simply took the opportunity to accuse him of being one of the chief inciters, although he knew he was innocent and had nothing to do with the

82

business. They made him kneel in the dirt and then the general himself shot my father in the back of the head. That terrible news was what made my mother scream. What neither she nor we children realised at the time was that the good Senor Castro y Argiz had a son in his late twenties who was the ringleader.'

'Fidel Castro?'

'Yes, Fidel Castro. The plantation owner was the father of Castro, our beloved Presidente. Castro hated Batista and anyone connected to him. That included Oliva. When he learned of my father's execution, Castro cursed the general and swore revenge before escaping into the Sierra Maestra. Six days later, they captured him and sent him to prison in the Isla de Pinos. During his incarceration, Oliva ordered an inmate called Carabrero to kill him, but Carabrero, beguiled by Castro's charisma and power of speech, failed to carry out Oliva's order. Less than two years later, Castro and the revolutionaries were released in a general amnesty.'

'Castro's a lucky guy.'

'There's no luck with Castro, Terese. The man is charmed. He may not see it that way, but for some reason fate smiles on him.'

She catches sight of her reflection in the passenger side mirror: pale, anxious.

I hope Castro isn't the only one fate chooses to smile upon.

11th July

A fiery sun bakes the roofs of the clump of houses on the western fringe of Santiago de Cuba. Here, in one of the quieter neighbourhoods of the city, people respect each other's peace, but there is an exception. In one of the larger dwellings lives a man who, it is rumoured, can make folk disappear with the snap of his fingers.

They let *him* rant and rave without complaint.

'Get off your lazy backside and help me gather in the washing, Eduardo,' yells the woman, hair tied in a tight grey bun and carrying a waistline that long ago outgrew her substantial bust. 'I've hardly enough time to get everything ready before they arrive, and I need your assistance. There's nobody running around on your every command now that you're *retired.*'

Carmen Fortunato says the last word as if she has sucked it out of a lemon.

An unruly tonsure appears as the reader lowers the spread pages of the newspaper. Steel-grey, penetratingly intense eyes glare at his wife from beneath bushy, salt-and-pepper eyebrows. Over the years, many have withered under the fierce gaze of those unblinking eyes, but she is not one of them. After forty-one years of marriage and the bearing of his three children, he accepts the fact that he will never cow her. 'El Toro Negro' has met his match.

Cursing under his breath, he heaves himself to his feet, tosses the paper on the table, fastens his jacket over his barrel-chest, slaps a forage cap on his bullet head and strides through the back door of the house.

'What are you shouting at me for, you old sow? Can't you see I'm busy?' he bawls across the scrubby lawn as he stands arms akimbo on the whitewashed porch.

'Busy with what?' she screeches back. 'Busy with reading your paper, you old goat, is that it? Call that busy! One of us has to do some work around here or the place would go to the dogs!'

'I have to keep up with what's going on, it's important. Anyway, I'm going for my walk before they arrive.'

'What about my washing?'

The question drifts in the air; there is nothing for it to settle on. Eduardo Fortunato is already out of the gate and away towards the city.

Put plainly, he is bored out of his substantial skull. Yet in truth, he has no cause to complain. He should have hung his boots up years ago like all his old colleagues, content to live out the remainder of his life smoking and reminiscing with other pensioned-off old men. Thankfully, five years ago, in the year Eduardo was due to retire, a prescient Castro foresaw new problems at the "open sore" (as the President terms it) of the US naval base at Guantanamo Bay. Eduardo begged to remain in active service so he could keep a close watch on the base known by many as 'Gitmo'. Raúl Castro agreed, granting him an extra five years. The Presidente's brother slapped him on the back and declared he was the only man who could handle it. Mere flattery, naturally. Times had moved on, and even five years ago nostalgia was slipping out of fashion.

Over the course of the five years he had fun playing cat and mouse with Gitmo's senior officers, most of whom were less than half his age and far less savvy. He enjoyed watching the world turn its eyes on the Yanquis with suspicion and more than a touch of cynicism after the revelations concerning the incarceration of Haitian refugees.

He was delighted with the spin put on that story by his propaganda boys.

Then, ten long months ago, on the day of his seventieth birthday, they finally shoehorned him into an unwilling retirement. This time Raúl would not countenance any argument. It was time for an old soldier to retire. Resigned to his future, Eduardo bought a house in Santiago and returned to the city of his roots.

His life has come full circle.

He finds it impossible to adjust to civil life, let alone retired civil life. Gardening and gossiping are not meat and drink to a man who is a bundle of energy, a firebrand whose beliefs as well as prejudices were forged in the white-hot crucible of one of the world's most successful revolutions.

Eduardo Erneido Luis Fortunato is a legend in his own time. From humble beginnings as the only son of a poor farmer from a diminutive patch of land on the lower slopes of the Sierra Maestra, he grew to become one of his country's most revered and feared soldiers. His father, Juan-Carlos, wanted him to train as a teacher, a calling he might have done well at, but the arrival of Fidel Castro in his life put paid to that and steered him in a direction Juan-Carlos could never have contemplated.

Eduardo first came across Castro when a pupil at Dolores School in Santiago. Many in his class talked with awe of a boy in a grade seven years higher than theirs. This particular boy was a favourite with the Jesuit teachers because of his athletic prowess and indefatigable skill in debate. He had arrived at to Dolores after a short spell at LaSalle, another highly regarded school. It was rumoured his father was a rich man who owned a large estate in Biran.

The boy's name was Fidel Alejandro Castro Ruz.

The tall and lanky Ruz could run like the wind and broke the school's long jump record that had stood unsurpassed for sixteen years. His legs were fast, but his mouth was faster. Ruz could hold his own in debate with most of the Fathers, who, rather than scold him for his argumentative ways, delighted in testing his sharp mind and powers of logic. He also had something none of them possessed: God had endowed him with a photographic memory. Although not one of Dolores's most brilliant students, Ruz's ability to remember and regurgitate facts and events made him a worthy adversary and the Fathers loved nothing more than a contest, whether it was in the boxing ring or on the debating floor.

Then Ruz disappeared from school, moved, it was said, to the Belen High School in Havana. Eduardo thought nothing of it. The imperious Ruz had not so much as spoken to the farmer's kid with the staring eyes. It was not until he turned nineteen that Eduardo was to meet Ruz again, this time under very different circumstances. Ruz had changed his name to Fidel Castro. Castro ignited an unquenchable fire in Eduardo. He drew Eduardo in and kept him close as he consolidated his position as Cuba's most powerful man. The pair of them had stood shoulder to shoulder through it all: Batista, the revolution, the US blockade, the Special Period, Khrushchev and Kennedy; enough adrenalin rushes for ten normal lives. Two men could not be closer. However, Eduardo, tough and willing, was no great officer. After the revolution, his promotion through the ranks was pedestrian, his leadership uninspiring. Younger men rose higher, quicker and sometimes

Eduardo feels his loyalty took second place to others' ambitions.

He saw less and less of his beloved Presidente as others inveigled their way into Castro's inner circle. He did not let his thoughts dwell on it. If that was how Castro wanted it, then Castro had his reasons.

Then Castro began to get ill and shut himself off from his public, claiming he was still in good health, but in reality suffering from the wear and tear his body and mind has endured for more than sixty years. The diminishing number of occasions they permit Eduardo to meet with his old comrade saddens him, as he knows neither Castro nor he will live forever. Castro jokes that when the Grim Reaper comes for him he had better come well armed; that bloody scythe he carries is not going to protect him if Castro gets his hands round his scrawny neck.

As for Eduardo's twilight years, what do they hold? Gut-wrenching adventures? Daredevil campaigns? Games of mental dexterity with an enemy that could grind Cuba into the dirt with an imperialist heel? No. Just an old soldier's tales that nobody wants to hear any more, not even his own grandchild.

His 'walk' has become an unbreakable daily routine, as addictive as any drug he has taken in his adventurous life. He does not always choose the same route, but there is always one unchanging, ultimate destination.

Moncada Barracks.

Moncada means a great deal to him. Every day without fail, on reaching the disused barracks, he stares wistfully at the bullet holes in the ochre-coloured walls, remembering that fateful July day in '53 when Castro and a band of ragtag rebels launched their doomed assault.

Those bullet holes hide many secrets. One of which he is soon to reveal.

To someone he has yet to meet.

On the second day of the journey, Terese breathes a sigh of relief as Felipe finally runs out of steam after a winding diatribe that explores most of the last fifty years of Cuban politics and economics. She is polite, asks just enough questions, nods frequently and makes a passing comment or two. Occasionally, Angelo joins in the conversation. She listens intently when he talks of his life, making a mental note of every scrap of information that might be of use when she faces his father. When he reveals Eduardo almost disowned him after he became a follower of Santeria, his face melts into sadness. Then he resigned his commission in the army, a mortal sin as far as his father is concerned.

They have been at loggerheads ever since.

She recognises parallels with her own life: an overbearing, opinionated father determined to impose his choice of career: a need to free herself from obligations: a wish to take control of her life.

Angelo's marriage is broken, that much is evident. Maria and he hardly speak and on the rare occasions when she wakes, they sit apart, distancing themselves from one another.

Is this how Peru and I are destined to end up?

'What business is your family in, Terese?' Felipe's question derails her train of thought.

'Oh, mostly hotels and shipping, although the business does have other interests.'

Hearing a rustling movement behind her, she glances in the car's rear-view mirror. Angelo is sitting upright and leaning forward slightly, clearly keen to hear what she is about to say. Maria's head rests against the window, rolling gently as she sleeps.

'Would I have heard of the company?' says Felipe.

'Groupe Rodriguez is the holding company trading on the Bourse. There are quite a few companies under it.' The words sound as if she is chewing on a month old loaf.

'Name some of them.'

'Lucitor, Oromundo, Embarcor, GarciaBro.'

Felipe rubs his five o'clock shadow with a slim, liver-spotted hand. 'Oromundo? Yes, I think that one rings a bell. I'm sure I read recently in the newspaper of a company with that name. Something to do with Varadero if I'm not mistaken. Remind me, what do they do?'

'They run hotels in unusual destinations such as Laos, Tibet, and Cuba.'

Laughter escapes his lips. '"Unusual." Is that what you think my country is?'

She silently curses herself for the careless choice of adjective. *Why doesn't he concentrate on driving the damned car instead of working his jaw muscles all the time?*

Again, her words have a razor edge to them. 'Yes. The world thinks that's exactly what it is.'

'The world? That's a lot of people. Please tell me why, I'm intrigued.'

She clamps her lips tight, jumps as she feels Angelo's hand press on her shoulder.

'Are you OK, Terese?'

'Fine. No problem.'

Felipe's eyebrow cocks. 'So, Terese. Why do people find this island of ours so unusual? As I said, I'm intrigued.'

Careful! Don't let him see how much you know, it could arouse his suspicions. The guy may just be curious, but it's best to be on the safe side.

'I guess because Cuba's so . . . untainted.'

'Untainted?' Felipe's eyes fly open. 'That's an interesting word given our country was corrupted for years by the Mafia and the tyrant Batista. Yes, *untainted* is certainly an interesting way of describing it.'

'I wouldn't know much about that. I'm just here to see the land, enjoy the weather and chill out.'

Seconds tick by, then Felipe says, 'I think you know a lot more about us than you admit.'

She clenches her fists, relaxes them. 'Then I'm sorry to disappoint you. What I know is what I've read in my guidebook. As I said, I'm just here to spend some time in the sun and see a beautiful country.'

'But you could do that anywhere, couldn't you? Haiti, Colombia, Peru, Brazil. Why choose Cuba?'

'It's . . . different.'

'Different? How is it different?'

'It has a history and culture unlike anywhere else in this part of the world, which many would say makes it unique. Personally speaking, I find Cuba evocative, romantic.'

'Romantic?' A broad grin creases his face. 'Ah, now I have it. You're looking for a young man. That's why you came to Cuba!'

'I don't need to look. I've a fiancé at home and we're in a very happy relationship.'

God, where is this going?

'Why isn't he with you?'

'He's busy at work.'

'I see. However, I must warn you . . . Cuba has a way of bringing out the devil in people. Sometimes she can turn their heads, even if they are already in love.'

'Thank you for your warning. I'll make a mental note to be careful.'

'It's my pleasure.'

He winks at Angelo in the mirror. Angelo winks back.

'If it isn't romance, then why are you really here? Are you working on a story? Will I find myself headlined in your paper? "Secrets of a Havanese professor"?'

'I came here because I wanted to see this country before it becomes a slave to tourism, as it ultimately will.'

Fuck, I shouldn't have said that! Those are Peru's words I'm spouting.

A deep furrow creases Felipe's forehead then he plays her words back to her. 'A slave to tourism? We've always been a slave to tourism right up to the time Castro foolishly decided he didn't need it. No, I think there's another reason you are here. Maybe—'

'Stop teasing her, Uncle Felipe,' cuts in Angelo. 'I apologise for my uncle's behaviour, Terese. He has a very wicked sense of humour not always appreciated by those who know him, let alone those who do not. When he's in the company of a beautiful woman, he can go a little too far. Take no notice of him.'

She turns round, sees a comforting look on Angelo's face. Heat rises in her cheeks. Maria is now wide-awake, almond eyes staring straight at her, mouth stretched tight as an elastic band.

Minutes before five o'clock in the afternoon, the taxi winds down the contours of a hill, closing in on its final destination. Pink-roofed and white-walled houses, scattered haphazardly in a dense mass of luxuriant trees, shimmer in the dying heat haze. High above them, vultures trace arabesques, riding the thermals of a darkening sky. Beyond the seaward fringes of the city, the Caribbean metamorphoses from aquamarine at the shoreline to indigo on the far horizon.

Felipe's hand sweeps across the windscreen. 'Santiago de Cuba. Beautiful, isn't she?'

An uneasy silence has settled in the car during the final hours of the journey. For a while, Felipe continued to press the conversation, but receiving only the curtest of replies fell into a brooding silence. As they draw near to Santiago, she rehearses in her mind the various scenarios that could take place.

'Where are you staying?' Felipe almost barks the question. No longer is he the cultured academic, the ambassador, the joker. Now he is like many of the taxi drivers in Bayonne: terse, rude.

'The Casa de la Mar on Costa de San Francisco.'

'OK, I know the place. I'll drop you off there.'

'No, no, Uncle Felipe,' protests Angelo from the rear seat. 'That won't do. I think we should invite Terese to join us for a bite to eat at Ma and Pa's first. Ma would never forgive us if we didn't show her how hospitable the Fortunato family is.'

Felipe opens his mouth to say something, stops himself, nods.

'You're right, Angelo. Forgive me, Terese, for forgetting my manners.'

'You really don't need to, I'll be fine. I wouldn't want to be an inconvenience.' Her objection is half-hearted. Decline the invitation and she might never get such a good opportunity to meet his father.

'No, no. I . . . we . . . insist. My sister's cooking is something you mustn't miss. I'll drop you off at the Casa de la Mar later, if that's OK with you. Then you'll be free of us and can be on your way again.'

'Thank you. It will be a welcome experience to enjoy some home cooking during my travels.'

Phew. That was a little too close for comfort. What would I have done if Angelo hadn't intervened?

'Look Terese, over there!' says Angelo. 'See the big house with the Cuban flag flying from the flagpole? That's the Casa del Toro Negro, my folks' place.'

The two-storey house he points at is set slightly apart from its neighbours on the brow of a low hill. From a large pair of sturdy gates guarding the front entrance, an unmade road winds its way downhill towards the denser packed houses of the city. Although not a grand house by any stretch of the imagination, the impression it gives is of a property boasting a superior status than those neighbouring it. Her eyes search for signs of life in the building, but see none. She half hopes the Major General is at home, half wishes he were a thousand miles away.

As the taxi approaches the house the rotund figure of a woman rolls out of the front door and waddles slowly down the gravel driveway. On reaching the gates she holds up her left hand in greeting, the right drawing a bunch of keys from her apron pocket. She selects one and inserts it into a heavy, dark green padlock that grips the end links of a rusty chain threaded through the gates. Unthreading the chain, she pulls each gate back in turn and waves the taxi through.

Felipe sticks his thumb in the air, drives slowly down the sweeping drive and parks outside the front door.

'Greetings, sister,' he says, stepping out of the car and walking over to hug Carmen Fortunato before she makes her way back to the house.

'You're too thin, Felipe. You're not feeding yourself well enough.'

He rolls his eyes. 'Sister, I cannot say the same for you.' That remark costs him a cuff round the ear.

'Hi, Ma.' Angelo wraps his arms around his mother and gives her a kiss on both cheeks.

She gently prods him in the stomach. 'I don't like the way this is hanging over your belt, son. You need to eat less.'

He holds his hands out, blushes. 'I know, Ma, I'm working on it. This is Terese. She's touring the island. I hope you don't mind, but I've invited her for dinner.'

'It's no skin off my nose. She can have half of yours.' Carmen takes hold of Terese's hand, squeezes it. 'Pleased to meet you, senorita. I'm only joking, there's plenty of food for all. We would be delighted to have you join us. Who's in the back of the car, Angelo?'

'Maria, Ma. She fell asleep.'

'Well, are you going to leave her there or do I have to wake her up myself?'

'I'll do it,' Felipe volunteers. 'She's been quiet all the way here. I hope she's not sickening for anything.'

'Where's Pa?' asks Angelo, trailing his mother into the house.

'Oh, he's out on his walk, as usual. He's probably at Moncada, reliving his glorious past.' She shakes her head and wipes a strand of stray hair off her forehead. 'You would think it was yesterday rather than nearly fifty years ago. He'll be along soon. The man can smell my cooking from five kilometres away and he has an uncanny knack of appearing just when food is about to be laid on the—'

'Is someone talking about me? My ears are burning.' The voice is deep, resonant and authoritarian. The kind of voice that is capable of reducing strong men to shivering wrecks.

'See what I mean?' says Carmen, tapping the side of her nose with her finger.

Terese feels the latent power of the old man as he enters the room and it makes her tremble. His eyes alight on her, screw up tight as if struggling to focus. She thinks he may be figuring why a complete stranger is standing in his front room in the midst of his wife, son, daughter-in-law and brother-in-law. For a second, silence cloaks them.

Then Angelo speaks. 'Hello, Pa. This is Terese. She's a journalist on holiday in Cuba. We brought her down from Havana with us.'

Eduardo looks in turn at Angelo and Felipe, as if they have a secret they are keeping from him. He walks up to Terese, removes his foraging cap and bows slightly. She smells traces of a smoker, but it is not the acrid, lingering smell of cigarettes.

'Welcome to Santiago de Cuba. I trust you are enjoying your visit to our wonderful island?'

He reaches out to shake her hand, his huge hand completely encasing hers. His handshake is accommodating, soft even, adjusting to the light pressure of hers, but she senses the hand, fingers the size of sausages, could crush hers effortlessly if its owner willed it.

'Yes, I am, sir.' Close up, his eyes remind her of a hawk; intense, unblinking, merciless.

'I prefer Major General. Where are you—'

'You're late back, Eduardo,' snaps Carmen, poking him in the chest. 'And we're hungry. You can continue your conversation over dinner. Come, let us eat.'

Carmen takes hold of Terese's elbow, steers her into the dining room. The furnishings are simple, stark. White-painted walls, several rush mats, a rough-hewn dining table, a handful of cane chairs. This is not a room for those craving luxury.

'You sit here, Terese.' Carmen slides out a chair from under the table and then disappears into the kitchen, muttering to herself. As the diners take their places, she shuttles between the kitchen and the dining room, setting down steaming tureens of vegetables and a large, oval plate piled high with fried chicken.

'Shall I serve?' asks Eduardo.

'You always do,' says Felipe, winking at Angelo.

Eduardo takes one plate at a time from a stack, doles out the food and hands it to Maria who passes it down the table until everyone has a plate. Serving himself last, he grips his knife and fork and immediately begins to eat, one eye on Angelo whose head is bent, hands clasped in prayer.

'So, what places do you intend to visit in Cuba apart from Havana and Santiago?' Eduardo asks, wiping his greasy mouth with the back of a large, hairy paw. 'Is there anywhere in particular you wish to see?'

She looks up to find his eyes once again locked on hers. Did she think she saw a bird of prey in them? No, on closer examination they are more like those of a rattlesnake; cold, calculating, deadly.

'I came to Cuba to have a break from the stress of work, Major General. My aim, if you can call it that, is simply to see as much of this wonderful place as I can. I've no fixed plans, so I'm open to suggestions. Trinidad and Guantanamo appear to be very interesting places from what I've read about them.'

Eduardo's fork hovers in mid-air. 'Guantanamo? Why would Guantanamo be of interest to you?'

'Guantanamo is the furthest east I want to go. If I go there I can honestly say I've travelled the island from one end to the other.'

He nods. 'Of course, how stupid of me. That makes perfect sense.' The fork continues to its destination. 'What do you plan to do in Santiago?'

'Oh, you know, explore the town, see the churches, absorb a little of the local history. Moncada Barracks sounds fascinating.'

'You know of Moncada Barracks?'

'Only what I've read in my travel guide, which isn't very much.'

One more lie. I spent hours researching Moncada. I'm becoming very good at lying. It isn't something that makes me feel good. Sometimes the lies make me so sick I want to grab the nearest priest and confess them all. Maybe I'll find God when this is all over.

Putting the fork down on his plate, Eduardo rests his elbows on the table, steeples his fingers and stares fixedly at her. 'And what does it say, this guide?'

'About the barracks?'

'Yes.'

'Mostly it's bland facts and figures. A few sentences covering Castro's involvement, a lot of bloodshed, routing by Batista, that sort of thing.'

'And would that be sufficient to satisfy a journalist's curiosity?'

'Not a good one, no.'

'And are you a good journalist?'

'I like to think so.'

'Then don't you want to know more?'

'Perhaps if I was working, but I'm on holiday and the journalist in me is taking a well-earned rest. I'm just another tourist for the duration.'

'Naturally, we all need a break from our real work from time to time.' He bounces his chin on his fingertips and then peers down the length of the table at Felipe. 'Is that not so, Felipe?'

Felipe does not reply, but the set of his face betrays his feelings. Clearly, dark undercurrents swirl around the two men that only those with an intimate knowledge of the family's dynamics would comprehend.

Eduardo resumes his eating, scooping up a forkful of vegetables and holding it in front of his mouth. 'So, I take it you would not be interested to hear what really went on at Moncada in '53?'

'I wouldn't be so rude as to say it wouldn't pique my curiosity.'

'Then I'll take you to Moncada, senorita, and make history live for you. You see, I was there.'

A tingle runs down her spine. This is what she hoped for: an opportunity to be alone with him and drop her bombshell. She glances around the table, sees Felipe winking at Angelo, Carmen glowering at Eduardo and Maria scowling at her.

As soon as Felipe drives off with Terese Carmen and Maria depart the dining room for the kitchen and the argument begins. Eduardo feels his hackles rise as Angelo passes a casual remark about the backwardness of his country.

'You ungrateful whelp, do you know what sacrifices we made for you and your generation?' he says, quivering with rage. 'Do you? Do you really?'

'All I'm saying, Pa, is that it's high time for a change. It's almost fifty years since the revolution. We need to move on. If we don't, we'll miss out on some great opportunities. You're stuck in the fifties and you've turned a blind eye to what's happening in the world. The rest of the region is booming and we should be too.'

Eduardo cups his left hand, smashes his right into it. 'Good people died for your generation so you could have a better life than we did. Better education, better medical facilities; those are the things people *really* appreciate. Now you repay us by craving big houses, shiny new cars and expensive boats . . . just like those stinking capitalists across the water.'

'Pa, this is 2006. We're stuck in a rut that's getting deeper and muddier. The Presidente is ill and, although nobody in government will admit it, we all know it's true. Old men, moulded by a revolutionary ideal, are bankrupting this country. Raúl offers a glimmer of hope, but he's also in the twilight years of his life.'

'Pah! If it wasn't for Castro we'd all be shovelling shit in the fields!'

Neither of them is ever going to win the same old, tired argument. They both accepted that long ago. Now it isn't about winning: now they're both addicted to the rhetoric.

'I pity you, my wayward son. You're doomed, like that traitorous friend of yours, Rafael.'

Sinking back in his chair, he plucks a large cigar from the cedarwood box that never moves from the large stone mantelpiece, and lights it. Deep down he suspects Angelo is right. Another revolution is brewing, but not the kind he comprehends or wants to understand. This time, there will be no guns, no violence, not even a political cause, simply the recognition that if his country is to survive in the modern world it will be necessary to give the people back what they once had before Batista—freedom to achieve their personal dreams. He hopes he's dead before that day dawns. Ever since he was a youth, he has believed the state should take precedence over the individual. Castro drilled that into him. It is understandable if Angelo's personal dream is to be wealthy and have what Rafael has. Understandable, but there's no way he'll condone it.

A silent revolution is already underway. No matter how strict the regime, ultimately the people will win. Already, he can see evidence of it in Santiago. Daniela, the sister of a friend of Carmen, runs a paladare out of her house. Outside her front door, she advertises meals with prices listed in Cuban pesos and inside, on the back of the door, she pins the paperwork from the government granting her permission to run her business. The government demands this paperwork from all entrepreneurs and, in addition, dictates she buys all of the ingredients for her restaurant in US dollars, but perversely, forces her customers to pay in Cuban pesos. Although the government insists the Cuban peso is worth one US dollar, the world currency market places the value of the Cuban peso at slightly less than four cents; so Daniela has to break the law to avoid losing money on each dish she sells. Out of sheer necessity, she buys the cheapest ingredients she can find. Often, she barters and trades with her neighbours to avoid the high prices of the government-run markets. She then sells her dishes for a profit in Cuban pesos if necessary, in US dollars when possible.

Eduardo is fully aware of this, but chooses to turn a blind eye. Daniela's food is out of this world.

Taking a deep draught of his cigar, he streams a lungful of smoke into the air, a sign of his anger. It swirls in a chaotic cloud and clings, limpet-like, to the smoke-stained ceiling.

'You know, Angelo, all over the world oppressed people still struggle, even in this enlightened day and age. Look at Zimbabwe and Ethiopia. They desperately need a Castro, Guevara or Cienfuegos. Without the vision and sacrifice of such men, change in those wretched places will never happen. I think that French woman understands this. My instinct tells me she sympathises with my views, unlike you. When *you* realise what we have in this country, I will personally arrange a street party in your honour.'

'What about the Basque Country?'

The cigar stops dead an inch from Eduardo's mouth. 'What about it?'

'Terese is from the Basque Country. Why didn't you ask her about the nationalist movement there? I thought you would have been a little more inquisitive.'

'Me? Why should I be? You heard her. She's here on holiday to escape the pressures of her job. I wouldn't be so rude as to talk politics over dinner.'

'Have you heard of an organisation called ETA?'

'Of course I have. Do you think I don't take an interest in what's going on in the world?'

'So, aren't you a little curious about them? Doesn't it sound similar to what took place here with the Spanish and the Americans?'

'I'm an old man, Angelo, and I don't think about such things any more. I'm more interested in taking my walk and enjoying a fine cigar and a shot of rum.'

'Come on, Pa, that's not true and you know it. You scour your paper from front to back, then you're on the phone for hours with Oswardo and I don't think you talk about baseball.'

'What Oswardo and I talk about is none of your damn business. He's a true son of Cuba. I'm no longer sure what *you* are. All you ever talk about is Rafael this and Rafael that. If you're so dissatisfied, why not go and join him? I'll tell you why you don't . . . you don't have the balls.' He spits a thick gob of phlegm onto the rough concrete floor. 'I sometimes wonder if you're really a son of mine.'

They are back on the well-trodden path of their perennial argument. Soon, Eduardo will mouth a spiteful invective regarding Angelo's aspirations, disloyalty and manhood. Then he will criticise his religious beliefs, sneering at how his son looks like a male version of Mother Teresa, dressed in white from head to toe.

The appearance of Felipe prevents him from launching his attack.

'Are you two at it again?'

'Ah, I see the man who would rather make money than educate our children has arrived. Are you sure you can afford the time?' says Eduardo.

'It's better than sitting on my arse pining for the glorious old days.'

'At least I have glorious old days, my friend, and days worth remembering.' Rising from his chair, Eduardo snatches his paper and storms out of the room, slamming the door behind him. He does not go far. Slipping into the adjoining room, he puts his ear to the wall and listens.

'Usual argument?' he hears Felipe say.

'When is it any different? I think Pa takes great pleasure in losing his temper with me. He always makes me feel as if I'm letting him down. It's got to the point where Ma won't enter the room when we're together.'

'Look Angelo, I know it's difficult, but try to look at it from his point of view. The revolution was the highlight of his life, it made him the man he is—you won't find a more patriotic individual. Sure, he has views that wouldn't bend in a hurricane, but he's also a father and a good one . . . otherwise my sister would not have remained by his side all these years. He has his peculiarities, but the old bear has a heart of gold deep down.'

'Then he has a strange way of showing it.'

'Do you know what I think?'

'Tell me, Uncle Felipe.'

'I think your father doesn't know what to do with his time and that must depress him. As long as I've known him he has relished a good argument, but there's no one to argue with any more, no one to confront. Your mother has learned how to cope with him over many years and she simply ignores him. He has my sympathy. Like him, I no longer have the mental stimulation I once had. Maybe that's why he perked up when he arranged to meet that young woman at Moncada?'

'It didn't escape my attention.'

'It didn't escape your mother's either, but it's nothing to do with her good looks. He's not so much as turned his head for another woman in over forty years. It's not even that he's desperate to recount his interminable stories about Moncada, Castro, Guevara and the Revolution, although he'll take pleasure in doing so. I know your father and his ways. He'll treat that woman as one of his pet projects. Something about her has sparked his interest and he'll want to know more. I haven't worked out what it is, but it will be interesting— very interesting—to observe what develops. Anyway, forget about him for the moment. You can bring me up to date with Rafael's news. I want to know every little detail, particularly concerning the Ferrari.'

Listening behind the door, a smile crosses Eduardo's face. Whatever else he might be, his brother-in-law is certainly not stupid.

12th July

The following morning, the owner of the Casa de la Mar hands a message to Terese. From Eduardo, written in a bold hand, it is brief and to the point. It states that if she wishes to learn more about Moncada he will meet her at the intersection of Los Libertadores Avenida and Paseo Jose Marti at midday.

The note concludes:

> Be sure to bring your notebook. There will be some interesting facts you may wish to write down.

A crucial milestone in the plan is fast approaching; one she has dreaded ever since she caught the Air France flight. If she plays her cards right, the burden will shift temporarily to the Major General's broad shoulders. But if she gets it wrong, what then? She dare not imagine. The reaction of the Major General could be unpredictable, but that of Peru needs no imagining. At best, it will signal the end of their relationship. At worst . . .

I'm between a rock and a hard place.
Her stomach churns. This is her first big test.
She has to succeed.

Moncada Barracks is imposing. Ochre-coloured, crenulated walls stretch between whitewashed columns. A perimeter walkway runs around the lower level, cast in shadow by the overhanging cantilever of a first floor landing. Staircases rise from ground level to this landing at regular intervals. Plain and simple, the barracks is nonetheless a beautiful structure.

Resplendent in full military uniform, a swagger stick tucked under his arm, the Major General is waiting for her. His barrel chest strains his tunic, making him appear almost as wide as he is tall. A row of medals reflects the light from the early morning sun.

His stance screams he is not a man you would willingly cross.

I can understand why Guevara was wary of him, she thinks.

'Good day, senorita. Welcome to Moncada Barracks, one of the most important places in the history of revolutionary Cuba. Shall we walk?'

As they stroll, she looks up at the walls of the silent building, no longer filled with the clamour of military personnel going about their business. Nowadays, it houses a much less menacing presence—the children of the City School of the 26th July.

'Many years ago,' he says, 'during the Spanish-Cuban-American War and before these barracks were here, a Spanish-built cruiser called the *Reina Mercedes* was scuttled to block Santiago's harbour entrance following the great naval battle of the third of July, 1898. After the war the US Navy raised her, but didn't restore her to operational condition. Instead, they converted her to a barracks ship. Later, on the same site, they built this garrison. They named it after Guillermo Moncada, one of twenty-nine generals in the Cuban War of Independence. There isn't much of interest then until the middle of 1956. The twenty-sixth of July to be precise; the date on which we tried to storm the stronghold.'

They pause in front of the barrack's massive main gate.

'Castro was meticulous with his planning. I suppose that's the lawyer in him. He had been working on the plan for months and drilled it into us, time after time after time, until we knew it in our sleep.'

'It must have been quite a complex operation.'

'On the contrary, it was simple and direct. Castro intended to attack the barracks with one group and capture weapons stored here, in order to arm a revolution to overthrow Batista. Another group under Castro's brother, Raúl, would attack other points around the city including the radio station. We were to strike in the early morning.'

'When the local population would be sleeping off the effects of the annual carnival?'

'You know about the carnival?'

'It's in my guide.'

'Minutes before dawn we drove a convoy of twenty-six cars down unlit streets towards the barracks. Inside, there were over a thousand heavily armed and well-drilled soldiers. They vastly outnumbered us: one hundred and thirty desperate and determined men. Castro figured most of the soldiers would be drunk from the celebrations and wouldn't put up much of a fight. He also assumed the garrison would be sympathetic to our cause.'

'I gather it didn't work out as expected?'

'It was one of the rare occasions when he was wrong.' He slowly shakes his head as if it is unthinkable that Castro could ever have made such an error of judgement. 'Our convoy became fragmented and the car carrying our heavy weapons got lost. As the first car reached the spot on which we are now standing, a roving patrol of soldiers approached from around that corner over there,' he points with the swagger stick, 'and challenged Castro. In a panic, he jumped from his car and set about them. We leapt out of our trailing cars and joined in. The soldiers stood their ground and didn't surrender. More and more joined in and fired on us from the barrack's windows and doors. Those in the lead vehicles who had managed to get through the gateway were quickly subdued and captured by the garrison.'

'I guess the soldiers were afraid of the consequences if they didn't resist.'

'Who knows? Whether they were patriotic, loyal to the regime or just plain scared didn't matter. They put up a spirited and successful defence. Eventually, we realised our attack had failed so we turned tail and fled. It was a complete disaster. Sixty-one good men lost their lives in the fighting. Many were captured and tortured to death, poor souls.'

'Clearly not Castro and you.'

'No. A small band of us escaped into the countryside, but we were caught later through our own carelessness.'

Resuming their walk, they reach Trinidad Street, skirting the southern wall where Eduardo points with his swagger stick at a scattering of pitted holes on the ochre-coloured walls.

'See those? Do you know what they are?'

Squinting, she focuses on the indentations. 'Bullet holes?'

'Well done. They are indeed bullet holes and those bullet holes hold many secrets. Let us look more closely.' He stretches his arm above his head, places the palm of his hand against the wall and inserts a stubby forefinger into the entrance of one small, crumbling hole. 'This one was mine. Those,' he nods at a group of five holes half a metre to the left of where his finger is, 'are fakes.'

She studies the holes carefully, unable to see any difference. 'Fakes?'

'Most certainly fakes and undeniably made by a power drill. The copies are very good, but look carefully at the angle of entry. You would have to be three metres tall to have made those holes with a gun.'

He is correct. The holes are at right angles to the face of the stonework. If rifle shots came from shoulder height, the shooter would need to be a giant.

'They fool almost everyone except those like me who know what to look for. Of course, for tourists and the younger generation it all adds to the romance of the tale, although I can tell you romance was the last thing on our minds that night.'

Frowning, she points to the genuine hole. 'You said, "This one was mine". But how can you be so sure?'

'Ah, I thought you might ask that. The reason I know it is mine is that years later I dug the bullet out of that hole. I had to ask Castro himself for permission to take it.'

'I'm sorry, but I still don't understand how you know that particular hole was made by you.'

'Then I'll explain. An old habit born out of boredom gave it away. You see, when I first joined up with Castro I used to scratch a tiny outline of a bull on the side of each lead bullet with the tip of my knife before we went on training manoeuvres. That could keep me occupied for hours on end whilst the others played cards. I don't like cards.'

'A bull?'

'Yes, a bull. After Taurus, my birth sign. That's how I got my nickname, El Toro Negro—the Black Bull.'

'Ah, I understand. But why black?'

He removes his finger from the hole and makes a grunting noise. 'You might not believe it now, looking at this shiny dome and clean-shaven jaw, but once I had the thickest, curliest black hair and beard. Much fuller than Castro's: he was quite envious of it. They knew I carved the bulls and came up with the nickname. It stuck.'

'What about the other holes?' She sweeps an arm across the expanse of the pockmarked wall.

'Oh, for the most part they're genuine. They needed the false ones down here, where the tourists can touch them and view them close up; it gives an authentic air to the old place. It's almost fifty years since we stormed Moncada and there will be celebrations next year. People will come here from all over the world, so I wouldn't be surprised if the authorities drill a few more. Are you interested in hearing more about the campaign?'

It is just as well the old soldier is thoroughly enjoying himself, given the bomb she is about to drop on him. She guesses it is quite some time since he last relived his revolutionary youth, spinning yarns to someone whom he thinks is keen to listen.

She pulls a notebook out of her knapsack. 'Do you mind if I write this down like you said in your note?'

Hesitating for a moment, he fishes a large cigar out of the top pocket of his tunic. 'I don't, but only if I can edit your notes, since I wouldn't want to discover your newspaper misquoting me, should that become your intention. I may be a close friend of Castro, but he still keeps his eyes open for potential enemies and I'm far too old to land in hot water. And,' he adds with a warning look, 'I'm too smart.'

Again, those eyes turn on her, fixing her with their magnetism.

A lump swells in her throat.

'I understand, Major General. It's a deal.'

His eyes narrow. 'I don't make deals. Over the years, many people have learned that. I will tell you more, but I must rest first. I can feel my joints beginning to stiffen and I would like to enjoy a cigar. Let us sit.'

As they settle on a pitted iron bench under the shade of a nearby acacia tree, she gazes at the bulk of the renovated barracks. Rows of new, tubular steel posts topped with opaque, spherical glass lamps line the weed-free footpath running around the full length of the perimeter.

'Have you ever felt passionate about a cause?' he asks, attention focused on a spot on the barracks wall. 'So passionate you would gladly lay down your life?'

His question throws her. It seems an odd one to ask.

'Not really,' she lies.

'Only I understand you live in Bayonne, no? Isn't that in the Basque Country and don't you have an organisation there that fights for the independence of your people?'

For one terrible moment, she fears he knows more about her than she thinks. Her instincts tell her that simply is not possible. If she is unknown to the authorities back home, then in Cuba they certainly will not have information regarding her sympathies and activities for a cause to which she has pledged her life.

'Yes, it's called ETA. They're freedom fighters.'

'Freedom fighters?' he echoes, cocking an eyebrow. 'Many innocent lives have been lost in the name of freedom. Some would call them terrorists as they seek to achieve independence by violent means. Do you sympathise with their cause?'

She bites her lip to stop herself from blushing. The last thing she wants is for him to draw her into a discussion of ETA. 'I would find it difficult to sympathise with anyone who would take an innocent life to further their political cause.'

'Not even in extreme circumstances? Not even when your country is being destroyed by a tyrannical and greedy regime?'

'That isn't the case where I live.'

'Perhaps not. Although I'm sure there are those who may say it feels like it.'

She lets the remark pass without comment. He might be showing his age, but the passing of years has not dulled the mind inside that bullet head. Here is a man who keeps himself well informed.

'The love of one's country is a marvellous feeling,' he says. 'It consumes one entirely. I'll put it into context for you.'

Producing a cutter, he snips the end off the cigar. Placing it between his stained teeth, he flips open the top of a battered Zippo lighter and repeatedly sucks hard until a shower of flame explodes on the cigar's tip. Drawing deeply, he expels a cloud of greyish smoke which whorls into the air above them.

'Do you know of Fulgencio Batista?'

'Again, only what I read in my guide. That is, not a great deal.'

'Then I will enlighten you. General Fulgencio Batista y Zaldivar was a bad man, a very bad man. He treated Cuba as his personal plaything in the forties and fifties. Like most politicians, he began on the right foot, but then developed a taste for power and a fascination for La Yuma—that's what we call the United States. In '44, Ramón Grau San Martin, a man who openly defied US domination and supported the struggles of the lower classes, defeated him. We thought that was the last we would hear of Batista, but we were wrong. Four years later, he won a seat in the Cuban Senate whilst living luxuriously in Florida. Four years after that he ran for president and, knowing he wasn't going to win, decided to stage a coup.'

'With the help of the Americans?'

'Undoubtedly. The '52 election was a three-way race. Roberto Agramonte of the Ortodoxos party led in all the polls followed by Carlos Hevia of the Autentico party, with Batista running a distant third. Both Agramonte and Hevia wanted Colonel Ramón Barquin, who was then serving as the Cuban military attaché in Washington, to head the armed forces after the elections. Barquin was a first class officer who commanded the respect of the army and who promised to eliminate corruption in the ranks. Batista feared Barquin would oust him and his followers, and when it became apparent he had little chance of winning he staged a coup with the backing of a nationalist section of the army. Once back in power he opened the way for large-scale gambling in Havana.' He spits on the ground. 'The city became the "Latin Las Vegas", a playground of choice for many gamblers and gangsters. Prostitution and corruption became rife. Batista and his cronies were having a whale of a time whilst the rest of the country starved. They were also growing incredibly rich by siphoning money off to bank accounts they held in La Yuma.'

'Then Castro came into the picture.'

'Castro wasn't the only one. He just happened to have the guts and the charisma, especially the charisma. I had known of Fidel since he was a little boy, although I had never spoken to him. His mother and my aunt were friends. They both used to work as maids for his father, Senor Angel Castro y Argiz, on his sugar plantation.'

'I'm sorry, I think I misheard. Did you say his mother used to work as a maid for his father?'

'Ah, there lies another tale, one that possibly explains the conundrum that is Castro. The senor had five children with Castro's mother, all out of wedlock. When Castro was seventeen the senor married Castro's mother and acknowledged him as his son.'

'Unbelievable.'

'Yes, it is. Years before Castro's father married Castro's mother, he sent him away to school in Havana. It wasn't until much later—'51 I think it was—that we met for the first time here in Santiago. He told me of his plans and I was astounded. The Castro I remembered was only interested in sport and arguing with the priests who taught us, but the Castro I encountered that day was different. There was fire in his eyes and silver in his tongue.

'At the time, many of my friends and their families were scraping a hand-to-mouth living and we young men were angry, very angry, like fuses waiting to be lit. Maybe it didn't help that there was almost no work at that time. We were all bored and I, a young hothead, was a willing recruit to Castro's revolutionary cause.'

'So then you hatched the plot to take Moncada?'

'Oh, no, that was already in train. Castro had been working on it for at least two years. His first thought was to do something dramatic in Havana, make a statement, but he ruled it out as being too risky. Santiago was sufficiently distant to escape Batista's reach, big enough for him to notice. Castro is clever, exceptionally clever. That's been proven by the undisputable fact that no one else in the world has outlasted nine American presidents.'

Thank heavens I'm not dealing with Castro, she said to herself.

'But surely he must have realised his plan had little chance of success? A handful of men outnumbered by a garrison of trained soldiers. On the face of it, it appears suicidal.'

'On reflection it was, but Castro had plenty of guts—still has—and an almost missionary zeal. We never thought for one moment we might fail. It was only after the tortures and killings that reality dawned. Some slunk away never to be heard of again. For the rest, and I was one, it strengthened our resolve. We were even more determined to rid the country of Batista, but without the leadership and vision of Castro, I don't think we would have succeeded. The man is blessed. Batista should have killed him whilst he had the chance, but he didn't and Castro lived to fight another day. Then we met Guevara in Mexico and convinced him to join the M-26-7. From then on, there was no stopping us.'

Terese braces herself. The mention of Guevara's name jolts the question out of her. 'Major General, I—'

His hand shoots out, fingers splayed. The quickness of the movement takes her by surprise. 'No more questions, it's time I returned home. My wife will complain bitterly if I'm late again for my meal.'

The hand, dominant and commanding, brooks no argument. It fills her vision. A thin white scar runs unbroken, from the mound of his thumb to a callous at the base of his little finger. There is strength in that hand, frightening strength: the kind of hand that can snap a neck with little effort.

With a supreme effort, she squeezes out the words through dry lips. 'I-I understand, Major General. Perhaps we c-could continue some other time?'

'I will consider your request, but I can't promise anything. Now, I must be on my way.'

They rise from the bench and those fierce eyes lock on to hers. 'If we do meet again, you will tell me the real reason why you are interested in Guantanamo.'

All is not well at the Casa del Toro Negro.

Angelo studies Maria as she turns in bed and glares at him. Dark rings fringe her eyes and unruly strands of hair lie strewn across the gentle swells of the bolster. Her look is familiar; pleading laced with desperation.

'Maria, what in Heaven's name is the matter with you?' he says. 'You mope around the house all day, you don't talk to anyone, our friends don't visit us as often as they used to. Now your behaviour is beginning to worry my mother.'

Settling himself on the side of the bed, he reaches out and tries to take hold of her hand. She snatches it away, hides it beneath the sheets.

'I'm sick, Angelo, sick and tired of living. There's nothing for me to live for. We've been round and round this for months and I've had enough. My life's worthless and if I disappeared off the face of the earth tomorrow no one would care.'

'Don't be stupid, Maria, you're being paranoid. What's the matter with you?'

Their rows are now frequent and vitriolic. In his army days they hardly quarrelled at all. On the rare occasions they did, he would escape to the mess, an exclusively male enclave. Back then, she did not occupy her mind with thoughts of children. That might have owed much to the fact that she had the company of other young army wives, many of whom were childless and pursued interests outside the home. Army life had suited her; probably would still suit her if he had not decided to resign his commission. That act was the catalyst for their constant bickering. She pleaded with him to remain in the army—as did his father—but he had other ambitions.

Ambitions neither she nor his father share.

They both know—all their friends know—that the flame of love has flickered and died. Close friends say they should either have children (a solution favoured by Maria), or seek a divorce (a solution rejected by him).

His response to having children is a flat 'no way.'

'If that's how you feel, divorce me,' she tells him. 'Then I can get on with my life and meet another who will give me children.'

Divorce is something he will not countenance. His faith does not tolerate it and it would give his father yet one more reason to despise him. His mother and father have remained together through a revolution, an embargo and countless occasions when there were shortages of even the most basic commodities. At times, they were apart for months on end, but they still managed to keep their marriage intact. If he chooses to join Rafael in Florida, no way would the Americans allow him to enter their country whilst Maria remains in Cuba. His father would disown him instantly, given his pathological hatred of all things American.

Three years now, he has wrestled day and night with this intractable problem, but to no avail.

As he rises from the bed and walks toward the door, her words catch him. 'I saw the way you were looking at that French slut and the eyes she was making at you. You disgust me, Angelo. You're a real piece of shit.'

Gritting his teeth he turns to argue, thinks the better of it. This is the latest development in her increasingly irrational behaviour towards him. If he so much as returns a polite nod or exchanges a friendly word with another woman, she spits infidelity at him. Admittedly, Terese is attractive, but then, so are many of the young women who sun themselves on the seawall along Malecon, waving to him as he passes by in the trap. Thank heavens Maria does not hear his replies that cause the girls to shriek and giggle behind their hands. All the drivers do it. The girls expect it, knowing the men would never act on what they say.

'Are you going to get up?' he asks, resting his hands on his hips.

'No,' she pouts and then squeezes her eyes to slits.

'Come on, Maria, you're not unwell.'

'I feel like shit.'

How much longer do I have to put up with this? he asks himself, rubbing the back of his neck.

'Don't be silly there's nothing the matter with you. Please get up and get dressed and we'll go for a walk down to the harbour. The exercise will do us both good.'

'I don't feel like walking. I want to go home.'

'We'll go home soon, I promise. Felipe will want to get back to Adriana and I need to earn some money.'

She peels the sheet away from the bed, revealing her nakedness. As he watches, she slowly and deliberately opens her legs to reveal a triangle of curly black hair. Sliding her finger across the curve of her left breast and down across the flatness of her stomach, she lets it dwell on the apex.

'Fuck me, Angelo,' she whispers. 'Come back to bed and make babies.'

'I can't, Maria. I can't do that. You know I can't.'

'Bastard!' she screams. 'I hate you!'

Picking up a shoe lying on the floor next to the bed, she throws it at him, striking him on his chest. Then she bursts into tears and buries her head in the pillow.

He shakes his head and kicks the shoe out of the way.

There has to be a way out of his predicament.

There just has to be.

On his return Eduardo finds Carmen in the garden, beating to a pulp the dust-ingrained rugs from the upstairs floor of the house. It is a physically demanding task, but Carmen is a physically strong woman. That strength helped her when she was a young recruit in M-26-7.

'Hello, my sweet,' he greets, slipping his hands around her generous waist. 'Have they deserted you?'

She brushes aside his hands. 'I'm worried about Angelo.'

'You're always worried about Angelo. What has he done now?'

'It's what he won't do. Maria has asked him for a divorce, but he says no.'

He harrumphs. 'Ha! If I was her, I wouldn't have waited this long to ask.'

'Don't joke, Eduardo. She says he won't contemplate divorce nor will he give her children. It's driving the poor girl mad. Whatever is the matter with him?'

Eduardo curses under his breath. That question is one he will not try to answer. The way Angelo's mind works is a mystery. He might sympathise with Maria, but he can do little to help her. She has made her bed: she must lie in it.

'Why doesn't he like children, Eduardo?'

He shrugs. 'Doesn't he? I'm not so sure of that. He appears to enjoy playing with Eduardo junior on the rare occasions he sees him. Maybe it's nothing to do with children. Maybe it's another woman.'

'Another woman? Why do you say that?'

'It's a possibility, isn't it? This Santeria nonsense might trouble his conscience but it can't suppress his desires.'

'Hmm, the same thought crossed my mind. So after breakfast, when Felipe and Angelo were carrying the rugs into the garden, I went upstairs and asked Maria if she still loves him.'

'What did she say?'

'At first, she didn't say anything and seemed a little embarrassed. Then she stared at me, a faraway look in her eyes. She said she doesn't get butterflies in her stomach as she used to when they first met and it no longer excites her when he returns home. She doesn't get goose pimples if he kisses her neck. She asked me if they were signs she has fallen out of love with him.'

'What did you say?'

'What could I say? I was wondering how to answer her when she screamed, "He only seems interested in what Rafael's doing. Rafael's bought this, Rafael's got that. Rafael, Rafael, Rafael. It's an obsession. If he wants Rafael's lifestyle that badly then he should divorce me and take off to Florida." She worked herself up into quite a state I can tell you.'

Eduardo shakes his head and sighs. 'Is he ever going to let it go?'

'Then I asked her if that's what she really wants, a divorce. She said she wants babies. Lots of babies before it is too late.'

He wipes his forehead with the back of a dusty hand. Maria is not the most intelligent of women and Eduardo often wonders why his son ended up marrying her. But to refuse her children? That cannot be right. Every woman deserves to bear children. Carmen gave birth to his three sons and he would never have foregone the pleasure of raising them and seeing them grow into young men.

He has his suspicions it isn't marriage that is troubling Angelo. His middle son is in the shadow of his brothers. Oswardo is the strong one, the leader, Eduardo's image in looks and temperament. Ramon, the youngest, reminds him very much of Felipe: clever, gentle. Both are content with their lots, both good citizens of Cuba. The only thing Angelo has is his dream, a dream that lies a mere ninety miles to the north of Havana. So close, yet so far.

He pats Carmen on her arm. 'Look my sweet, if it helps, I'll have a word with him, but I can't promise anything. I would be surprised if he even listened to me.'

He turns to walk away.

'There's more,' she says.

'Go on.'

'She says if he won't divorce her or give her children she'll kill herself. Then she did this.' Carmen slowly draws a fingernail across her neck, leaving a faint white mark from ear to ear. 'I'm worried, Eduardo, really worried. What do you think we should do?'

'Let me think about it, my love, whilst I'm having a smoke.'

He pecks her on the cheek and strolls to the edge of the garden, where he lowers himself on a rickety canvas chair beside the chicken run. From here he has an uninterrupted view across the expanse of the town to the hazy blueness of the sea. Taking a cigar out of his top pocket, he lights it and thinks of Carmen's words. He does not dwell on them for long. Angelo can sort out his own problems. He is more interested in the French woman. Something about her troubles him, something he cannot put his finger on. He might not have much experience of journalists, but he is very knowledgeable about human behaviour. All through their meeting, she was edgy, nervous, as if she wanted to say something, but could not bring herself to do it. He knows he can be intimidating; intimidation is a facet of the persona he has cultivated. When they met, however, he set out to be approachable, friendly, willing to share his stories and experiences. She should have been at ease instead of anxious. Out of curiosity, he asked about ETA and she reacted as if he was accusing her of some crime. Then, as they were about to part, he noticed her body language. She wrung her hands and took quick breaths, stammering from time to time. He is familiar with the trait. She was steeling herself to say something; something that would anger him.

But what? His gut tells him it has to do with Guantanamo and if it has, then who better than he to find out what it is?

Beforehand, he thought one meeting would suffice to tell her about Moncada and then he would forget her, stow her away with other fleeting memories. Now he knows he will have to meet her again.

She is in Cuba for a reason and that reason has nothing to do with sightseeing.

The next time they meet, he *will* uncover her real reason for being there.

He is very good at that.

15th July

Three long days have passed since her meeting with
Eduardo. It feels more like three years. Terese finds it
impossible to relax, her mind wrestling with ways in
which she could contrive to meet him again should he fail
to contact her. Should she stroll around Santiago on the
off chance their paths will cross? Possibly, but that might
never happen. Should she turn up on his doorstep with
some fabricated story about Guantanamo? He seems
very interested in the place. No, that would set his family
to wondering, especially Maria, who glowered at her all
through the meal that first night.

*As if i was interested in her man, stupid bitch. There
are enough men in my life without any more to
complicate it further, thank you very much.*

Time is ticking away. The Casa de la Mar's owner is
curious as to how long she intends to remain in Santiago.
He is aware she has only three weeks' vacation—she told
him so when she arrived. He must know it is barely
enough time to see the whole of the island if she does not
move on soon.

Those three dead days turned her mind once again
to Peru and the morality of her mission. Without inviting
it, she has become the key player, the foundation taking
all the pressure, something she neither enjoys nor wants.
How Peru and she have changed! Once, she would have
done anything to please him: a serious, focused young

man with brooding looks, who wore passion on his sleeve. They fitted together like pieces in a jigsaw, a couple of young ideologues with a common aim. As soon as ETA got under his skin, he talked incessantly about what he was going to do to bring about the independence of his people; what sacrifices he was prepared to make; what risks he would have to take. His talk began to scare her, but talk could do no harm.

Then she met Salbatore Vasco and for the first time realised just what she was getting into.

In those early days Peru had hero-worshipped Salbatore, with his fervour, charisma and clear-sightedness. Salbatore is a veteran of the cause, a witness of death at close quarters. A hard-bitten man, he has spent time with some of the most unscrupulous freedom fighters the world has ever known. His experience and ruthlessness qualify him well for wearing the mantle of leadership. He is completely insensitive to whatever mayhem the application of his skills brings about. She has always been frightened of Salbatore, frightened and wary. At times, he leans towards megalomania and displays symptoms of a schizophrenic mind with his mood swings and unpredictable rants and raves. Disturbingly, Peru is becoming more and more like a Salbatore clone. He has lost what little sense of humour he once had and now, like Salbatore, is indifferent to the carnage and grieving caused by their bombings, kidnappings and assassinations.

A sharp rap on the door interrupts her thoughts. She opens it to find Gerado, the owner, standing in the hallway, holding a folded slip of paper in his hand and wearing a worried look on his face.

'Good morning, Senorita Rodriguez. I have a note for you, left by a Major General Fortunato.' He passes the slip to her.

'Thank you.'

He shifts his weight from foot to foot, rocking sideways. 'Is there a problem?'

'A problem?'

'I am rarely visited by such a powerful man, senorita. In my experience, when a man such as this Major General lands on your doorstep, trouble always follows.'

'No, there's no problem. I happen to know the Major General purely by accident after having met his son. Don't worry.'

'Will you be leaving soon?'

'Very soon.'

Closing the door, she unfolds the note and reads:

> Senorita Rodriguez, I thought you might like to hear the truth about the events of 1959. If you wish, meet me by the main entrance of Moncada at noon today.

'I certainly do wish, Major General,' she mouths, relief washing over her. This time she will not miss her chance to say what she has to say.

In her mind's eye she pictures his massive paw, closing over her face, squeezing it like an overripe tomato until it bursts. Her stomach lurches. She turns and sprints for the bathroom, hand clamped over her mouth.

Time seems to have stood still. There he is, striking the same confident pose in the same pressed uniform as when last they met. This time, though, he looks a little puffy around the eyes, as if he is suffering from a cold or lack of sleep. His left hand holds a half-smoked cigar; the right, one end of the swagger stick tucked under his arm. She wonders if he might have been waiting for some time.

'Good afternoon. Still in Santiago, I see. I was certain by now you would have continued your journey.'

'Good afternoon, Major General. You're right, I should be on my way by now, but it's so beautiful here, isn't it? There is so much to see. However, I can't stay here forever. Tomorrow morning I'll be on the road again.'

'To Guantanamo, I assume?'

'That would be my intention.'

'Ah, I thought so. Come, let us walk.'

This time they turn so the barracks are at their back. The crescent of Santiago opens out like a hazy white sickle before them, floating in the heat rising from the sun-scorched earth.

'I think '56 would be a good year to start. Are you taking notes? Good. We should continue our story in November of that year. Castro had devised yet another plan and was determined this time not to fail. He chartered a yacht in Mexico on the twenty-fifth of the month. Eighty-two of us set sail for Santiago. The journey took longer than planned; seven days riding an angry, foaming sea. We aimed to rendezvous with a group under the command of Frank Pais, with the objective of attacking the police headquarters, the Customs House and the harbourmaster's offices. Bad luck struck one more time and we lost communications with Pais.

'Three days later, as we were on the verge of rendezvousing, Batista's troops surprised us as we rested on the edge of a cane field at Alegria de Pio, not far from the Sierra Maestra. They killed or captured nearly all of our party, but a handful escaped including the Castro brothers, Che Guevara, and I.'

Invisible fingers wrap themselves around her throat. This is the defining moment, the tipping point. In the next few minutes, she could end up dead. Her heart begins to race—Baboom! Baboom! Baboom! Her mind

126

screams at her, begging her not to loose the words caught on her tongue.

Trembling, her lips spew them out. 'Major General, I know about your wife's bastard child. The one she had by Che Guevara.'

He strides on without missing a step, as if her words might simply be a throwaway remark on the weather or the peaceful tranquillity of their surroundings. Then he halts, stands stock-still. She watches, petrified, as he slowly cups his ear with that huge hand.

'Excuse me, but my hearing must be failing me. What did you say?' His words are calm, but tempered with an edge of steel.

Her legs begin to shake uncontrollably. Fighting an impulse to turn and run, she braces herself and repeats, 'I know about your wife's bastard child.'

His eyes, when they turn on her, blaze with anger. Lightning-quick, he whips the swagger stick from beneath his arm and swings it in a horizontal arc until its brass tip touches her throat.

'If you were a man,' he growls, 'I'd kill you for that insult. Damn it, I knew from the moment I set eyes on you, you were up to no good. Pack your bags and leave Santiago right now. Don't think of travelling to Guantanamo. If you do, I'll make damn sure my son's watching out for you and he wouldn't have any hesitation in ruining your impudent face. Now fuck off!'

Lifting a shaking finger, she slowly pushes the stick away from her throat, drawing on every ounce of strength she can muster to make the movement.

'I-I can't do that, Major General. You need to k-know I have a Guevara diary describing in detail what went on between your wife and him only weeks after you married her. His writing is very graphic; it certainly made m-me blush. This diary chronicles the twelve months after their

. . . coupling. He mentions her pregnancy at least twice. There is also a reference to what you and your wife decided to d-do with the child. It has a genuine provenance, written in Guevara's own hand. I have deposited three copies of this document in the safe custody of a colleague and he has strict instructions to deliver a copy to each of your sons if instructed by me. I imagine they know nothing of this liaison or the existence of their bastard sibling. If my colleague fails to r-receive a daily telephone call from me then he will—and I mean will—deliver those documents immediately. If you d-deny all knowledge of this liaison, I'll phone him this evening and he'll immediately make the deliveries, without hesitation.'

His mouth compresses to a tight slit as he lowers the stick. 'I don't know what you're talking about. Have you taken leave of your senses? My wife and Che Guevara? Ridiculous! Now, go, before I kill you right here.'

'It was a one-night stand. They f-fucked each other. He records you knew nothing about it until your wife's belly began to swell.'

The swagger stick begins to rise and then stops. For an instant, she catches a flicker of doubt in his eyes. This is what she gambled. His curiosity will buy her the precious seconds she needs to try and convince him.

He snorts, shakes his head. 'You're mistaken. I have read Guevara's diaries many, many times and they do not refer to either my wife or a bastard child. Guevara was meticulous with his records. If it happened, he would have recorded it.'

It is her turn to force a tight smile, as she feels her confidence building. 'That's where you're wrong, Major General. As you say, the *published* diaries do not mention Carmen Fortunato or even Carmen Caraballo as she was before you married her. The *unpublished* one does.'

'Impossible. They were all published, every one of them. Guevara told us that himself.'

'Then he must have had a reason for not publishing the one he sent to a distant relative of his in Bilbao. Maybe he was embarrassed. I finally tracked this unpublished diary down after years of searching. The original manuscript is now in the vault of the most secure bank in the Basque Country. Let us say I acquired it from the person who possessed it, but for some reason, fortunately for me, never had the time or inclination to read it and uncover its secrets. I was much more diligent and discovered this diary contained information I could use to my advantage.'

Shaking his head, he brings his face close to hers. 'Nice try, but my gut tells me you're bluffing. No one I know has ever heard of an unpublished diary.'

'Don't you want to hear why I'm risking my life telling you this?'

'No.'

'Did you know his forefathers came from the Basque Country?'

'His diaries say so. It's common knowledge.'

'And that he sympathised with ETA?'

'The man was an incorrigible revolutionary. Guevara sympathised with all revolutionary causes, wherever they happened to be.'

'Did you also know that he planned to offer his expertise to ETA after his involvement in Bolivia? His unexpected death may have been the reason why he never published this particular diary. I can only assume that he may have been curious about his roots and sent the handwritten draft to a trusted, if distant, relative in advance of publication.'

'I stress again, there is no diary and I deny all knowledge of the ridiculous accusation you're making. Now, return to your lodgings, pack your bags and be on your way. This is not your home. You are in Cuba and in this country people have a habit of disappearing without trace.'

Hand trembling, she reaches into her pocket and pulls out a thin sheaf of folded papers.

'Perhaps you'd like me to read it to you? This is a photocopy of the relevant pages. For the sake of modesty, I won't describe the night of passion.'

Unfolding the papers, she begins to read. *Today was a bad day. It started well enough with the chosen men drilling enthusiastically in the pleasant warmth of an early summer sun. That was all that was good about it. In the afternoon, the captain of the* Granma *informed us that the provisioning of his ship would probably take longer than expected, causing us to delay our date of departure. We did not like that and told him so. We think he is angling to squeeze some more money out of our arrangement. Are there blood-sucking capitalist leeches everywhere? Three of the men are suffering stomach ache and Raúl, who is among them, blames it on the over-spicy food. At the best of times, there is a lingering smell about the camp. We buried Ricardo Camargua at noon, taken by the good Lord at twenty-two. The priest gave such a beautiful service and the camp women draped great bunches of tulip poppies on the coffin. The doctor and I think it may have been a heart attack. Poor soul, so young; he could not wait to get back to Cuba.*

'Then it got worse, much worse. That hothead Eduardo Fortunato burst in on me during my siesta, grabbed me by the throat and dragged me on to the floor, screaming "Bastard! Bastard! If Castro didn't

need you so much I'd kill you now, you filthy cunt!" I did not know what had come over the man, but I had no chance to speak as his arm was pinning my throat. "When did you do it, Guevara, eh? When did you do it?" My mind struggled to recall what 'it' might be, then I remembered and it hit me like a punch in the solar plexus. The one night I had slept with his girlfriend, Carmen, (no, I'm wrong; I think at the time they might have recently married), who had come on to me strongly a couple of months after we arrived in Tuxpan. We all had a little too much to drink that particular night and well, it just happened. I am only human after all, despite what the men think sometimes.

"'She's pregnant, you bastard! She's pregnant with your child!" Fortunato screamed down my ear, his fearsome eyes boring into me. At that instant, I knew I was an inch from death. Then he removed his arm and a tear rolled down his cheek. "Cunt," he repeated, stood up and stormed out of the tent.

'Does that bring back any memories, Major General?'

His face remains impassive.

She flips to another page. 'This is later, November of the same year. I'm sure this may also bring back a few memories.'

His eyes narrow.

'10th November 1956. I detest ships and I will be glad when we land in Las Colorados. I am too active to be confined to a boat that is little more than twenty paces from end to end. This morning Fortunato and I discussed what to do about his wife's baby when it is born and, after much debate, we concluded that, for the sake of all, he should send it to a relative of his in Spain. Thank God that's settled; we can now both concentrate on the difficult job in hand.'

She folds up the papers, returns them to her pocket.

His hand begins to jiggle the swagger stick. 'Is that all there is? Ha! A fiction! Anyone could have made it up.'

'It's enough for you to listen to what I want of you.'

The swagger stick rises, this time pointing straight at her left eye.

'You're a fool,' he hisses. 'And by the end of this day, you'll be a dead fool.'

She never takes her eye off the stick as he lowers it.

Spitting a gob of phlegm between her feet, he turns and strides away.

After they separate, Eduardo exhumes a memory buried deep in his subconscious. There is no doubting the truth in what the woman read out to him. Ricardo Camargua's funeral service was something only a few people would be aware of and only those who were present would remember the tulip poppies. The image of his hands around Guevara's throat flashes back to him. He thought the incident was lost in the labyrinth of his mind, but her words have shown it the way out.

He ponders the consequences if she were to leak the contents of Guevara's diary to his wife and sons. The scandal would split his family like rock fracturing under intense pressure. Carmen, who has never once mentioned the baby, would lose the respect of her sons. Angelo might see a way out of his predicament. Worse still, Eduardo would lose the love of Oswardo and that would ruin him. He considers his options. Perhaps he should dispose of the woman. If he kills her now, nobody would dare to step forward as a witness, but that would put in motion a train of events he would be powerless to stop.

If he does not kill her, could he hide her? He dismisses the idea immediately. As an ordinary citizen, he no longer has access to the myriad of secret locations where once he could have held her indefinitely.

Should he force her to place the daily call to her contact so as not to arouse suspicion? That would buy him time until a solution presented itself. But how long might that continue?

If he does nothing, she will certainly send those damning documents to his boys. It took a great deal of courage to say to him what she did. Threatening words and a little horseplay with his stick is not going to deter her.

Bloody Guevara, why couldn't he keep his cock in his pants?

He knows why not. The man was a magnet for women. He did not even need to make an effort. Alberto Bayo was astounded all those years ago in Mexico at how the young Argentine could find the energy to bed the local girls after a punishing day's intensive training. It worsened after Castro made him up to Comandante. A heady cocktail of animal attraction and latent power meant women literally threw themselves at him. Some said it was the passion that ran deep in his veins, the mixed blood of Irish rebels, Spanish conquistadores and Argentine patriots. Carmen was less romantic; she said it was his eyes. Eyes that slowly and tantalizingly peeled every vestige of clothing from a woman and caressed her naked skin, making her sex itch with longing. Whatever it was, she too, resist as she might, found her legs wrapped around the man after he enchanted her by reciting the whole of Hernandez's *Martin Fierro* from memory after a mammoth bout of drinking, two weeks after her marriage to Eduardo. Now he thought about it, maybe that was what women found so irresistible about Guevara; his obsession with poetry. He was forever spouting verses from either Macado or Lorca. But why,

why, did the vanity of the man mean he had to write everything down in those bloody diaries? Carmen let down her guard for one night and the man's seed took root in her belly. Eduardo could have killed him. Perhaps he should have, but he worshipped Castro and Castro wanted Guevara. Carmen gave birth with Guevara's knowledge. There was no way she and Eduardo could have kept the child; Eduardo's pride would not let him. Carmen and he did the only thing they could at the time and then they forgot about it.

No, he has no choice. No alternative but to listen to what the woman wants.

Firstly, though, he will wait and see what move she makes next.

He is a past master at playing this particular game.

Shaking like a leaf, Terese closes her room door behind her, still thinking what damage the swagger stick might have inflicted. Pictures of an innocuous cylinder of wood used as a deadly weapon of death or mutilation flash through her mind. In the Philippines, they showed her how easily, in experienced hands, it could dole out unbearable, lingering pain.

There is no doubt in her mind that the Major General's hands *are* experienced. The speed at which he brought the swagger stick to the point of her throat astonished her. His reactions are those of a man thirty years his junior. She quakes when she recalls the stick's cold, brass tip pricking her skin. One quick thrust was all it would take. It would have left her in agony, a hole the size of a peso in her windpipe, air hissing out like a punctured tyre.

He terrifies her. Before reality dawned, she imagined herself reducing a frail old soldier to a pleading, compliant wreck. Perhaps the photographs in her guidebook of elderly men sitting on street corners sucking toothlessly on their cigars misled her. Those men were benign, peaceful, their leathery skins crinkling as they smiled for the camera. The only thing they have in common with the Major General is their age.

Collapsing onto the bed, she covers her face with her hands and begins to cry; great wracking sobs that shake her body. It feels good, as if all her unwanted emotions are leaching out in the tears. Unmoving, she remains prone for almost a half hour. Then, sliding off the bed, she rummages around in her bag and digs out her mobile.

Peru has instructed her to make the call only if absolutely necessary.

It is necessary now.

Wiping away the tears with her fingertips, she presses the numbers, puts the phone to her ear and walks over to the window. Outside, rain patters on the glass, making tiny channels as the droplets cut through ancient layers of dust. Breathing deeply, she waits for her contact in the French Embassy in Havana to answer her call.

'Jerome Leroy. Who's calling, please?' The voice is soft-spoken, cultured.

'My name is Terese Rodriguez.'

'What can I do for you? '

'I, er . . .'

Her heart stutters. *The phrase, what is it?*

His voice is suddenly insistent, edgy. 'Hello? Hello?'

'Don't forget to meet your wife's cousin in Havana,' she blurts out.

'A moment please.'

The line goes quiet for several seconds and then Jerome asks, 'Did she enjoy Peru?'

Terese smiles at the double meaning. Perhaps Peru has a sense of humour after all.

'Yes. She found it fascinating.'

His tone hardens. 'When do you want me to call him?'

'As soon as it's safe.'

'I'm on it.'

She stabs the button to end the call. A call she hoped never to make.

Instead of returning home directly, Eduardo wanders down to the waterfront and stares out across the dappled waters of Santiago Bay, oblivious to the raindrops bouncing off his face. His mind mulls over those far-off days in Mexico. All he can recall of the child is the infant's wrinkled face peering up at him, its tiny fist clinging tightly to his index finger. Carmen watched stoically, holding back the tears, as the unknown couple took the infant from her. He does not remember their names. The only thing he does remember is the hour or two he passed nattering to the man about their shared interest in hunting and shooting. He worked as a gamekeeper on some big estate. Then, as quickly as they came, the couple disappeared taking the baby with them. Guevara made a decent gesture, paying for the couple's round trip to Mexico. Probably out of shame for what he had done, or maybe his wife gave his conscience a prod. Oh, yes, that was another remarkable thing about Guevara. His dalliances took place under the noses of his wife and children. Eduardo dismissed the whole incident and neither he nor Carmen ever mentioned their first born again.

Shortly after six, he walks through the gates of Casa del Toro Negro, sees a note pinned to the front door. He recognises the handwriting immediately.

Major- General Fortunato (retired),

136

Your wife and family finally ran out of patience
waiting for your magisterial presence. Did you
forget that Juanita had invited us all to Alberto's
birthday party this evening? If you get hungry, you'll
find your meal in the cold store. I hope you know
how to warm it up.

He curses, having forgotten completely about the arrangement.

Deciding that remaining at home is his best course of action, he opens the door and strides into the house with the intention of changing out of his wet clothes. As his boot settles on the lowest stair, the phone rings. In two minds whether to ignore it or not, he hesitates and then turns back. It might be Oswardo with some juicy news from Guantanamo.

'Hello?' he says, picking up the handset.

'Major General Fortunato?' A man's voice, smooth as silk with only the faintest trace of an accent and certainly not belonging to Oswardo.

'Yes.'

'I have a message for you.'

'Who is this?'

'You don't need to know. I'm calling you as I've received an instruction from my client.'

The hairs on the back of his neck stand on end.

Instruction? Client? Who is this, and what the hell is he talking about?

'You have the wrong number,' he says.

'I don't think so. My client has instructed me to arrange the personal delivery of an important document to each of your sons, first thing tomorrow morning. Apparently she doesn't believe you're taking her seriously.'

Eduardo's body stiffens. It does not take a genius to figure out who the client is.

'What kind of document?'

'I'm not at liberty to say, but I believe it reveals some interesting information about a certain famous person and a woman whom you know very well.'

Guevara and Carmen.

The voice continues, 'My client is very reasonable, Major General. She understands this must be very difficult for you, given the circumstances. If you agree to listen to her, she will rescind her instruction. By the way, do not worry about anyone listening in to our conversation. This is a secure diplomatic line.'

A diplomatic line. That means it must be from one of the embassies.

'Three copies of this document have been deposited in safe custody and I have strict instructions to deliver a copy each to Colonel Oswardo Fortunato, Doctor Ramon Fortunato and Senor Angelo Fortunato if I'm so directed.'

'Are you calling from the French Embassy?'

'That's irrelevant, Major General. Now, are you prepared to listen to what my client has to say?'

'Don't be ridiculous. Tell your client to make sure she's on the next plane back to where she came from if she knows what's good for her.'

'I'm afraid that's not possible. If you think she isn't serious, then you can expect to hear from your sons soon. I am sure they will find the document enlightening. Goodbye, Major General—'

'Wait! What does this document contain?'

'This is no time for games. You know full well what it contains.'

'I'm concerned about its provenance. I admire your client for her creativity, but there is no way it can be real. It's a fiction, a fabrication.'

'That's where you're wrong. It's genuine, I can assure you.'

Eduardo thinks hard. There has to be some detail that proves the document a fake. He casts his mind back to Mexico again. Then it strikes him—Guevara's pet name for the baby. No one can possibly know it apart from Carmen, Guevara and himself.

'Then I have a question for you, ' he says. 'What did Guevara call the baby?'

The line falls silent for a moment before the voice resumes. 'I will need to consult my client for the answer to that. Please put down the phone and I will call you back shortly.'

As the call terminates, a smile creases Eduardo's face. She is clever, damned clever, but no match for him. It is impossible for her to come up with the name. That will be the last he hears from her.

Adios.

Five minutes later, as he is stripping off his shirt, the phone rings again. Ignoring it, he lets it ring. After a dozen rings, he descends the stairs to the hallway.

'Fortunato!'

'Good evening, Major General.' Her voice is unexpected. This time the words are firm, confident.

'What the hell do you want?' he barks.

'I have a name for you.'

'I've warned you for the last time. You—'

'Chiquito.'

Colour drains from his face, his shoulders slump. Guevara had heard the name on his travels with Alberto Granado. The woman is telling the truth after all. The unpublished diary must be genuine, as she claims. There is little point in continuing to play cat and mouse. For the first time in his life he finds himself with his back to the wall, all escape routes cut off. His only option is to go along with her.

But what could she possibly want from him? Money? Surely not, that would be laughable. Information? Something about Guantanamo for a scoop? She knows he would never do that. Castro would have him shot without question. His mind flicks through the reasons she could be so desperate to pressure him and comes up with the one thing that makes sense.

'Am I correct in assuming you're from ETA?' he asks.

'Yes.'

'I thought so. What do you want from me?'

'Not *from* you. You don't have what we need, but I know you can find a way of obtaining it. Otherwise, I will have no alternative but to release the document. I regret having to put you in this position, but I have no choice. Now listen very carefully.'

Pinning back his ears, he listens with rising incredulity. This must be a dream. He cannot believe what he is hearing.

How in the name of God did they discover its existence? And how come I don't know where it is? In Guantanamo! Right under my bloody nose all these years!

Then beads of sweat bubble on his forehead as she makes her demand.

'That's impossible! They don't allow retired officers access to those places, even if they've served in the most senior ranks. And even if they did, there wouldn't be enough time to get the virus. It can't be done!'

'I'm sorry, impossible is not acceptable, otherwise . . . well, otherwise you know what I must do. As I already said, I've no choice in the matter, as I'm sure you understand.'

Yes, he does understand. During the course of a long military career he had been in a similar position many, many times.

Terese is simply a foot soldier carrying out her orders to the letter.

'You have precisely two minutes to agree, Major General. Otherwise the documents will be delivered.'

Disbelief binds him tight as a shroud. He forgot about the virus years ago. When it suits them, the Russians and Americans spread rumours it is in Cuba's possession; but even if they did believe their own tales, they would have no idea where it was or how they could get their sticky fingers on it. The only explanation is that someone must have leaked the information. Someone very important and very well informed. Someone with the highest security clearance.

Who could it be?

A memory rises through the murkiness, fighting for breath: 15 May 1979, the day he arrived with his battalion in the Angolan capital of Luanda. His emotions were in turmoil, torn between the excitement of another tour of duty on foreign soil and sadness at having to leave his wife and three growing boys back home in Havana.

Two weeks later, Operations HQ in Havana ordered him to lead a cross-border mission into Zaire. He was to take a small party across the Congo to the outskirts of Boma where they would liaise with a band of Zairian rebels. The mission should be trouble-free in a part of the country where foraging parties had crossed the border bisecting the mighty river many times since Cuba had involved itself in Angola's internal affairs. The rebels would hand them two small boxes. These he was to handle carefully and bring back to Luanda where a transport plane would be waiting to freight them to

Havana. It was a simple enough task, but the commandment was worded strangely:

Comrade Colonel Fortunato,

It is imperative you yourself lead this important mission. The two boxes in question must be handed to you personally, must be in your sight at all times, and are not, repeat not, to be tampered with under any circumstances. Handle them with extreme care.

We wish you success in your mission.

The order for him to go in person puzzled him. Normally, such an apparently routine operation without a combat objective would fall to a First Lieutenant or Captain, not a high-ranking officer like himself. However, if that was what Havana ordered he figured there must be a reason for it and he would, as he always did, follow orders.

On the morning of 9 June, they set off from Luanda in two trucks, eleven soldiers and him in one, the other laden with four two-man kayaks. Taking the neglected, rough road that hugged the coast for much of the way, they passed through Cacuaco, Barro Do Dande, Capulo, Ambriz, Musserra, and N'zeto. At N'zeto they turned inland onto an even rougher road, which wound its way up to Mepala and on to Pedra do Feitiço, close to the southern bank of the river. Thankfully, the weather was dry and cool at that time of year and the soldiers were in good spirits as they sang and bantered whilst bouncing around in the back of the stiffly-sprung transport.

Once they left Pedra do Feitiço in their wake he instructed the drivers to position their trucks as close to the languidly flowing waters as was considered safe. He split the men into two groups. Seven of them would paddle across the river with him; the remainder would stay and guard the trucks.

The river was wide at the point of embarkation and although the current wasn't strong it took the kayaks some time to tack across to the far bank. A ragtag bunch of men awaited them, the leader standing at the water's edge, a padlocked wooden box at his feet. The coal-black man was sweating profusely and clearly agitated. As the men beached the kayaks the Zairian pointed at the box, shaking his head rapidly from side to side. After the traditional greeting of exchanging kisses on both cheeks, Eduardo's scout listened to a string of rapid-fire Portuguese. Eduardo, unable to understand the language, asked the scout, an Angola veteran, to translate for him.

'He's not very happy, sir. Swears there's a curse on the box. Says there were fifteen men when they picked the boxes up in the north of the country almost three weeks ago and now there are only six of them alive. He can't understand it. Men have been falling sick for the past eleven days and dying in utter agony. Demands we take them with us to be treated for whatever it is they've caught.'

'Ask him if he thinks it's malaria.'

The Zairian's eyes swivelled to Eduardo. He saw fear in them, real fear.

'He says if it is it's unlike any malaria he's ever seen. It starts with uncontrolled vomiting, bloody diarrhoea, headache, dizziness, and troubled breathing. Within four or five days, they begin to bleed from nose, mouth, and anus. Soon after that they die.'

'Wait a minute; I think I might have missed something. Did he say "boxes"?'

'He did, sir.'

'Are you sure?'

'Yes, sir.'

'Then ask him where the second box is.'

The Zairian's words erupted thick and fast, spittle flecking the corner of his mouth.

'He says it was dropped and damaged, so they opened it to see if they could repack what was inside. All they found were several broken glass vials. Whatever was in them had soaked into the packing and couldn't be recovered.'

'What did they do with the box?'

By now, the Zairian was gesticulating wildly. Eduardo didn't need words to get the meaning.

'They burned it.'

Suddenly, there was a piercing yell and, as one, the Cubans crouched low into the firing position. One of the rebels had pitched face down on to the river's muddy bank, a dark stain spreading out from the crotch of his ragged trousers. As he sprawled, writhing and moaning on the ground, Eduardo snapped the order.

'Get the box! Quickly now! Into the kayaks!'

A shot rang out and one of his soldiers screamed. The rebel captain had drawn a revolver, firing at Eduardo, but the bullet narrowly missed him, finding instead the soft flesh of one soldier's groin. All hell broke loose. It was a one-sided affair, over within seconds, the bloodstained and shredded bodies of six Zairians propped at broken angles, caught in the gnarled roots of the mangroves lining the dark river.

'Get the box, corporal. Let's get the hell out of here.'

'Yes, sir. I've got it.'

The atmosphere on the way back to Luanda was very different to the outward journey. Questions began to circulate among the men. What was in the box? Eduardo made a swift decision and threatened the next man to mention it would be cleaning out the latrines for the next month.

It piqued his curiosity, though. At first, he wondered if the boxes might be connected to his country's ambition to one day have a nuclear weapons programme. But Cuba wasn't North Korea or Iraq. Sure, there were plans afoot to build the country's first pressurized light water moderated reactors near Juragua in Cienfuegos province, but they were light years away from any kind of nuclear weapons capability. He dismissed any idea of a nuclear trigger.

His mind questioned briefly what it was that had struck the Zairians down and whether it might have been in the abandoned damaged box. He didn't pursue the answers to his own questions. He was a soldier, and they trained soldiers to carry out orders without thinking. Once they arrived back in Luanda he handed over the box to a captain of the Cuban Air Force.

As far as Eduardo was concerned, that was the end of the matter.

Then the scout who had kissed the rebel leader on the cheeks in greeting fell ill, seriously ill. Eleven days after showing the first signs of illness, the scout died. The same day, two more soldiers complained of headaches and vomiting. Ten days later, they too were dead.

General Ortega, the most senior officer in Luanda, commanded the sealing of the barracks until they could ascertain the cause of the deaths. A team of medical specialists flew in from Havana to deal with the situation. Eduardo, fearing for his own safety and not a man afraid of facing up to his superiors, collared Ortega.

'What's going on, General? Why the hell has Havana got involved?'

'Ah, Eduardo, you know how it is.'

'No, sir, I don't. Tell me.'

'This must go no further, Eduardo, do you hear? I trust you. We've known each other since Moncada, but if this gets out we can kiss goodbye to any future Cuban involvement in Africa as well as our own careers. In addition, the Russians would come crawling all over us.'

'The Russians? It's that important?'

'Yes, it's that important. OK, this is how it is. Have you ever heard of Ebola?'

'Ebola? It doesn't ring any bells.'

'It wouldn't unless you were a medical specialist and a very knowledgeable one at that. It's a virus, Eduardo, a very virulent virus. It turns people into soup.'

'Jesus Christ.'

'It only came to light four years ago in Yambuku, a town in the north of Zaire. A schoolteacher named Mabalo Lokela entered the local hospital with a high fever that they diagnosed as possible malaria and they gave him a quinine shot. He returned to the hospital every day, but a week later his symptoms included uncontrolled vomiting, bloody diarrhoea, headaches, dizziness, and troubled breathing. Soon, he began bleeding from his nose, mouth, and anus. Two weeks after the onset of symptoms he died.'

'God Almighty.'

'Then more patients began to arrive with varying but similar symptoms including fever, headache, muscle and joint aches, fatigue, nausea, and dizziness. Like the schoolteacher, their condition deteriorated. The medics thought the initial transmission was due to the unsterilized reuse of the needle for Lokela's injection. They also thought further transmission was due to care of the sick patients without barrier nursing and the traditional burial preparation method, which involved washing and gastrointestinal tract cleansing.

146

'Two nuns working in Yambuku as nurses also died in the same outbreak. The world had discovered Ebola, the planet's deadliest virus, named after the Ebola Valley where it first appeared. There are no vaccines or treatment available for this one. Catch it and you can start praying you won't suffer too much on your journey out of this world.'

'Don't tell me. Those two boxes—'

'They contained the Ebola virus.'

'How was the scout infected?'

'There isn't a person in the world who knows. We can only assume it was sweat on the rebel's cheeks when he kissed him. Rest assured though, we have some of the finest doctors in the world and we *will* find out more about this thing. From their research so far they've concluded that Ebola definitely isn't airborne.'

'What about the other men who died?'

'They don't know, Eduardo. The experts' best guess is contaminated needles.'

'Needles?'

'Needles used in self-injection. You know it goes on. Men get bored in this country so they turn to anything to take their minds off the godforsaken place. In our day it was pills—now they use needles then they pass the needles around without sterilising them.'

'Why do we want the bloody stuff anyway?'

'Isn't it obvious? We're the plaything of the two most powerful nations on earth. We don't have the expertise or resources to develop our own nuclear weapons and even if we did it would take years. The only other threat that causes nations to quake is germ warfare and we don't have a Fort Detrick tucked away doing its dirty work. Ebola is too good to be true: a silent killer against which there is no known defence. Of course, we have only a tiny amount. We would never use it and it isn't much of a threat in its present form, but that's not the point. It could come in very handy one day.'

'Are the Russians doing anything with it?'

'You can bet your life they are. They'll be working night and day to get it into a state suitable to use as a weapon. Our experts estimate that will take at least another fifteen years, but the Russians certainly wouldn't leave any in our hands if they got wind we had some. They would squeeze Castro's neck tighter than a starving boa.'

'Where did the rebels get the Ebola?'

'Eduardo, my friend, you are now asking questions to which I do not know the answers. Probably no more than a half dozen people do. We both know who they are and we should leave the political manoeuvrings up to them. We're just soldiers doing what we're told to do, that's all.'

Eduardo left it at that. His focus was on things that were more important. Before long other campaigns consumed his time and the Ebola incident slipped to the back of his mind.

Only twice since returning from Angola has he come across a reference to Ebola in the documents that passed across his desk. Three years after returning from Africa, on his promotion to Major General, an 'Eyes Only' made reference to the transport of an 'exceptionally dangerous' substance from Havana to a highly secure establishment, location unspecified.

Now where might that be? he asked himself at the time, but again there were more pressing things to occupy him. Then, late in '92, he skimmed another 'Eyes Only' which suggested that the Russians in their Sverdlovsk facility were close to developing an Ebola-based agent suitable for weapons use.

Fourteen years on, Ebola invades his world again. The woman is desperate to have it and he must acquire it if he wishes to avoid his sons learning of his long-buried secret.

His heart races as it used to whenever he was on the verge of putting one over the cursed Yanquis. At first, he was furious with the French woman and even angrier with himself for not being quick enough or clever enough to outwit her. Then, as he pondered her demand and weighed the logic behind it, he softened, feeling more than a little sympathy. Is she not in a similar position to the one he found himself in all those years ago, fighting powers that stamped on his people and dipped their fingers in the bowl of plenty? The world will never recognise her people's language and culture unless ETA does something about it. He finds it easy to understand why the organisation exists and employs such extreme methods, the same methods M-26-7 used all those years ago. They were prepared to take innocent lives in the name of their cause. Every revolutionary movement in the history of the world will in order to achieve its aims.

That's just the way it is.

Is it pure coincidence the Basques founded ETA in the same year as Castro kicked Batista out of Cuba? Are The Fates sending him a message? Perhaps *this* is his destiny, to help the woman as he helped Castro all those years ago. Damn it, his life has to have some purpose otherwise he will petrify. At last, here is something worthwhile in which he can sink his teeth.

Her voice cuts into his thoughts. 'Major General, your two minutes are up.'

'All right, I will do it. I will do it for your organisation because I understand what they are going through and why they have to do this thing. But I must have more time.'

'I'm afraid that's not possible. I have to leave in ten days.'

'But I can't—'

Click.

'You're getting worse, Eduardo.' Carmen gives him a look that could shear off the side of a mountain. 'Juanita didn't say it, but I know she was wondering why she even bothers asking us around.'

Lips clamped tight, he follows her into the bedroom.

'How did your meeting go with the French woman?' she says.

'OK.'

'OK? You spent two hours with her and all you have to say is OK? What did she tell you? I want to know all the details.'

'She didn't say much.'

Carmen crosses her arms over her substantial bosom and narrows her eyes. 'Eduardo Fortunato, you haven't been able to lie to me since we first met, so I do hope you're not going to start now.'

'Well . . . I . . . she . . .'

Suddenly, he is a small boy again. Memories flood back of the morning he sneaked two sugary apple cupcakes from his mother's pantry, and then hunkered down amongst the thick green stalks and armadillo cobs in the cornfield at the back of his parents' tiny house, feasting on the cakes. Armena, with her good head for numbers, knew very well how many she had baked, and on his return asked him if he had taken any.

'*No, Ma.*'

'*I'll ask you again. Did you take my cakes?*'

'*No, Ma.*'

150

'*This is the last time of asking, Eduardo, and then we'll let your father deal with it when he comes in. Did you take my cakes?*'

'*Yes, Ma, I was hungry. Please, don't tell Pa.*'

'*That's better. Next time, ask. If you ever lie to me again it will be your father you have to answer to. Do you understand?*'

'*I understand, Ma.*'

'She didn't say much, Carmen, because I did most of the talking, explaining the history of Moncada and what went on in '53.'

'And that took two hours?'

'There's a lot to tell. I only touched upon it. We may have to meet again.'

'And no doubt you dressed it up.'

'Don't be ridiculous, woman. It's a marvellous story. Why, I might even write a book about it one day.'

She shakes her head and tuts. 'You're full of wind, Eduardo Fortunato. Speaking of which, did you have a word with Angelo?'

'I mentioned it in passing, but he was very guarded, as I expected. I asked him why he wouldn't give Maria children.'

'As subtle as ever, I see. What did he say?'

'Exactly what I knew he would say. He told me they couldn't afford it, not on what he makes. He said it's bad enough scraping a living and perhaps if the powers that be allowed him a little freedom to make more money it might be different and then they could have children, like Rafael. He could have a house full and still be able to afford it.'

'And I suppose at that point you lost your temper.'

'Close, but not quite. I did wonder how long it would take before Rafael was mentioned. What do I have to say or do to make Angelo realise the man is a traitor? Rafael deserted his family and abandoned his roots. What would happen if we all followed suit and sailed off to Florida? What would happen to this country then?'

'No doubt that triggered the same old argument.'

'I told him he should listen to you more often. I said you know him almost as well as he knows himself. But you think there's something apart from the money, don't you?'

She unfolds her arms, places her hands tenderly on his cheeks. 'Yes, Eduardo, I do. It's not simply a lack of money. I don't think he loves her and I know she doesn't love him. How could he contemplate bringing a child into the world in that situation? I couldn't do it, I simply couldn't. It would be morally wrong in my book.'

A long-forgotten image of Carmen, kneeling before him, begging for his forgiveness, flashes across his mind. She didn't love Guevara and yet, if not for Eduardo's insistence, she would have kept his child. What goes around comes around.

'What about divorce?' he says.

'That might be the best solution. If it's what he wants.'

'Does he know what he wants?'

'I think he does, but his conscience won't contemplate divorce and his religion won't condone it. I really don't know what he'll do. Worse still, I don't know what Maria will do.'

'What do you think he should do?'

'I think he should speak to her, Eduardo. My guess is she's on the verge of a nervous breakdown.'

16ᵗʰ July

'Don't expect me back for lunch today, my little chicken. I've some important business to attend to.'

Carmen pauses in her washing of the breakfast dishes, her eyebrows knitted. 'Are you all right, Eduardo? You seem a little . . . lightheaded.'

'I'm perfectly fine. Never felt better. It's a beautiful day to be alive.'

Stretching his arms wide, he balls his fists and beats them on his chest. When he awoke, he felt as if he had hijacked the body of a man twenty years his junior.

Her eyes flash as she fishes a knife out of the sink and points it at him. 'Don't tell me you're off to see that French woman again to finish your discussion? Is she the 'important business' you have to attend to?'

He holds his hands above his head, palms towards Carmen. 'No, no, my turtle dove. She left for Guantanamo, so I don't suppose I'll see her again.'

He knows Carmen will not press him further. They have an understanding, woven into the fabric of their relationship, from a time when it was necessary for him to keep secrets from her for fear of compromising state security.

'Then make sure you're not late if you don't want your meal to go cold again. I promised Juanita I would help with cleaning the church this evening. It's in a terrible state.'

'Your wish is my command.' Doffing his cap, he bows.

'Go on, go, before I ask you to feed the chickens.'

She scowls at him as he exits the back door.

Head held high, he strides purposefully down the gravel path towards the wrought iron gates. This morning, the barracks are off his itinerary. Moncada will have to do without him for once.

Instead, he will head down to the harbourside where someone is waiting to meet him.

Eduardo spots the man, elbows resting on his knees, squatting on the low, whitewashed wall fronting the harbour. Dressed in the blue uniform of the Cuban Air Force, he pours coffee into the cup of a polished-steel vacuum flask. His head is hatless, revealing a mass of thick black curly hair showing the first signs of thinning at the crown. His jowls are blue and heavy.

There is no mistaking his son, even though he stands a good six inches taller than Eduardo.

Laying his hand gently on Oswardo's shoulder, he kisses him on the cheek. He is immensely proud of his eldest son. A born leader, Oswardo imposes his will with his fists and physique. When he was a boy, very few dared challenge him and he was never bested by the local youths. Eduardo treated him like a protégé, working day after day to perfect his fighting and wrestling skills. By the time he was fifteen he had the strength, guile and agility of a well-honed athlete and showed real promise as a boxer, not losing a single bout until one fateful evening at the Rafael Trejo gym in Old Havana in a contest with a seventeen-year-old. It was clear by the end of the second round Oswardo had the measure of his opponent and, eagerly springing out of his corner at the beginning of the third, he smashed a right cross into the ribs of the older boy and his hand snapped. Gritting his teeth he carried on, but the pain blunted his clinical efficiency and the other boy took the advantage offered him. Oswardo lost the bout and his opponent went on to win an Olympic gold medal at the next Olympics.

The hand injury never set properly and the doctors advised against aggravating it with the stresses imposed by boxing. Oswardo, stubborn as a mule, complained bitterly, but Eduardo had the last say. From that moment on, the worm of disappointment ate into Oswardo. For two years, he made a career of acting as minder for his youngest brother, drumming up trouble at the slightest excuse. In the surrounding neighbourhoods he acquired a reputation as a juvenile thug. Without the strong, corrective hand of Eduardo, he would most likely have ended up in gaol. The worm was expunged when Oswardo enlisted in the tough regime of the air force, where another latent talent surfaced—his motivational skill. The ability to get the most out of his men coupled with a burning desire for personal advancement ensured a series of promotions through the commissioned ranks, much to the delight of Eduardo.

However, Oswardo's single-mindedness cost him his marriage. In his unrelenting pursuit of advancement, he passed most of his off-duty hours socialising with his peers and superiors in the officers' mess. Even a newborn child could not encourage him to spend more time with his wife. Eventually she decided enough was enough. Carina gave him a piece of her mind and stormed out of the house with Eduardo junior in tow. Since her departure, almost twelve months ago, she has not deemed to contact him and he has not bothered to call her.

'Hello, son.'
'Hello, Pa.'

'Much happening at Gitmo?'

Oswardo spits a gob of phlegm into the sea. 'Yeah. The Brits have taken a keen interest in the place after the film *The Road to Guantanamo* was released earlier this year. The Yanquis are taking a lot of flak at the moment.'

Eduardo racks his brain. The film does not strike a chord. 'I haven't heard of this film. What's it about?'

'It's about what we want to hear, Pa. We've a mandate to show it regularly to the enlisted men. The story revolves around four British men of Pakistani descent. Five years ago, they travelled from Britain to Pakistan for a wedding and stupidly decided to visit Afghanistan. One gets killed and the other three are captured by Northern Alliance fighters and handed over to the Yanquis who take them to Gitmo. In Gitmo they're interrogated and tortured to make them confess to being terrorists. The film makes it clear they're being set up to appease the Yanquis' thirst for revenge.'

Eduardo rubs his hands together. 'It sounds almost good enough to be true.'

'It's reckoned to be true. Even if the happenings aren't exactly as shown in the film its objective was achieved. It's put the Yanquis on the back foot and in a position where they're on the defensive in the face of criticism from the international community, especially from the British, their most trusted ally.'

Eduardo chuckles. 'I can see their dilemma. Had these men been Cubans the Presidente would have raised the roof, but the world at large wouldn't give a damn. Mind you, neither would the Brits if Asians weren't so important to their economy. From what I read, they run most of the taxi firms around the country and quite a slice of local government. I guess that's the price to be paid for subjugating two-thirds of the world. Imperialists deserve everything they get if you ask me. Eventually things will come back and bite them.'

'There's more. Only yesterday, there was a very interesting development. We think the Yanquis are using shock techniques on some of the detainees. A plant of ours reported one stubborn individual was forced to wear women's underwear on his head, confronted with snarling dogs and had a leash attached to his chains. Swig of coffee?'

'Please.'

He settles himself on the wall next to his son and stares out across the calm flatness of Santiago Bay. They remain silent for several minutes, each in turn taking a sip of the thick, black fluid from the cup. At this time of day, before the searing heat of the sun softens the tarmac roads, few people are on the streets.

Oswardo breaks the silence. 'I take it this isn't a social visit?'

'No, it isn't. I have a favour to ask.'

'It must be a big favour if I have to come all the way here to talk to you. Couldn't we have spoken on the phone?'

'No, it's too important and you never know who might be listening.' His eyes scan the waterfront. The only soul in sight is a man wearing an ill-fitting suit and sunglasses, disinterestedly looking out to sea, standing some hundred metres or so distant. Eduardo inclines his head in the man's direction and chuckles. 'It looks like someone's keeping an eye on me, even in my retirement.'

Oswardo turns his head and looks past Eduardo. 'I wouldn't worry, Pa. Looking at him, I don't think he's anyone official.'

Eduardo lowers his voice. 'Have you heard of Professor Jaime Hornedo?'

Oswardo pulls his earlobe. 'The scientist?'

'The virologist to be precise.'

'I've heard the name mentioned. What about him?'

'He's not who he appears to be.'

'Oh?'

'His real name is Zviad Makashvili, and he's a dissident Russian scientist. Actually, he's a dissident Georgian scientist who used to work for the Russians at Sverdlovsk.'

'Sverdlovsk? Isn't that the germ warfare facility?'

'The very same.'

'No kidding. Why did he change his name?'

'Twenty years ago, he escaped from Russia after an anthrax experiment went horribly wrong, killing more than sixty people and almost causing an international incident between the Russians and the Yanquis. The KGB blamed him for the accident and obliterated all traces of him. That scared the shit out of him, so he boarded a boat to Cuba leaving his fiancée and friends behind. For a while he laid low, but a suspicious CDR official reported him to the authorities.'

Oswardo's brow creases. 'Why didn't we send him back? The Russians would have played merry hell if they'd known he was here.'

'Ah, a good question. That was Fidel's first thought, but Raúl had a brainwave after Makashvili told him of his work at Sverdlovsk. Raúl knew the development of nuclear weapons was decades away and would cost a huge amount of money, but the harnessing of germs with the potential to be almost as devastating—well, that was a different story. It would be cheap, very cheap. Until Makashvili arrived on these shores there was no one with the level of expertise to direct a germ warfare research programme. They gave him a new identity—Jaime Hornedo—and left him no choice but to stay and rekindle his research. However, he told them there was an insurmountable problem. He lacked the raw material: a killer virus. Development was impossible if he didn't have the micro-organisms with which he could create lethal biological agents. He would need anthrax spores, botulinum toxin, and Lassa or Ebola cultures to work with. They had heard of anthrax and botulinum, but not Lassa or Ebola. When he explained what Ebola was and that it could be found in Zaire, they realised their luck. We were fighting a war in Angola and often made incursions into Zaire in the pursuit of rebels.'

Oswardo's eyes spring open. 'Don't tell me we brought Ebola to Cuba.'

'We did. They set up Hornedo in a high security lab in Guantanamo and he carried on with his research. Nothing much came of it for years—until he made a breakthrough.'

'What kind of breakthrough?'

'I remember reading there was an intractable problem with the way the virus is transmitted. Apparently, it can only spread in infected blood and bodily fluids or by contact with contaminated medical equipment such as needles. That would make it extremely limited as a weapon of germ warfare. Hornedo convinced the Castros he could solve that problem, given time. It has taken him nearly twenty years, but recently he cracked it. Not only that, but during his years of research working closely with the virus, he's managed to develop a strain even deadlier than the original Ebola. Now, we have a viral weapon with the potential to cause excruciatingly painful death and large scale panic.'

'What are we going to do with it?'

'I don't know, but I bet there are some very impatient people keen to play with their new and deadly toy. Exactly how they propose to do so is beyond me. I don't really care anymore. That's their business.'

'How did you find this out?' asks Oswardo, his fingers drumming on his cup.

'Ah, it's best you don't know. Put it this way, it came to me from an unexpected source.'

'A source you trust?'

'Yes.'

'Why are you telling me this?'

'I want you to remove some of the virus from Hornedo's lab.'

Oswardo jerks upright, as if harpooned. 'Me!'

Eduardo recounts the tale of his meetings with Terese, omitting the information she holds about Guevara's bastard child. Oswardo nods occasionally. When Eduardo finishes, Oswardo shakes his massive head and frantically rubs his chin with a calloused hand.

'Christ, Pa, that's one hell of a risk I'd be taking and you won't even tell me why you want to help her?' He draws a cigarette packet from his pocket, flips open the lid, takes out a cigarette and sticks it on his lower lip.

'It's in a good cause, son, you can see that.'

This isn't going to be easy, Eduardo thinks. *Oswardo is the one with everything to lose, but if it can be done then he will have to be the one to do it. I may be determined, but no longer can I manufacture the opportunity or acquire the means. Besides, his reason for being in Guantanamo is unquestionable, unlike mine.*

Oswardo caresses his luxuriant black moustache with the thumb and forefinger of his left hand. 'I'm sorry, Pa, but I don't see how it can be done. A place like that would be highly secure. For God's sake, I can't just waltz in and ask nicely for the stuff.'

A grin splits Eduardo's face from ear to ear. 'You won't need to.'

'What do you mean?'

'Don't you think the Castros keep a close eye on Hornedo? The man's not allowed to leave the confines of the facility given the knowledge inside his head.'

'So?'

'So he's provided with everything he needs. Russian books, music, films, documentaries and the finest Russian vodkas. And girls.'

'Girls?'

'Apparently he has a voracious appetite for young girls of a particular type. Heavy breasted, long-legged with jet-black hair; oiled and swept back into a tied tight bun and young, no more than sixteen or seventeen at most. Professor Hornedo specifies his girls almost as painstakingly as his formulae.'

'I still don't follow.'

'Bear with me. One of the guards at the facility is the youngest son of an old colleague of mine. He told me Hornedo is particularly fond of a young tart called Eva, who visits him two or three times a week. You won't take the virus, Eva will.'

'And why would she do that?'

'That, my son, I will leave to your fertile imagination.'

Oswardo rakes his fingers through his hair, rubs the back of his neck. 'How long have I got?'

'Ten days.'

A low whistle hisses through Oswardo's teeth. 'Ten days! That's no time at all. What's her hurry?'

'They have an operation planned for next month and it depends on the virus.'

Oswardo sucks hard on his cigarette. 'What type of operation?'

'She wouldn't say, but I assume it's something big if she needs this kind of stuff.'

He studies his son's face, puckered in concentration. Brow furrowed, his eyes tracking a distant tramp steamer chugging across the indigo waters of Santiago Bay. Eduardo can almost hear the gears slowly but firmly engaging in that massive head.

'There's something you're not telling me, Pa.'

'Why would I do that?'

'To protect me, or,' Oswardo swivels his head and raises his eyebrows, 'to protect yourself. Does this woman know something about you, something I don't? If so, you should tell me now.'

Eduardo lays his hand on Oswardo's arm. 'Don't be so melodramatic. I think hers is a just cause, that's all. Hell, I remember what I was like at her age when justice was all we cared about. I know I'm asking a big favour, but what's the worst that can happen?'

'I could be court-marshalled and we could both be shot.'

'That will never happen. I have friends in high places.'

'Pa, your friends are getting older and there's a new generation of rising stars, all eager to have their names in the history books. It's common knowledge the Castros can't hold the reins of power much longer, especially now the Presidente is on his sickbed most of the time and I tell you, the new regime will *not* huff and puff when they're in the spotlight of the world media. They know which side their bread is buttered on.'

They lapse into silence again, the only sound waves lapping gently against the shore. Oswardo is the first to speak.

'It's not ETA. It's Al-Queda, isn't it?'

'Al-Queda? Don't be ridiculous. What makes you think that?'

'They're a bunch of crazies and this is the kind of stuff they'd be very keen to get their hands on. And I tell you, Pa, if they're involved it stops right here and right now, do you understand? I won't be the fall guy for what might happen, whether or not you're my father.'

He ruffles his son's hair as he used to when Oswardo was a boy.

'It has nothing to do with Al-Queda. I wouldn't be that stupid. Do you think I don't know that would bring a ton of bricks down on all our heads after 9/11? It would give the Yanquis a perfect excuse to trample all over us once more and this time there isn't a Khrushchev to make them think twice.'

'That's why I asked, Pa. I love this country, I love my job and I'm not about to ruin one and lose the other because of a bunch of lunatics, whether or not I agree with their motivation.'

'Oswardo, if I were struck dead this instant, there is no Al-Queda involvement, trust me. This isn't about worldwide terrorism at any cost. This is about a people who have been denied their identity for almost seven hundred years. That's why we fought Batista fifty years ago. He was just a puppet of the Americans and we ordinary people were subject to the whims of a greedy, imperialist power that messed—and is still messing—with people's lives all around the world. That is why you keep an eye on the base, to make sure Bush and his cohorts never think about repeating what Kennedy tried at the Bay of Pigs. I'm willing to help the woman because it proves to me that I still have balls, that there is still a reason for living and that I am not passing my retirement with the sole purpose of doing your mother's shopping.'

Oswardo throws the stub of his cigarette into the crystal-clear waters of the bay.

'OK, Pa, I'll do it. I'll do it and be damned.'

17th July

Mid-afternoon, following a teeth-gritting, roller-coasting, two-hour taxi ride from Santiago, Terese arrives in Guantanamo. Thankfully, she has not had to endure an interrogation this time. Her morose driver has not uttered a single word during the entire journey, remaining silent, his jaw chomping on chewing gum, as they yomped up and down in his ancient, battered Chevrolet.

After the nostalgia of Havana and the tranquillity of Santiago, her first impression as they drive towards the city centre is of a sprawling, hectic place that lacks redeeming features. She is surprised to see so many people lounging at the side of the road: standing in knots or sitting down on whatever obstacle they can find to accommodate their backsides. She wonders if it has something to do with Guantanamo's population explosion. Her ever-present guidebook states the city has more than trebled its population in the past fifty years and now supports over two hundred thousand souls: a sprawling mass bursting at the seams.

After paying the driver, she scours the surrounding streets looking for a casa particulare. Hoping not to draw attention to herself, she has exchanged the ubiquitous female tourist garb of shorts and singlet for a pair of faded jeans and a long-sleeved, white calico shirt, uncomfortably heavy for the time of year. The change of outfit will probably prove to be pointless. In a place like

Guantanamo, away from well-trodden tourist routes, people are bound to notice her. Their eyes and ears are always on the alert, given the continuing existence of the CDR.

Besides, she is well aware that the sexual radar of the Cuban male is always on the look out for the blip of a pale-skinned woman.

The part of the city she finds herself in is grim: a repetitive pattern of blocks, identical to each other as far as she can see. Neglected, dirt-encrusted buildings pack together tightly, skirted by potholed, crumbling roads. Stumbling across one casa, a quick look inside convinces her that Guantanamo falls way short of the standards expected by tourists, even those of an adventurous disposition.

Oh, well, if I have to stay here awhile, I might as well be comfortable. And that means I'm not going to stay in a dump like this.

Stopping to ask a passing woman where she can find a decent hotel, she is directed to the Hotel Marti, one of the city's only three decent establishments, located opposite Jose Marti Central Park and tucked into the corner of Calixto Garcia and Aguilera. It goes against her better judgement to stay in a luxury hotel, visible to many comings and goings, attracting attention she does not want to invite. But it is stretching the imagination to label the colonnaded, hotchpotch building a 'luxury' hotel.

As she checks in, the weasel eyes of a desk clerk with tombstone teeth and nicotine-stained fingers glue themselves to the swell of her shirt where it sticks to her breasts. He insists on explaining, almost apologetically, that the hotel will be closing soon for renovation under new ownership. He says they rarely accommodate tourists, but the hotel is a popular destination for the locals when they flood into the city at weekends for the cultured Nochas Guantanameras.

These, she later discovers, are no more than a flimsy excuse for prolonged bouts of wild and excessive drinking.

She climbs a rickety staircase to the first floor. Here, the dozen or so rooms fan out in a horseshoe. Turning to her left, she strides purposefully and locates her room at the far end of the landing. She enters, firmly closes the door, locks it, slings her rucksack on the room's one threadbare chair and walks over to the single window across which a colourless curtain is drawn. Pulling it to one side, she peers through a dusty pane of glass on to Calixto Garcia, an unremarkable and uncared for road.

The view would not make the cut for a picture postcard.

Releasing the curtain, she moves the rucksack on to the floor and sinks into the chair. In the next room, an argument starts. A man raises his voice and the banshee wailing of a woman rails against it. It builds in intensity then stops abruptly with the slamming of a door and the scurry of footsteps across the landing. The peace lasts for a full ten minutes, then is shattered by the ear-splitting noise of a dogfight in the street below, joined by shouting as people try to separate two animals seemingly hell-bent on tearing each other to pieces.

The sooner I'm out of here the better, she thinks.

She told the Major General he had three days to work out a way to secure the virus. If he fails to come up with a plan in that time, she informed him, then she will instruct the delivery of the damning documents to his sons.

He tried to argue, saying three days was unrealistic, but she was immoveable. Reluctantly, he agreed, saying he would be in contact again when he had a plan in mind. Under no circumstances should she call him.

This is a time for trust, but she cannot bring herself to trust him. What if he arranges to have her killed, caring nothing for the consequences? What if he changes his mind and comes clean about Guevara's bastard? Unlikely. The old man is cast in the same mould as Peru. A puffed-up alpha male, protective of his position and needing to be respected.

He would do anything to keep it.

Wouldn't he?

20th July

Three days later and she has still not heard from him. Twice a day, she asks The Leer (the name she secretly calls the man behind the Hotel Marti's reception) if he has any messages for her. He always answers with a slow shake of the head, his eyes riveted to her breasts. He never checks and she wonders if this is a game he plays to amuse himself. Or maybe he is that engrossed performing his other duties as bellhop and barman it slips his memory.

She spent the first morning staring at the architecture of the Salcines Palace, taking in the paintings in the Art Gallery and studying the artefacts in the Museum of Decorative Art. Then, in the afternoon, she walked the short distance to the Ruben Lopez Sabariego House of Culture, the old Spanish casino, thinking it wouldn't be out of place on the main street of some hick town in the Wild West. She retired early, only to be awakened by the noise of a fistfight outside the hotel entrance, the cheering of a crowd encouraging the brawlers. After that, she found it impossible to fall asleep, the fracas setting her nerves on edge and, just as she was on the point of dropping off, another heated argument exploded in the adjacent room.

On the second day, she toyed with the idea of taking a taxi out to Guantanamo Bay to satisfy her curiosity, but decided against it. It might fuel suspicions and the Major

THE CIGAR SEED

General said something about his son 'looking out for her'—a threat on which he might make good. What she read about the naval base intrigued her; the fact that the Americans had leased it for more than a hundred years and even Castro was powerless to force them out of his country. It must annoy the hell out of him. Yet strangely, it seems to be of little interest to the population of a city going about its daily business. Instead, she visited the Museo Municipal with its quirky collection of pre-revolution passes to the base and antique, ugly-green Harley-Davidsons commissioned to convey secret messages during the revolution.

This, the third morning, she is pacing her room like a caged lion. In the absence of email, internet and watchable programmes on her room's decrepit TV, the screen of which suffers from a permanent magenta cast, she feels isolated and cut off from the modern world. Used to the frantic hustle and bustle in meeting a busy newspaper's schedule, she finds it impossible to adapt to such a glacial pace of life.

Minutes before ten o'clock, the phone rings.

'Yes?' she says, picking it up.

'A call for you, senorita,' croons the voice of The Leer. 'A man who won't give me his name. Do you wish me to put him through?'

'Yes, please.'

'Good day, Senorita Rodriguez. This is a call from Cubanacan. We trust you are enjoying Guantanamo?'

She recognises the Major General's voice immediately and smiles at his subterfuge. 'Is there much to enjoy?'

'Ha, I see you have a good sense of humour. Would you be available to meet your representative? He would like to discuss your onward itinerary with you.'

'Yes, I can do that. When and where?'

'Would today at noon in the Plaza del Mercado Agro Industrial on the corner of Los Maceos and Prado be convenient?'

'It would. How will I recognise him?'

'He'll be carrying a Cubanacan flight bag.'

'OK, I'll look out for him.'

'Goodbye.'

'Bye.'

Before the call ends, she hears a faint click on the line. The Major General was right to be cautious. The Leer must have been listening in on the conversation.

She feels exposed, standing on the pavement at the junction of Los Maceos and Prado. The heat from the gleaming white walls of the market building reflects on to her back. Damp patches darken the underarms of her cotton shirt and rivulets of sweat trickle down her ribs, moistening the waistband of her jeans.

Heat is not the only thing causing her to sweat. She will never forget how she felt the last time she came face to face with the Major General.

At midday precisely, she spots him working his way through the thickening crowd towards her.

He dips his head in greeting, his face wearing a trace of a smile.

'Major General,' she utters, a lump snagging her throat.

'A beautiful building, isn't it?' he says, angling his head upwards at the red cupola peeping out of the white balustrade high above them.

His words are spoken more as a statement than a question, delivered in a relaxed, friendly manner, unsettling her.

'A fine example of what we Cubans can do when we set our minds to it. This building was designed by Leticio Salcines, a local man.'

She fights the lump, steels herself. 'With respect Major General, I don't have time to discuss architecture. Can we talk about the virus?'

He sighs, shakes his head. 'That's the problem with young people today; always in a hurry. You should learn to make time to appreciate the things around you. Why not imbibe some of the sights and sounds of our beautiful country?'

The man's like a chameleon. This can't be the same man who, less than one week ago, told me to be on the next plane out of the country, or he would kill me.

'Thanks for the advice, I'll bear it in mind. However, as I said, I'd like to hear about the virus.'

He crooks a finger. 'Follow me.'

They cross to the far side of Los Maceos, away from the shoppers. His eyes scan the length of the street and then he sits down on a low wall facing the market building's façade. She sits down beside him.

'You'll need to be patient; there's much you should know about.' He taps the side of his nose with his finger. 'Much of it I myself did not know until very recently.'

She wants to say *Are all the men in this country in love with the sound of their own voices? I don't want another history lesson. I want the Ebola and the hell out of here.*

Instead, she says, 'You have my full attention, Major General.'

'We should go back in time, to a place called Sverdlovsk.'

She tries to recall the name, but it eludes her. It sounds Russian. 'Sverdlovsk? I've never heard of it.'

171

'Years ago, it was a suspected biological warfare facility, located in the town of Sverdlovsk in Russia, now known as Ekaterinburg. There was no hard evidence to support such suspicions, not until an unusual incident occurred in April '79. There was an outbreak of anthrax, allegedly affecting almost one hundred people. Reports said more than sixty subsequently died. The first person affected died after four days, the last six weeks later. Intestinal anthrax from tainted meat caused the deaths or so the Soviet government claimed. It was the height of the Cold War. Officials in the White House claimed the outbreak was caused by an accidental release of anthrax spores from a biological weapons facility. The Yanquis accused the Soviets of violating the Biological Weapons Convention and made their suspicions public. The Soviets denied any activities relating to biological weapons and stuck to their contaminated meat story. Nothing was conclusively proven and the superpowers returned to their tit-for-tat chess game.

'Then we move forward to '92, after the collapse of the Soviet empire. Boris Yeltsin was in power and admitted, without going into details, that the anthrax outbreak was the result of military activity at this facility. He allowed a team of Western scientists to go to Sverdlovsk to investigate the outbreak. In Cuba we assumed the Russians would continue their offensive biological warfare program unabated.'

The morning sun climbs towards its zenith as Eduardo takes a cigar from his pocket, lights it, sucks in deeply and wipes his sweating forehead with the back of his sleeve.

'Although the KGB confiscated hospital and other records after the incident, the scientists were able to track down where the victims were at the time of the anthrax release. Their findings were interesting. They

172

showed that on the day of the incident all the victims were clustered along a straight line downwind from the facility. Livestock in the same area also died of anthrax. After completing their investigation, they concluded the outbreak was caused by a release from an aerosol of anthrax pathogen at the military facility, but they couldn't determine what caused the release or what specific activities were conducted at the facility. What they didn't know, was that before their arrival the KGB removed all record of a brilliant young Georgian virologist named Zviad Makashvili. Not only did they destroy the facility's personnel file, they also extirpated every document connected to Makashvili—birth certificate, driving licence, communist party card, everything. In effect, it was as if he never existed.'

'I don't understand. If all the records were destroyed, how do you know about this man?'

'Ah, this is the interesting part. Makashvili was a genius but a flawed genius. He displayed dissident tendencies and was prone to voicing his opinions in public, making him very unpopular with his colleagues and superiors. When the anthrax incident occurred they took the opportunity to point the finger of blame at him, claiming it was his carelessness with an atomizer that led to the release of the anthrax into the environment. He got wind of their intention to notify the KGB and simply didn't turn up one morning for work. He was never heard of in Russia again.'

'But that still doesn't explain how you know of him.'

The smile starts slowly at the corners of his mouth and spreads upwards, like the smile of a man who has finally cracked an indecipherable code.

'Zviad Makashvili is now Jaime Hornedo, one of our most gifted scientists. When he fled Russia, this was the most obvious place to head for. In the '70s it was hard to get out of this country, but not too difficult to get in. He tried to go unnoticed, but he was soon in the custody of some very important people keen to get truthful answers to their direct questions. Makashvili was a scientist, not a hero, and it wasn't long before he blurted out the whole story.

'They debated what they should do with him. Should they send him back to Russia where he would be condemned as a traitor and most likely shot, or make use of his prodigious talent? The request for a decision went right to the top. They gave Makashvili no choice. Work for the Communist Party of Cuba, like it or lump it.'

'Weren't they worried the Russians would find out?'

'At the time the Russians had bigger fish to fry. They were involved in an impossible war in Afghanistan. The hunting down of one elusive scientist didn't merit the use of their resources.' He rubs his knees. 'Let's walk. I'm not used to sitting for so long.'

As they stand, he whispers, 'Someone is watching us.'

'I don't see anyone.'

'Neither do I, but then, I don't need to. I can *feel* it when someone's eyes are on me.'

As they turn away from the market, he resumes his story. 'Where was I? Ah, yes. Having Makashvili in their grasp set some powerful men's minds to thinking. Men who made the decision to engage Cuba in other people's wars in Africa, the first so-called 'Third World' country to do so. Here was an excellent opportunity to make the most of a first-class mind and put it to good use. Makashvili had worked with state-of-the-art equipment in a no-expense-spared facility and had access to some of the Soviet Union's best-guarded biological warfare secrets. We would gain all that knowledge for nothing. Why shouldn't we have a biological warfare programme?

174

The top brass puffed themselves up at the thought of it. If nuclear weapons were a pipe dream, harnessing of germs with the potential to be almost as devastating was irresistible. Also, it would be extremely cheap. Then reality brought them down to earth. They had the man with the ability to realise their dreams, but they lacked the raw material: a killer virus.'

'Ah, now I'm beginning to follow you.'

'Finally the threads come together in the weave. In '79, I was stationed in Angola. I remember well one particular mission, to liaise with a group of Zairian rebels. My instructions were to collect two boxes; what they contained was unspecified. When we rendezvoused, I knew there was something wrong. The Zairians looked ill and agitated. When I stepped forward to greet him the leader started to shout and gesticulate wildly at a box on the ground in front of him. My scout asked where the other box was and the man said that they had abandoned it after dropping it and looking to retrieve what was inside. All they found were smashed glass vials so they left it behind. As we were talking, one of his men doubled up on his knees, screaming with pain.'

'And at the time you had no idea what was in the boxes?'

'How could I? Besides, it was no business of mine. When they gave me my orders, I thought it might be a nuclear trigger, but I soon ruled that out. What possible use could we have for a nuclear trigger? Apart from that, I couldn't hazard a guess, and when I saw the size of the remaining box I knew for certain that it couldn't be a trigger. It was far too small.'

Terese lets out a low whistle. 'Well, well. We know *where* the stuff is kept; we have sources you wouldn't believe. But we didn't know *how* your country had managed to get hold of it. Your story is very enlightening, but of no importance. All I want to know is how you're going to get the Ebola for me.'

His eyes flash and he raises a finger. 'Ah, that's where I have a plan. I'll explain it to you. I believe you'll find it quite ingenious, if I say so myself. Even as we speak the first steps are being taken.'

She listens as he outlines his plan. The scientist has a penchant for young girls and is infatuated with a young prostitute. The plan is for the girl to steal the virus. It sounds too simple and not at all promising. If she understands correctly, it depends on the girl's ability to dupe a senior research scientist and steal the virus from under his very nose.

'Are you sure it will work?' Doubt clouds her mind. 'She might not go through with it.'

They halt whilst he lights another cigar. 'My son assures me she will and I know and trust my son. If he says she will, then she will. But there is a small issue.'

'Ah. I wondered if there might be.'

She has the Major General at a disadvantage, but is smart enough not to fool herself into thinking he won't try to salvage something out of his situation. Her mind tries to figure out what quid pro quo he will demand and ice runs in her veins as she recalls Peru's words.

Think about it. You did promise to do anything—anything—for the cause.

She shudders, braces herself, not wanting to imagine.

'In order for my plan to work, the girl will be able to steal only a single shot of the virus.'

The ice melts, but now she is confused. A single shot?

'I don't understand, Major General. A single shot?'

'That puzzled me, also. I pictured the virus in some sort of glass container, perhaps a vial, as I imagined it all those years ago. But this Hornedo is a genius. The prototype ammunition for a weapon is in the shape of a small, plastic cylinder, roughly five millimetres in diameter and no longer than fifty millimetres. It contains the virus and fits inside a modified, commercially available aerosol gun. My son says it won't be too long before a production facility will be in full operation.'

'And you think she can steal a single cylinder?'

'If she fails she will die. And that one cylinder will have to be sufficient for your purposes.'

'How effective is one cylinder?'

'According to my sources, Hornedo boasts that, if properly dispersed on a reasonable breeze, it has the capability to cause hundreds of fatalities.'

She nods. One will be sufficient for their needs. 'When can I expect to have it?'

'My son says the girl will be with the scientist tomorrow evening. If she does what is expected of her the virus will be in his possession the day after. I cannot be sure how long it will be before he delivers it to me. Two, three days, maybe. It all depends if he can get away. You must realise as well how difficult this is for me, making excuses to my wife. She must wonder why I visit Guantanamo so frequently. I tell her I have business here, but I think she's beginning to disbelieve me.'

'Once I have it, how will I get it out of Cuba?'

Beaming now, he holds out his cigar. 'Ah, that is where my old friend, Hoyo de Monterrey, comes in.'

She shudders. Is this a trick? Why does this person have to be involved? Is he some kind of courier?

'Who's he?' she asks.

He chuckles. 'You will soon find out. He will take the starring role in my ingenious plan. Now, I must go as I have an important appointment this afternoon.'

The girl is on her way home to a run-down hovel on the outskirts of Guantanamo when Oswardo waylays her and drags her, kicking and squirming, into a disused building. Eduardo is already waiting, a gun in his hand. Waving the gun at her, he forces the terrified girl to strip.

He tilts his chin at his son. Oswardo closes the door as he exits the room, leaving Eduardo alone with the girl.

Discovering the existence of Eva is a godsend. Recently turned sixteen, she touts for business at the US base. Her body is stunning, making a mockery of the straight line. She has curves where no curve has a right to exist. His calloused hands are tempted to caress those curves and he wonders if he should have a little fun himself then decides against it. There is far too much at stake and the girl might be astute enough to use any impropriety against him in the future.

There is no harm in looking, however.

With her long legs spread wide and hands clasped behind her head, she stands exposed in front of him. A gold nipple ring, dancing up and down on her heavy left breast, catches his attention. From time to time, he gently slides his swagger stick along the softness of her sex, forcing her to shift weight.

'So, my little one, we've been entertaining the Yanquis have we?'

'No, sir.'

In a flash, the stick whips across the girl's left thigh, leaving a bright red weal. She screams with pain and surprise. Slowly, the stick returns to its previous position.

'Try again shall we? It would be a shame to mark such a beautiful body. I hear you've been performing acts of a sexual nature with soldiers of an aggressive, imperialist regime. Am I correct?'

'Y . . . yes, sir.' She begins to shake, making the ring dance uncontrollably.

'Do you know what the punishment for that is?'

'N . . . no, sir.'

'Then let me educate you. At best, it's five years locked away in a stinking prison with only rats for company. At worst, it's execution by firing squad. Most people who do time wish they'd been shot.' He feels the pressure on his wrist as the girl's body settles lower on the stick. 'What you do is regarded as an offence against the state, a very serious offence. Some would say it amounts to treason.' He begins to jiggle the stick. 'But there may be a way for me to, let us say, turn a blind eye in return for a favour from you.'

A knowing look crosses the girl's face. She unclasps her hands, starts to crouch. He administers another stinging blow across her right thigh and her hands snap back behind her head.

'Not that kind of favour, little one. This favour concerns your friend or should I say client, Professor Hornedo. Turn around.'

He lowers the stick as she turns to face the wall, full of ragged holes where the plaster has come adrift. Applying the tip to the back of her neck, he traces a path down the length of her spine, stopping when it reaches the valley of her buttocks.

'Listen carefully, I will tell you once only. This is what I want you to do, and do it you will, if you know what's good for you and your family. And you'll do it tonight.' As he gives his instructions to the girl's beautiful back, he feels his resolve crumbling.

'Fuck it,' he mutters, unbuckling his belt and undoing the buttons of his fly. It is a long time since Major General Eduardo Fortunato has had the pleasure of such a magnificent body.

A very long time.

.

21st July

Inside the whitewashed walls of the single-storey, concrete building the flickering fluorescent light tries with all its might to trigger, but the tube is having none of it. The white-coated figure of Professor Jaime Hornedo hunches forward on a swivel chair, swears under his breath.

Not again. Where do they buy them?

He is heartily sick of the tubes. Given the money they spend on laboratory equipment, it is unfathomable why they skimp on the lights. Another department's responsibility no doubt. It is more than annoying; it could end up causing him severe headaches as it did two weeks ago. On that occasion, he was forced to take the day off and shut himself in the darkened bedroom of his small villa on the complex until the hammer inside his head stopped pounding on his skull. They did not take kindly to that, of course, impatience bursting out now he has cracked the seemingly impossible problem of how to disperse the virus in air. Almost thirty years of trying and failing hundreds and hundreds of times, but he knew, knew in his heart that it could be done. In fairness to the men in uniform, they never gave up believing in his ability to do it. Then finally, he made an unprecedented breakthrough. Success, though, is bringing its own problems. They are growing impatient, keen to play with their new and deadly toy. Where exactly they propose to try it out and in what manner are beyond him. He does not really care; that is their business. He has done the hard work and now it is a matter of manufacturing, not science. His next task is to work with the engineers and his close-knit team to implement the plans for a small-scale production facility.

Then the military men can play until their hearts are content.

He congratulates himself now he has realised his dream, pursued in such a single-minded manner: a viral weapon with a lethal potential, cheap to produce and unbelievably destructive. Ah, how he loves that word, *destructive*. That word defines his genius. Naturally, the Russians with their head start, limitless resources and well-staffed facilities were there before him in solving the problem of how to spread the virus by means of an airborne agent. That is only to be expected. However, now they have cracked that problem, they seem content to let it rest and focus their attention on other projects.

Professor Petrov and his incompetents never could see the grand picture.

As he thinks of Petrov, he recalls the time he demonstrated his innovative techniques with anthrax. Yes, the accident happened, but neither his science nor the method of dispersal caused it. They should have cancelled the demonstration after he warned them about the unseasonably strong westerly tearing through the plant that day in July. That is the problem with Russian scientists; they are pigheaded and arrogant. If his native Georgia ruled the republics, the political map of the world would be a whole lot different.

'Please cancel it, Professor Petrov. The wind's too strong to proceed.'

'Are you mad, Doctor Makashvili? I've invited all the top brass and I mean all. No, we'll carry on.'

'There may be unforeseen consequences, dire consequences.'

'The only dire consequences will be the slashing of my budget if the brass leaves believing we've wasted their time. Don't worry about what might happen, Doctor. Carry on as planned and if there's a problem I'll take care of it.'

There was a problem—precisely as he feared. A problem which resulted in the deaths of sixty-four innocent people six weeks later and which escalated to the point where it further widened the already unbridgeable chasm of mistrust between the superpowers.

Petrov certainly did take care of it as he promised he would. The slimy bastard covered his own backside by laying the blame squarely on Makashvili's shoulders. He had no alternative but to disappear.

A knot twists in his stomach as he thinks of what might have befallen him owing to Petrov's buck-passing. Scared to death, he quickly scraped together a few personal belongings and stowed away on a boat bound for Cuba, without speaking a word to his fiancée or his friends. If he hadn't secreted himself on that boat it was a certainty he would have wound up dead, his body disposed of in a lime-filled pit like some infected animal carcass. Thank heavens he was in possession of specialist knowledge and skills the Cubans found useful. They installed him in his own lab, allowed him to select his own team and provided the necessary means to continue with his research. Those means are not as generous as the lab in Russia, but they are sufficient. Unlike the Russians who are impatient for results, the Cubans understand it can take years before they see the fruits of scientific endeavour. They have always been good to him, but with strings attached: unlike an ordinary citizen he does not have the freedom to travel within the country and is forced to live his life under supervision on a secure complex. But they give him everything he can possibly want. Russian books, music, films, documentaries and the finest Russian vodkas.

And a constant stream of girls.

Oh, yes. They know precisely what kind of girls he favours.

Life could be a lot worse for a man grappling with the world's deadliest virus.

He glances at the black hands of the clock on the lab wall. They tell him it is ten thirty-five. This is to be a short day and that puts him in a good mood. He has a meeting with Perez and the engineering team at one o'clock. At three-thirty, the security people will carry out their daily check. After that, and unusually, business in the lab will be concluded for the day. He will then spend a few hours in his villa writing up his notes until Eva arrives later that evening, dressed in one of her impossibly short skirts. The girl is the best they have provided for him; she can drive him crazy. His mind drifts to the rounded contours of her young breasts and the shiny gold ring that pierces the peanut of her left nipple. Already, he can imagine the soft caress of her full, red lips as they roll over his shiny tip and slide slowly and teasingly down his shaft until she holds him fully engorged in her sensuous mouth.

He begins to get hard.

As soon as the duty corporal departs, his hands reach out to explore the geography of her incredible body.

She locks her fingers in his. 'Wait, Jaime, we have all night. Do you know I've always wanted to be made love to in a laboratory?'

'In a laboratory? I never heard of such a thing. Come on now, little one. Eat me.'

'It's all that apparatus and everything virginal white. It makes me really hot when I think about it.'

It's the most unusual thing he has ever heard. Sex in the laboratory? Then again, she is an unusual girl.

'It does? How strange, I think Jung would have something to say about that.'

'Forget Jung, whoever he is. Take me there Jaime. I'll do things we haven't done before.'

He likes it when she says that. It never ceases to amaze him what sexual surprises Eva can spring on him.

'Oh, all right, I don't suppose it'll do any harm. What things?'

'I'll show you, but don't forget to bring your drink.'

Entering his lab in the evening will not arouse any suspicions. The sentries are aware he is a poor sleeper and that he often returns to the lab at odd hours to work. If they happen to notice the light peeping through the wooden shutters, all they do is nod to one another and continue playing cards.

Stealing across the narrow courtyard separating his villa from the lab, he leads her by the hand down the short flight of steps to the rear entrance. Punching a code on the numbered security pad, he enters.

'Sit down over there, under the window,' he says. 'I'll pull the shutters closed so security won't be suspicious.'

'OK, but don't be long. I'm beginning to get wet.'

Closing the six large wooden shutters takes some time and only heightens his anticipation of new pleasures he is about to experience. He switches off the main lights leaving only the annoying strip lights above his worktop.

'Wow, this is some place,' she says. 'Why don't you show me around?

'What for? Come here, I want you.'

'Be patient, Jaime. Let's make a game of it. A sex game.'

A tingle runs down his spine. 'A sex game? I like the sound of that.'

It proves to be one of the most erotic experiences of his life. Each time he shows her a piece of apparatus— centrifuge, Petri dish turntable, homogeniser and finally the climatic test chamber— she allows him to explore a different part of her body with his mouth. By the time they reach the freezer where the virus is stored, he is ready to throw himself off a cliff for the taste of her body.

'What's in there?' she asks, pointing at he enamelled door of a metal cabinet.

'The freezer? Nothing of importance.'

'Let me see.'

'No, it's not for viewing.'

'Are you sure?' Unbuttoning his fly, she rolls his underpants over his engorged penis. Pushing him on to his back, she pulls his trousers down to his knees. As he closes his eyes, she puts her mouth over the purplish head and purses her lips so they just brush the shiny dome.

'Go on! Go on!'

'Let me see what's in the freezer first.'

'For Christ's sake, Eva!'

'I told you you'd enjoy this game.'

He feels the tip of her tongue glide down the underside of his bulging shaft until it touches his balls. By now, he is shaking like a leaf.

'Do I get to see inside? Perhaps I should stop?'

'OK, OK. The key is in the drawer under the worktop, I'll get it for you.'

'Oh no, not now I have you where I want you. Close your eyes.'

A warm hand grasps his manhood. Slowly it begins to slide up and down.

22nd July

When Hornedo awakes the next day, his head feels like it has been cleaved in two by an axe, but he does not care; the taste of the girl is still on his tongue. The alarm clock on the dressing table in his bedroom shows seven o'clock: time to get thinking and work off the headache. He dresses quickly, splashes his face with cold water from the kitchen sink, skips shaving and strides quickly to his lab, retracing last night's steps.

His mind drifts back to the previous evening.

Intriguing. I've never heard of anyone wanting to make love in a laboratory. Wherever does she get her ideas? With a mind as creative as that, she could be the next Mata Hari.

As is his custom, he opens the wooden shutters to admit the natural light and flicks the switch for the fluorescent lighting. One of them begins to flicker. He curses under his breath and makes a skywards gesture with his middle finger.

The next step in his routine is to check the viral prototypes in the freezer. Opening the door, he counts the slim cylinders in their plastic rack. One, two, three . . . then it hits him like a truck. One is missing.

It can't be, he tells himself. *The vodka must be confusing me.*

Recounting them, he realises there is no mistake; the rack contains eleven cylinders. His hands begin to shake and sweat beads on his forehead. His fuddled mind screams it has to be the girl who took one of the cylinders, but his logic refuses to work out how or why.

All he knows for certain is that trouble is going to crash down on him later that day.

Trouble with a capital T.

Before Terese and he separated, Eduardo informed her that the phrase he will use when the virus is in his possession is, 'the tobacco is good this year'. When she hears this, they will schedule a rendezvous, again in the Plaza del Mercado Agro Industrial.

For the time being, until he hears from Oswardo, he will enjoy the benefit of the Castros' generosity. That morning, a small truck arrived laden with boxes of food; a privilege afforded him for his years of military service. Unlike most ordinary citizens of Cuba, he has no need to endure deprivation. During the difficult years of the Special Period when people had to eat anything they could lay their hands on, when nothing on four legs was safe, Eduardo was assured of a ready supply of more than life's essentials, thanks to the Castros.

He glances at his watch: a quarter past two. Carmen and he are enjoying a moment together as they stack the boxes in the Casa del Toro Negro's storeroom. The phone interrupts their conversation. Eduardo excuses himself and takes the call.

'Fortunato speaking.'

'Hello, Pa. Oswardo here.'

'Hello, son. How are things with you?'

'Never better thanks. I've managed to find you a birthday present. Sorry it's late, but as they say, better late than never.'

'Will you be bringing it over?'

'Yes, but not until the twenty-fifth. That's the earliest I can get away. I'll make sure it's wrapped well.'

'I'll see you on the twenty-fifth then.'

'You will. I'll be there around midday. Bye, Pa.'

'Bye, son. Take care with your present.'

Grinning broadly, he replaces the phone in its cradle. Oswardo has come through, as he knew he would.

'Who was that?' asks Carmen, poking her head round the doorway.

'Oswardo. He's coming over later in the week.'

'Oh? What's the occasion?'

'No occasion. He just needs a change of scenery, I guess. Perhaps Gitmo is driving him crazy.'

'That wouldn't surprise me; it's already turned one member of this family loco.' She stares at him wide-eyed, making a circling motion with her index finger at her temple.

Springing forward, he chases her as she runs into the kitchen, screaming.

25th July

The day after her meeting with Eduardo, Terese informed The Leer she was leaving Guantanamo for a few days. If she had to wait, she thought, she might as well try to enjoy a few days sightseeing. After she leaves, nothing will convince her to set foot on Cuban soil again. Outside the busy centres the island is a treasure, as yet unspoilt by commercialisation but certain one day to succumb. Set in a string of enchanting islands stretching all the way from the Gulf of Mexico to Trinidad and Tobago, it is the brightest gem among a sparkling clutch.

She chose a route with cacti-studded fields on one side and the lapis lazuli Caribbean on the other that winds itself to the coast at Cajobabo, a large, scattered village where she discovered a small, clean casa particulare.

Today, a steamy, hot day tempered by a capricious sea breeze, she strolls into the village and calls in at a sleepy cafe. Sleepy that is until a five piece band springs to life and serenades the morning with foot-tapping rhythms, their sweat-coated bodies swaying in time to the salsa. Four songs later, as the band lapses into silence, a young girl tries to sell CDs to a handful of customers and then slides behind the counter.

As Terese is on the point of ordering a coffee, her mobile phone vibrates in her pocket. She fights her natural inclination to answer it. Not being able to use it freely makes her feel peculiarly isolated. Periodically, she is tempted to make a quick call to Peru simply to let him know her progress. On one occasion, acting without thinking, she composed a brief text message to him and was on the point of pressing the SEND button when she stopped herself, realising what she was about to do. That lapse of concentration might have had unexpected consequences. Without doubt, Cubacel would keep detailed records. If the Secret Police demands to see them, Cubacel would hand them over willingly.

No call, no record, no problem.

Giving in to the phone's persistence, she takes it out, sees FABIEN flashing on its tiny screen. Now she receives at least two calls from him every day. Considerate as ever, the poor man must be sick with worry. She has not contacted him since leaving Bayonne; not even a text to say she arrived safely. Although she asked him not to phone her, it is a measure of the man that he respected her wishes for the first two weeks. Then, five days ago, the calls started, one a day at first. Three days ago, he started leaving text messages. She has not answered any of them, but she dare not switch the phone off. If an emergency call from Peru does come through, she will have to answer it immediately.

Still, she thinks, *it won't hurt just to look at Fabien's texts.*

She scrolls through the menus, finds the message inbox and selects the last message received.

> Hello, darling, please call. Worried to death. Your
> father also very concerned. Wants to know how you
> are. Text if can't call. Fabien xx

Instantly, her hackles rise. Her cursed father is sticking his big nose in again. He made a massive error of judgement when he sent Jacques Oreaga and his cronies to spy on her. Neither he nor Oreaga is aware of the skills she has acquired: even if they managed to tail her, her unseen 'shadow' would soon flag up any suspicious behaviour. The 'shadow' is an innovation of Salbatore's, another avoidance procedure devised by the man when he was at his brilliant best. At all times, two members of the commando are 'paired' taking it in turns to be the 'shadow', rotating at two-day intervals. It is inconvenient, at times mind-numbingly boring, but extremely effective. For the past year, Martina and she have been each other's shadow. A fiery biologist whose grandfather fought against Franco in the Civil War, Martina lives and breathes ETA. Her father has contacts in terrorist organisations all around the world. Through his sprawling grapevine, he learned of the purported existence of a secret laboratory in Guantanamo, reputedly experimenting with the deadly Ebola virus. Reports reaching him suggested a scientist had developed an airborne means of transmitting the virus. This was a remarkable revelation. When Martina told Terese, they agreed to share the information with Peru. His fertile imagination readily grasped the knowledge and sketched it into the outline of a plan.

How could I have been so stupid? she thinks.

Maybe Oreaga has found out about her engagement to Fabien. If he has, she can write the script. Oreaga reports to her father. Her father then requests a meeting with Fabien, all nice and cosy at first. Then he applies pressure, wringing out every drop of information about their relationship. Her father works like that. If he cannot get what he wants one way, he will try another and another and another until he does. She wonders if it explains Fabien's frequent phone calls. If so, the poor man's life will be a misery.

Her mobile flashes again and 'FABIEN' replaces 'CUBACEL'. She ignores it. Thirty seconds later, the phone vibrates. Another voice message on her answering service. She slips the phone back into her pocket.

Should I call Peru to let him know what's happening?

She considers the risk so close to the US Naval Base. Providing strategic logistics support to both US Navy and Coastguard vessels and aircraft, it must have very capable communications technology. Who knows what else it might monitor? There are tiny remnants of the Cold War strewn all around the globe and Guantanamo is unquestionably one of them.

No call, no trace.

Peru's cold, dispassionate words float back to her. *'Never call or text me whilst you're in Cuba, Terese, do you hear? Never. Just remember what we're fighting for. Remember, this is war.'*

She should be relaxed, warmed by the burning sun, waiting for the signal that flags the beginning of her journey back to Bayonne, but the question still nags her. Why did Peru choose her in preference to Martina for the mission? Martina was hurt and disappointed when he announced Terese would be the one to go. He said Terese was the one who discovered the diary so she should be the one to confront the Major General. None of the others raised an objection, not even Salbatore whom she thought might have demanded to be the one to go. However, as egotistical as he is, Salbatore is no fool. He knew—they all knew—it had to be a job for a woman.

As if responding to an invisible signal the band springs to life, takes up its position and again cuts the air with mesmeric rhythms of salsa.

Waving at the girl, she mouths *coffee, please.*

Her mind moves from her father to the Major General. Could his words be a bluff, a ruse to buy time to think his way out of his predicament? Peru and she spent hours discussing how he might react, but it was impossible to imagine every scenario. Then again, his intentions may be genuine, but his plan might fail. She has doubts about his plan all right, deep doubts. What if the girl fails to steal the virus from the scientist? What if they catch her in the act? What if she betrays them? What if the Major General and his son are being interrogated right now?

The not knowing is playing havoc with her mind.

Her phone buzzes again. This time it is a text message, but not from Fabien.

Senorita Rodriguez, this is a message from DHL. We have a package for you awaiting collection in our Guantanamo depot. Please call us back to confirm collection details.

It confuses her for several moments, then she realises it cannot possibly be a message from DHL. It is a coded instruction to call immediately. There must be a development.

After paying for the drink, she thanks the girl, gives an enthusiastic thumbs-up to the band and quickly makes her way to a quiet corner of the street.

The deep voice of Eduardo answers the call. 'Good day.'

'Good day. Is this DHL?'

'It is, and we have a package for your collection. The man who left it said it was for you to take back to your father. He said to tell you *this is a good year for tobacco.*'

A tingle runs down her spine. He has done what he promised he would. His crazy plan to obtain the virus has succeeded and now it is time for her to prove herself once more. Again, she will need to test herself and see if she has the temperament and courage to succeed.

'Where are you?' she says.

'Opposite the Mercado Agro Industrial. We open at ten o'clock.'

She leans against a stuccoed wall and breathes a sigh of relief.

Soon, she will be home.

The scene reminds her of the film *Groundhog Day* in which a TV weatherman wakes up every morning to find it is identical to the previous one. That is how it feels sitting once again next to the Major General in Guantanamo. He is dressed in the same clothes and they are sitting in exactly the same spot, opposite the same market building, the same hot sun blazing down on them. Only this time, the scene contains an object that was not there before. Between them, on the wall, is an item that can be found anywhere in Cuba. So ubiquitous is this item, that the locals continuously pester tourists to buy it.

A cedarwood box, perfectly designed to hold twenty-five cigars.

Very clever, she thinks. *Anyone watching him would think he was just another tout offering me a cheap deal.*

'In here,' he caresses the box with the tips of his fingers, 'you will find the stuff of your dreams.'

She studies the box's oval logo, next to which is a small white label with indecipherable black words printed on it. 'Cigars?'

'I told you Hoyo de Monterrey would play the starring role in my plan. These are not just cigars, they are Hoyo de Monterrey Double Coronas, a *wonderful* smoke, my favourite. You'd be amazed at what goes into them.' He chuckles and pats the box lovingly.

A puzzled look creases her face. 'I don't follow, Major General.'

He taps the box. 'Then allow me to explain. In this box are two rows of cigars: thirteen in the upper layer and twelve in the lower. Don't ask me why the factory doesn't produce them in boxes of twenty-six. They must have their reasons. However, that's irrelevant. Twenty-four of the cigars are exactly that—cigars. However, one of them is special, very special. It has been rolled in a particularly, shall we say, unique way.'

A light flashes on in her head. 'Ah, now I understand.'

'Good. This one cigar is the one you must protect at all costs if you wish to achieve your aims. Listen carefully, for I will say this only once. Then we must never, I repeat never, meet again.'

Involuntarily, she leans closer to him.

'This particular cigar is the fifth from the left on the bottom layer. Airport security will be unable to discover what it contains as it has been prepared in such a way as to be undetectable by normal scanning equipment. The only means to determine its structure would be to unravel the tobacco leaves by hand. A most unlikely occurrence, I think you would agree.'

She nods.

'I doubt very much if anyone would even notice. Almost without exception, tourists depart Cuba with one or two boxes of cigars, whether they smoke or not. They're so cheap to buy here nobody can resist such a bargain.'

'Ingenious. I'm very impressed.'

'There is, however, a proviso.'

Her head snaps up. 'Oh? And that is?'

He points at the white label. 'You must never break the seal on the box whilst in Cuba. That would immediately arouse the authorities' suspicions.'

'How do I know you're not lying if I can't check the contents?'

'You don't, but I think I know how your mind works. I assume you have instructed your contact, whoever he is, to deliver the documents if it turns out not to be what you want.'

Her mouth clamps. She guessed this is what he might say, but he is mistaken. Jerome may be a patriot, but he is not a brave patriot. One call is all he promised Martina's father he would make—one and one only.

'I thought so,' he says. 'However, I, too, have a problem. How do I know you will not deliver the documents regardless? I have the most to lose, have I not?'

'I won't do that, you can trust me.'

'Ah, trust; a small word that makes such huge demands. Do I have an alternative other than trust you? I expect not. But I will tell you this. If things should go wrong and you attempt to connect me to this little box, I'll kill you, no matter where you are. You can trust me on that. Now, take it, and never cross my path again.'

Cold, menacing eyes stare into her soul. At that moment, she knows he could and would do what he threatens. She puts it out of her mind. She has what she came all this way for. The old man is of no further use. Finally, it is time to go home. All that remains is for her to spirit the virus out of the country and deliver it safely to Bayonne.

'*WELCOME TO CUBA. THE TEMPERATURE OUTSIDE IS THIRTY-TWO DEGREES CENTIGRADE. PLEASE REMEMBER TO COLLECT YOUR LUGGAGE FROM THE TERMINAL. WE DO HOPE YOU ENJOYED YOUR FLIGHT. THANK YOU FOR TRAVELLING WITH AIR FRANCE.*'

A stream of passengers jostles impatiently inside the glistening tube of the Airbus A340-300. Bending his lanky frame as he descends from the opulence of the plush haven that is first class, Viktor tilts his head at the cabin crew as he stands by the open door of the plane squatting on the shimmering tarmac of Jose Marti International Airport. Then he steps into the blinding light of a still and cloudless Havana day, pausing briefly at the top of the rolling steps. Reaching into his jacket pocket, he pulls out a pair of Roberto Cavalli sunglasses to shield his eyes against the glare of the airport's smoked glass skin.

The flight was a long one and he does not like flying at the best of times. More specifically, he does not like airports. Once in the plane he finds it tolerable, cosseted in a sumptuous, fully-reclining leather seat with his own workstation and TV, an obsequious attendant fussing over him and plying him with champagne and gourmet food. Airports are another matter altogether. In his view, nobody but a sadist could design an airport with its tortuous, start-stop processes. A straight-to-the-point man, he cannot understand the need to be subjected to such a complexity of security procedures before finally reaching the peace and quiet of the VIP lounge, where he can relax in comfort before departure. Normally, he would simply climb aboard his company's Gulfstream G500 with as little fuss as possible, but long hauls such as this one do not afford him such convenience.

Thank God, I'm not forced to travel economy like those poor devils, cramped and uncomfortable in their crowded deck.

After passing through passport control and collecting his luggage, he spies Manuel Suarez, Groupe Rodriguez's 'representative' in Cuba. Built like a sumo and sporting a bristling black moustache that completely conceals his upper lip, Suarez has a reputation as a very effective local fixer. There is very little he cannot procure in the name of business—one way or another. All Viktor has to do is wave sufficient money under his nose and Suarez will get it for him. He recognises the same resourceful character in Jacques Oreaga, except money is the last thing to motivate his Head of Security. Oreaga likes to get things done, likes to face a challenge. That is what gives the man pleasure.

Recently, Suarez smoothed the way for the Punta Hicacos development deal. He did an excellent job, but it cost Viktor a lot of money—one hell of a lot of money. The number of palms Suarez supposedly greased amazes him, although he suspects the lion's share remains in the pocket of the sharp-suited man whose gold-filled mouth is now beaming at him.

They shake hands and he hands his suitcase to Suarez.

'Good day, Senor Rodriguez. I trust you had a pleasant flight?'

'Hello Manuel, it's good to see you again. The flight was tolerable. How are Carlota and the boys?'

Suarez shrugs his fleshy shoulders. 'You know how it is. My wife is fine, but the boys . . . well, boys will be boys.'

'Not just boys, Manuel, children in general. They're a joy when they're small, but once they grow up they seem to delight in causing their poor parents heartache.'

'That's true, senor. However, let us not talk about them on such a beautiful day. The limousine is waiting outside and I know you are keen to talk about . . . business.'

Ten minutes later, they ease themselves into the back seat of a big silver Mercedes and set off en route to the Hotel Nacional in the suburb of Verdado.

'What have you discovered? Do you know where she is?' says Viktor.

'I will tell you everything I know, senor. My investigations have revealed your daughter checked in at the Hotel Telegrafo, which is close to the old part of the city, on her arrival in Havana three weeks ago. She kept herself to herself on the first day and remained in the hotel. She did not make any telephone calls from her room according to my sources and she did not meet with anyone. Around mid-morning on the second day, after a late breakfast, she showed the hotel porter a photocopied photograph of a man and enquired if he knew where she could find him.'

Viktor frowns. Whom can Terese possibly seek in a place she has never visited? Moreover, how does she happen to have a photo of that person in her possession?

'Do you know this man, Manuel?'

'He's a local man well known to the porters in the Telegrafo. His name is Angelo Fortunato. I don't know him personally, but I do know of his father, as do many of my compatriots. The father is somewhat of a legend in Cuba, having fought alongside Castro and others in the revolution, in return obtaining a senior position in the army. This man was formidable when doing his military duty, but we no longer need fear him. Recently, he retired to his hometown of Santiago. No doubt, we'll soon forget him, as we have many of the old revolutionaries. People here are learning to move on.'

'What about the son?'

'Angelo is a very different personality. I understand he followed his father into the army, but now plies his trade driving tourists around Havana in a pony trap. Quite a religious man, I believe.'

Viktor scratches his head. 'Why on earth would my daughter be looking for this man?'

'I'm afraid that is a question I cannot answer. I can only pass on the information I have received. Please permit me to continue. One of the porters informed her there was a good chance she would find Fortunato over by the Hotel Parque Central, as that is where he has his pitch. She thanked the porter and went out of the hotel. Curious as to why a foreigner would be looking for this particular individual, the porter watched your daughter from the doorway of the Telegrafo as she crossed the street. She appeared to look around a little, and then went into the Hotel Parque Central. Sometime later, she reappeared and walked quickly around the perimeter of the park. He saw Angelo approach her, no doubt trying to convince her to take a pony ride. She refused and walked on as if she intended to visit Old Havana on foot. That intrigued the porter, as less than an hour before she had waved Fortunato's photograph under his nose. It was apparent from Fortunato's behaviour that he didn't know her, according to the porter. Then a peculiar thing happened. As he was returning to his pony, she retraced her steps; they engaged in a brief conversation and then separated once again. After that, Fortunato found another couple whom he helped on to the trap. Your daughter continued on her way into the old part of the city.'

'Your porter is unusually observant, Manuel.'

'Many young men in this country are ex-military, senor. During their time in the forces they acquire certain skills that can be very useful in civilian life. The porter was a scout in the army at one time.'

'Ah, I see. I sense there is more. Please go on.'

'There is more, and it becomes more intriguing. The porter says your daughter returned to the Telegrafo at about midday and had a light lunch and a drink in the hotel bar. At one forty-five or thereabouts, she left the hotel once more, again in the direction of the Hotel Parque Central. This time she was met by Fortunato who assisted her into the trap and the pony trotted off in the direction of Central Havana.'

Viktor rubs the side of his nose with a long, bony forefinger, an old habit when wrestling with a problem. 'There may be nothing in it. Maybe she simply wanted to see the city and had booked his services.'

'I agree, senor, there is nothing unusual in what she did. Taking a ride in a pony trap is a very common tourist activity in Havana. However, five days later, the same porter was on duty when a taxi arrived to collect her. She booked out of the hotel and he naturally assumed she was embarking on the next leg of her journey. It was the people in the taxi who greeted her like a long lost friend that caught his attention.'

'Not this Fortunato character again?'

'Yes, it was. He was with his wife and uncle. In this part of the city, everyone knows the uncle. Felipe Caraballo is a very clever man. At one time, he was a professor at the university, but now he makes far more money driving a taxi than he could ever make teaching students. Fortunately for you, he likes the sound of his own voice. The porter overheard him tell the receptionist they were on their way to visit his brother-in-law and sister in Santiago. The brother-in-law in question is the retired military man I mentioned, Fortunato's father, Major General Eduardo Fortunato. The trail then goes cold, I'm afraid.'

Viktor does not want to hear this. He has not planned to chase Terese all over the island. A quick in-out visit to check on her, using the excuse of giving the local bigwigs a photo opportunity, is all he wants.

'Santiago is some distance from here, isn't it?' he says.

'Senor, it's a long drive and it would take the best part of two days to get there. However, if you wish to get there quickly, you can catch a plane to Holguin. From there it's a short drive to Santiago.'

'Do you have people in Santiago?'

'I have a very good man there, senor. Nothing escapes his attention.'

He makes an instant decision. 'Book us on the first available flight tomorrow to Holguin and tell your man to meet us at the airport. By the way, I would like you to join me for dinner this evening. I want an update on the Punta Hicacos project and who we will be meeting for the contract signing.'

'I would be delighted, Senor Rodriguez.'

27th July

Terese feels as if a headstone has been lifted off her chest. Although his reputation goes before him, she never expected the Major General to be so ingenious in his planning, so efficient in his methods.

Relieving him of the cigar box, she spent the remaining hours of yesterday at her lodgings in Guantanamo, carefully repacking her rucksack and stashing the cigar box halfway down the khaki-coloured cylinder. Again, Peru proved to be correct, advising her to carry the bare minimum required to undertake her mission; sufficient so she would not arouse suspicion and not enough to burden her.

Earlier this morning, she took a taxi to Holguin's Frank Pais Airport. She paid cash for a ticket on the eleven o'clock flight to Havana. Paying by cash is another of Salbatore's unbreakable rules. The source is impossible to trace and therefore secure. She was surprised to discover the airport has tighter security than Jose Marti. Groups of armed military patrol its periphery; perhaps owing to its relatively close proximity to the naval base. The dour and stony-faced immigration and customs officials prove to be much more diligent in their work. It is one of those rare occasions when she is glad she is not a blue-eyed blonde with an hourglass figure. The men, diligent or not, would certainly take much more notice of her.

She holds her breath as the conveyor carrying the rucksack slowly rolls beneath the black curtain of the luggage scanner. Seconds later, the rucksack rolls out the other side without a flicker in the eyes of the watchful woman glued to the screen.

An hour and forty minutes later, the Aerocaribbean ATR 72-210 softly kisses the steaming runway of Jose Marti.

Terese again pays cash at the Air France ticket counter and books a seat aboard the next day's eight thirty-five flight to Charles de Gaulle. Once at Charles de Gaulle it will be a simple matter of passing through customs with nothing to declare. That leaves a five-hour train journey from Paris to Bayonne. By nine o'clock tomorrow evening she will be on familiar territory, safely back in her own home.

Now all she has to do is book into a hotel close to the airport and then try to grab as much sleep as she can.

The worst is over.

At the same time Terese is registering in her hotel in Havana, a seedy looking individual waits for Viktor and Manuel Suarez in Holguin Airport's utilitarian car park.

'I must apologise for the transport, Senor Rodriguez.' Suarez points at a battered Lada and shrugs his shoulders. 'It's not what you're used to, but it's essential to be more discreet here than in Havana.' He tilts his chin at the man waiting in the car. 'This is my man, Adelmo. He may not look much, but he's good, very good.'

'Senor,' greets the driver, looking up at Viktor over the top of a cheap pair of sunglasses. Viktor peers down at him along the length of his nose.

'Take us to the Hotel Melia, Adelmo,' says Suarez.

'OK, senor.'

Forty-five minutes after checking in, Viktor finds the two men in the hotel's lounge. He thinks Adelmo would be better suited to a home for down-and-outs. Spotty-faced, hair that appears unacquainted with shampoo and wearing a timeworn, creased suit of a nondescript style and indescribable colour, he presents a stark contrast to the immaculately dressed and neatly manicured fixer sitting in the armchair opposite him.

They rise from their seats as he walks towards them.

'Sit down, sit down,' he says, waving his hand.

Suarez snaps his fingers and a waiter appears.

'Would you care for a drink, Senor Rodriguez?' says Suarez.

'Double shot of the best brandy, as it comes.'

'For you, Adelmo?'

'Mojito please, Senor Suarez.'

After the waiter brings their drinks, Suarez relates the conversation he had with Adelmo whilst they sat waiting for Viktor. 'It seems a woman fitting your daughter's description was seen near Moncada two weeks ago with Major General Fortunato, senor. Adelmo here and his . . . friends . . . keep a close eye on a number of, let us say, interesting individuals in the city.'

'Moncada? Where's Moncada?'

'Moncada is the name of a famous barracks in Santiago, no longer used. It's now a school. The Major General spends a lot of his time looking at Moncada and it is almost unknown for him to pass a day without walking to the place. He is always on his own, without exception. So it came as quite a surprise to find him meeting with this woman, who we assume to be your daughter, as I said.'

'Why would she want to meet him? And why there?'

'We have absolutely no idea, senor. Perhaps it was a coincidence.'

Adelmo snorts and then coughs as Suarez shoots him a warning look.

'Adelmo thought the Major General was showing her a piece of history, pointing at the bullet holes where the revolutionaries exchanged fire with the garrison during the revolution. He seemed to be enjoying the attention she was paying him. In the politest way, of course.'

'She listened very attentively, senor,' Adelmo added.

'Three days later,' continues Suarez, 'they were seen again at Moncada. The Major General and your daughter met in exactly the same location and appeared to continue where they previously left off. They walked round the building with your daughter taking notes and the Major General pointing out the occasional sight with his walking stick.'

'Swagger stick,' Adelmo corrects. 'He was dressed as before in full military uniform, which was unusual.' He turns to Viktor. 'Unusual on account of the fact that he is now retired, senor.'

'Swagger stick, yes, such a peculiar name,' says Suarez. 'Anyway, his mood suddenly changed. According to Adelmo, he started shouting at her. He raised the—swagger stick—and pointed it straight at her throat. At this point, your daughter should have been terrified, but the strange thing was she reacted almost as if she expected it. Clearly, she must have said something that made him extremely angry. Then she calmly pushed away the stick and he lowered it to the ground. After that incident, they went their separate ways. Adelmo followed the Major General down to the waterfront, where he stood in the pouring rain for some time, looking out to sea.'

Viktor rubs the side of his nose with his finger. He does not like the sound of what he is hearing, not one little bit. What in hell is Terese doing meeting not once, but twice with a retired high-ranking Cuban officer? He wonders if he should have let Oreaga voice his concerns when he suspected Terese's connection to a secret organisation. No, he is getting ahead of himself. There must be a logical explanation for her actions.

'The following morning,' Suarez goes on, 'Adelmo observed the Major General meeting with his eldest son on the seafront in Santiago. To what ends, we don't know. It may have been coincidence or simply an innocent discussion, but in our experience when two men such as these meet, it's not usually to talk about Major League baseball.'

'The son's name is Oswardo,' cuts in Adelmo. 'A colonel in the air force. A brute of a man and some say a very nasty piece of work.'

Suarez shoots him a filthy look. 'The next morning, your daughter checked out of the Casa de la Mar where she had been staying and we lost track of her for a while. She's very good at losing people, it seems.'

Oreaga's words echo in Viktor's ears. A cold finger traces his spine.

'Five days later, the Major General didn't take his daily constitutional to Moncada. Instead, he asked a friend of Adelmo's called Leonardo to drive him to Guantanamo.'

'Guantanamo? Isn't there an American naval base there?'

'There is, senor, and there is also a lot of Cuban military keeping a watchful eye on it. And one of the sharpest happens to belong to Oswardo Fortunato.'

Viktor turns to Adelmo, pins him with his eyes. 'Did your friend ask this Major General why he wanted to go to Guantanamo?'

Adelmo shrugs. 'Senor, Leonardo is a man of few words; that is his strength. The Major General chose not to talk. It would have been out of character for Leonardo. He prefers to listen.'

'Then in future I think you should use somebody who does talk,' spits Viktor. 'Then we would all know what the hell is going on.'

Suarez raises his hand. 'Please, senor, there is more. Four days later, Leonardo again drove the Major General to Guantanamo. This time, his instincts told him that this was way out of the ordinary, so he decided to keep a discrete eye on the Major General. He said the Major General met with a foreign woman outside the market building and they sat together, deep in conversation, on a wall opposite it.'

'Don't tell me it was Terese?'

'Yes, it was your daughter. Leonardo also observed two men watching them closely.'

'Not the Secret Police, surely?'

Suarez puts his finger to his lips and casts his eyes around the room. 'Please senor, nothing so dramatic. It was Angelo Fortunato and his uncle. It was clear to Leonardo they did not want the Major General to see them. Your daughter and the Major General's meeting was very brief and according to Leonardo, quite terse. Before they separated he passed something to her.'

'A package, senor,' says Adelmo. 'It was a small package.'

More questions pile on Viktor. This man met his daughter on at least four occasions: two in Santiago and two in Guantanamo. Why? If Suarez and his sidekick are to be believed, the initial meetings were tense and laced with threats. Yet this Major General gave her a present during their last meeting. Was it a present, or something else? Something he wants her to deliver for him?

It is time to find some answers.

Viktor turns his wrist, glances at his Rolex Oyster.

18:25.

'Make the call,' he says.

Opposite him in his hotel room, Suarez picks up the handset and asks for an outside line. In his hand, he holds a scrap of paper, numbers scribbled on it. He reads them and then his stubby fingers stab the keypad.

On the fourth ring, a woman's voice answers the phone. 'Hello, Carmen Fortunato here.'

'May I speak with Angelo, please?' says Suarez.

'Who shall I say is calling?'

'It's a business acquaintance of his.'

'One moment, please.'

'Hello.'

'Good evening, Senor Fortunato. You don't know me, but I've been asked to deliver an important message. It concerns the daughter of a very powerful friend of mine. The man is French and—'

'Who is this?'

'Please don't interrupt. This man's daughter is in Cuba on vacation. He believes she took a ride on your trap.'

'What if she did, that's—'

'Please . . . I asked you not to interrupt. Does the name Terese Rodriguez mean anything to you?'

'No.'

'Are you absolutely sure, Senor Fortunato?'

'I couldn't be more certain. Now, if you don't mind I'm in the middle of my dinner and—'

'Do you know your father met with this young woman on a number of occasions?'

'As I said, I've never heard the name.'

'Do not lie to me, Senor Fortunato. You've been seen spying on your father in Guantanamo, accompanied by your uncle, I believe. Your CDR might find that of interest.'

The line falls silent for several seconds. 'How did you—'

'It doesn't matter. The point of my call is simply to arrange a meeting between you and this man. Meet him in the lobby of the Hotel Melia tomorrow morning at eleven. I would advise you to be there if you know what's best for you.'

'Just a minute, I don't know if—'

Suarez slams the phone down and turns to Viktor. 'He'll be there, senor, I can guarantee it.'

Rue Vasserot is the ideal place for one of their safe locations. Forming the bar of the letter 'H' between the uprights of Rue du General Bourbaki and Rue du Capitaine Pellot, it is close to the Adour and the curve of the railway on the north side of the river, yet far enough away from the city centre. A sympathetic supporter of ETA owns the house; a sea captain who is seldom at home and thus not subject to scrutiny. It is a shifting neighbourhood with constant comings and goings, where people mind their own business and where nobody pays much attention to the periodic gatherings at the little house.

Peru takes in the excited faces. He has not seen them this way for some time, certainly not since the Chamartin Station debacle. There is a buzz, a feeling that something momentous is about to take place. Now that he has wrested control from Salbatore his attention is focused solely on a single objective, one with which he has become obsessed: the mass killing of civilians at Barajas International Airport. The location struck him when he noted the density of human traffic during the month of August, a time when almost the whole of the region takes its vacation and when a national disaster will have maximum impact.

All the planning is finalised. The members of his commando have rehearsed their roles repeatedly. They know the operation like the backs of their hands. They will use the well-tried-and-tested diversion of a small incendiary, planted close to the offices of *El Mundo*, which will whip the authorities into response mode. Meanwhile, out at the airport, Peru himself will release the Ebola into a tightly packed destination lounge with devastating results. The authorities won't have a clue how to deal with it. They drill relentlessly for bombings; they have procedures in place for bombings; they have bomb disposal specialists aplenty. Would they have procedures to cope with an airborne virus? Not a chance. They will be clueless as to what has happened. By the time they figure it out, the virus will have done its deadly work.

What if the authorities think it is a ruse, a bluff? They would never imagine ETA to have Ebola in its possession: that is supposed to be the sole preserve of the superpowers. If the authorities do think it is a trick, God help them. Hundreds of innocent people will die because of that miscalculation.

When ETA lays its demands on the table, France and Spain will face a real moral dilemma. Disbelieve and have death on their hands, or believe and give up a territory they have held sway over for hundreds of years.

The commando was unanimous in its agreement to carry out mass murder if it goes down to the wire. They did not hesitate, although he was sure he detected concern in Terese's eyes.

'This is the dawn of a new era,' he says. 'Finally, after years of struggle, we will gain the advantage. There is a moment, not too long off, when our ancestors will be proud of the people in this commando. Posterity will record our names in the history books as the liberators of our nation. Future generations will bestow great esteem on our children and our children's children. France and Spain will be pariahs in the international community, written off as the last imperialist powers in Europe. Not only will we free our land, but we'll be hailed as an example to all peoples struggling to throw off the yoke of a bully.'

A cheer rises from the assembled company. Bottles of wine are uncorked, poured into proffered glasses.

'To liberation!' he yells.

'To liberation!' chorus the commando.

28th July

As she stands in line at Jose Marti airport, the cold fear she felt when she arrived in Cuba grips Terese again. Entry into the country was slow enough; waiting to exit it is glacial. The officials seem to delight in pulling as many passengers as they can to one side, in order to rummage through their luggage.

Maybe they won't be interested in a rucksack, she thinks.

She thinks wrong.

A severe-looking woman, face caked in makeup, points at her and indicates a space on the counter.

'Hello,' greets Terese, forcing her mouth into a wide smile in an attempt to mask her nervousness.

The woman says nothing and motions for Terese to open her rucksack. She fumbles with the drawstrings as the woman's eyes bore into her. The instant she places the knapsack on the counter, claw-like fingers tipped with crimson nails dig inside. She watches as, item by item, the woman extricates the contents and spreads them out. Then the hands pause, halfway down, grasping something.

Terese knows what it is.

As the woman pulls out the cedarwood box Terese's heart skips several beats.

Accusing eyes stare at her. 'Carlos,' the woman calls, beckoning one of the security guards.

Terese freezes. She recognises the man instantly. He is the one who confronted her on her arrival in Havana.

'Yes, Consuela?' he says.

'I have something for you.'

'Ah,' he says, studying the box. 'Hoyo de Monterey. A nice smoke. If only I could afford them.'

Fuck. He's going to take them for himself.

The woman points to an office behind her. Frosted glass, impossible to see what lies inside. She hands the box to the guard. 'Take this to Silvio and ask him to check it.'

She turns to Terese, boredom written all over her face. Clearly, this is something she has done many times before. 'Do you have a receipt, senorita?'

'I . . . I don't, no.' She can't take her eyes off the guard when he looks at her. Is there a flicker of recognition in his eyes?

The woman's voice is insistent. 'They should have provided you with a receipt. Where did you buy them?'

The words are the first to enter her head. 'The market in Santiago.'

'What was the merchant's name?'

'I don't remember.'

'I see.' The woman points to the end of the counter. 'Please wait there.'

Her body begins to shiver, even though the temperature inside the terminal must be in the thirties.

There is nothing she can do except wait.

But wait for what? Did she really think they wouldn't dig into her luggage? Didn't think a problem might present itself at the airport? An unforgiveable oversight. Now she is trapped, caught by a woman who is probably interested only in looking at any fancy underwear she might find in the luggage she searches.

The queue grows shorter. Soon she will be the only one left.

She tries to focus on her watch, but her anxiety won't allow her.

Then the guard returns holding the box.

'It's OK, Consuela. Silvio checked it and the seal hasn't been tampered with.'

The woman grunts, cheated, and instructs the guard to place the box on the counter. Then she beckons Terese and gives a flick of the wrist, which Terese takes to mean she should pack her belongings herself. She stuffs her rucksack as quickly as her shaking fingers permit.

Then she senses the guard closing in on her.

'I remember you, senorita.'

Her stomach shrinks into a tight ball. She glues her eyes to the rucksack, inserts the last item and pulls the drawstring.

'You're a very pretty girl,' says the guard. 'I always remember pretty girls, especially those who don't turn away when my rifle is pointed at them.'

'I'm sorry, but I have to go. I have a plane to catch.'

His hand settles on her forearm and begins to rub it gently. The corners of his mouth turn upwards into a vulpine grin. His breath is rasping, acidic.

'What's the hurry? There will be another one tomorrow. I'll show you a side of Cuba you won't have seen.'

'Corporal Figuera!' barks a gruff voice.

The guard jerks upright as if skewered with a barbecue fork. 'Sir!'

'A word. Now!'

Terese throws the rucksack over her shoulder and sprints for the departure lounge.

29th July

Hotel Melia is located on the corner of Avenidad de Las Americas and Calle M, in the Reparto Sueno district. Built in the early nineties, the fifteen-storey building towers over the city and is Santiago's most prominent landmark. Three hundred rooms cater almost exclusively for foreign visitors. The hotel's Bar Colmadito and the Santiago Café are popular venues where local politicians and officials regularly meet to discuss their affairs.

Viktor spots the man dressed all in white as he enters the lobby of the hotel and attracts the attention of the receptionist, a common-looking girl who for some reason has chosen to dye her black hair an absurd blonde. The girl reflects for a minute, casts her eyes over the few people standing in the lobby and then points a slim finger directly at where he is standing.

'Senor Rodriguez?' the man enquires, looking up at Viktor, who looks haughtily down the length of his aquiline nose at the new arrival. Viktor holds out his hand in greeting and feels a fleshy hand grasp his. The grip is strong and firm. He guesses the man is in his mid thirties or thereabouts.

'Ah, Mister Fortunato, I presume? Yes, I'm Viktor Rodriguez. This is my associate, Senor Suarez.'

'I'm pleased to meet you, Senor Suarez.'

Suarez beams, the gold in his mouth reflecting the lobby lighting. 'My pleasure also, Senor Fortunato.' He shakes Angelo's hand.

'Shall we take coffee?' asks Viktor.

'Sure,' says Angelo.

Once seated in the lounge, which is beginning to fill with tourists and a few locals who can afford the price of the Melia's cuisine, Viktor takes control of the conversation.

'Thank you for meeting with us. It's very important. I'll come straight to the point, Angelo. Do you mind if I call you Angelo?'

'No, please do.'

'Mister Suarez here informs me that your father has met with my daughter on a number of occasions and I find that extremely intriguing. Perhaps you could enlighten me?'

He watches Angelo closely as he asks the question, but there is no sign of a reaction. Clearly, it is not going to be easy to intimidate this man.

'With respect, I think there may have been a mistake. Perhaps it's somebody who looks like my father?'

He inclines his long body towards Angelo. 'Don't take me for a fool, Angelo. People have made that mistake before and they usually regret it.'

'Are you trying to frighten me?' Angelo retorts, rising to his feet.

Suarez gently grips the sleeve of Angelo's shirt. 'Gentlemen, please. There is no need to get excitable. It will focus attention on us. In this place, discretion is essential. Please sit down, Angelo, and listen to what Senor Rodriguez has to say.'

Viktor leans back in his chair and crosses his arms over his chest. 'I apologise, Angelo. It is the action of a concerned father. Do you have children?'

'No,' Angelo squirms in his chair. 'Not yet.'

'A great pity, they bring such joy into one's life, but they also need to be protected. Try to imagine how you would feel if your daughter appeared to be associating with a retired high-ranking officer of a foreign army. You would be worried wouldn't you? And if your daughter was simply taking a vacation wouldn't you be a little ... curious?'

Angelo hesitates and then answers, 'I would be, yes.'

'So you see why I consider it a little strange for your father to be consorting with my daughter, whom, as far as I know, she had never met until she arrived on these shores. And whom he singles out to give a package the contents of which we have no idea?'

Angelo's eyebrows knit. 'A package? What kind of package?'

'A package small enough to be carried by hand and that wouldn't attract much attention. Drugs, perhaps?'

Paling visibly, Angelo holds out his hands in protest. 'No, no, he would never be involved with drugs; that would be against his principles. It must be something else. Perhaps it's a present?'

Viktor eyes blaze. Before he can mouth the next sentence, Suarez cuts him short.

'Senor Rodriguez, please, we will have a much more effective meeting if we lay our cards on the table, no?' Suarez bends his head towards Angelo. 'The fact of the matter is your uncle and you were seen watching your father when he met with Senor Rodriguez's daughter in Guantanamo and your actions suggested you did not wish him to know of your presence. I am sure you have your own reasons to behave in such a manner—they are no business of ours. Senor Rodriguez is merely trying to protect his daughter and any assistance you can offer would be most welcome.' He reaches into his inside pocket and extracts a bulging leather wallet, which he places on the side of his armchair. 'Most welcome.'

Angelo's eyes stray to the wallet. Unconsciously, he licks his lips.

Will he take Suarez's bribe? thinks Viktor.

He soon has his answer.

'I won't be bought, Senor Suarez.' Angelo leans closer to Viktor. 'For your sake, because you are her father, I will tell you what I know. Although you may be disappointed it is so little.'

Suarez slides the wallet back in his pocket.

'Over the past weeks, I have wondered myself why my father was meeting with Terese. That is your daughter's name, isn't it? I could see no reason why he would want to see her again after she departed Santiago, but something in his behaviour aroused my suspicions. My mother told me he informed her that Terese's next stop on her travels would be Guantanamo. Early one morning, a few days after her departure, a local taxi arrived at a ridiculously early hour to pick him up. Now, that also amazed me, as my father never takes a taxi, he always insists on driving himself. I asked my mother where he had gone to, but she implied she didn't know, guessing it may have been Guantanamo to meet my brother Oswardo. Again, that took me by surprise, as in his retirement he has never returned to Guantanamo, a place where he spent the last nine years of his working life watching the comings and goings of the Yanquis. So why would he want to meet her there? Having nothing better to do, my uncle and I decided to follow him and saw him meet with Terese, but we decided not to follow them as they might have spotted us. The very next day, I sought out Leonardo and asked him where he took my father, knowing full well he went to Guantanamo.'

'Leonardo?' queries Viktor, well aware who Leonardo is.

'Leonardo the Limp, our local taxi driver. We call him that as he was born with one leg shorter than the other. Anyway, Leonardo wouldn't tell me and merely tapped the side of his nose with his finger, which I assumed meant that it was something he had been told to keep quiet, undoubtedly by my father. I found that very puzzling. I still do. There should be no reason for secrecy, now that he's no longer on active duty.'

'Go on, Angelo,' urges Suarez.

Angelo holds his hands palms upwards and shrugs his shoulders. 'That's all I know. I'm afraid I have no answers for you, only more questions.'

A waiter arrives with a cafetière, which he places on the table. There is a temporary lull in the conversation whilst he pours coffee into three small cups.

'What do you do for a living, Angelo?' asks Viktor, his tone softening.

'I drive a pony trap, which I use to take tourists on trips around Havana.'

'Do you make much money?'

'Enough,' answers Angelo, guardedly. 'Why?'

Viktor ignores the question. 'How much is enough?'

'I don't see—'

'Indulge me. How much do you earn from this activity?'

'If I make three rides a day I bring in forty, maybe fifty pesos.'

'Approximately fifty dollars, Senor Rodriguez,' chips in Suarez.

'And after expenses?' continues Viktor.

'Half of that,' says Angelo.

'So, let me see. In a year you end up with about seven thousand dollars maximum?'

221

'Possibly a little more.'

'Then let's say ten thousand for argument's sake.' Viktor picks up his coffee cup, takes a gulp and then nods to Suarez who produces a thin sheaf of paper from his inside pocket and lays it face down on the table.

'Is it enough to pay the bills and run a car?' asks Viktor.

Angelo's eyes stray to the paper. 'It's sufficient to pay the bills. I cannot afford to run a car.'

'Would you like to be in a position to run a car?'

'Of course, who wouldn't?'

'And I presume you're good at what you do?'

'Some say I am the best. I know Havana like the back of my hand.'

'Ten thousand dollars, eh? How would you like to earn ten times that amount, Angelo?'

'Another bribe?'

Viktor remains impassive. He looks at Suarez who takes up the conversation.

'You misunderstand us, Angelo. Have you ever visited Varadero?'

'I know of Varadero, although I've never been there myself. All I know is that many tourists end up in the big hotels there after flying in to Havana.'

'Varadero is the future of this country, Angelo. It is where clear-sighted men will generate new wealth. It will be a model for Cuba's economic recovery when the next revolution takes place, but it won't be a bloody revolution this time. When it happens, and it certainly will, we will need commercially astute and ambitious men to lead the country into the next stage of its development. Men like you, maybe?'

Angelo shuffles in his chair. 'You flatter me. I'm just a pony trap operator.'

'We believe you would like to be much more,' says Viktor, noticing Angelo's tongue flicking across his lips.

'Having money like that would raise suspicions,' says Angelo. 'It's too much.'

'Of course it is, but sixty percent of it would be paid into an offshore account. We believe within the next five years the changes that will occur in Cuba will allow you to access these funds and buy the life you so desire. That would please you, no doubt.'

He can imagine what is going through Angelo's mind. In five years' time, the young man could find himself with some three hundred thousand dollars in savings. Never in his lifetime could he accumulate that amount of money offering pony rides. Nowhere near.

Bending forward, Suarez flips the thin sheaf of paper over and slides it across the table. 'This is a contract of employment, Angelo. It is for the post of Operations Manager at Oromundo's prestigious Punta Hicacos development. As you can see, we made it out in your name. All it requires is your signature and your agreement to perform a small favour.'

'Ah, I see. What kind of favour?'

'As I mentioned, our sources inform us that Senor Rodriguez's daughter was handed a small package by your father. We would like to know why that was and what the package contained. That is all. No more, no less.'

Suarez draws a fountain pen out of his pocket, unscrews the top and holds it in front of Angelo.

As he makes his way to the Casa del Toro Negro, Angelo's legs are on autopilot, there are that many thoughts careering wildly inside his head. On the one hand, he has been offered a once-in-a-lifetime chance to achieve many, if not all, of his dreams. In five years' time, he might be in a position to join Rafael in Florida under a completely different set of circumstances. If those circumstances herald a change for the better, he will have a nice stash to begin a new life—with or without Maria. On the other hand, he would have to spy on his own father, reporting to people he has only just met and who are not beyond bribery if that is what it takes to get their way.

He wonders what his father gave to Terese. Could it be something as simple as a memento of Cuba? Impossible. Eduardo would never give a stranger a bauble. Rodriguez and Suarez clearly didn't think it was something so innocent.

The business with the wallet and then the contract of employment intrigues him. Does his father have something they desperately want, and if so, what? Why can't they get the information themselves? He imagines Suarez is a resourceful man with a web of informants. Why is Rodriguez so keen on tracking his daughter's every move anyway? That does not strike him as the kind of thing a normal father would do. Would he have flown all the way to Cuba just to keep an eye on her? Unlikely. Other motives are at work, motives Angelo does not understand. They must be party to other information they didn't reveal in the meeting.

Not my business, he thinks. *All I have to do is find out what's going on and let them know. Then the world could be my oyster.*

As he arrives at the imposing wrought iron gates protecting his parents' house, he spies his father outside the kitchen door, sitting on a chair propped against the wall. On the floor next to him are several well-thumbed books. Eduardo is skim reading them as if searching for some hidden words of wisdom.

'Hello, Pa, looking for something?'

'I'm refreshing my memory. It helps to remind me of this country's more glorious moments. Unfortunately, moments you will never appreciate.'

Glancing at the books piled at his father's feet, he can just make out the title of the top volume.

THE MOTORCYCLE DIARIES: NOTES ON A LATIN AMERICAN JOURNEY BY CHE GUEVARA

Shaking his head, he enters the kitchen where his mother is peeling potatoes.

'Did you have a good walk?' she asks.

'Pleasant. Not much changes here, does it?'

'Thank goodness for that, son. If you want to see change I'm told you need to go to Varadero.'

'Who would want to do that, Ma?' he says, grinning.

As the train pulls into Bayonne railway station, Terese spots him waiting on the end of the rain-lashed platform, struggling against the wind to hold a green and white golf umbrella above his head.

The journey from Paris was a nightmare. The weather in France is unseasonably wet, coming as a shock to her system after sun-soaked, balmy days in Cuba. A torrential downpour has hammered the country ever since she stepped on board TGV 8525 at Paris-Montparnasse. On the outskirts of Poitiers the train was delayed by fifty-five minutes owing to the outage of a signal and failed to achieve its usual breathtaking speed, causing it to arrive an hour and a quarter late in Bayonne.

She looks at her watch. 18:22.

As she alights from the train Fabien rushes forward to meet her and guides her under his umbrella. His lips brush her cheek as she turns her head.

'Hello, darling,' he says, a hurt look on his face. 'I've missed you. I gather the train was held up. Come on, let's get you home so you can freshen up before we eat. I've booked a table at the Moulin-à-Vent for nine o'clock.' Linking his arm through hers, they hurry beneath the station's triangular, glass-covered roof.

'I missed you terribly,' he says, as they pause at the station's exit.

'I missed you, too. Would you mind if I give this evening a miss? I've been travelling for what seems like an age and I'm absolutely dog-tired. Maybe we can do it tomorrow, yes?'

The disappointment dulls his eyes. 'Of course. How remiss of me. I should have realised how worn out you would be. Come on, let's get you home.'

How typical of Fabien, she thinks. *He's far too good for me.*

There was no need for him to brave the elements to meet her, but that is just the way he is: kind, considerate, and thoughtful. Even if it were possible, Peru would never have met her at the station. He would expect her to catch a taxi in spite of the fact she has been absent for a month.

'How was Cuba?' Fabien asks, as they squeeze themselves into the constricted space of his Audi TT.

Her rucksack is crammed into the tiny compartment that passes for a boot and she cannot help thinking how easy it would be for someone to shatter the car's rear window and grab it. It has happened before. Only the previous year her paper ran a series about a smash-and-grab gang operating in the city.

She is tempted to ask him to pull over so she can retrieve it and sit with it on her knee, but how crazy would that appear?

'Cuba was marvellous, absolutely marvellous,' she says. 'It's such a beautiful country and the people there are so accommodating, so very accommodating.'

'That's nice. I want to hear all about it, from the very beginning.'

'Tomorrow, my love, I'll tell you all about it tomorrow.'

As he concentrates on driving, peering through the rain lashing in torrents across the car's windscreen, she leans her head against the side window and pretends to fall asleep.

Thank God for the bad weather, she tells herself.

But Fabien is in a talking mood. 'Did you happen to see your father whilst you were there?'

She jerks upright. 'Where? In Paris?'

'No silly, of course not Paris. Did you see him in Cuba?'

An electric charge passes through her body. 'He went to Cuba? Why would he do that?'

'It was a last minute thing. I think he wanted a break from the office. Oromundo is on the point of signing its first contract with the Cubans and I guess he wanted to show them how important it is by being present. That's to be expected. He is Chairman of Groupe Rodriguez after all. Didn't he contact you while he was there?'

She takes a deep breath before replying, trying to keep a lid on the nascent anger rising inside her. 'No, but the mobile network isn't very good. I didn't pick up any of your messages until after I landed in Paris. You must have sent at least twenty.'

The corners of his mouth curve gently into the trace of a smile. 'I knew that was the reason you didn't answer the calls. I told your father it must be the network they have there when he kept asking me why you hadn't responded.'

Her jaw tightens as anger boils over. 'Why the hell would he keep asking you? What's he been saying? Has he been pushing his bloody nose into my affairs again? Is that the real reason he went to Cuba? To spy on me? Tell me, Fabien!'

Face flushed, he begins to drum his fingers on the steering wheel. 'Why don't you ask him? I'm sick of being piggy-in-the-middle between you two.'

Stunned by his unexpected words, she turns away to watch the reflections of passing lights in the oily blackness outside whilst he concentrates once more on the road. His sharp words are so out of character. Fabien is normally an even-tempered, unflappable man. She can imagine the pressure her father would have applied. It must have been relentless for Fabien to snap like that.

Poor man, what am I putting you through?

'Piggy-in-the-middle?' she says. 'I don't—'

'Forget it!'

They drive on in silence.

'I'm sorry, Terese,' he says as they turn in to the road that leads to her house. 'I'm under a lot of pressure at work at the moment. That outburst was unfair and I'm ashamed of myself. I've missed you so much and as soon as you're back, I rat off at you. I'm so, so sorry.'

She lays her hand on his arm. 'Forget it. It's as much my fault. It's not you I'm angry with, it's my damned father. Being tired doesn't help, either.'

They part with a cursory kiss and a brief exchange of 'Goodnights'. Once inside her house, she digs out her mobile as quickly as she can and punches the unforgettable numbers on the keypad.

Her call is answered on the third ring.

'Did you get the stuff?' asks a husky voice on the other end.

How like Peru, she thinks. *No "How are you?" Or "I missed you" or what at one time I would have hoped to hear, "I love you". Business always comes first.*

'Yes, no problem, it's safe with me,' she says.

'Meet me at Rue Vasserot. Get there as soon as you can and bring it with you.'

'OK.'

'Be quick.'

'I'm on my way right now.'

As she steps out of her house she fails to see the pockmarked man sitting low down in a Renault Safrane parked on the far side of the street. She climbs into the back seat of the waiting Mercedes taxi, her rucksack glued to her lap. As the taxi drives off, the Renault pulls out and follows at a discrete distance.

On Rue Vasserot she slides out, says a few words to the taxi driver and enters an unlit house. The Renault parks fifty metres down the street and then the pockmarked man kills the lights.

Once inside, she places the rucksack gently on the floor and then throws her arms around Peru's neck. Pressing her lips to his, she can smell the salty tang of sweat on his neck and feel the tautness of his body as she crushes him to her.

'God, Peru, I missed you so much. I was beginning to go crazy.'

He gently pushes her away. This isn't quite the homecoming she is expecting after four weeks' absence.

'You were already crazy before you met me, Terese.'

'Let's go to bed right now. I want to fuck the brains out of you.'

'I need to see the stuff first. Where is it?'

'Can't it wait? It's in the rucksack. We can take it to bed with us.'

'Don't be stupid, woman. I don't want to get caught unawares.'

'Get caught unawares? What do you mean?'

His look is hard, accusing. 'I'm worried you might have been followed. You didn't stick to the normal procedure, did you? Why did you take Jean-Paul's taxi?'

She feels her hackles rise for the second time that evening. 'Christ Almighty, Peru! I've been halfway round the world to a country not known for its liberal attitude to human rights to steal one of its most closely guarded secrets. Do you know what they would have done to me if they had caught me? Do you?'

'You would most likely have been tortured and disappeared off the face of the earth. You knew that before you went. It doesn't alter the fact that you've jeopardised this location by not following procedures.'

She grits her teeth, willing herself not to scratch his eyes out. 'I didn't think it was necessary. Fabien thought I would be in Cuba for two more weeks and the weather is so awful you can hardly see your hand in front of you, let alone tail a car, and nobody would ... would ...'

Before she finishes the jumble of excuses, she realises they won't cut any ice with him.

'Grow up, Terese, this isn't some James Bond movie. You go to bed if you're tired, but I'm staying here to keep watch. And don't unpack whatever you do. If we have to move, we'll have to move fast. I'm not going to blow this now just because you made a thoughtless mistake.'

30th July

The morning after their meeting with Angelo, Adelmo drives Viktor and Suarez a short distance from Guantanamo to the mid level of a small hill overlooking the naval base. The two men get out of the car and leave Adelmo, cigarette in hand, waiting by the side of the dusty road. Viktor strides purposefully to a spot where he can get a clear view of the sprawling facility. It takes some time for Suarez to heave his bulk in the tall man's wake and he arrives puffing and panting, his hands resting on his knees.

'Yesterday did not go as planned,' says Viktor.

'No, senor, it did not. Maybe we should increase the offer?'

'Don't be bloody stupid, man, he's not for buying. There must be another way. What do you plan to do?'

Suarez straightens himself. Runs his finger round the inside of his collar.

'I need your answer, Manuel, and I need it *now*.'

The fixer's next words take him by surprise. 'I took some actions last night after you retired, Senor Rodriguez. I have good news for you.'

'Good news, eh? Let's hear it then. I've a business empire to run. Time spent away from my office is costing me a lot of money.' He looks round at the wilderness surrounding them. 'Why have you brought me to this godforsaken place, anyway?'

Suarez points to the base. 'Down there is where I found a nugget. Adelmo has a cousin who, shall we say, provides entertainment for the troops.'

'Cut the niceties. You mean he runs a prostitution racket.'

'Please, senor, show some discretion. It is a capital offence if they find out. Yesterday evening, I asked Adelmo to contact this cousin and see if any of the girls might have seen a foreign woman. Nothing much happens around here without their knowledge and tourists in these parts are rare. It was a long shot, in fact a shot in the dark, but surprisingly it turned up some useful information.'

'Which is?'

'It cost me money to get this information, senor, a lot of money.'

Viktor recognises this game. 'OK, I get the picture. How much?'

'Let us say five thousand dollars, senor.' Suarez licks his lips. A fleck of spittle lodges itself in one corner of his fleshy mouth.

'This had better be worth it, Manuel.'

'It is, senor. I assure you, it is.'

'Go on. I'm listening.'

'I think we should return to the car before I speak.' He inclines his chin towards the base, nestled in an inlet of Guantanamo Bay. 'I don't trust those people. I wouldn't be surprised if they can hear every word we're saying.'

Instructing Adelmo to wait outside the car, they settle in the back seat.

'What I'm about to say may surprise and even shock you,' says Suarez. 'It must not, and I stress must not, be revealed to anyone. If certain people suspect me of knowing what I know, it would be touch and go if I see my next birthday. I doubt also if they would allow you to leave Cuba. They would devise ways and means of implicating you.'

The change in his demeanour is remarkable. No longer is he obsequious, keen to please. Now he is like a cornered rat, prepared to fight to the death.

'I get the message, Manuel.'

'Good, then we understand each other. A girl recently performed a service for a certain officer. Apparently, the girl is almost as afraid of this officer as she is of Adelmo's cousin. Even after a little physical encouragement, she still would not tell the cousin what she had done, not unless he promised to give her and her mother safe passage to Florida. Those girls can be very stubborn, such a pity.' He sighs, shakes his jowls. 'Adelmo's cousin knew how important it was so he agreed, although I have no idea how he will carry out his promise.'

He draws a cream silk handkerchief from his breast pocket and wipes it over his glistening forehead. 'This particular girl not only works the base, she is also a favourite of a small number of local clients in public service. She is very young, very voluptuous, and gives an impression of innocence, which I suppose is the reason she is so much in demand. One of those clients is a senior scientist. The girl has bewitched this particular client and he will do anything she asks, according to her. When the officer approached her with a specific request, that belief was put to the test. No, I correct myself. It wasn't a request: he commanded her. He instructed her to steal a particular item from the scientist's laboratory and bring it to him. He didn't care how she did it as long as it was done. The fact that she did it without argument suggests to me this officer must be very senior and very powerful.'

Viktor's forefinger taps like a woodpecker on the side of his nose as he absorbs the information. He holds back from asking the obvious question. What did she steal?

Suarez continues. 'Somehow, the girl managed to secure this item and passed it to the officer. He threatened that if she ever told anyone what she had done it would be the end for her and her family. That is why she was so reluctant to say anything to Adelmo's cousin.'

Viktor cannot contain himself any longer. 'What was the item?'

Suarez rolls his shoulders. 'That I do not know, but I do know two things for sure. One, the scientist's area of expertise is virology. Two, the officer in question is Colonel Oswardo Fortunato, son of the Major General.'

Peru bangs his fist on the table and curses silently. He is busy repacking the contents of Terese's rucksack when his mobile rings. On the other end of the line, a giggling Martina warns him that two suspicious men are in the vicinity; a giant of a man trailing Terese, who minutes before left the house, and another sitting in a midnight-blue Renault Safrane at the end of the road.

Peering out of the window, he watches a dark-skinned man climb out of the Renault just as Martina passes his front door, flicking her head backwards. Hastily, he slings the rucksack on his back, shoves an empty red wine bottle into the garbage bin and sneaks out the back door just as the front door creaks open. Climbing over the back garden fence, he crosses the enclosed parking quadrangle and slips down an alleyway, emerging on to Rue Benoit Souriges.

He curses again. Next time he sees Terese he will tear a mighty strip off her. Thanks to her carelessness, the safe house is now compromised and they will need to find another. That doesn't worry him overly much—there are plenty of trustworthy sympathisers in the city—but the two men agitate him.

Who are they and for whom are they working?

The phone call from Suarez demanded Angelo meet him and the Frenchman at the Hotel Melia that evening. He protested, making the excuse that he needs more time to consider their very generous offer. Suarez was not to be put off. He said the purpose of the meeting is not about the job in Varadero. He has some information concerning Angelo's brother that Angelo really needs to hear.

Alarm bells rang in his head. Ramon? Oswardo? To which brother is Suarez referring? What has he discovered? Why call him?

Luckily, he was the nearest to the phone when it rang. Thank God it wasn't his father; there would have been a Spanish Inquisition. He had to use another of his excuses, claiming it was a friend looking after the pony in his absence.

His simple life is suddenly becoming very complicated.

He enters the hotel and heads straight for the bottle-blonde receptionist who directs him to the Lookout Pico Real on the 15th floor, where he finds the two men waiting, huddled in a quiet corner. There must be a problem with the air-conditioning. The air in the bar is heavy as a damp blanket, a precursor to the hurricane season. He prays one is not on its way. Nobody wants a repeat of last year when Hurricane Wilma took a tentative nibble out of Havana and then unexpectedly veered off to sea. Not much later Hurricane Dennis arrived, taking a giant bite out of the south of the island. According to the Cuban weathermen, generally regarded as the world's leading experts on hurricanes, another monster is rising. This one could herald a frightening new trend: it might be the first to form in the eastern Caribbean.

'Ah, Angelo, thank you for coming at such short notice. Would you like a drink?' says Suarez, his face set like concrete.

'A glass of water please, Senor Suarez.' He nods at Viktor. 'Senor Rodriguez.'

The Frenchman dips his head. 'It's a pleasure to meet you again.'

It doesn't feel like a pleasure to Angelo. 'I didn't imagine we would meet again so soon,' he says to Viktor, taking a seat opposite the two men.

'Nor did I. However, we urgently need to discuss a development of great importance to us all. It concerns your brother, Oswardo.'

'Oswardo? I don't understand.'

'Manuel, please tell him what you know.'

Suarez wipes his glistening forehead with the back of his hand. He leaks sweat. Damp patches darken the underarms of his beige suit and he is clearly agitated, unlike the calm and unflustered person Angelo met for the first time only twenty-four hours previously. Something must be troubling the man greatly.

'This is a very delicate matter,' Suarez says. 'If ever anyone finds out—'

'Tell him, Manuel,' Viktor growls.

The previously assured, confident fixer wrings his hands and shifts nervously in his seat, constantly looking around the room before he speaks. When he does so, it is in such a quiet voice that Angelo has to strain his ears to hear his words.

'We have some . . . information.'

'Information? What kind of information?' asks Angelo. 'What are you talking about?'

Suarez shushes and places a finger on his lips. 'Your brother is involved with something that could get him shot.'

Ice forms in Angelo's veins and a nervous tic attacks his right eyelid. Involuntarily, he crosses himself and puts his hands together, as if in prayer.

What has Oswardo been up to now? Can it be anything to do with Pa?

An irreconcilable gulf exists between his father and him and yet, despite their deep-rooted differences, he still loves the man who served his country so honourably.

'There has been a development since the last time we met,' says Suarez, sweat continuing to bubble on his brow. 'Senor Rodriguez and I have it from a trustworthy source that your brother was involved in the stealing of a sensitive item from a highly classified research establishment in Guantanamo last week. Not directly, of course, but it appears he constructed the plan to obtain the item.'

Angelo's jaw drops; he cannot believe what Suarez is saying. 'No, no, there must be some mistake. Oswardo would never steal from anyone, let alone the government. You don't know him as I do. He's incorruptible.'

Viktor cuts in sharply, 'No, Angelo, I'm afraid there is no mistake and I may be jumping in with both feet, but I'd like to know why your fucking father and brother are involving my daughter in whatever it is they're scheming. Perhaps you'd like to try and join the dots for me?'

'I . . . I really don't know.'

'Don't you? Then let me make it simple for you. Your brother travels all the way from Guantanamo to see your father in Santiago. Why would he do that? A social visit? If that was the case your brother would have called in to see your mother, wouldn't he? Not long after, your father has a meeting with my daughter, also in Guantanamo. Then a certain item goes missing—is stolen—from a highly secure government laboratory. A senior officer in the Cuban Air Force arranges the theft of this item. Guess who? Sometime later, my daughter again meets your father in Guantanamo and, as you know from our recent meeting, he hands her a small package. Now maybe I'm putting two and two together and coming up with five, but maybe, just maybe, whatever it was that was stolen might just be the same thing that your father passed to my daughter.'

'I'm sorry, Senor Rodriguez, but I'm completely confused. Why would Oswardo steal this item and what is it? He never—'

'We don't know,' butts in Suarez. 'What we do know is that it was stolen from under the nose of an eminent virologist.'

Angelo's eyebrows knit. 'A what?'

'A virologist. That's someone who studies the diseases caused by viruses and the techniques to isolate and culture them. Viruses have the potential for use in research and therapy.'

'And germ warfare,' adds Viktor, eyes narrowed.

'Shit! You don't think Oswardo—'

'We don't know.'

Angelo's mind attempts to string events together in their correct chronological sequence. His father's meeting with Terese in Santiago, his visits to Guantanamo and the tête-à-têtes with Oswardo. He can slot a number of pieces of the puzzle in place, but just as many are missing. Nobody is more patriotic than Oswardo; he would die for his country. So why would he do something that could have devastating consequences? What cause is so compelling that he steals from his own government? Had he really stolen a virus from this lab? Who would want to use it as a weapon?

Viktor's voice brings him back to the conversation.

'I think you should have a word with your brother for all our sakes, Angelo.'

'But I don't—'

'For all our sakes!' hisses Suarez, smashing his fist on the table.

No matter how hard he tries, the pieces of the mental jigsaw Viktor is struggling with simply will not fit together. He marshals the facts, tries again. Eduardo, Angelo, Oswardo, Terese, the tart and the scientist. These are the actors in this complex play. Havana, Santiago and Guantanamo are the settings. Meetings, threats, a package and a terrorist organisation are elements in the plot. He tries one more time. No, still no good, it simply does not make sense. Some crucial piece of information must be missing and he doesn't have any idea as to what it might be. In some ways he is glad he doesn't. He is more comfortable on his home turf where he knows the score and calls the shots. Cuba is an unknown entity and, apart from Suarez, he has no one he can trust. Then again, can he trust Suarez when the chips are down? He saw another side to the fixer during the last meeting with Angelo Fortunato. Something scared the man, scared him badly, and if Suarez was scared, it could only mean one thing.

He is terrified of being spirited away in the night never to be seen again.

What's Terese up to?

Jacques Oreaga's words keep haunting him. *'I thought you might say such a thing, monsieur. That's why I had Henri and Paolo follow her at different times on different occasions. Same result. She lost them both.*

Are you sure she's not involved with . . . Shall we say . . . any clandestine organisations?'

To the best of his knowledge there are only two subversive organisations operating in the Basque Country: ETA and Al-Qaeda, and he can rule out the latter immediately.

That leaves ETA.

The idea that she is part of a terrorist organisation is frankly ridiculous. Why should she, a well-educated, talented woman embarking on a rewarding career in the field of journalism want to be involved with crazy people who are prepared to blow their fellow men to smithereens in order to pursue their misguided aims? Are they blackmailing her over something her journalistic sniffing has uncovered? If she had showed any militant tendencies surely he would have noticed, wouldn't he? He makes it his business to know everything she does, watching her closely since she graduated from the Sorbonne.

'Are you sure she's not involved with . . . Shall we say . . . any clandestine organisations?'

The words dog him. He ticks off the unanswered questions in his mind one more time.

One: why did she travel to Cuba alone in the first place? A holiday break is the simplest and most obvious answer. But why not ask Fabien to accompany her? OK, he says he is too busy, which makes sense. But why didn't she ask him to join her later? If, as Fabien said, she would be in Cuba for six weeks, she could have asked him to join her after the August holiday peak was past.

Two: how did she happen to have a copied photo of Angelo Fortunato in her possession? Where did she obtain it and for what purpose? Why had she immediately sought him out as the porter reported? Had she planned to meet him beforehand? If so, why?

Three: what was her purpose in meeting with Fortunato's father, a retired Cuban officer? Did it have something to do with an assignment for her paper? If that was the case, then why did she tell Fabien she was in Cuba on holiday? She met with the Major General on at least three occasions to Suarez's knowledge. If she is researching a piece for *El Correo* then surely three meetings wouldn't have been necessary. Why did she travel to Guantanamo when it would have been much more convenient to conduct an interview in Santiago where the retired man lives?

Four: why did he pass a package to her and what did it contain?

Lastly, and most important of all: where is she now?

Her whereabouts would be the easiest to discover and he resolved to get an answer as soon as possible. After his meeting with Angelo, he despatched Suarez and Adelmo with a single objective: to find her whereabouts. Tomorrow, he plans to attend the contract signing ceremony with the Cuban officials in the Capitolio Nacional in Havana, to formalise the relationship for the Punta Hicachos project. Afterwards, thank God, he will be free to fly home and brief Oreaga. There are things to be done and soon.

The phone's shrill ringing interrupts his machinations.

'Yes?'

'It's Manuel, Senor Rodriguez. I have the information you seek. Your daughter boarded the eight thirty-five evening flight to Paris yesterday.'

'She left the country?'

'Yes, senor, she did.'

Another unanswered question joins his list. Why has she cut her holiday short? It can only be something connected to that damned package. It is time to return to Bayonne and find out exactly what she is playing at.

'Manuel, would you book me on a flight to Paris? Make it the first available after the signing. I must take my leave and return to Bayonne. You can explain my hasty departure to the joint venture people—say there's been a family emergency and I've had to go home at short notice. I'm sure they'll understand.'

'I am sure they will, Senor Rodriguez. I will make the flight arrangements first thing in the morning.'

'Oh, and by the way, Manuel. Next time we meet you can tell me what the hell is worrying you so much about the Fortunatos.'

Replacing the handset, he paces the length of the room. Taking his mobile out of his pocket, he punches in the numbers. Nothing happens. He glances at the display: EMERGENCY ONLY. The room must be in a dead spot.

He picks up the room phone.

A deadpan voice answers. 'Yes, senor?'

'I'd like to place an international call to Bayonne, France.'

'Could I have the number, please?'

'0033-5-59-55-00-31.'

'Would you say that again, please?'

He slowly repeats the number.

'Thank you, sir. One moment.'

Impatiently drumming his fingers, he waits for the call to connect. On the fifth ring, the voice of Jacques Oreaga answers.

'Groupe Rodriguez Security.'

'Jacques, it's me. I need you to do something for me. Find out what you can about any ETA activities in Bayonne, anything they're rumoured to be planning in the region. It doesn't matter how unimportant or insignificant—document it. Assemble a dossier and have it on my desk in the office by tomorrow evening at the latest.'

The tinny voice on the other end of the phone is barely audible. 'ETA, Monsieur Rodriguez? Did you say ETA?'

Viktor swears, shouts down the line. 'ETA, Jacques! E.T.A . . . ETA! Do you hear me?'

'I hear you, Monsieur Rodriguez. I'll see what I can do.'

'That's not good enough, Jacques, you'll do more than that and if my daughter should happen to turn up in Bayonne you're to stick to her like glue. Like glue, do you understand? I don't care if she sees you; do not let her out of your sight for a single second. Is that clear?'

'Clear as daylight, monsieur. I will see to it.'

'Make sure you do, Jacques, make sure you do.'

He slams down the phone.

31st July

Angelo feels like he has been rolled up from the inside. Last night was the most disturbed night's sleep since those inerasable, traumatic days serving in Angola. There, it was the high-pitched whine of a bullet and the dull thud as it struck its human target that tormented his sleep.

He was lucky. His country's involvement was at an end and his time there was only short. Nonetheless, it took a long time for him to stop hearing that whining at night after he returned to Cuba. At one stage the nightmares were so bad that he abandoned the marital bed completely and took to sleeping in the living room of his cramped married quarters at the barracks. Even then, his and Maria's lovemaking was declining dramatically in its frequency and intensity.

No bullets whined in his ears last night. Last night the spectre of a wraithlike figure refused to leave him in peace. It persisted in floating in and out of his consciousness. The wraith morphed into a blurry image of Oswardo that swirled about, crowing; a dark figure with a sneering, cavernous mouth full of gleaming white teeth. It evaporated and gave way to the distorted figures of Viktor and Suarez, screaming and pointing at him. Oswardo reappeared and shook a ham-sized fist at Angelo. Then a deadpan Suarez drew a glinting knife and sliced it viciously across Oswardo's sneering mouth.

Blood spurted everywhere, spraying the scene in a fine red mist, but the mouth went on laughing, louder and louder and louder until everything began to spin, faster and faster until Angelo jerked awake, sweat streaming out of every pore.

Oswardo terrifies Angelo; has done since they were kids. When there were just the two of them in the days before Ramon was born Oswardo made certain Angelo knew who was boss, sometimes delivering a sly punch to his younger brother's stomach where it wouldn't leave a telltale mark. Perhaps Oswardo considers him a threat to his father's favour; perhaps he simply has a nasty streak. It doesn't matter. Angelo avoids his brother whenever he can. When Ramon came on the scene, Oswardo, maybe because of the opportunity to throw his weight around, took it into his mind to treat the slightest remark to Ramon as an excuse to confront Angelo. He was quick with his fists was Oswardo and when he hit Angelo it hurt, *really* hurt. All these years later he still thinks of Oswardo as the teak-tough boy he grew up with. It is as if all his childhood memories have frozen and grown old with him, unchanging. Nowadays they seldom speak to each other, not even when thrown together in the bosom of the family. Under normal circumstances they largely ignore each other. But these are not normal circumstances and Angelo knows it. It is a great shame that Oswardo and he are not on better terms. It would seem his brother is a lock that only his father is capable of picking.

There is only one course of action available to him and that sends shivers down his spine.

He will have to face up to Oswardo himself. There is simply no alternative.

As dawn breaks, he calls Oswardo, saying they desperately need to meet. A surprised Oswardo attempts to make a joke of it, saying if Angelo wants a marriage guidance counsellor then he is talking to the wrong man and why is he calling him at that time of day? Angelo informs him there is something Oswardo needs to know, something that cannot be discussed over the phone. Oswardo scoffs, but takes notice when Angelo says it could threaten his career.

Angelo borrows Felipe's taxi and finds Oswardo on the highway, midway between Santiago and Guantanamo. The road is empty when he espies a dark green jeep, nestled against a field of sweetcorn. He pulls over, cuts the engine. Stomach churning, he climbs out of the car and walks slowly to where his brother is inspecting the long, tightly shrouded, green-leaved cobs.

'It's been a good crop this year,' he says, nerves jangling.

Oswardo turns and glares at him without saying a word, then resumes his examination.

'I need to talk to you, Oswardo.'

'So you said. Talk away, brother.'

'There is a woman—'

'Don't tell me you've fallen in love? Whatever would Maria say?'

The vein in Angelo's temple begins to twitch. It is no use going round the houses to get to what he has to say. Best to get straight to the point no matter what Oswardo's reaction might be.

'Who was seen receiving a package from Pa outside the market building in Guantanamo.'

Oswardo's back stiffens. 'So? Perhaps she's an admirer of his.'

'The package may have contained something that was stolen.'

Oswardo's lip curls. 'Perhaps he's making a little money on the side to boost his pension.'

'They say a virus was stolen from a highly secure research facility in Guantanamo. They say you stole it.'

This time there is no smart quip from Oswardo. He turns to face Angelo, straightens himself and puts his clenched fists on his hips, elbows jutted. '*They*? Who are *they*?'

'A Frenchman and a Habanero called Suarez. They know you're involved somehow.'

'You've lost me. I don't know any Frenchman or a Suarez. I think you must be having bad dreams. Perhaps it's guilt at not fulfilling your marital duties, eh?'

'At least my wife didn't abandon me.'

As soon as the words are out of his mouth, he knows he shouldn't have said them.

Lightning-quick, Oswardo leaps at him and clamps a meaty hand tightly around his neck. 'Why, you piece of shit, I should kick the fuck out of you for that.'

Angelo claws at the hand, but it's like trying to open a crocodile's jaw. Forcing the words out of his mouth he says, 'The girl squealed on you. I wouldn't be surprised if there's a reception committee waiting for you back in Guantanamo.'

Oswardo's hand springs open as if a size 12 boot has kicked him in the balls. 'What girl?'

Angelo sucks in air, coughs, massages his neck with his hand. 'Look Oswardo, listen to me for once will you? I don't know what you and Pa have got yourselves mixed up in, but it links back to the Frenchman's daughter. I know this because I've met him and Suarez. The Frenchman is a powerful man, a very powerful man. He's connected to some very ruthless people in Cuba. Suarez is some kind of agent who works for him. It was his people who found the prostitute at the base. She told them about the scientist and then she told them about you. What are you up to?'

Oswardo's shoulders slump and he lets out a keening noise. Gripping his head in his hands, he shakes it viciously from side to side.

'Christ, what's Pa done? What have I got myself into? This wasn't supposed to happen. He said it was for a cause, a good cause!'

Angelo's head spins at the words, unable to process what he is hearing. Never has he seen his brother react in this way.

'What wasn't supposed to happen, Oswardo?'

'We'll all be disgraced! Fuck! Fuck! Fuck! They'll kill me!'

'Who?'

'The Castros! The minute they find out, that's it. We're done for!'

Gingerly, Angelo places his hand on Oswardo's quaking shoulder. 'I don't think the authorities will find out.'

The look he receives is one of utter loathing. 'Don't be so stupid, of course they'll find out! They'll seek out the girl then go straight to me. I'm dead meat.'

'They won't find the girl. The girl's gone. All her family is gone.'

Oswardo's eyes fly open. 'Gone? Gone where?'

'Florida.'

'How the hell would they get to Florida?'

Angelo shrugs and shakes his head. 'I don't know, but I suspect it might be Suarez's doing. Now don't you think you should tell me all about it?'

Oswardo scratches the stubble on his lantern jaw and nods. 'I knew it was a strange request Pa was making, but he said he needed it and so I agreed to get it for him.'

'Strange? Stealing a lethal virus from a secret government establishment? That's not strange, that's bloody suicidal. What was going through your head? Didn't you question Pa as to why he wanted it?' Angelo's brazenness surprises him. Not for many a long year has he dared to speak to his brother in this way.

'Oh, he told me exactly why he wanted it. The woman's on some kind of a mission. He knew straight away that she was connected to a terrorist organisation and it didn't take him long to put two and two together and figure out that the organisation in question was ETA.'

'ETA? What's ETA? I've never heard of it,' Angelo lies.

'A very committed organisation that believes their country—the Basque Country that sits in both France and Spain—should have its own language, governance and culture. They'll use whatever means to achieve their aims.'

'Oh, my God, this gets worse. And you still went ahead and did what he asked?'

'Sure I did. Haven't you noticed how the old man is rotting inside? No, I don't suppose you have since you only ever argue with him. It was the passion in his voice, the sparkle in his eyes when he asked me for the favour, Angelo. It was as if he had found something to breathe new life into him in his retirement. You wouldn't understand, but it was something he needed to do and he wanted me to help him to do it. How could I refuse?'

Sometimes Angelo finds his brother impossible to fathom. Oswardo's logic can be flawless, yet fatal at the same time.

'Weren't you afraid the girl might tell someone?' he asks.

'I took steps to ensure she didn't.'

Angelo doesn't want to hear any more. He has no appetite to gain an understanding of whatever 'steps'

Oswardo took. Now he realises the truth in what he has always suspected; that his father and brother, both cast in the same mould, are capable of absolutely anything without regard for others.

'Well, she did tell someone, Oswardo, and that someone told this man called Suarez, who in turn passed it on to the Frenchman. What if that someone also passed on what he knew to others?'

'That isn't possible.' Oswardo's eyes harden. 'I wasn't telling the truth when I said I don't know anyone named Suarez. We sometimes use his services when the need arises and we don't delve into his means. If Suarez got the information from his network, I can assure you it won't leak out as it would cost him his reputation and place him in a very uncomfortable position with certain people he would have no desire to cross.'

In the name of God, it's another world, thinks Angelo.

'I've been thinking,' Oswardo continues, stroking his moustache. 'There is a way out of this. We have to prevent the Frenchman's daughter using the virus for whatever purpose she has in mind. If we can do that, then—'

'Wait!' Angelo holds up his hand. 'You mean find her and take back the package?'

'It's not that simple.'

A cold finger runs down Angelo's spine. *Where is Oswardo's twisted logic taking him now?*

'Oh? Why not?'

'It's Pa. He insists she has the stuff.'

Angelo's brow furrows. 'Why?'

'I didn't ask and he didn't say.'

'Don't you find that strange?'

'I don't poke my nose into his business, but this time perhaps I should make an exception.' He looks Angelo in the eye. 'We have to find the woman.'

'And how exactly do *we* plan to do that? I wouldn't be surprised if she's left Cuba by now and is halfway to France, if that's where she's heading.'

Oswardo smiles, lips curling over his teeth. 'I won't—you will. You'll have to tell Rodriguez the whole story and trust his conscience will lead him to do what's right.'

'Do what's right? Are you crazy? This is a man without a conscience, and if he did have one, how do you think he would react to the news that his beloved daughter is carrying a deadly virus back to her homeland in order to carry out chaos? Because that's the only reason I can see that she wants the stuff. Now, I do understand why Pa sympathises with her, but he's way off beam this time. In his mind, he's still living the revolution, but he doesn't realise the game's different now. This time it's not guns against the army in the cause of removing a greedy and corrupt regime. This time it's an invisible killer disease inflicted upon a civilian population. You got us into this mess and I don't see why I should be the one who tries to get us out of it. I would—'

'Think about it, Angelo. Pa can't be seen to meet with the Frenchman—we both know the bigwigs still keep a close eye on him. How does the saying go? "Keep your friends close and your enemies closer". And I have no reason for so doing, whereas you have a perfectly good excuse in discussing the offer Suarez made you.'

A fist grips the inside of Angelo's stomach. 'What offer? How do you know he made me an offer?'

'I told you, we sometimes contract the services of Suarez.'

His eyes bulge. 'I don't believe it! You've been spying on me, your own brother?'

Oswardo shrugs his shoulders. 'Let's say the welfare of our family is my first priority. I take certain precautions to ensure it's well protected. Unfortunately you are the weakest link.'

'You patronising bastard! What if I refuse to tell the Frenchman?'

'You won't, because I know your conscience won't leave you in peace if you do. Do it, Angelo. Do it now, for the family.'

Viktor is halfway through packing his case when the call comes.

'Yes?'

'It's Angelo Fortunato, Senor Rodriguez. It's an urgent matter. I have something you need to hear. Please do not ask Senor Suarez to join us.'

'Why not?'

'I have a good reason. This is for your ears only.'

He looks at his wristwatch. 8:20.

'I'll meet you here in the bar at nine o'clock.'

'I'll be there.'

A little over forty minutes later, the two men sit facing each other in a quiet corner of the lobby bar. It is completely empty, save for the presence of a barman, stomach bulging over too-tight trousers, chatting in English to two elderly women.

Viktor cannot believe his ears. It is too bizarre to imagine. 'Are you implying my daughter is in possession of a virus,' he says, incredulous, 'that was stolen from your government and passed on to her by your father?'

Angelo splays his hands. 'I know it sounds unbelievable, but yes, that's exactly what I'm saying.'

'How did you find this out?'

'I had words with my brother.'

'The colonel?'

'Yes, Oswardo.'

'And he volunteered the information, just like that?'

'It wasn't quite that easy. But when I faced him with a few home truths, he told me.'

Viktor doesn't articulate the thoughts racing through his mind. Is Terese really a member of ETA? What could possibly have motivated her to join it? Wouldn't Oreaga have picked up some giveaway clue? How could she possibly keep it secret even if it is true? Then again, how can it *not* be true? Everything fell into place when Angelo gave him the information about the package's contents. That was the final piece needed to complete the jigsaw. Nevertheless, even with that knowledge, he still finds it impossible to believe she could be implicated.

Think it through Viktor, think it through, his brain tells him.

'Does either your brother or your father know you're here?'

'My brother is aware of our meeting, but my father has no knowledge that I know you.'

'Good, let's keep it that way and then there's one less person to worry about.'

'Excuse me, I don't follow you?'

Before he can reply, a group of men and women disturb the stillness of the bar, laughing and talking animatedly as they work their way around the bar's tables, taking up residence at one close to the two men. This is the time when many of the tourists are making ready for their excursions into Santiago and the surrounding areas. A couple, wrapped tightly around each other, follow the group. The woman whispers coyly into the man's ear as they glide across the floor.

'I think we should continue this conversation in a less public place,' says Viktor. 'Follow me.'

They look an odd couple as they cross the floor of the hotel: the gangling, grey-haired man in a formal, dark-blue pinstripe suit and his shorter, slightly pot-bellied companion wearing a white fedora and dressed in a white T-shirt, white trousers and white sneakers.

They halt under a palm tree some twenty metres away from the glass-roofed tube leading to the lobby of the hotel.

'Let me get this perfectly clear in my head, Angelo. It's a little hazy right now. My daughter meets your father four times: twice in Santiago, twice in Guantanamo. During their last Guantanamo meeting, he's seen handing her a package. You now tell me the content of that package is a highly deadly virus that your brother arranged to have stolen from a top government scientist. So, in summary, it reads to me like this: my daughter knows of your father before she comes to Cuba. She knows he has access to something that she wants. He, willingly or unwillingly, agrees to obtain it for her and enlists the help of your brother, who then 'acquires' the virus from this scientist and then passes it to your father who parcels it up and gives it to her. How does that sound?'

'There is one thing missing, Senor Rodriguez.'

'Oh, and what might that be?'

'My brother told me why she wants the virus. According to what my father told him, she requires it to carryout an operation.'

'An operation? You mean an operation as in a terrorist plot?'

Angelo winces and holds up his hands. 'Steady, senor, I didn't say the words "terrorist plot"; you're putting them in my mouth. My brother surmised the virus was going to be used to further your daughter's organisation's ambitions.'

'Organisation? What organisation might that be?'

'My brother said he doesn't know for sure, but his guess is that there could be only one organisation that would go to these lengths.'

Viktor's mind races. If they aren't sure which organisation is behind Terese it would be best to let them pick the obvious scapegoat. If they are stupid enough to believe an Islamist movement would recruit a Catholic woman, he isn't about to convince them otherwise.

'Of course, I should have known it would be Al-Qaeda,' he says.

'No, that wasn't the name he gave me. The name he told me was an organisation named ETA. Do you know this name?'

It is pointless answering the question with a lie; it is clear the Fortunatos aren't fools and they certainly aren't stupid. Now Terese has what she came for, he is convinced they will decide it best to bury the whole episode. He doesn't care what happens to them. All he cares is how he will alter the course on which his daughter is set.

'Of course I know of ETA,' he says. 'It's a terrorist organisation in my country.'

'Then why is your daughter in such an organisation?'

He moves closer, looming over Angelo. 'That's not a question that should concern you. It's *my* business and *my* business alone. If I were you, I would ask yourself this: what is it that would motivate your father to obtain a highly dangerous substance for a woman whom he has never previously met? Why go to all that trouble and take such risks? She clearly has information about him that he doesn't want the world to know.'

1st August

Viktor's mood is dark. That morning he landed in Paris and immediately chartered a private helicopter to Bayonne. As soon as his feet touched the ground, he dashed to his Bentley and instructed his chauffeur to drive him to Groupe Rodriguez Tower. During the journey he berated the poor man for driving too slowly, threatening to sack him if he did not floor the accelerator.

Tension in his office is tangible, the dry air crackling with static as Jacques Oreaga stands in front of Viktor's desk like an errant pupil awaiting his headmaster's punishment.

'What kind of incompetents are you employing, Jacques?' he screams, jabbing a finger at Oreaga. 'My instructions were very simple. "Do not lose her," I said. What part of that didn't they understand?'

Oreaga remains motionless, his unblinking eyes meeting Viktor's.

'With respect, monsieur, my men are not incompetents. They are first class operatives, handpicked by me for their skills and experience. We have worked together for many years and I can assure you this has never happened before. I have no excuses, only a suggestion and one that I know you won't want to hear.'

Viktor groans, sensing what Oreaga is about to say. 'Don't tell me Jacques, let me guess. I have an awful feeling you're about to inform me that Terese is involved with a terrorist group.'

'I have considered every possibility and I keep returning to that, monsieur. They must have devised a procedure for losing a tail that, taken together with a deep knowledge of the local geography, enables them to evade pursuit. It will take us a while to come up with a way to crack this procedure, but I assure you, crack it we will.'

'How long, Jacques? How long will it take?'

'Not long, but we have to be careful. DGSE and the Spanish Secret Police will also be snooping around ETA. You wouldn't want those people to turn their attention to your activities, would you?'

He is quick to grasp the implication in Oreaga's words. Should Groupe Rodriguez appear on the radar of the authorities they might pry into other things that shouldn't concern them. If they do, and happen by chance to turn over a few choice stones, the whole of his business empire would be in danger of tumbling down around his ears.

'You're right, Jacques, of course. I bow to your expertise in this matter. Now tell me, did you uncover much about the local commando?'

Oreaga slides a thin manila folder across the desk. 'There are volumes and volumes in print and in official records about ETA, and the internet is a mine of information. To begin with, I have concentrated on building a profile of the local organisation, together with some background information.'

'Will you summarise it for me? I'll read the details later today.'

'Certainly, monsieur.'

Oreaga retrieves the file and clears his throat. From his top pocket he extracts a pair of gold-rimmed spectacles and hooks them over his ears.

'ETA used to be organised in a hierarchical manner with a leading figure at the top. However, in recent years they have completely changed the structure to one based on commandos, largely owing to the fact that they are more difficult to infiltrate and, if one is, it doesn't result in the whole organisation being put at risk. The military wing of ETA operates through armed commandos of between three and seven members, whose objective is to conduct attacks in a specific geographic area. Currently, there are many itinerant commandos not linked to any specific area and thus more difficult to capture, like the one here.'

'Do you know that for sure?'

'I have an old colleague in the DGSE who does me the odd favour from time to time. He provided me with some of the individuals suspected of being members. May I show you?'

Viktor nods and Oreaga walks round the desk to stand next to him. He lays down the folder, flips over a couple of pages and taps his finger on a grainy photograph.

'This man is Doctor Salbatore Vasco. Single, thirty-three years old, born in San Sebastian. Father a pharmacist, mother a teacher. His parents divorced when he was seventeen. He studied chemical engineering at the Bilbao University of Deusto obtaining an excellent grado. He then stayed on to obtain a doctorado in chemical and catalytic reaction engineering. Currently employed by AgraChem in Bayonne. Attends mass every Sunday, as regular as clockwork. No criminal convictions, as clean as a whistle. On the face of it, Dr Vasco appears to be a model citizen. Intelligence has it that he may be the leader of the commando and its explosives genius.'

Oreaga turns over the page.

'Martina Trevino, twenty five. Single, born in Saint-Jean-de-Luz. Mother died in childbirth; father a dockhand and a known ETA sympathiser. She left school to join Cordoba Communications where she still works as a networking specialist. Football fanatic, attends Athletic Bilbao matches whenever she can. Nothing adverse on her record, apart from the usual teenage stuff—drinking and experimenting with drugs.'

Viktor studies the girl's photo. The Groupe Rodriguez building is in the background. She is tomboyish, ponytail poking through a baseball hat, combat trousers, trainers and an Athletic Bilbao football shirt. He turns over to the next sheet in the folder. This time there isn't a close-up photo, just a couple of long distance shots of a lean, tanned man, smoking a cigarette.

'And this is?'

'I'm still piecing this one together, monsieur. We know this man regularly associates with both Vasco and Trevino. As yet, we haven't been able to identify him. DGSE assumes he lives somewhere near the quays as that's where he's been seen on three separate occasions. He doesn't appear to have a job judging by the times they've spotted him, although that doesn't rule out the possibility that he could be a shift worker.'

'Any idea at all who he might be?'

'It would be too early for me to guess and I can only ask my contact at DGSE for so much at a time, without arousing suspicion.'

'I understand, Jacques. Keep at it and let me know immediately anything develops.'

'I will, monsieur. Enjoy your reading.'

Before leaving for work, Peru stows the cigar box in the false bottom of a suitcase tucked away in the loft of the house he shares with his father. In a little over half an hour, he will be supervising the night shift working on the new CCTV and building management system for the Port of Bayonne. The system will provide a state-of-the-art, integrated communication and security solution for the port. In order to meet an aggressive deadline, the project is running around the clock.

He is still annoyed with himself and fuming with Terese. What was she thinking? She knows the procedure. Never, ever move around without the shadow. Never. It is written in stone. A cardinal rule. Why didn't she contact Martina on her arrival at the railway station? If she couldn't get in touch with her, why not call one of the others? She made an unforgivable mistake, one that could cost them their freedom and jeopardise the project and his future. God knows what could happen if they are exposed.

Thank heavens Salbatore devised what he considers a foolproof procedure and the men spotted by Martina hadn't taken Peru by surprise.

'There are two of them', she said when she called him. 'A huge guy following Terese and one with dark glasses heading straight for you. I'll deal with the tail; you'd better make yourself scarce.'

Yes, it was a narrow escape.

Whoever these people are, they are good, very good. He was foolish to underestimate them and now the commando will need to be doubly cautious. The men must have been watching Terese's every move, although why they would do that is beyond him. He knows the authorities have their suspicions of Salbatore as his connections with ETA go back well over a decade. Yet in all that time suspicion is all they have and without proof they are dead in the water. Salbatore has always been very careful and that has paid dividends. Peru assumes they will also have Martina in their sights, given the openly declared sympathies of her father, Noel. Noel is a strong trade unionist and a hardened worker, not afraid to voice his opinions and one of his strongest opinions is his support for an independent Basque state. However, he has never gone so far as to turn his opinions into actions and although the authorities listen to his ranting they consider him to be all noise and no substance. If only they realised how mistaken they are. Noel has a worldwide network, the strands connected by the many seamen passing through the Port of Bayonne. Seamen whose hands, if examined closely, would reveal they have never undertaken manual work. Strange to think the customs and immigration people pore over their papers and scrutinise their faces, but never have the wherewithal to ask to see their hands.

Apart from Salbatore and Martina, Peru always considered the rest of them to be invisible as far as any connection to ETA is concerned. They all keep a low profile and are careful where they go and who they meet. Without exception, none of them has ever been in real trouble with the police.

So why have these men latched on to Terese, the least likely person to be involved with ETA, given the standing of her father in the community? Has she let something slip to Fabien in an unguarded moment? Has Fabien engaged someone to watch her? No, surely that is too fanciful. Fabien wouldn't know how to go about it. On the other hand, it is a possibility and one Peru will need to explore.

He resolves to give Terese a dressing-down in the next meeting and remind her how a loose tongue can have devastating consequences. Never again will she make the same mistake.

He will make sure of that.

Viktor still cannot believe it. His youngest and most promising daughter is a member of one of the most reviled terrorist groups in existence.

Oreaga dispelled any lingering doubts the previous day.

'We've cracked the way they operate, monsieur. They work in pairs. It's like the way the old Stasi used to operate, but owing to resource constraints it's rarely used nowadays. They've altered it a little and mobile phone technology has afforded some refinement, but essentially, it's the same. This morning, Paolo and two of my men who hadn't worked on this operation tried out a counter measure. I won't bore you with the details, but they confirmed that your daughter is paired with Martina Trevino, the woman in the ETA file. Only unlike the last time, this time your daughter was the lookout for Trevino. Trevino met with Vasco and later on with an individual named Miguel Iparagirre. Iparagirre isn't known to the security services, so I can't say for sure if it wasn't simply an innocent meeting of friends. If you want him watched I'll have to put more men on the case.'

'That won't be necessary, Jacques. Maybe you should tell your friend at the DGSE about Iparagirre.'

'And what should I do about Terese, monsieur?'

'I'll deal with her. And Jacques . . . find out what you can from this Vasco. Pull out all the stops. Do it tonight.'

All day, Viktor wrestles with the question of whether or not he should tell Marie-Louise. One part of him argues it is a mother's right to know; another argues if he can make Terese see reason then there will be no need to worry his wife. The question is, how is he going to make his daughter see reason? For the past four years they have indulged in their personal version of the Cold War, neither willing to, figuratively speaking, come to the table, share their grievances and negotiate. Perhaps he goes a little too far at times with the snooping and use of Oreaga, but nothing can persuade him it is anything other than his duty as a father. They have their differences, but which parents and offspring do not?

Deep down, he knows it isn't entirely concern for, or protection of his daughter that forces him to confront her. It is the business. Building Groupe Rodriguez into the empire it is has taken him a lifetime of hard work, astute decisions, and tricky manoeuvring and he desperately needs Terese to carry the torch. He has achieved unimaginable wealth and he craves to have his name live on long after he departs this earth. She really has no say in the matter; it is her destiny. He has to make her give up this ETA foolishness, grow up, accept her responsibilities.

This time around, he won't give her a choice.

As she waits for Fabien to arrive, Terese studies her reflection in the gilded mirror in her hallway and applies a spot of lip balm to her puckered lips. Dabbing at the corners of her mouth with a tissue, she smoothes her bob of hair, straightens the seams of her pencil skirt and slips into a camel-coloured jacket. The clothes feel strange after spending the time in Cuba in jeans or shorts and loose-fitting vests and shirts.

These clothes are too formal, too feminine.

As she fastens the last button on her jacket, there is a knock on the door.

'Hello darling, I'm ready,' she calls and opens the door to find Fabien propped against the jamb.

'May I come in?' His words are slurred, tripping over one another.

'Have you been drinking?'

Brushing her gently aside without answering the question and not bothering to give her his customary kiss, he makes his way into the small kitchen at the back of the house.

'Can I get myself a drink of water, please?' he asks.

'Of course. Is something the matter?'

For the second time he ignores her. Reaching into the fridge he takes out a bottle of still water, unscrews it and half fills a glass lying on top of the work surface.

'We have to talk, Terese.'

She spreads her hands in apology. 'I know. I'm sorry about last night. I can be a moody bitch at times, can't I? There's plenty of time to talk over dinner. I'll tell you all about Cuba. Come on, I'm starving.'

He squirms, doesn't look her in the eye. 'I've cancelled dinner. I don't think it would be appropriate to say what I have to say in a public place.'

Alarm bells start to ring and a hot flush creeps steadily up her neck. This isn't like Fabien.

'OK . . . but can we sit down?' she says. 'You look as if you might faint at any minute.'

'Yes, I think it would be better if we did.'

She leads him into the lounge and sits down next to him on the leather sofa. She holds her breath as he takes her hand in his.

He shakes his head, looks into her eyes.

'Darling, you do know I love you very much, don't you?'

'I do, Fabien. And I love you, too.'

'And that I would do absolutely anything for you.'

'I know you would.'

'Well, I've given it a lot of thought since you were away and—'

Oh God, she thinks, *I'm on the wrong tack. He's been stoking up the courage to set a date for the wedding. Foolish girl, I should have known.*

'Darling, I'm sorry. I don't want to hurt you, you're too good a man for that. If this is about the wedding, it's too soon. It's me. I'm not ready for that sort of commitment just yet.'

His eyes widen and his hands spring open. 'The wedding? No, no, you've got it wrong. That's not what I want to talk about.'

'Then what's the matter?'

'It's over, Terese. I've come to tell you we're finished.'

Her mind goes into freefall. *No! No! Not now! Not when I need you most! Peru will kill me. Jesus! Make yourself cry, girl. Turn on the tears!*

She scrunches up her eyes, tries to force the tears.

'Don't cry Terese, please. I hate to see you upset.'

'But I love you, Fabien! How can you do this to me? I *will* marry you I promise, you're the love of my life, but it will have to be when I feel the time is right.'

He stiffens. 'I'm sorry, but I've made up my mind.'

'Why? What have I done to deserve this?'

He takes a deep gulp of air then lets it out slowly. 'As much as I love you, I cannot contemplate having to tolerate your father as my father-in-law. He's an interfering bully and I'm resolved that if he makes my life a misery at work, he's going to make it one at home as well. You know as well as I do that he'll meddle in our lives from dawn to dusk and, frankly, I'm not going to put myself in that situation. There, I've said it and I hope you understand.'

His head drops into his hands.

A tiny hand tugs at her heartstrings. Poor man. Fabien isn't weak as Peru joked. He is sensitive and caring and in her eyes that doesn't equate to weakness. They are qualities she respects; qualities that far too few men possess. Qualities that none of the other men in her life possess. They are certainly absent in Peru and her father. When she first engaged in the deception with Fabien, she managed to remain detached, as if viewing life in a terrarium, observing, but not participating. Fabien was a tool she would use, simple as that. Their relationship was purely a sham to serve Peru's purpose. Then Fabien began to get serious. His honest affection is genuine, no strings attached. Unlike Peru, he doesn't play mind games with his emotions; he wears them on his sleeve. She would have had to be blind not to see that he has fallen in love with her. Then, completely unexpectedly, he produced the engagement ring. What choice did she have but to say yes? If she refused him there might have been a chance he would have broken off their relationship and she couldn't have allowed that to happen. Fabien is a man of breeding. He would probably have taken her refusal as a failure on his part and walked away to save her further embarrassment. So she agreed, and he had slipped the beautifully crafted silver ring on to her third finger.

She wonders if she has become merely 'Peru's woman'. Nowadays, he takes her for granted. Their lovemaking has virtually ceased to exist. His mind is stuck on a single track and it isn't her. ETA consumes him, burrowing its way into every aspect of his life. She will never be able to compete and is destined to play the role of mistress to his real wife—the cause to which he is married.

Does she blindly follow Peru solely because she is afraid of losing him if she doesn't? Probably. Does she feel as passionate about Basque independence as he does? Possibly. Is she as committed to ETA as he is? She is full of doubt after her time in Cuba. Is she prepared to kill for the cause as much as he is? The answer truly tortures her.

She really doesn't want to lose Fabien. Not because she needs a cover, but because she realises she quite enjoys the attention of a good and open man who treats her with respect. He is proud for her to be on his arm and he will never need to live his life in the shadows. For the first time in her life, here is a man who is prepared to give her the love she is missing.

She likes that and wants it to continue.

'Please Fabien,' she says, taking hold of his hand. 'I know my father's not the easiest of people and I don't think that much of him myself. You and I both know he's an old man and old men don't live forever. We've all the time in the world. Please don't do this to me, please.'

He turns to her, face etched in pain. 'Sorry, Terese, it has to finish here and now. There's no other way.'

Her stomach churns.

Christ, I've had it when Peru finds out.

The windowless room is black and airless, pierced only by the spotlight focused on the rough surface of the wooden table. A skeletal man sits in the shadows, dressed in black and wearing a woollen balaclava, holes exposing a pair of lifeless, grey eyes. The single beam picks out three objects: two manacled hands and a meat cleaver.

The hands belong to Salbatore Vasco.

Earlier that evening he was paired with Jorge, Salbatore the spotter. There was an unusually long queue waiting for the bus to arrive from the city centre and, as usual, Jorge and he stood some ten passengers apart, ignoring each other as the procedure demanded. The bus arrived late, almost full, the light fading. As the passengers began to climb aboard it became clear to Salbatore, standing at the back of the line, that there was a good chance of Jorge and he becoming separated. Gently pushing his way up the queue, he found his way blocked by a huge man and was unable to push past without causing a scene. Everyone managed to get on the bus except the man, Salbatore, and an almost-as-large man behind him. As the bus drove away he felt something hard and round push firmly into the small of his back. At the same time, the man in front pulled a knife from his pocket, the shiny blade catching the reflection of the streetlights.

So much for all the training in unarmed skills. They caught me in a human sandwich, he thinks.

Bundled into the back of a black Range Rover, they forced him to lie on the floor. Earplugs were jammed into his ears and one of the men placed a sack over his head, disorientating him. Then they taped his hands and feet. After that, they drove around for a good half hour or so. He sensed the G-forces as the vehicle swung round a series of bends before finally coming to an abrupt halt. Strong arms lifted him out of the car and carried him supine, like a sack of potatoes. After a short time they dumped him on a hard, cold floor. Minutes later, they dragged him to his feet again and made him sit on what he assumed was a chair. They then untaped his hands, pulled them out in front of him palms down, spread eighteen inches apart. He felt the coldness of metal as they clamped his wrists, pinning his hands to a hard surface. Then they removed the sack from his head.

He is utterly helpless, but determined to remain defiant.

Whoever you are and whatever you want, you won't break Salbatore Vasco.

'Good evening, Monsieur Vasco. I trust I find you well?' The voice is reedy and caustic. 'I'm sorry to interrupt your business schedule, but there are a number of questions I'd like you to answer for me.'

A bony hand slowly appears from beneath the table and rests gently on the handle of the cleaver. Its skin is almost translucent and he can see crazed blue veins beneath the surface.

'But before I do, I'd like to say a few things. I know that you're an important figure in the local ETA commando. I also know you're planning a, shall we say, very unpleasant activity in the very near future. I believe in that activity you intend to use a lethal virus in order to achieve your misplaced aims of a liberated Basque nation. How am I doing so far?'

He stares defiantly at the eyes, jaw clamped.

'I take it then I'm right on all counts. Now, listen carefully to what I will say next. I am not a member of either DGSE or indeed any security service. If I were, I would be bound by international conventions regarding interrogation protocol and technique. But personally, I don't give a damn for either protocol or technique. All I care for is results.' The hand lifts the cleaver an inch off the table and then puts it back down.

You don't scare me.

'Now, I will ask my questions. I'd like to know exactly when and where you plan to release the Ebola?'

'Fuck you, whoever you are. I don't know what you're talking about.'

'Oh, dear, I see you're going to need a little encouragement.'

The man's other hand appears, glides across the table and tenderly grasps Salbatore's right hand.

'You know, Monsieur Vasco, the hand is a wonderful instrument; so precise, so versatile, and so very sensitive. Imagine all the wonderful things your hand has done for you during your life. You have eaten with it, constructed things with it, felt your lover's heartbeat with it. All by using those marvellous things called fingers. However, the truly ingenious aspect of the hand is not the finger; it's the thumb. Do you know we are the only species on earth that can rotate its thumb? Such ability permits the hand to hold objects in such a way that would be impossible otherwise. Can you imagine life without a thumb?'

'You're making a mistake. You must be talking about another Salbatore Vasco.'

The eyes narrow. 'I won't ask you again.'

'Go to hell.'

Light glints on the blade of the cleaver as the bony hand raises it. For a split second, it disappears from the circle of light and then Salbatore hears a whooshing followed by a dull thud as the blade meets the unyielding resistance of the table. Silence falls. A thick, sticky liquid begins to pool on the table by the side of his hand. Another hand, meatier and hairier, reaches into the light and plucks his detached thumb from the table.

He stares at his mutilated hand in disbelief. Then the pain hits him, lancing along his nerves and exploding in his brain. He screams, a high-pitched, animal wail that reverberates round and round the empty space. The meaty hand shoves his thumb viciously into his open mouth. Involuntarily, he bites down on it. A split second later, he spits it out where it lies, grotesquely, on top of his other hand.

'Shall we try again? You have only nine digits left, Monsieur Vasco and believe me, I will get my answers.'

2nd August

Viktor stares out of the window as he listens to the feet of the man behind him shuffling nervously on the carpet. Now Terese is back he will need information from her and fast, and the best way to do that is through Fabien.

Without turning, he puts his question. 'How was dinner last night, Fabien? Did Terese and you enjoy yourselves? I expect you had a lot of catching up to do.'

For a moment, there is no answer. Then the faltering voice of Fabien speaks. 'We didn't have dinner, monsieur.'

Viktor smiles. It was the couple's first evening together. Perhaps they spent a cosy evening in her house. 'I expect you had other plans, eh?'

'No, monsieur, we didn't. We had some important business to discuss.'

'Ah.' He takes his eyes off Boucau and slowly turns to face Fabien. 'Something connected to a wedding, maybe?'

'Not exactly, monsieur. Another personal matter.'

'Might I ask what that matter was?'

'As I said, it was personal.'

'Personal, eh? As I've explained to you on several occasions, there's no such thing as "personal" in my family.'

'I thought you might say that.'

'Did you?'

'I did, monsieur, but you see I'm not your family and I don't intend to be your family. Therefore you have no right to know my business.'

Viktor feels his back stiffen. His employees don't dare talk to him like this.

'You're not making sense.'

Fabien crosses his arms over his chest. 'Terese and I . . . it's over.'

'Over? What does 'over' mean?'

'The engagement is off, monsieur. In fact our relationship is finished.'

'Did she finish it?'

'No, I did.'

'Well, you can make it back on again.'

'I probably can, but I'm not going to.'

'I don't think you understand me. I'm ordering you to reinstate your engagement.'

'*Ordering* me?' Fabien clenches his fists, nails digging into fleshy palms. 'I'm sorry, but as far as my personal life is concerned I don't take orders from you or anyone else for that matter. Terese and I are finished. Not that it's any bloody business of yours.'

Viktor feels the heat rush through his body. 'Do you know who you're talking to, young man?'

'I know exactly who I'm talking to. I'm talking to the most arrogant, self-centred, manipulating individual that I've ever had the misfortune to meet. *That*, monsieur, is who I'm talking to.'

Willing himself to relax, Viktor breathes in, cracks his knuckles. 'If you remember, when I gave you your promotion I said what goes up can always come down. Well, Fabien, not only have you come down, you've come down *and* you're going out. Clear your desk, you're no longer an employee of mine.'

Fabien shakes his head. 'If you want the truth, that's a huge relief. I don't think I want to be associated with you or have anything to do with you or your company. You may be wealthy, but you're low class and it shows. I wouldn't insult my family by foisting you upon them.'

Turning on his heels, he heads for the door.

'Oh, I almost forgot to tell you, Fabien,' Viktor calls after him. 'Terese has a secret lover. No doubt he's twice the man you'll ever be, you stuck-up little cunt.'

As Fabien slams the door, he lifts the intercom and calls his PA. 'Argine. Is Oreaga there?'

'Yes, he's here, Monsieur Rodriguez.'

'Send him in.'

'Was that Fabien Mendiola who just stormed out?' asks Oreaga on entering. 'He was as pale as a ghost.'

'I'm not surprised, Jacques. The little shit has just informed me that it's over between him and my daughter. That will make your job a little more difficult now, won't it?'

Oreaga's face, as ever, remains untroubled. 'That's a great pity, monsieur. He would have been a valuable source of information.'

'I'm not so sure about that, Jacques. Fabien's weak and Terese knows how to twist him round her little finger. She probably tells him a pack of lies much of the time. There's a key to this whole business somewhere and we will find it, I assure you.'

'If I may be so bold, monsieur, you haven't told me yet what you suspect she brought back from Cuba.'

'Haven't I? Well, all in good time, Jacques, all in good time.'

274

Terese tries without success to meet the eyes of the four men and one woman gathered in Le Chat Noir. She senses an electric charge in the air, a crackling. Once more, the food and drink on the table are hardly touched. She avoids Peru's gaze, recognising his dark mood, a mood that makes her feel like an errant child. Instead of praising her for her efforts, the first thing he did when they assembled was to give her a degrading dressing-down in front of the entire group, followed by a droning lecture on how important it is to stick to procedure.

Embarrassed, she bit her tongue, deciding it wise not to tell him the news of Fabien.

After her public humiliation, she watches as he reaches into his rucksack and, with a dramatic flourish, brings out an item that he places on top of the table. An innocuous aerosol can no different to a million and one others.

All eyes stray to the can.

'Our weapon of choice,' says Peru.

'A can?' says Martina.

'Not any old can. This one has been modified by Philippe, our resident genius.'

'What did you do to it, Philippe?' asks Miguel.

'The hard part was done by the Cuban scientist,' says Philippe, grinning from ear to ear. 'The virus is sealed in an airtight plastic vial about this long.' He indicated the size by holding apart his thumb and forefinger. 'At one end of the vial is a thin, non-porous membrane. At the other is a chamber containing a tiny amount of propellant. I inserted a copy of this vial filled with perfume into a slightly modified commercial aerosol and then tested it. It works just like a normal spray.'

'Simple, but effective,' says Peru.

Moving the aerosol to one side, he rolls out a plan of Barajas International Airport on the table and gathers the others around it. 'Our day has finally arrived,' he crows. 'The day after tomorrow, the number of holidaymakers passing through Barajas will be at its greatest. After I release the virus into the main air conditioning outlet servicing the passenger hall, there's no way of stopping it doing its deadly work.'

'How many people will it kill?' asks Martina.

'My guess would be five hundred or so.'

Someone lets out a low whistle.

'OK,' says Peru. 'One last time then we go our separate ways.'

He points to an area circled in red on the plan. 'This is the main air conditioning duct above the booking hall. I'll disguise myself as one of the airport's maintenance men, seemingly carrying out a routine inspection inside the system. Of course, I shall be wearing protective clothing at the time and you will all have left the building before I do my work. I'll simply spray the virus into the outlet in the main duct and there will be no effect—until later when people begin to go down like flies. At some point they'll identify it as Ebola, but an unknown, much more virulent strain. Of course, they won't have a clue as to how so many people came to be affected. The authorities will have to spend time taking statements and trying to get a clear picture of what happened. When the Grim Reaper starts his grisly work, we'll announce to the world that ETA is responsible and the airport is just the beginning of a new wave of terror. I don't think they'll be too keen to call our bluff the next time around. We'll have them by the balls.'

'Brilliant,' says Jorge. 'I have to hand it to you, Peru, that'll make one hell of a statement. Dead holidaymakers, eh? The government will certainly be much more interested in having a dialogue with us.'

'Is there a contingency plan?' asks Terese, nervously scanning the others' faces. 'When Salbatore was in charge there was always a fallback option.'

Peru shoots her a filthy look. 'Like what, Terese? Call for The Mad Hatter? There's no need for any contingency. My heart tells me we will not fail this time.'

'Speaking of Salbatore, where is he?' says Martina.

'We became separated,' says Jorge. 'We were in a long queue waiting for the bus to arrive from the city centre. I got on the bus and he didn't.'

'Shouldn't we wait for him?' says Terese, thinking if he were there Salbatore would surely object to a plan with no safety net. If he does, he might also question Peru's gung-ho attitude and then there is a chance the whole crazy scheme would be abandoned.

'No,' Peru snaps. 'Now, can we focus and run through it for the last time?'

'Wait a moment.' Terese takes a deep breath. 'Do we really want to go through with this? I mean, there may be pregnant women and children in the terminal.'

Five pairs of eyes glower at her.

'Don't you recall, Terese? *No matter what it takes*,' says Miguel.

Before she has time to speak, Martina's hand grips her elbow. 'It's just nerves,' she says. 'Terese has been through a hell of a lot. She'll be OK.'

Peru grunts and spreads his palm on the map. 'As I was saying. This is the last time. Listen carefully.'

3rd August

14:00hrs

Oreaga did well, thinks Viktor. Vasco lost a thumb, but in a few days' time he will lose his freedom when DGSE get their hands on him and loosen his tongue further. For the time being though, until he has a word with Terese, Oreaga's men will keep him out of the way.

Now that all the pieces of the jigsaw are in place, it is time for him to bring this nonsense to an end and time for her to stop all the foolishness before it gets her into serious trouble, very serious trouble. She could lose her life if she goes through with this madness. The powers that be might make it a capital offence. It doesn't matter if they abolished the death penalty more than twenty years before. For premeditated mass murder the public will bay for blood, forcing the authorities to do a U-turn. He can't allow that to happen. There is no way on earth that his reputation is going to go down the pan because of his daughter's misguided ideology.

He has worked out how he will do it. Marie-Louise will be the means.

Opening the door to his office's anteroom, he calls out to his PA. 'Would you put a call through to Miss Rodriguez at *El Correo*, Argine?'

'I'll do it this minute, Monsieur Rodriguez.'

'Hello, *El Correo*. Terese Rodriguez speaking.' Her tone is soft, friendly.

'Hello Terese, this is your father. Are you available to meet this evening?'

Her voice hardens. 'Why?'

'There's something I must talk to you about.'

'Can't we talk on the phone? I've an important meeting this evening.'

'No we can't, it's something that has to be discussed face-to-face. Cancel your meeting. I'll pick you up from your house at eight o'clock.'

'Now just a minute, you can't tell me what to do. I—'

'Oh, I think I can. It's about ETA. More specifically it's about you and ETA and a certain individual named Peru Echeverria.'

The line falls silent for a moment before she speaks again. 'ETA? I don't know what you're talking about. And I've never heard of any Peru whatsisname.'

'Please don't treat me like a fool, Terese. A certain Salbatore Vasco has kindly volunteered information about the Bayonne commando and your involvement in it. In fact, he was so keen to talk it was difficult to keep him quiet.'

'Have you been sticking your fucking nose into my business?'

'If it threatens the family, it becomes *my* business. I've your mother and sisters to consider, and you should watch your language young lady.'

Another pause before she speaks. 'OK, I'll reschedule. But I want you to know I'm not doing it willingly.'

'I don't care if you're doing it willingly or not. And I would counsel against contacting Echeverria, as that would be very ill-advised.'

Viktor winces as she slams the phone down. He opens the manila folder lying on his desk. It has grown like a Russian vine in the past six hours, thanks to the sterling work of Oreaga, who came up trumps yet again. He begins to scan the names. Salbatore Vasco, Martina Trevino, Miguel Iparagirre, Jorge Gorriaran, Peru Echevarria, Philippe Sagastizabal.

The last page contains a photo of the face he knows so well.

Terese Rodriguez.

16:00hrs

Terese rests her elbows on her desk and reflects on the brief conversation with her father. Her initial reaction was disbelief. How could he have found out about Peru and Salbatore? Then annoyance followed and turned into anger, which finally subsided into shock at the realisation of what his discovery could mean for her. She has never known him speak in such menacing tones. He might be bullying and overbearing, but not usually given to menace.

Two hours after his unexpected phone call she still cannot untangle her knotted feelings. Fear, panic, desperation and helplessness, all mixed in a potpourri of emotions. Out of nowhere, her world has suddenly and without warning begun to implode. She hoped to be able to come up with a way of gradually disengaging herself from the commando, but now that option has evaporated thanks to her meddling father.

When rationality starts to kick in, her first thought is to phone Fabien. Then she takes a more detached view and realises that might not be a particularly clever call to make. If she confesses to her association with ETA it will be like tiptoeing across a minefield wearing clogs. There is no telling how he will react to the revelation that the woman he loves is a despicable criminal in the eyes of the law. Should she tell Peru her father knows? Forget it. If she does, circumstances would force him to abandon the plan for Barajas, which would leave him one very enraged and vengeful man.

Last time it was just a tongue-lashing. Next time it could be worse, far worse.

Steady girl, take your time, you need to think this through.

Firstly, she needs to ask herself some questions. Does her father know Salbatore? If so, Salbatore has never mentioned it. If her father does know him, why would Salbatore bring Peru into the conversation? Is it because he is seeking revenge even though he hides it well? Perhaps Salbatore thinks by leaking the news of her relationship that her father will send in Oreaga's thugs to warn Peru off, as he did with Damien Parnasseau. That would certainly put Peru in a difficult situation.

Wait. Her father also knows about her connection to ETA and there is no reason why Salbatore would have mentioned that as far as she can see, not to her father, a man who has never shown the slightest sympathy with their cause.

Unless ...

She freezes as the thought strikes her. Maybe she is thinking along the wrong lines. Maybe Salbatore doesn't know her father. She tries to recall the words of their telephone conversation. 'Kindly volunteered' were the words her father used. That isn't the Salbatore she knows. Salbatore plays his cards close to his chest and wouldn't 'kindly volunteer' anything.

Unless ...

Unless her father forced Salbatore to tell him.

She doesn't like where her train of thought is taking her. Her father is a ruthless businessman who might readily employ a little intimidation, but it would take more than that to prise anything out of Salbatore. A whole lot more. If Salbatore has given up Peru, then what else has he revealed? Has he spilt the whole can of beans?

She made one mistake. One mistake in all these years and one made because of her longing to please Peru, a longing he threw back in her face. Why didn't she think before rushing off to meet him? It would have taken only one quick phone call to either Martina or Jorge. If she had done that, whoever was watching them would have passed a wasted night. Did that small error of judgement lead her father to Salbatore?

It had to be Oreaga's stooges who followed her the night she arrived back in Bayonne. They must have cracked the champagne when they realised she screwed up. However, that still doesn't explain how they came across Salbatore. That puzzles her, as does her father's directness. He is a master of mind games and bluntness is a departure from the norm. This time, he came straight to the point: no chicanery, no sleight of hand.

There is only one person she can turn to. The one person she has already deceived enough. The one person who says he would do anything for her.

She picks up her mobile phone, recalls the number, hits the connect button.

18:00hrs

People are beginning to arrive in the neighbourhood, many walking home from their places of work in the evening balminess. The area surrounding the *El Correo* office is very much sought-after, populated by aspiring couples and singles in their late twenties to mid forties.

The phone on Terese's desk rings.

She picks it up, presses the handset to her cheek. 'Hi, Frantziska.'

'There's a Fabien Mendiola waiting in reception for you, Terese. He says you're expecting him.'

'Thanks. Tell him I'll be right down.'

Her stomach clenches. She never expected events would turn out this way. The hunter has become the hunted, and the man she needs might or might not turn her away.

She thinks about changing her mind, but decides against it. Striding quickly along the corridor leading down to reception, she halts at the top of the stairs. From here, she can see him talking to the receptionist. He looks up at her and languidly lifts a hand in greeting.

'Come on up,' she says.

He climbs the stairs, gives her a weak smile. 'You look well, Terese.'

She doesn't feel it.

Taking hold of his hand, she leads him back along the corridor and ushers him into a small meeting room, closing the door behind them. Then she motions him to take a seat on one of two chairs separated by a circular, glass-topped table.

'You look beautiful,' he says again. 'I'm really sorry I upset you. I can't help thinking it must have been such a shock.'

His look tells her he really means it.

Just like Fabien, to put my feelings first.

Pulling out the chair, she settles herself opposite him and lays her forearms, fists clenched, on the glass tabletop.

'Did you wonder why I wanted to see you?' she says.

'Of course I did. I've thought of nothing except you since we . . . well, since we . . . you know.'

'I know. I'm sorry, too. I didn't ask you here to discuss our relationship. What I'm about to tell you mustn't go outside these four walls. If it does, there's every chance you might never see me again. Perhaps no one will ever see me again. You're the only person I know I feel I can trust. Please, give me your word you won't say anything.'

'I . . . I give you my word.'

She unclenches her fists, places her hands palms down on the cold surface and begins to recount her story. As she talks, she catches sight of his right knee beneath the table, bouncing rapidly up and down, his foot tapping out a silent, metronomic beat.

'There are a lot of things you don't know about me, Fabien. You may find them rather disturbing, possibly repulsive. I am not what I appear to be. To understand that, I must tell you about a man called Peru Echeverria.'

'Who's Peru Echeverria?'

'Peru is . . . was . . . my . . . lover. We met at the Sorbonne when I was nineteen years old. At the time, I was very impressionable and Peru, well, Peru is a very passionate and charismatic individual. He is the first man I met who thinks about the world as I do and who shares similar beliefs to my own. My young and idealistic mind was filled with hatred for any political regime that subjugated and exploited people in order to serve their own selfish and grasping needs. Only my hatred was undirected, and I didn't have a hook on which to hang it. Peru showed me that hook. He had committed himself to the liberation of the Basque people. Do you mind if I pour a cup of water?'

A small water cooler stands in the corner of the room. She rises, fills two white plastic cups and places them on the table before returning to her seat.

Fabien's jaw is slack, as if his chest has lassoed it. She knows he must be feeling as if he is looking down on their conversation from above, detached from his earthly body, floating invisible above it.

'The more Peru took me into his confidence the more I came under his spell. Soon I was completely bewitched. The beliefs he held became my beliefs, his purpose my purpose. It was as if we'd become one. Not long after I met him, we became lovers. It wasn't the sex; there was never any raw animal craving that begged to be satisfied. I know it sounds strange now, but it was as if we didn't need to enjoy each other's body to reach a climax. Just the thought of how we might change the world was sufficient for us. Like me, Peru was born and raised in Bayonne, but unlike me, he comes from a poor and uneducated family that hates privilege. You might think that would have set him against me immediately. It didn't. When he listened to how my father treated me and how I'd turned against him and all he stood for, any misgivings that he might have had melted like snow in the spring.'

She pauses, takes a sip of water.

'I guess our relationship might have run its course if it hadn't been for the intervention of an old school friend of mine, who had gone up to the Sorbonne the year before me. Peru had a cause, but he needed the resources of a well-organised operation. My friend provided the means for him to obtain them. She introduced us to one of the tutors, not much older than we were, who ignited Peru like a match to dry kindling. He was a member of ETA and he recruited Peru and me. After graduation, fortunately for us, we both managed to secure jobs here in Bayonne and were taken under the wing of the local commando, where we carried out a series of campaigns against the authorities.'

Fabien's lips are now flapping like a landed fish. 'I can't believe what I'm hearing, Terese. If I understand you correctly, you're telling me you're a terrorist?'

She flinches at the word. 'That term carries all kinds of connotations, Fabien. I don't see ETA as terrorists, more as freedom fighters.'

He shakes his head from side to side. 'I'm sorry, but people who bomb indiscriminately and condone assassination are terrorists in my view.'

Her instincts tell her what is coming next.

'What purpose was I meant to serve? Did you use me?'

'Please, this is very difficult for me. Let me finish and then I'll answer your questions. After that, do what you will. If your conscience tells you to go to the police, then that is what you must do.'

He shakes his head again, leans back in his chair and pinches the skin above the bridge of his nose into a deep vee.

'Unfortunately, some innocent lives were lost, but by and large the operations we carried out were mostly ineffective. Hoaxes designed to keep the authorities on their toes and ETA in the headlines. Do you remember the Estadio San Mames scare? That was a prime example. If we'd really wanted to kill on a mass scale we had the means and opportunity on that day. It was all propaganda, designed to frighten people and keep the organisation and its objectives at the forefront of their minds. Like so much of what we do it was blown out of all proportion by the journalists, me included. ETA always makes a powerful story and the call for freedom for the Basque Country is guaranteed to make emotions run high, whether one agrees with it or not. Then the situation changed. Peru grabbed the leadership—it's not important to know why or how—and revealed something that scared the life out of me: a plan for the murder of more than five hundred passengers in Barajas Airport.'

Fabien straightens as if struck with a cattle prod. 'Mother of God!'

'But the plan depends on one crucial element and that was only to be found in Cuba, which is why I had to go there. You see, I discovered by accident a link between Che Guevara and a certain retired, high-ranking Cuban army officer. We already knew the Cubans had the particular thing that we needed, so all I had to do was convince this man to get it for me. Peru chose me for the mission because of my knowledge of the circumstances of the link and because he considered a woman would be better placed to pull it off. Myself, I didn't think I stood a chance. One young woman pitted against a hardened veteran? I wouldn't have placed a bet on my succeeding. In truth, I had hoped I wouldn't succeed, as I would rather have suffered Peru's wrath than be instrumental in providing him with the means for mass murder. I was in for a surprise. This man had been close to Castro in the revolution and could relate to our cause. Not only that, but he seemed to display an enthusiasm for it. If he really wanted to he could have had me killed, or killed me himself. I got what we wanted.'

'Terese, you're really frightening me. What did you bring back, for God's sake?'

'A virulent new strain of Ebola.'

'What? What's Ebola?'

'The world's deadliest virus.'

For a long moment neither of them speaks. Then Fabien breaks the silence.

'Why are you telling me this?'

'Because I need your help.'

'My help? Why would you need my help?'

'I'm frightened, Fabien. Frightened and sick at the thought of what Peru is about to do. Yesterday evening, the commando held a meeting and I honestly thought that now they had the virus they would come to realise how mad this plan is. I was wrong. When I saw their faces, I realised they were all as crazy as Peru. Not one of them raised an objection to what they were about to do. That decided me. I want no part of it.'

'What do you expect me to do? And why should I help you, anyway? This isn't my mess, Terese. This could land you in gaol. Or worse.'

'Fabien, if you love me and I believe you do, then you'll help me. Please.'

He crosses his arms over his chest and nods. 'Ah, there we have it. Of course, I love you. I've loved you since the first moment I set eyes on you. But look at it from where I'm sitting. My fiancée, the woman I worship, has been deceiving me by having a lover. If that's not devastating enough, her lover happens to be a terrorist. Not only that, but she's been using me as a tool in some sick plot to murder innocent people. What would you do if you were me?'

'I would take my leave right now, walk straight to the offices of the Bayonne police and tell them all I know.'

'You would? Then why shouldn't I do the same?'

'Because I'm not you and it's not my decision, Fabien. It's yours. And what you decide within the next few hours will determine the course of my life.'

She stares at the honest face of the man who holds her future in the palm of his hand. He returns her stare and then looks away. In that fleeting moment, she knows she would willingly marry him if she ever extricates herself from the mess in which she finds herself.

20:00hrs

When Terese meets her father, it is with a cursory exchange of nods. Climbing into his car, she sinks into the deep softness of the leather passenger seat, not a single word passing between them on the journey south towards the centre of the city.

Unusually, her father has dispensed with the services of his chauffeur for the evening. After crossing the river at the Pont Saint-Esprit, his driving is hesitant as he negotiates the big Bentley around the winding and dimly lit streets in the quieter part of Bayonne. He makes a hash of parking off the Rue de Lisses and she almost loses patience with him, but thinks the better of it.

The charming Auberge du Cheval Blanc isn't normally the kind of place her father would choose to dine. Tucked into a quiet corner on the Rue Bourgneuf, the former post-house oozes character. Paintings by local artists hang on the pastel walls of the dining room. Some dozen circular wooden tables, each sufficient for two diners, are neatly arranged in the small dining room. A slim glass vase containing a single red rose decorates each table. The fragrance of the flowers mingles with the aroma of garlic and onions drifting in from the kitchen.

She assumes he has chosen this location for three reasons. Firstly, there is a very good chance nobody will recognise him in this part of town. Secondly, it is almost certain to be bereft of diners on a Thursday evening. Thirdly, the Auberge du Cheval Blanc is reputed to offer the widest choice of fine Irouliguys wines. He can afford better, but the region of his birth produces a vintage pleasing to his palate.

As soon as they enter, the maître d'hôtel, a short, rotund man with a clipped moustache and the whitest teeth Terese has ever seen, minces over to them and shepherds them to a table, where he pulls out a chair for Terese. She slides onto the chair, folds her arms over her chest and stares at her father.

He has aged considerably since their last meeting and it surprises her to realise that the man for whom she holds such hateful feelings must now be approaching his mid-eighties. His thick white hair is thinning and the skin beneath his eyes hangs in folds. She imagines anyone seeing them together would think she is his granddaughter. They might also speculate why her body language doesn't suggest closeness.

As soon as the wine waiter takes the order from her father for a bottle of Omenaldi, she buries her head in the leather-covered menu, oblivious to the dulcet tones of the soothing background music. It is only after ordering that their conversation begins, her father breaking the strained silence.

'Your mother's dying, Terese. She has an inoperable brain tumour. The doctors give her two months, maximum.' He says the words casually, as if reviewing one of his meetings.

The heavy menu slides out of her hands and onto the stone floor. She shivers involuntarily and her stomach lurches as she experiences a moment of nausea. This isn't the subject she is waiting for him to raise. She is steeling herself for a grilling over her involvement in ETA.

She puts her hand over her mouth and the words slip through the gaps between her fingers. 'No, it can't be true, it can't be.'

'I'm afraid it is. I've asked for second and third opinions from the finest specialists in England and America and they agree entirely with Professor Lamont at Pitie-Salpêtrière. They're researching a procedure that uses keyhole laser surgery, but they say it's a good two years away at least. Unfortunately, there is nothing they can do for her. All you and I can do is guarantee the time remaining to her is as pleasant and stress-free as possible.' His shoulders droop and a tear wells in the corner of his eye. He sniffs and immediately wipes it away with the back of his hand.

'How long have you known?' She doesn't intend it to be a question.

'About six months.'

Her eyes spit hatred. 'And you didn't tell me? What kind of father are you? No, don't answer that. I know what kind you are.'

'Your mother begged me not to let you know. I wanted to, naturally I did, but I also wanted to respect her wishes.'

She shakes her head slowly. 'But when we spoke on the phone she never mentioned it. Why?'

'Perhaps you should ask her that question. You never come to see us. You haven't been up to the house for more than two years. Do you hate me that much?'

Blood throbs in her temples and her hands begin to shake. 'Will you take me home? I've lost my appetite.'

'All in due course, but I'm going to ask you some direct questions first, to which I'd like some honest answers. I know these past few years have been . . . difficult, but that's because your mother and I care so much about you.'

As she sinks back in her chair, the maître d'hôtel arrives at their table. Before he has chance to speak,

Viktor brushes him away with an imperious wave of his hand.

'You may not like it, but when your mother is no longer with us,' he chokes on the words, 'I will continue to care about you and that's something you won't really understand until you have children of your own.' Pausing, he takes a sip of the blood-red wine from his glass. 'I'm a plain speaker, Terese, so I'll get straight to the point. The facts are these. I know you're involved with ETA and I can sympathise with that. I'm a Basque myself, aren't I? But they're misguided, they belong to the past and, quite frankly, people have more pressing concerns on their minds nowadays. What are you personally hoping to achieve? Then there is your relationship with this Echeverria fellow. What's that all about? He's some low-life from the poor side of town and, although I understand he's an educated man, nobody can make a silk purse out of a sow's ear.'

'How dare you say—'

'Before you fly off the handle I would beg you to consider the effect on your mother of any actions you propose to take in the near future.'

'You planned this didn't you? You planned it so I'd be torn between my love for Mama and a cause I deeply believe in. You're an evil man, Papa, and I hope you rot in hell!'

'Please hear me out. Look, I didn't know of your connection to ETA and what you planned to do a month ago, let alone six, so I couldn't have "planned" it as you say. You misunderstand me yet again. What do I have to do to stop this infernal feuding between us?'

'Try getting out of my life. Permanently.'

'Is that what you want me to tell your mother?'

Events rewind in Terese's mind. What he says is believable. There is no way he could have known. If he had, this conversation would already have taken place. To hell with ETA, her mother is dying. Terese loves her deeply and knows her father is the only reason they have become strangers. Marie-Louise worships Viktor, and she herself must feel torn between the love for an absent daughter and duty to a beloved husband. If she is going to die then surely she deserves to die happy in the knowledge that Terese and her father have buried the hatchet. On the other hand, if Terese now comes clean and tells her father everything, then there is no knowing what he will do with the knowledge and it might deny Fabien the time to make his decision.

She needs time to think, the walls of a shrinking room pressing in on her.

His fingers begin to drum on the tabletop. 'I want answers to my questions, Teri, and I want them now. Tomorrow will be too late. You will not be involved with this murderous plan. I'm not prepared to let you ruin your life for two reasons. One, I love your mother and two, believe it or not, I love you. If you don't come to your senses, I promise you I will call the authorities and warn them about this virus and what ETA intends to do with it. Firstly, though, I'm curious to know why you would want to be involved with such people. Where did your mother and I go wrong?'

This murderous plan. With those three words she realises he knows exactly what they are planning to do at the airport. Once again, he is the one holding all the aces. Well, maybe she can wipe away some of his smugness.

'I'll tell you why I felt the urge to join an organisation like ETA. It probably started when I was fifteen or so, at a time when I needed the ear of a father who was interested in listening to me.' She shoots him an acid look. 'People say it's a very impressionable age. Most young girls are impressed by boys, but you, you sent me away to a school where there were no boys to be impressed by. So I became inspired instead by the passion and intelligence of a girl. A girl who became my best friend at school and later at the Sorbonne introduced me to ETA. I also met Peru to whom I became attracted. He had a burning hatred of privilege after an aristocrat dished out some rough justice to his family and forced them to live in squalid circumstances. The three of us were kindred spirits and became inseparable, sometimes even sharing the same bed. Oh, yes, Papa, that was how much we loved each other. Then the girl died tragically for the cause. From that moment, Peru and I threw ourselves into the separatist fight. All that mattered was thinking how we could force the government to give up control of the Basque Country. With the airport plan, we have a chance to make that elusive vision a reality.'

Her father shakes his head, reaches across the table and places a cold, sinewy hand on hers. Strangely, his touch is comforting and she leaves her hand where it is. It is a long time since they last had physical contact.

'You must understand I can't let ETA go through with this, Terese. I fought in the last war to save our country from an aggressive tyrant and to save the lives of people from whatever it was he had in mind for them. I didn't kill innocent people because of misguided aims. It doesn't need to be done this way; you only have to look at Northern Ireland to see that. After all those years of death and destruction, the people there are beginning to build a new world, one that was unimaginable ten years ago. I know the situation is very different here, but given time who knows what might happen? People shouldn't die on account of someone's personal ambition.'

His words strike her across the table. Does he also know about Peru's struggle with Salbatore? She recalls what Martina whispers to her whenever Peru and Salbatore engage in an argument.

'Here they go again, Terese. They'll be comparing dicks soon to see who's got the biggest.'

'What do you intend to do?' he says, his hand squeezing hers. The grip is surprisingly strong for a man of his age. 'Possibly shorten what's left of your mother's life and risk being locked away for the rest of yours, or expose a madman and his crazy plan and save the lives of hundreds of innocent people?'

She hesitates before answering. 'I don't know.'

'Then I'll help you. Nobody need know of your involvement tomorrow. If you're not at Barajas, they can't arrest you. If the others try to implicate you . . . well, we'll deal with that if and when it arises. Now that I know you're appealing to your conscience and not to your emotions, I'm sure you'll come to the only decision that's right. Whatever happens afterwards is out of our hands, and I mean *our*. Let's order food and at least pretend we're enjoying each other's company.'

'Are you going to tell Mama?'

'If you force me to, I will.'

Looking in the direction of the hovering waiter, he beckons the man with a crook of his forefinger.

Oh, God, this is going from bad to worse. Should I tell him about Fabien?

'And I understand Fabien has terminated your relationship. I'm pleased about that. I always thought he was after our money. The Mendiolas might think they're the high-and-mighty, but they're going to get their come-uppance soon, I can tell you.'

'What do you mean?'

He smiles, takes a sip of wine. 'A little bird tells me they're about to lose everything. Rumour has it the bank has finally tired of them and decided to call in its loans.

In the not-too-distant future *all* the Mendiolas will have to work for a living like the rest of us.'

She feels the heat rising in her neck.

'What have you said to Fabien?'

'Said? I did more than say. I fired the insignificant worm. He isn't worthy of the Rodriguez name. The husband of the future Chief Executive of Groupe Rodriguez will be someone of my choosing.'

She curses herself for having let her guard down. They are back on familiar territory. Even the thought of her mother's imminent death can't prevent her reaction.

Pushing back her chair, she stands up and throws her napkin on the table. 'Fuck you. Fuck you and fuck everything connected to you, you evil bastard,' she screams, then storms past him out of the restaurant.

20:50hrs

On returning home, she locks the doors of her house and retreats to her bedroom where she takes refuge, trying to close out the thoughts that crowd in on her. It proves impossible. There are just too many demons toying with her mind. In the past twenty-four hours, her nerves have been stretched that tight she can play a tune on them.

The ringing of her mobile makes her jump. Questions leap out at her. Is it Fabien? Has he gone to the police? Is he phoning to warn her?

In her haste, she snatches up the phone without looking at the display.

'Hi, Terese.' Peru's voice is cheerful, relaxed, like someone without a care in the world. Peru, who specifically instructed there is to be no contact before they assemble at Barajas.

His tone freezes her. A prickly sensation crawls up the nape of her neck. Peru and carefree is like David and Goliath sharing a picnic. Tension, tight as a rubber band, pulls her shoulders down to her toes as her body seeks to find safety in the foetal position.

Why is he calling me when he issued strict instructions there was to be no communication?

'P-Peru,' she stammers.

'Are you OK?'

'Yes. Why?'

'You sound a touch worried, that's all.'

Control yourself, Terese. It's only a phone call.

'It's n-nothing. Probably nerves, that's all. It's a big day tomorrow.'

'Understandable, but you needn't worry.' His voice is calming, oily. 'There's absolutely nothing to be concerned about. I guarantee there's no way anyone could possibly know what we're planning to do. Maybe we should meet, just to settle your nerves. Yes, the more I think about it, the more I think that might be a good idea. Why don't you—'

'No, we can't do that.' Her rushed reply is too abrupt and she knows it. She also knows his finely tuned instincts will sense it in a flash.

'Oh? Why not? I'll ask Miguel to cover me. We can meet on the Quai de Lesseps in half an hour. There won't be anyone about at this time of night.'

'I d-don't think that's a good idea.' Her breath comes hard and fast.

'Are you sure you're OK? You normally jump at the chance of seeing me. Like you did when you returned from Cuba, remember? You couldn't wait to get into my pants then.'

'Please, Peru, not tonight. Let's get tomorrow over with and then we'll see.'

His mood changes abruptly. 'And then we'll see? What the hell does that mean?'

'Peru, I don't want to argue. Not now, please.'

The line falls silent. When he speaks again there is a hard edge to his voice. 'OK, suit yourself. I'll see you at Barajas. Bye.'

Before she has time to reply, the line goes dead.

Seconds later, the mobile rings again.

Christ, he knows, she thinks. *He knows something's wrong. He's got a sixth sense for trouble. Pull yourself together or you're screwed.*

This time she looks at the display.

FABIEN

Relief washes over her. Is he phoning to tell her he has decided to go to the police or that he is prepared to help her? It is a black and white decision with no room for shades of grey. Whichever way he jumps, she will have to live with it.

She punches the button to take the call.

'Terese, it's Fabien.'

'I wasn't sure I would hear from you again.'

'I have to speak to you, immediately. There may be a solution to your . . . problem. I'll be round in half an hour.'

'Please hurry.'

'Why? Is something the matter?'

'I'm scared, Fabien, really scared. I think Peru suspects I'm having second thoughts. If he does, there's no knowing what he might do.'

'Don't move a muscle. By the way, I'll have someone with me.'

She tenses.

He's spoken to my father. Oh, why did you have to do that, Fabien?

'I can't believe you would have been crazy enough to tell my father.'

'It's not him I'm bringing with me. It's your mother.'

As he finishes the call, Peru's instincts kick into red alert. Terese isn't just nervous which would be understandable. She is scared, really scared. She tried to cover it up, but she cannot fool him so easily.

The more he chews it over, the more a pattern begins to emerge. He has been that focused on the operation of late that he hasn't had time to think about her. A maggot of doubt was already eating away inside him. Was it really a lapse on her part when she 'forgot' to contact

301

Martina before she arrived at the safe house that night? Terese isn't new to the game—she understands the importance of following procedures and knows how he will react if she doesn't. He gave her a public dressing-down right enough, but perhaps he dismissed the incident too quickly. Maybe it wasn't a lapse, as she claims. Then she questioned the morality of the plan during the group's last meeting. When he comes to think of it, he should have realised what her doubt could lead to.

It could lead to treachery.

Something is clearly wrong. The maggot buries deeper. Has she confided in Fabien Mendiola? Worse, has her father found out?

Then his mind takes a twisted turn in logic as it did with the Comte's son all those years ago. Why didn't he think of it before? The men who so nearly trapped him had to be her father's thugs. That explains why she failed to call Martina that night. She *wants* him caught. She must have leaked their plans to her father, the father she professes to hate.

He makes his decision. He will dispose of her and quickly. There is no time for argument or denial. Terese has served her purpose. He has the virus. He has waited years for this moment and he isn't going to risk her denying him his moment of glory. Independence for his country is paramount: she is dispensable. The operation is not going to fail. His future rides on its success. At some point, his superiors might even invite him to join their inner circle.

This time he will strike first. This time he will make certain she can't play Judas to his Jesus.

He punches the numbers in his mobile. Jean-Paul Legarreta answers the call in his taxi. An ETA sympathiser, he helps the commando whenever the need arises.

'Where are you?' asks Jean-Paul.

'I'm in Rue Neuve. How long will it take you to get here?'

'I'm not sure. There's been an accident on Avenue Duvergier de Hauranne and the traffic's snarled up. I'll be there as soon as I can.'

When the taxi finally arrives, Peru is pacing up and down the pavement, wound up tight, taking drag after drag on his cigarette.

Jean-Paul leans out of the car window. 'Not working tonight, Peru?'

'Not tonight, I've swapped my shift. They can do without me for a change.'

'Where to?'

'Drop me at Rue Albert Mora.'

'OK.'

They sit in silence as the car speeds towards the northern suburbs. Peru's impatience is fizzing into anger by the time they reach their destination.

'Shall I pick you up later?' asks Jean-Paul.

'No, it's OK. I'll find my own way back.'

The streets of Boucau are devoid of life. It is that dead time of the day after people have dined and before they settle for the evening. As he turns the corner into Terese's street, he spots a car parked on the road at the front of her house. A car he recognises immediately as the black Audi TT of Fabien Mendiola.

What the hell is he doing here on the night before the operation? Is that why she doesn't want to see me? Jesus, she must have told him!

His anger is now at boiling point. If he has to get rid of Fabien as well, then so be it. He is an excellent shot and all it needs is a couple of rounds fired from his choked Millennium PT145 to do the job.

He reaches inside his jacket, fingers seeking the gun's grip.

No gun.

Stupidly, in his hurry, he forgot to bring it with him. Now he will have to do things the hard way with his knife. Fabien will be a pushover, but Terese has learned the tricks of self-defence. If faced with the two of them he might have a problem.

It could be messy and risky.

He takes several deep breaths and waits for his heartbeat to steady.

Should he bide his time or go in now?

Terese hardly recognises the woman slumped in the armchair next to her. Her mother looks as if she has been folded up in the middle. Marie-Louise's unblemished skin has developed a jaundiced cast and the weight has dropped off her. Sunken and yellowish eyes peer out at Terese from under the dark green pashmina draped around her mother's head.

Marie-Louise's voice is rasping, feeble. 'I'm dying, darling. It's a tumour that's growing inside my head.'

'Oh, Mama . . .'

'It's all right, I've come to terms with it. I've led a marvellously healthy life so far and I've no complaints. It looks like death was prepared to grant me a stay of execution, but now he's impatient for my soul. My only regret,' she wipes away a tear in the corner of her eye, 'is that I will always blame myself for causing you to be sent away when you were so young. That was thoughtless, so, so thoughtless.'

'It wasn't your fault, Mama. It was Papa's. He's the one who put me on that train without even so much as a kiss goodbye.'

'I can see why you think that way, my love. Your father's not the most demonstrative of people, not even with his nearest and dearest. I was the one who said either it was a case of the two of you resolving your differences or I would end up seriously ill. Your father took it too literally, I'm afraid.' She dabs the beads of sweat on her brow.

'I had dinner with him earlier this evening. Did he tell you?'

Marie-Louise unfolds slightly. 'I haven't seen him today. He left the house before I awoke this morning. This infernal illness leaves me that drained. I hardly ever rise before eleven nowadays.'

'He told me about the tumour, Mama.'

A startled look springs on her mother's face. 'I don't understand. Why would he do that? I asked him not to tell you until the last moment. I didn't want you to feel any . . . obligation.'

'I think he was trying to put pressure on me.'

'Pressure on you? Why? I don't understand.'

Terese shoots a look at Fabien.

'I haven't told your mother everything,' he says. 'I thought that was best left to you.'

She sits down at her mother's feet, wraps her arms around her knees and rests her head on her lap.

'Has Fabien told you about Peru?'

'He has. I don't know how you could have done such a thing to poor Fabien. It's so unlike you. I never thought you would turn out to be duplicitous. It's just as well that Fabien is such an understanding man. There aren't many like him in this city.'

She takes her mother's hands in hers, squeezes them. 'There's something else, Mama. Something that's far worse than being unfaithful. I don't think you'll ever forgive me when I tell you.'

Her mother reciprocates the squeeze. 'Darling, my life is coming to an end. I am not about to sit in judgement of my only daughter. I'm listening.'

'It all began at the Sorbonne . . .'

Crouching behind the wing of the Audi, Peru can make out the top half of Fabien standing inside the front room of the house. Knowing where he and Terese are is a stroke of luck. Surprise is on his side. Seconds ago, he wondered if Fabien spotted him as he bent double and scuttled across the tarmac road to squat behind Fabien's car, but Fabien turned and now faces inwards.

His mind runs through the house's security system. Not exactly Fort Knox. One of the first things he did when she moved to Boucau was insist she install an alarm and window locks. She might have to keep sensitive information there from time to time and he doesn't want some two-bit thief accidentally discovering that the quiet young woman who keeps herself to herself is not quite who she purports to be. The front and back doors might be locked—sometimes Terese locks them when she is inside.

He rehearses two possible courses of action in his mind.

One: he can wait until Mendiola departs, which would leave Terese on her own for him to deal with. She will not invite Mendiola to stay overnight—he knows she made it clear to Fabien there would be no doing that until after they were married. A grin twists the corner of his mouth.

Marriage? You'll be waiting an eternity, my friend. There's no way you'll taste the fruit of that particular tree.

If Mendiola does not depart soon, it will be cutting things fine. Soon he will have to be on his way to Madrid. Jean-Paul is not in on the plan, so he cannot call on the taxi driver to transport him. Peru plans to take the ten-thirty bus to Biarritz, where he intends to stay overnight before catching the early morning train to Irun, departing from the station shortly before seven. That gets him into Irun at seven-thirty, where the train stops for almost three-quarters of an hour. It leaves Irun at quarter past eight and arrives at Madrid Chamartin at a quarter to two, giving him ample time to get over to the airport.

Glancing at his watch, he sees it is almost quarter to ten already.

Not much time.

Two: the direct approach, taking out both of them. Terese won't have set the alarm yet. There is always a possibility she has left a window or door open at the back of the house. If so, he will catch them unawares, using the knife to dispose of Mendiola first. This, too, has its risks. She may scream for help, but in a neighbourhood where everybody minds their own business, nobody will take any notice.

He chooses the direct approach, deciding to double check to see where exactly they are in the room before he makes his move. He looks up and down the street. Empty. Inside the house, Fabien hasn't moved position. Bent double, Peru scurries round the front of the Audi and darts across the small rectangle of grass separating the house from the footpath until he is directly below the corner of the window. Raising his head slightly, he peeps into the room.

307

He can't believe his eyes. Another woman is sitting next to Terese.

'Oh, Mama, what have I done?'

For several seconds, Marie-Louise doesn't answer. Then she cups Terese's chin in her hand. 'I think I must be having a bad dream. I thought you said you were involved with ETA?'

'I was Mama, but now I'm not. The experience in Cuba shocked me. I've never known such fear. And I never thought anyone would be crazy enough to try and commit mass murder. But I blame myself. I didn't have the courage to say no when Peru sent me to get the virus. I'm a coward.'

'It doesn't matter, darling. What does matter is that you've come to your senses and realised you've done wrong. Now we have to consider how we distance you from these people. Isn't that so, Fabien?'

Fabien looks at Marie-Louise and nods. 'Yes, Terese, we have to get you out of the mess you're in. I've been thinking and I've come to the conclusion your father should be the one to advise us.'

'No, no way. I don't want him meddling in this. Mama, you can't expect—'

Marie-Louise holds up her hand to stop the flow of words. 'I'm afraid you don't have a choice in the matter. I've been married to your father for a long time and he has an uncanny knack of working out exactly what to do in situations like this. God knows how he does. I don't know and I don't want to know. But if anyone can protect you from these people, your father can.'

'No, Mama. Please.'

'Do you have an alternative? Do Fabien and I have an alternative?'

Terese slowly shakes her head.

A thread of steel runs through her mother's words. 'Then I think it's about time you and your father reconciled your differences, don't you? Unless you want me to go to my grave with my heart full of shame.'

The words cut Terese. 'All right, Mama. I'll do as you say.'

'I knew you'd see sense.'

Then Fabien springs his surprise. 'I took the liberty of speaking with him before I collected your mother. He should be with us anytime now.'

As he finishes the sentence, he turns back to the window.

'Perfect timing. His Bentley has just pulled up outside.'

Peru wheels round to see the car's headlights cutting through the descending darkness. Scrambling on all fours, he secretes himself behind a large rhododendron bush at the side of the house just as the Bentley rolls up and parks directly behind the Audi. Within seconds, the driver douses its lights. The doors open and four men climb out. Three stand by the car whilst the fourth strides into the house.

He listens as the tallest of the three men speaks.

'You two wait here while I join Monsieur Rodriguez inside. Keep your eyes peeled for anyone acting suspiciously. Do not let anyone within twenty metres of this house.'

Both men nod and one smacks a gloved fist into his palm. 'That won't be a problem, boss,' he says.

Peru curses. *I was right. Rodriguez and his goons. She's betrayed me, the bitch.*

Now he will have to abandon any thoughts of stealing into the house. Time is racing on. Tomorrow is going to be an historic date in the calendar and he isn't about to miss his date with destiny. The operation will continue with or without Terese Rodriguez. There will be another opportunity to deal with her when tomorrow is over. Even if Rodriguez knows about the plan, he will be powerless to stop it going ahead. Not without implicating his own flesh and blood.

Padding quietly along the side of the house, he scrambles beneath a hedge and makes his getaway.

There is frostiness in the room as Viktor enters. Fabien edges away from the window and stands directly behind Terese, hands resting on her shoulders. She sits, head down, right palm pressed to her forehead, elbow resting on her knee. Marie-Louise grips Terese's left hand in both of hers.

No one speaks until Marie-Louise breaks the silence. 'She has agreed for you to help, Viktor.'

Terese raises her head and peers directly at him. He can see she is no longer the quick-to-flash hellcat he has fought with so many times over the years. This is a woman with a look of beaten resignation in her eyes.

'And why is he here?' he asks, tilting his chin at Fabien.

'Because I love her, monsieur,' says Fabien. 'And I would do anything to protect her.'

Viktor snorts and is about to say what he thinks of that when Oreaga stops him.

'Monsieur, Miss Rodriguez will be safe as long as she remains here. Damien and Guy will take up positions outside and watch the house. By this time tomorrow evening it will be over and then you can all forget about it and carry on as if nothing has happened.' His eyes lock on Terese. 'We have a plan for how the attack tomorrow can be prevented. It is not necessary or prudent for anyone other than my men and I to know the details.' He turns to face Viktor. 'And that includes you, monsieur.'

Oreaga's voice is calm, reassuring, but it doesn't convince Viktor. His instinct tells him that Jacques Oreaga is deeply worried. Normally ice cool, Oreaga's mannerisms betrayed a concern that Viktor is biting off more than he can chew. His old comrade visibly paled when he ordered him to prevent a terrorist attack. Oreaga would realise that is impossible. His small band of men could never carry it off successfully. It is crazy even to think of attempting such a thing. If they try and then mess up, the DGSE will slide all over them like an omelette in a non-stick frying pan and they will ask some testing questions. Tough as he is, Oreaga will not be able to hold out. Physical torture nowadays is a crude way of getting at the truth: advances in modern psychoactive drugs have seen to that: much quicker, cheaper and far less messy.

'Do you all understand?' asks Oreaga.

Heads nod.

'I'll be on my way, then. There is much to do.'

'Don't fail us, Jacques,' say Viktor. 'You have a lot to lose if you do. Take Madame Rodriguez and Monsieur Mendiola with you. Leave them at the house with a couple of your men in attendance.'

'I'm not going anywhere,' protests Fabien, tightening his grip on Terese.

'Come, monsieur, it's for the best,' says Oreaga, taking hold of Fabien's arm.

'Don't tell me what's for the best, I—'

'In the car now!' barks Viktor. 'I am sorry, but this is no place for bravado. Do as the man asks you.'

'You can go—'

'Fabien, please! Do as he says.' Terese's voice brooks no argument.

Viktor scowls as Fabien marches out of the room, followed by Marie-Louise, a shrunken figure holding on to the arm of Oreaga for support. As the front door closes behind them, he stands squarely in front of Terese, hands on hips.

'Enough is enough, Terese. There are lives to be saved and I don't mean just at Barajas.'

'How did you know about Salbatore Vasco, Papa?'

'I have my sources.'

'And what did you do to him?'

'Do? What do you mean?'

'You had him tortured, didn't you?'

He gives a shrug of his shoulders. She may as well hear the truth. 'I had to know what was going to happen, Terese, in order to protect my family.'

'Using any means?'

He sniffs. 'Well, of course, I would have preferred a philosophical debate, but I don't think he would have given me the pleasure.'

'Did you hurt him?'

'Does it matter? My intervention will save the suffering of innocent people. I don't have a problem with the methods I employ.'

She rises from the floor and walks up to him. 'Maybe you don't, but I do.'

'Meaning?'

'Why do you think I joined ETA?'

'You already told me it was an infatuation with this Echeverria fellow and the romantic schoolgirl notion of freedom for the Basques.'

Her face blackens. 'I did it because I knew that if I did, you would never be able to fulfil your dream for me. Before long, my name would be under suspicion. Can you imagine? The daughter of the great Viktor Rodriguez suspected of being a *terrorist*? You could never ask me to join your business then, could you?'

He reaches out to put his arm around her, but she pulls back.

'I want you to join the business, Terese. I won't be around much longer and when I'm gone, Groupe Rodriguez will be vulnerable. You're strong; you'll be able to keep it together.'

'But can't you see? I don't want to. I'm not you, Papa, as much as you would like me to be. I don't want to be tied to a corporate office. All I want is my freedom, the freedom to run my life as I want to run it. And it's you who has denied it to me all these years. That's why I joined ETA. I knew you would find out eventually. But it surprised me you found out as quickly as you did.'

For the first time he recognises the steely spirit that mirrors his own. In that instant, he realises she will never succeed him in his business.

But this is no time for regret.

'If you are to come out of this untainted, I'll have to call in some costly favours and I don't want any surprises, do you hear me?'

'Yes, Papa, I hear you.'

4th August

Jacques Oreaga glances at the luminous figures on his wristwatch.

01:53.

'I see he's making you work for your money, Jacques. At your age you should be tucked up in bed at this time of night, dreaming of that house on the Côte d'Azur you've always wanted.'

Jacques Oreaga and Serge Lemouller sit in the front seat of Oreaga's BMW 525e, parked in an unlit spot on the Quai de Lesseps. After leaving Viktor's house, Oreaga drove the Bentley back to its daytime resting place deep in the ground beneath Groupe Rodriguez tower. The car is far too conspicuous and too easy for people to remember, particularly the kind of people who cruise the city streets in the early hours of the morning. He collected his own, much commoner car, a marque favoured by most of the professional classes in the city. It won't merit a second glance, especially at this time of night when the local police enjoy a coffee and swap tales before the next shift takes over.

'I normally would be Serge, but not tonight. Then again, after tonight I might just make that dream a reality. I'm beginning to feel it's about time I stepped off the treadmill. Smoke?'

'I thought you'd given up.'

'I have.'

Lemouller could be mistaken for a clerk in any one of the city's several banks. Of average height and average build with no distinguishing features, he would be a nightmare for any witness to describe. Nothing about his appearance is memorable. Bespectacled, although he has perfect eyesight, and thin as a rake, although he can bench-press twice his own body weight, truth is Serge Lemouller is not what he appears to be. That is the secret of how he manages to go about his work in such an efficient way.

When they were in the Legion, Oreaga had been a sniper and Lemouller, several years his junior, was his spotter. Oreaga's job was easy in comparison to that of his sidekick. All he had to do was take aim, shoot and kill using his keen eyesight and rock-steady forefinger. Lemouller had it much harder. In his role he had to locate the target, talk Oreaga on to it, and make a judgement call on the range and influence of the wind and then look for the trace. If Oreaga missed, Lemouller had to calculate corrections in a fraction of a second in order for Oreaga to make the next shot count. It was pressured work, but Lemouller excelled at it.

'Serge has a mind like a calculator,' Oreaga used to say. *'except a calculator can only do one thing at a time and only what you tell it to. He can do three at the same time without being told.'*

The two men forged a close bond owing to the symbiotic relationship upon which both their lives depended: a relationship that endured when they demobbed and joined DGSE. Years later, after Oreaga's resignation from DGSE, Lemouller continues to be in discreet contact with his old buddy, trading favours and information which helps both of them to be one step ahead in their respective jobs.

Against all the rules, naturally.

Lemouller was in bed with his latest girlfriend when the call from Oreaga came through on his mobile.

The voice was urgent, pressing. 'Serge, it's Jacques. Something big has come up, something really big. I need to meet you tonight and the sooner the better. It could be a matter of life or death.'

'Give me half an hour, my friend. Where do you want to meet?'

'Usual place. I'll be in my car. Flash your lights twice when you see it.'

Lemouller made his excuses much to the annoyance of his girlfriend, and drove a circuitous route to the river's edge. Once he was sure he wasn't being followed, he turned onto the Quai de Lesseps, parked his Citroen a hundred metres away from Oreaga's BMW, walked the short distance and climbed in.

For the first five minutes, Oreaga says nothing, smoking his cigarette and staring across the oily blackness of the river. Then he turns to Lemouller.

'We've known each other a long time, Serge.'

'More than twenty-five years by my reckoning. Longer than you were married to Michelle.'

Memories flood back to Oreaga. Michelle was his ex-wife, the woman to whom he gave his heart. Then she threw it back at him following several acrimonious months after he made the decision to leave the DGSE. A bitter divorce battle ensued, leaving him in need of money and a job. That was when he had entered Rodriguez's life for the second time: not willingly, but out of necessity.

'Perhaps I should have married you, Serge,' he quips.

'Perhaps you should. The company would have been good, but I don't think the sex would have been great.'

Oreaga lights another cigarette.

'Are we going to sit and smoke all night, or are you going to tell me what's on your mind?' asks Lemouller. 'I have a hot, naked woman in my bed who thinks I'm more interested in my work than I am in enjoying her body. Talk, my friend, I'm all ears.'

Blowing a stream of smoke through the open car window, Oreaga raps his fingers on the rim of the steering wheel. 'What I'm about to tell you must never, ever be traced back to me. If it is, any thought I have of retiring to the Côte d'Azur would go up in smoke. I would spend the rest of my days in a ten-by-eight looking at the sun through a row of bars. Do I have your word?'

'Do you need to ask?'

'No, but I'm asking anyway.'

'Of course you have my word.'

'That's good enough for me.' He squeezes the nape of his neck with his fingers. 'Tomorrow, at five o'clock in the afternoon or thereabouts, an ETA commando will release, without prior warning, a deadly virus into the air conditioning system at Barajas Airport. The commando's leader will be disguised as one of the airport's maintenance men, doing a routine check on the system. They plan to release the virus so it is blown out onto the passengers in the booking hall. Other members of the commando will create a diversion, disguised as a party of friends on a backpacking holiday, during which the leader will gain access to the ducting system above the hall, wait for them to leave and release the virus. He will be wearing a facemask and protective clothing whilst he does this. Nobody will notice a thing until two weeks later when everyone in that hall will be either dead or dying. There will also be a diversionary incendiary placed beneath a car close to the *El Mundo* offices.'

Lemouller slowly shakes his head. 'Are you right about this Jacques? It's not ETA's usual MO. Bombs and assassinations are more their style, normally with a clear warning beforehand—often very late, but with a warning nevertheless. What you've described is more akin to the way Al-Qaeda operates.'

'Believe me, it's ETA. I know that for a fact.'

'May I ask how you can be so sure?'

'Ask away, but I won't tell you. The less you know the better for your own safety. Let's just say I got it from the horse's mouth.'

'How will I say I came by the information?'

'Shortly after you arrive for work this morning, I'll make an anonymous call asking for you. No doubt, you will ask your DGSE colleagues to listen in as protocol demands. I will disguise my voice and I'll make my message short, to the point, and believable. It will give full details of the Barajas plot.'

Lemouller whistles through his teeth. 'God Almighty, Jacques. That doesn't leave us much time.'

'I'm sorry, Serge. It's the best I can do.'

'Do they have a contingency plan should we apprehend them?'

'Ah, there you have luck on your side. They will have one chance to pull this off and one only.'

'And if we fail?'

'You'll have a major crisis on your hands. It won't be confined to the people at the airport. I'm told this virus can spread like wildfire through direct contact with blood, saliva, vomit, urine and faeces.'

'Jesus Christ.'

'Now, listen very carefully and I'll run through everything I know.'

Philippe Sagastizabal tenses as he looks along the length of the empty street. Soon people will be heading for their cars, their working day over. If the owner of the car he has in mind happens to show up, no way can he fabricate an excuse to explain what he is doing. That shouldn't happen, not if Terese is keeping watch whilst he rigs the car.

But where is she?

He checks his phone messages just in case she has sent a text. She hasn't. He thinks about phoning her, but Peru's instructions are clear—under no circumstances are they to make a voice call on a mobile phone. He is adamant on that point.

Glancing at his watch, Philippe makes a mental note of the time. 16:40. If he waits any longer before firing the incendiary, the diversion could fail and he will have to ignore orders and call Peru, who would play hell. Months of planning will go down the plughole and Philippe knows who will carry the can.

He makes his decision. Hang Terese. He will have to do it alone and trust the driver doesn't catch him.

Taking out a pair of oily, faded overalls from his holdall, he quickly slips them on. The car he chooses on the quiet street is an old, rust-covered Renault 4. Anyone happening to pass by it would take him for a mechanic struggling to maintain an old banger. Crawling beneath the rear of the car, he pulls his bag in beside him. Taking out a screwdriver, he stabs it into both the car's rear tyres, puncturing them. Should the driver return, he would be unable to drive the car away. Carefully, he removes the small incendiary device from within the bag. The bomb is crude and not designed to cause widespread damage, just sufficient to create a minor panic. Taking a penknife out of his top pocket, he concentrates on scraping away flakes of rust from the car's floor pan. Satisfied with the result, he attaches the magnetic device to the underside of the car and carefully sets the timer.

The bomb will explode at 17:10.

Job done, it is time to go home.

As he slides out backwards, two pairs of hands grab his arms, drag him to his feet and frog-march him to a car parked twenty metres away on the opposite side of the road. The hands pinion him against the car's door and then splay his arms on the roof. Rough hands frisk him and press the side of his face against cold steel.

'Doing a spot of scrapping are we, monsieur?' asks a burly man, a mocking grin on his bearded face.

The small group blends in with the hundreds of passengers milling around the departure hall of Barajas Airport. Two young men and a woman, nervous with the anticipation of flying away for a backpacking holiday, appear no different to many others around them.

'Where's Salbatore?' whispers Jorge to Martina.

'I don't know. Nobody has heard from him for days.'

'Maybe he's got cold feet,' says Miguel.

Jorge shakes his head. 'Salbatore? Cold feet? Never. Something's wrong, I can sense it. There's ill luck about.'

'Nothing's wrong,' she hisses at him. 'Stop thinking negatively and concentrate on what you've got to do. Now go and do it.'

Hoisting his backpack on his shoulder, Jorge makes his way towards the escalator leading up to the balcony overlooking the crowded open space. His job is to look out for any suspicious activities that might jeopardise the operation when Peru makes his move. Opposite him on the far side of the hall, Miguel will take up a similar position. Once in their vantage points, they can cover any unusual activity that takes place.

As Jorge steps on the escalator, two pairs of eyes, already stationed on the balcony, look down on him.

Ten seconds later Miguel makes his move. The same eyes turn their attention to him as he steps on the same escalator.

At the top of the escalator Jorge turns left, Miguel right.

Martina takes a deep breath, ready to create the diversion.

Standing by one of the access doors to the air-conditioning shaft, Peru curses inwardly. The non-appearance of Salbatore does not come as a surprise, but to have him there would be additional security. By now, the incendiary should have gone off and both Jorge and Miguel should be in place. He looks up at the balcony for the agreed signal and sees Jorge wave to Miguel. This is the 'all clear' to proceed.

The digital clock on the lounge wall shows 17:04 and then rumbles to 17:05.

Dressed in dark green overalls and carrying a canvas tool bag, nobody takes any notice of him as he pulls on a pair of surgical gloves and quickly springs the lock on the door to enter the access shaft. Closing it behind him, he places the bag on the floor, opens it, and takes out an aerosol and facemask. He stuffs the facemask into the left top pocket of his overalls and the aerosol into the large right thigh pocket. Slowly and with deliberation, he climbs the aluminium ladder leading to the main horizontal feeder duct that stretches across the entire width of the departure hall. When he arrives at the duct, he heaves himself into a horizontal position and begins to crawl carefully along the dull grey rectangular tube.

Right on cue, a piercing scream echoes around the open spaces of the concourse.

'THIEF! THIEF! HELP!' A space quickly clears around Martina, as she yells at a bemused Indian man standing two metres away from her.

'HE'S TAKEN MY BAG! HELP! HELP!'

For some inexplicable reason the man panics and, throwing his laptop bag on to the floor, hares off toward the exit doors of the concourse, roughly shoving people aside as he attempts to reach it. Martina races after him, still screaming. Before long, the crowd's full attention focuses on the two people as they streak out of the exit. Outside the building Martina stops and smiles inwardly as the man dodges between a line of waiting cars and vaults over a metal guard rail, narrowly avoiding a startled driver on the other side of the barrier.

Miguel was right, he said to pick an Indian. Immigration is always extra careful with Indians. They keep an eye out for false documentation and suspicious travel documents.

'Ill luck, Jorge?' she whispers to herself. 'You're wrong there.'

Any minute now she should hear the chilling wail of sirens, the city springing to alert after the incendiary explodes.

Working his way along the duct toward the main air-conditioning outlet, Peru takes the facemask out of his top pocket and straps it over his nose and mouth. One metre away from the main outlet, he slips the aerosol out of his trouser pocket and holds it against his right thigh. In seconds, he will hold the aerosol at arms length and spray the Ebola down into the main concourse.

Then he hears an almost imperceptible scraping behind him, turns his head sideways and looks down the length of his body.

What he sees almost stops his heart.

Ten metres away, the tip of a suppressed Heckler & Koch MP5SD is beginning to rise vertically from the top of the ladder.

Christ, we've been rumbled! Fuck! Do it Peru, just do it!

As he rushes to bring the aerosol up to the level of his face, the sleeve of his overalls snags one of the bolts holding the sections of ducting together. The sudden resistance to his hand's upward momentum results in an involuntary reflex action, causing his fingers to open and fling the aerosol to his right.

Time stops, but the MP5SD doesn't.

Fight or flight.

Fighting is out of the question, he has nothing with which to fight and he knows when he sees the suppressor that whoever is holding that gun will be under instructions not to take any prisoners.

As Miguel runs towards the escalator, three men surround him in closed formation and, without a word, bundle him along the length of the balcony to where a group of armed police officers wait, guns lowered, but ready for action at a moment's notice. At the other end of the balcony, Jorge finds himself in a similar situation.

Outside the exit doors, a group of concerned backpackers form a closed circle around Martina Trevino. The one closest to her partially opens his fleece to reveal a holstered Glock.

Eight o'clock that same evening, there is a thunderous knocking on the front door of Giles Echeverria's house as he is readying himself for bed after another backbreaking day at the docks.

'Open the door, Mr Echeverria, it's the police,' shouts a voice from outside.

No please, no reason.

As he walks down the short hallway the knocking and demand are repeated, more urgently this time. On opening the door, he is confronted by five armed police officers, grim faced and determined.

'What the—'

'Giles Echeverria?' enquires a pale-faced, ginger-haired man who appears to be the leader. He holds up his identification. 'Gaston Deschamps, DGSE. Are you Giles Echeverria?'

'I am, yes.'

'We'd like to have a word with you, if you don't mind. Inside.'

'I'm not sure I want to—'

'Inside or at the police station. Your choice.'

Quickly casting his eye over the weapons, Giles decides it would be unwise to argue. As he stands aside, four men rush past him. Two go up the stairs, repeatedly swapping positions with each other, gun held in an outstretched arm whilst the other hand grips and supports the gun hand's wrist. The other two emulate the movements downstairs.

'Are you the father of Peru Echeverria?' asks Deschamps.

Giles nods.

'Is he here?'

'No.'

'Are you sure?'

By now, Giles has recovered from his initial shock. 'What's going on? Who the hell do you think you are, bursting into my home?'

'I'll ask you again, Mr Echeverria. Is your son here?'

'I heard you the first time and I gave you my answer. No he's not.'

As he finishes the sentence, one of the armed men appears at the top of the stairs. He points his finger skywards.

'Does this house have an attic, Mr Echeverria?' says Deschamps.

'Yes, why?'

Deschamps nods to the man who disappears. Seconds later, there is the sound of a chair scraping across a wooden floor, followed by creaking as an attic trapdoor is opened.

'What are you doing?' asks Giles.

Deschamps looks blankly at him.

One of the men who disappeared into the back of the house reappears, shaking his head. Seconds later the upstairs man reappears, also shaking his head.

'We have reason to believe your son was involved in an attempt to kill innocent civilians at Barajas airport.'

Giles feels his knees go weak. He leans back on the wall for support. This isn't happening. Soon he will wake up and wonder why he has been plagued with this nightmare. Surely that's all it will be, a nightmare.

'No, not Peru. You must be mistaken.'

'We don't make mistakes. Do you know where he is?'

'No.'

'I'll ask you again. Do you know where he is?'

'No.'

'Were you aware of his involvement with ETA?'

This is too much for Giles. He slides to the floor. He thinks of Peru, his only son, the light of his life and his sole reason for living. The son he is now informed is a . . . what? A terrorist? Everything he does, he does for Peru.

Everything.

Deschamps' questioning continues. 'When did you last see him?'

For a moment, Giles' mind blanks, then he remembers the taste of the mutton stew he shared with his son. 'Yesterday evening.'

'What time?'

'Eight-thirty, nine. Something like that.'

'Did he remain at home?'

'No. He went out to work.'

'At nine o'clock?'

'He works shifts. Down at the harbour on the new building works.'

'What time did he return this morning?'

'I don't know.'

'Didn't you see him?'

The questions seem relentless.

'No.'

'Why?'

'I'd already left for work. We don't see much of each other. He comes in often after I go out.'

'And he hasn't contacted you?'

'No.'

'Why not?'

'Why should he?'

'I think you're lying, Mr Echeverria. Your son's in very serious trouble. I would advise you to tell the truth.'

'I am telling the truth, for God's sake!'

'Did you know he was in ETA?'

'You just asked me that and I told you, no, I didn't.'

'I find that hard to believe. Do you sympathise with their cause?'

The change in tack throws Giles. 'I . . . I . . .' He knows his hesitancy condemns him. Of course, he is sympathetic to the cause. What true Basque isn't? Why, the pale-faced police officer is probably a sympathiser himself.

'Do you?' he asks his interrogator.

'Irrelevant. It isn't my son who is hell-bent on murder. I think we should take a trip down to the station after all. Meanwhile, my men will remain here, just in case your son takes it upon himself to return.'

6th August

Thirty-six hours later, Jacques Oreaga stands in front of his boss in Groupe Rodriguez Tower, hands clasped behind his back, muscles twitching in his jaw.

'You disobeyed my orders, Jacques, says Viktor. 'I told you to clear this mess up and quietly. Now it's splashed all over the newspapers.'

Holding up a copy of *El Correo*, he shows the morning headlines to Oreaga.

MURDEROUS ETA PLOT FOILED BY POLICE
HUNDREDS OF LIVES SAVED AT BARAJAS AIRPORT

'I made a judgment call, monsieur. In my opinion we would not have been successful in our endeavours, and that would have compromised the identity of your family, me and my men.'

'You can't be certain of that.'

'No, monsieur, I cannot. What I can assure you is that it is highly unlikely that any of this will lead back to you or me for that matter.'

Viktor leans back in his chair, joins his hands behind his head. 'How did you do it, Jacques? I'm intrigued.'

'I'm afraid I cannot reveal that, monsieur.'

'Come on, man. We've known each other for a long time.'

And I wouldn't trust you now any more than I did when we met for the first time, thought Oreaga.

The day after the Barajas plot was foiled he received a call from Lemouller, thanking him for his tip-off. The operation had gone smoothly without panicking the public. DGSE had notified the Spanish Grupos Operativos Especiales de Seguridad who executed the counter-terrorism manoeuvre. Those arrested are now being processed and Lemouller expects they will soon be incarcerated permanently, facing the maximum penalty the law can throw at them.

Then Lemouller dropped his bombshell.

'There is just one problem, Jacques.'

'Problem, Serge? What do you mean problem?'

'We didn't catch Echeverria. He escaped.'

'How the hell did that happen?'

'I can't tell you. It's classified, you understand. And when I say classified I mean classified with a capital C. Put it this way—the shit's hit the fan and the GOES boys have got some explaining to do.'

'I don't like the sound of that, Serge, not one little bit.'

'That makes two of us. If the guy's on the run he'll turn up somewhere else. Same maniac, different crew. We can only hope it's not on our patch. What happened to Vasco's hand, Jacques?'

'Who?'

'Salbatore Vasco. He used to lead the commando before Echeverria ousted him. He claims he was tortured by someone who wasn't official.'

'Sorry, Serge, I've never heard the name. Tortured, you say? That's terrible.'

'He was made to eat his own thumb.'

'Christ, how barbaric. Who would do a thing like that?'

329

'Indeed, who would?'

'Maybe it was internecine. These people are crazy.'

'They certainly are. Anyway, I'll let you know how things progress.'

'Thank you, Serge, I would be much obliged. By the way, I've decided to take your advice.'

'My advice? What advice would that be?'

'I'm retiring, this time for good. That little place on the Côte d'Azur has been waiting far too long for me.'

'I think that's a very wise decision, Jacques. Don't forget to invite me to visit. A break would do me the world of good.'

'You'll be my first guest, Serge. You and whichever woman you're screwing at the time.'

Bringing his hand out from behind his back, he slides a single sheet of paper across the wide expanse of Viktor's desk.

'What's this?' asks Viktor.

'It's self-explanatory, monsieur. It's my resignation.'

'Don't be foolish, man. You made a mistake, but I'm prepared to forget it. This time.'

Always the hidden threat, he thinks. *The man will never change.*

'My mind is made up, Monsieur Rodriguez. It's time for me to hang up my boots.'

'I'll double your salary.'

'That's extremely generous of you, but it's not the money. I have sufficient for my needs. I'm sure you'll manage very well without me.'

'What will you do?'

'Do? I think I might write a book. My life has been full of stories, stories that people would find fascinating. But why stop at one book?' He taps the side of his head. 'There's a whole shelf full in here.'

'Are you certain I can't . . .'

'Positive.'

Viktor sighs and Oreaga knows it is not with relief. There is an awful lot he knows about his boss. An awful lot that Viktor doesn't want the world to know about.

'I've been good to you, you know Jacques. If it wasn't for me your life after DGSE might not have turned out as well as it has. You owe me.'

'I owe you nothing, monsieur. I have paid my debt to you many times over. If you are worried that you may end up in my little book, then don't. There are many more people I know who are far more interesting than you.'

The look on Viktor's face says he doesn't know whether he should be insulted or flattered.

'But if I am ever tempted, monsieur, it would only be because you refused me one last request.'

'Oh? What might that be?'

'Stop meddling in Terese's life. Let her make her own choices whether they are right or wrong. Accept that if she doesn't want to follow you into the business, then that's her decision. If you can't think of anything else to occupy you, then take up fishing, or God help you, golf.'

Viktor nods and laughs. 'You have my word, Jacques, I agree to your request. But I insist you leave with a generous bonus. Just make sure all the loose ends are tidied up before you go.'

'I'm afraid I won't be in a position to do that.'

'Oh? Why not?'

'Unfortunately, the police didn't manage to catch Peru Echeverria.'

Beneath the shadow of Groupe Rodriguez Tower, Terese and Fabien sit in the same cafe where Fabien sat the evening he went to visit Marie-Louise. Terese's fingers stroke the back of the hand spread on top of the table in front of her.

'I don't know how I could ever have treated you like that, Fabien. Will you ever forgive me?

He pauses before he answers. 'Terese, it's not a matter of forgiving. You had a path, which you believed you had to follow, regardless. I will never understand your reasons for so doing as long as I live, so I'm not going to torment myself by trying. But in the end, your conscience told you it was wrong, and your heart told you it was wrong, and you did what was right. I will always wonder if you will ever love me as you loved Echeverria, but again, life's too short to let that eat away at me. I love you with every fibre of my being; I think I always will. I can only hope and pray that perhaps one day, you will come to love me, too.'

'Oh, Fabien, I might have been in love with Peru at one time, but the Peru I see now is not the Peru I knew then. I was blind to the way he'd changed. I could never love any man who was prepared to do what he was prepared to do.'

'And now? Now what happens to us, Terese?'

'I would like it to be as it was before. Only this time openly and honestly.'

'I broke off the engagement, remember?'

'How could I forget?'

'It was because of your father.'

'I know.'

Fabien leans forward. 'He phoned and asked me to meet him first thing this morning. I said to myself why not? When I met him, he apologised profusely and asked me if I would like my job back. I asked him on what terms? Same as before he replied. I said that wasn't good enough. He asked me did I want more money. I said no, not more money. I wanted him to swear to keep his nose out of my . . . and your . . . personal lives. I was astonished when he agreed.'

'He agreed? I find that unbelievable.'

'So did I, but then he told me that Jacques Oreaga has retired and I wondered if that might have something to do with it.'

'Will you take the job?'

'Yes, I will. I like the people I work with and I'll need the money for the wedding.'

'What wedding?'

Fabien looks deeply into her eyes. 'I've changed my mind about the engagement. If I were to ask you to marry me, what would your answer be?'

She doesn't hesitate. 'I would say yes. I'd be proud to be your wife.'

'Then that's settled. Now let's order, I'm famished.'

16th August

Angelo closes the door of his empty apartment after returning home from a tiring day plying his trade. There is no Maria to greet him. Two weeks ago, after the mother-and-father of a row, she called him every name under the sun, filled two cases with her personal belongings and stormed out, swearing never to return.

A solitary letter lies on the floor. He picks it up. The postmark indicates it was posted eight days previously and the franked stamp, depicting a sculpture by Constantin Brancusi, identifies it as originating in France.

Sitting down on the arm of his favourite chair, he slides his thumbnail along the top of the crumpled envelope. Taking out a single, neatly folded sheet of paper, he unfolds it and reads.

Dear Angelo,

I am writing to inform you that the venture in which your father and brother played such an important part has now come to an abrupt and unsuccessful end. Undoubtedly, you must have asked yourself what reason your father could have had for embarking on such an unwise course of action, and possibly, you may have raised the question directly with him, but I doubt it. Men of your father's character and resolve do not give up their secrets willingly, especially to their own children. I have taken it upon myself to fill in the blanks for you.

Many years ago, when your father and mother were newly married, your mother had a moment of passion with a senior figure in M-26-7. This figure, a brilliant, wild and committed revolutionary became the global face of hope for oppressed people all around the world. It isn't surprising that your mother found him so alluring and irresistible. The fruit of their coupling was a boy child who, with the consent of this man and your father, was sent far away to a distant relative in Bayonne, France. The boy grew up oblivious to the fact that his parents were not his genetic parents. In due course, he himself married and had a child, again a boy.

This boy, the son of your mother's bastard son, inherited some of the qualities of his brilliant paternal grandfather, but didn't quite have the same canniness in the manner in which he applied them. Foolishly, as he grew into manhood, he devoted his time and energies to a terrorist organisation and pursued their ridiculous and patently unachievable goals. I have to admit, he devised a brilliant plan involving the blackmailing of your father, the duping of your brother and the use of yourself as a go-between. However, the real credit for obtaining a deadly virus and sneaking it out of Cuba must go to your father and brother Oswardo—true patriots.

This—I will use the term 'half-brother'—of yours now finds his misguided son to be a fugitive on the run from the authorities in both France and Spain after he had the temerity to try and release this virus into the air conditioning at Madrid airport. When he is finally apprehended, and I assume it will be when rather than if, he will find himself locked away for a long time; so long I doubt if he will ever see the world outside of a prison for the rest of his life.

I feel I owe you my gratitude for informing me of your father's involvement in this intrigue. Were it not for you, things might not have turned out too well for the people in Madrid. However, my gratitude to you must be secondary to my duty as an upright and honest citizen of my country and I have briefed the Cuban authorities—through the appropriate channels, of course—on the whole sordid business.

With respect to the position that Senor Suarez discussed with you, I am sure you will agree that, given your situation and under the circumstances, it would not be prudent to progress the matter further.

Regards

Viktor Rodriguez

Chairman, Groupe Rodriguez

The paper slips from his fingers, floats to the floor. Pulled out of his thoughts by a sharp and persistent rapping on the wafer-thin front door, he rises slowly from the chair and drags his lead-heavy feet across the darkening room. On opening the door, he is surprised to find himself confronted by half a dozen po-faced soldiers wearing the uniform of the Cuban Army.

The gravelly voice of a bearded sergeant assaults his ears.

'Angelo Fortunato? Please come with us. There is a matter that requires some urgent clarification. I suggest you do not try to resist; if you do we may be forced to take an action you will regret.'

At the same time as Angelo is being escorted from his home, a military jeep containing four similarly attired soldiers pulls up at Eduardo's house. As he opens the gate to meet them, he is puzzled and surprised as to why they have chosen to call on him.

'Good evening, sir,' greets the captain, saluting him.

'Captain Canavero,' replies Eduardo, returning the salute. 'To what do I owe the pleasure of this visit?'

'I have orders from the top that your presence is required in Havana, sir. I am to drive you to Holguin where a plane will take you to meet the Presidente himself.'

Eduardo beams with the pleasure of expectation. Finally, they are to reward him for all the faithful years of dedicated service to his country. Castro must think it is high time to decorate his old comrade in his retirement.

'Give me fifteen minutes, Captain, while I pack my valise. I've been waiting for this moment for a long time.'

The captain gives him an icy stare and the soldiers sitting behind him raise their rifles.

'I wouldn't bother packing, sir. You won't be coming back.'

'At best, you know this is the end of your career, don't you Colonel?'

Words won't form in Oswardo's desert-dry mouth. Half an hour before, he was summoned to see his commanding officer who is now patiently and impassively reading a list of accusations from a charge sheet. His body is like a balloon that some naughty child has let the air out of; slumped, as if a hand has pulled his skeleton out through his mouth.

'And at worst, Colonel? At worst, it could mean a firing squad. You're finished, I'm afraid. God help you.'

Walking over to him, the officer viciously rips the epaulettes off Oswardo's uniform.

Epilogue

On the morning of 30th December 2006, an explosion took place in the car park building attached to Terminal 4 of Madrid Barajas International Airport. Reuters distributed a wire story on the event, but with sparse details. The story stated that a bomb threat was phoned in at approximately 08:15 local time with the caller stating that a bomb would explode at 09:00. After receiving the warning, police were able to evacuate part of the airport.

The Spanish Interior Minister confirmed that the almost-new car park had been damaged. (Three of the four storeys were demolished by the explosion.) The terminal also received some minor damage. Two people were killed and twenty-six others sustained injuries, mainly damaged ears because of the explosion's shock wave.

The explosion was from a van bomb, a Renault Trafic containing between 500 and 800 kilograms of explosives stolen from a Spanish national in France, who was abducted and then released shortly after the bombing. Entry was restricted to all airport terminals by the Spanish national police, but air traffic resumed at Terminal 4 soon afterward.

Responsibility for the explosion was claimed by an anonymous male caller claiming to represent ETA.

★

After forty-nine years at the helm, on 19th February 2008, Fidel Alejandro Castro Ruz stepped down as Cuba's president and handed the reins of power to his brother Raúl.

Castro, eighty-one years old, has witnessed the terms of office of nine American presidents.

★

On Tuesday 20th May 2008, leading ETA figures were arrested in Bordeaux, France.

Peru Echeverria, also known as 'Le Fanatic', had been on the run before his arrest. A final total of arrests brought in six people, including ETA members and supporters. The Spanish Interior Ministry claimed the relevance of the arrests would come in time with the investigation. Furthermore, the Interior Minister said that those members of ETA now arrested had ordered the latest terrorist attacks, and that the man considered to be the head of the terrorists, Peru Echeverria, was 'not just another arrest because he is, in all probability, the man who has most political and military weight in the terrorist group. He has already admitted he was the mastermind behind a previous failed attempt to kill hundreds of people at Barajas airport by means of a deadly virus.'

★

**EL CORREO
15TH JUNE 2008
MARRIAGES**

On 9th June 2008, on a gloriously bright and clear afternoon, Miss Terese Rodriguez and Mr Fabien Mendiola were joined in matrimony in the beautiful Cathedrale Sainte-Marie de Bayonne. The bride radiated happiness as she was given away by her father, Mr Viktor Rodriguez, one of the city's most prominent businessmen and benefactors. Best man was Mr Andre Mendiola, (groom's younger brother) bridesmaid was Miss Louisa Mendiola (groom's sister) and maids of honour were Miss Lorea Rodriguez and Mrs Kalara Lizardi (bride's sisters.) Mr and Mrs Mendiola will be living in the Mendiola family chateau until the building of their new house in Saint-Martin-de-Seignanx is complete.

*

On 20th January 2009, Democrat Senator Barak Obama was sworn in as the 56th President of the United States of America and the first black man to hold such a position. Hours after his inauguration he called for a halt to the Guantanamo war crimes tribunals, a move that heralded the long-awaited process of dismantling the detention centre itself.

It is now August 2011, and the world is still waiting.

Made in the USA
Charleston, SC
28 May 2014